Missing Matisse

Missing Matisse

A NOVEL BY

JAN REHNER

Inanna poetry & fiction series

INANNA PUBLICATIONS AND EDUCATION INC.
TORONTO, CANADA

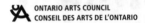

We gratefully acknowledge the support of the Canada Council for the Arts and the Ontario Arts Council for our publishing program.

We are also grateful for the support received
from an Anonymous Fund at The Calgary Foundation.

Cover design: Val Fullard
Interior design: Luciana Ricciutelli

Library and Archives Canada Cataloguing in Publication

Rehner, Jan
      Missing Matisse / Jan Rehner.

(Inanna poetry and fiction series)
ISBN 978-1-926708-21-8

      I. Title. II. Series: Inanna poetry and fiction series

PS8585.E4473M57 2011   C813'.6   0C2011-900731-2

Printed and bound in Canada

Inanna Publications and Education Inc.
210 Founders College, York University
4700 Keele Street, Toronto, Ontario, Canada M3J 1P3
Telephone: (416) 736-5356 Fax: (416) 736-5765
Email: inanna@yorku.ca Website: www.yorku.ca/inanna

To the next generation of women:
Lisa, Kate, Jo, Amy, and Carrie

All things considered, there is only Matisse.
—Pablo Picasso

To be Matisse's model is to mediate between the artist and the dream.
—Lydia Delectorskaya

Henri Matisse *(French, 1869-1954),* Rumanian Blouse *(also known as* Woman in a Blouse, Dreaming*), 1936, pen and ink, 490 x 368 mm. The Baltimore Museum of Art: The Cone Collection, formed by Dr. Claribel Cone and Miss Etta Cone of Baltimore, Maryland.* BMA *1950.12.48.* © Estate of H. Matisse / SODRAC *(2011).*

Part I
Woman in a Blouse, Dreaming

COTTON, SOFT AS SILK, CARESSES *my skin. Embroidered threads of scarlet, sunflower yellow and black, against a background of snow white, dance across the sleeves and bodice of the blouse. It has become, I have become, a garden of delicate flowers and swirling leaves.*

My face is the still point. I hold his gaze, only blinking when he looks down to guide his pen. When he lifts his eyes, I understand he sees beyond the blouse to my flesh, and beyond my flesh to my bones. I am angle and shape, only form. If I move, even slightly—touch my hair, tilt my chin—I will break the harmony of the line.

For a moment, our eyes meet. I pour myself into him, and he is open, receives everything. The pen moves silently. He draws my mood, my musing, my hopes, my dreams. He draws the light in the room and the scent of the sea in the air.

After a long stillness, he lays down his pen and beckons to me.

I see myself transformed. He has drawn three flowers on the bare skin of my right arm, as if I were blossoming.

S HE'D STALKED HIM FOR THREE weeks, ducking around corners, careful to avoid a pattern. She'd seen him jogging in the early morning, collecting his mail, leaving for his office. She knew his car. She'd followed him to the research lab where he worked, noted the hours he kept. At night, she'd timed when his lights went on and off. She knew his habits. She knew his clothes: fine tailored suits, dark blue denim jeans and black leather jacket, jogging pants and windbreaker.

His name was Adam Jensen. Tall, athletic-looking, with short, curly hair the colour of sand, a slightly protruding nose, a strong chin. His suits looked expensive, even from a distance. His jogging clothes were designer label. The shoes alone probably cost more money than she could hope to make in a month.

The stretch of Millbank Avenue where he lived didn't have many houses. Ten on the east side, Jensen's side, and eight on the west side. They were all handsomely large, mostly stone or brick, immaculately kept. Like the thick maples and chestnuts that lined the avenue, the houses were well-rooted, solid, and mature.

The street followed a slight incline, curving into Glenayr Road at the bottom, and the entrance into the Cedarvale Ravine. The houses on the east side enjoyed the privacy of deep back yards, ending in a fringe of trees and the steep, slick banks of the ravine below. She'd taken the walking path behind Jensen's house, but it led downhill, meandering well below street level. Patches of spring snow dotted the ground, melting in pools and icy rivulets across the muddy path of the ravine. While she was inconspicuous among the other walkers on the path during the day, she would be noticed if she tried to climb the slippery banks. During the night, floodlights illuminated the back yard.

Despite the privacy afforded by the ravine, she knew she could not attempt to enter Jensen's house from the back.

The puzzle of how to gain entry had occupied her mind for several weeks. She'd hoped to gather enough information from his life style and habits to form an idea, but she hadn't learned as much as she'd hoped from her surveillance. If she pitched a rock through a window, she would be sure to trigger an alarm. But what she wanted was inside that house, and she was determined to get it back.

The house was beautiful freestone, trimmed in black, with a winding stone path to the arched front door. It was too large for one person, yet Jensen lived there alone. Two sets of leaded-glass windows flanked the wood door on the ground floor. The windows on the left probably graced a dining room, while the larger set of windows, with five panes forming a squared bay, suggested a living room. The ground floor seemed to be mainly in darkness, at least during the times she passed by. If Jensen had a social life, he conducted it mostly elsewhere.

At night, she had noted light shining from the second and third floors. When he was at home, he occupied the upper storeys almost exclusively, where he would certainly have a bedroom, and perhaps a reading room or study.

She knew from her father that Jensen was a scientist, a medical researcher for a government-funded laboratory in Toronto. She'd stolen some of his garbage once, spreading out its contents on newspaper on the kitchen table of her Crang Avenue house, but she'd gleaned little from the messy exercise of picking through a heap of mango peels, coffee grounds, and a chicken carcass. The recycling bin had seemed more promising. She'd hoped for a personal letter or two. Instead all she'd learned was that he had a healthy bank balance at the Toronto Dominion, that he had no pets, and that he didn't recycle tuna cans or juice cartons. Not very useful information for her purposes.

She turned and headed back up the street. She was at a stalemate. If he was clever, and she had every reason to suppose he was, he would know from seeing her that she was Sammy's daughter. While she had inherited her high cheek bones, narrow nose, and dark eyes from her French mother, the long mane of unruly auburn curls was unmistakably from Sammy Rea. She needed a way to enter the house that would not be immediately alarming, something she might explain plausibly if she were caught.

She'd passed Jensen's house for the second time and had reached the path that lead to Suydam Park at the edge of Spadina Village when she saw a catering van turn into Millbank. She stopped and watched it park in front of Jensen's address. Immediately, she retraced her steps. It was risky, but it might be her only chance.

She waited a minute or two, but no one emerged from the van. *Taste of the Town, Fine Catering.* Male driver. Female passenger. She glanced up the street. Was Jensen planning on meeting them? If so, she didn't have much time.

She approached the driver and waved, waiting until he'd lowered his window. "Hi. I'm one of Dr. Jensen's neighbours. Can I help?"

The driver looked at his watch. "I guess we're a bit early. We're here to set up for the party tonight. Dr. Jensen's meeting us at six."

"Oh, great. Well, I'll leave you to it, then." She turned as if to go. She had only a few minutes before she could expect to see his car. She looked back at the driver who was still watching her. "See you later. I'm one of the guests tonight. If it's not too nosy, what are you serving?"

"Hot and cold hors d'oeuvres. Do you like tiger shrimp satay?"

Hors d'oeuvres. That meant it wasn't a dinner party. Her plan might just be possible. "Love it. Will there be a big crowd?"

"Between fifty and sixty, according to the order sheet. But the shrimp goes fast."

She heard Jensen's car enter the street. "Thanks. See you later."

Head down, she walked quickly back to the entrance to the park and took her customary short cut home.

Three hours later, she was back. She'd brought her rusty Volkswagon this time, parking it a fair distance from the house. She'd had to guess at what to wear—a simple black dress, black heels, a gold and black woolen shawl cut on the bias. Evenings were still cool in April, but she needed the voluminous shawl for more than just warmth.

She paused, checking to see no other late-comers were approaching, then walked up the path, grasped the door handle, and entered as quietly as she could. She hoped Jensen would be busy with his guests. If she could just keep to the periphery of the gathering and make her way through the house, she should be unnoticeable.

No one approached her in the vestibule and she slipped silently into the dining room. There were maybe twenty people chatting in small groups, balancing plates and wine glasses. A few faces glanced up when she entered the room, but glanced away again when they failed to recognize her. If anyone asked, she would say she was with John. There were always two or three Johns in a party this size.

She scanned the layout of the room, noting its beautiful mahogany table laden with flowers, crystal, and platters of food, her eyes lingering on the three watercolours arranged on the far wall, and then edged her way to the door at the end which she guessed would lead to the kitchen.

It was brighter in this room, and for a minute her heart raced. The kitchen formed a long rectangle opening onto a sunken sun-room where another group of guests buzzed with conversation. Jensen was there, his back toward her. As if in slow motion, he began to turn.

She spotted the driver from the van, giving thanks that he was a tall man when he was standing up. She ducked in front of him. "Hi. I'm late. Got any shrimp left?"

He took just a moment to remember her, and then smiled. "Sure. I saved you some."

"Thanks. But first I'd like to leave my shawl. Is there a room somewhere for coats?"

He led her through a side door into the hall. The foot of the staircase was about five meters away from the vestibule. She'd been too anxious to melt into the crowd earlier to notice it.

"Straight upstairs. The first door to the right. I could take your shawl up for you, if you'd like."

"No thanks. I need to freshen up a bit."

She started up the stairs, trying not to move too quickly. She'd thought her timing was perfect, but now she worried that she may have arrived too late. Cocktail parties, by definition, ended early. Soon guests might be coming up to retrieve their coats. And Jensen would be at the front door to bid his guests good night.

She looked around her and groaned audibly. The open concept of the kitchen area was extended to the second floor of the house. Instead of a neat series of discrete rooms, there was only one small guest bedroom, its bed piled with coats, and a cozy TV room to the left. The rest of the floor was an expansive reading room with floor to ceiling oak bookshelves, and couches for lounging. The soft light came from several lamps on low tables, and half a dozen couples had escaped here from the chatter below for more intimate conversations. There were paintings on the walls, but she was too far away to study them. She couldn't cross the room without announcing her presence.

She looked around for another staircase, less grand, that would lead to the third storey of the house, and found it just to the left of the TV room. Some of the couples might notice her, but she had no other option. She lifted her head and tried to look as if she had a right to wander the house.

On the third floor, her nerves settled. It was in darkness, but street lights glowing through several skylights allowed her to explore. A master bedroom with an adjacent bath. Several stunning modern oils. She saw an Emily Carr that looked original, and a watercolour of cascading flowers by Molly Bobak. She stood before the closed door of a room roughly above the reading room below.

The knob turned easily and she entered the study, closing the door gently behind her and slipping off her shoes. She found the light switch and flicked it on. The room was smaller than the reading room, but still sizable. There was an Oriental silk rug on the hardwood floor, more bookshelves, a reading chair, an L-shaped computer desk. She scanned the walls—a series of mounted historical maps of Canada, a grouping of photographs.

And suddenly, there it was, just as she remembered it. The pen and ink drawing, unmistakably by Matisse. *Woman in a Blouse, Dreaming*. It was tucked into a small panel above Jensen's desk. He must look at it every day, as she had all through her childhood.

Immediately, she longed to touch it, to hold it again. But first, she had to look through his papers, just in case the letter was there. She didn't care any longer if she was caught. She felt reckless. The drawing didn't belong to him. He had no right to it. Now that she was this close, she wouldn't let it go. But she was careful and quiet. She found the desk files and began scanning them rapidly. Most of them were work files, sheets of paper filled with chemical formulas and government memoranda that she didn't understand. Nothing personal. She abandoned the files for the desk drawers.

In the third drawer, at the bottom of the desk and deeper than the others, Jensen's orderly filing system had been abandoned. She scooped out a jumble of papers, postcards, and envelopes with two hands and laid the shifting pile on the desk.

There were loose photographs, and she recognized several of Jensen and his brother. She would never forget his face. She picked up one photo and studied it. James Jensen was standing in front of the Eiffel Tower, an arm around the shoulders of an older woman. She looked vaguely familiar, but Chloe couldn't place her. Quickly, she sorted through theatre programmes and personal letters, but none had handwriting that she recognized. She would have to give up. The letter wasn't here.

She stuffed the material back in the drawer, and slowly reached for the framed Matisse. She caressed it with her fingers. It was not large. She lifted it gently from the wall and tucked it under her shawl, holding it against her body with one enfolding arm. She put on her shoes, shut out the lights, and listened at the door for a moment.

Then she slipped into the hall, down one staircase, down the next, and out into the night. No one stopped her. No one noticed her. She was dizzy with exhilaration.

For several days afterwards, Chloe combed the newspapers, searching for any mention of Jensen or the missing Matisse. The Sunday papers were always a bit thin, mostly filler stories and advertising flyers, and she found no references to her Thursday evening exploits. As she'd hoped, Jensen seemed not to have reported the theft, either because he didn't wish to have his guests interrogated or, more likely, because he lacked proof of ownership.

There was, of course, a third possibility.

If he remembered the letter he might have easily worked out what had happened. She knew he'd not seen her in his house, but others had. A few probing questions to his guests here and there, a phone call to Sammy, and he could surmise who had claimed the Matisse. Sammy would be shocked, indignant. Not his daughter, not his good little Chloe. But what could Jensen do, after all? She knew that he had no provenance for the drawing. He would be caught in his own brother's lie.

She was not surprised at her shamelessness. In fact, she was well-satisfied with herself, especially when she gazed upon the drawing. She liked to prop it against her living room wall and stretch out on the floor in front of it, her chin resting on her folded arms. Unconsciously, she adopted the same posture she'd had as a child, when looking upon the drawing anchored her amidst the turbulent emotions of her parents' disintegrating marriage. The sketch was her talisman, her link to her past, unalterable and romantic.

She knew every sweep of the pen, every intricate line. The woman's right arm lounged against the back of a chair, as if to make a pillow for the square, strong face that leaned against it. The elongated fingers of the right hand curved gently around her left wrist. Her left hand was tucked under her chin. The full sleeves of the blouse were all glorious pattern, a grid of straight lines in one patch that echoed the tight background of the sketch, and a profusion of multi-sized flowers and swirling leaves that spilled across the foreground. This, Chloe knew, was the famous Rumanian blouse that Matisse would paint again and again.

But it was the woman's face above the bursting detail of the blouse that arrested Chloe. It was drawn with only four clean, curving lines. The eyes did not confront the viewer, but seemed focused elsewhere, perhaps on the painter, perhaps on some dreamed about future. Her expression was tranquil, reflective. The slightly parted lips seemed almost about to smile. The shape of the face gave it strength, but it was gentle too. Chloe saw it as loving and open. In part, she knew this impression was a testimony to the skill of Matisse—the viewer's eyes were naturally drawn to the simplicity of the face in contrast to the decorative whirls of the blouse.

But Chloe also felt the way she did because the woman belonged to her. In the drawing, the woman wore a large, oval-shaped ring on her right hand, the same ring that Chloe now wore on hers. No, she couldn't feel ashamed of bringing the woman home. The legitimacy of her claim lay in her ancestry and on her finger, even though neither would go unchallenged in a court of law.

Chloe's reverie was interrupted by a sharp rap at the door. Her heart stuttered, and her first instinct was to hide the drawing. But, no. If she was to repossess it, she would do so proudly. It had been hidden from her sight by Jensen for too long.

The second rap was accompanied by a querulous voice. "Chlo. Open up."

Chloe smiled. It could only be her neighbour, who always pronounced her name as plain Chlo, rather than adding the final syllable. Chloe invited her in, and settled her on the sofa beneath her front window, taking care to place her cane within reach.

Mrs. Rosatti, Luciana, was always dressed in black, with thick black stockings and house slippers no matter what the weather. Her hair was cropped in a gray bob, and her face was webbed with a network of fine wrinkles. But she was endearingly vain of her appearance. Chloe had never seen her without lipstick, although some days, if her arthritis was acting up, it was applied a bit crookedly. As usual, two tiny gold crosses dangled from her pierced ears, and being Sunday, Luciana wore her rosary. Blessed by the Pope himself, or so she had told Chloe about a hundred times.

Her sharp eyes darted around the room, missing nothing. Chloe saw them pause briefly on the drawing.

"You painting again, Chlo? Is nice. But it needs colour. You should hang it."

Chloe smiled. "No, I didn't draw it, Luciana. Can I get you some tea?"

"No time. I come for Amber, poor little dog. No walks. You been busy? She waits for you, three days now." Luciana counted off the days one by one on her fingers as she spoke, and then shook her head and sighed, as if in deep sorrow.

The performance was overkill, but Chloe did feel abashed. "I'm sorry, Luciana. I'll take her for a walk right now, okay?"

"Okay. But no rush." Luciana grasped her cane and began to rise, shooing away Chloe's helping hand. "No, no, I'm not old yet."

She had never told her age, but Chloe guessed she must be in her mid-eighties, at least. While Luciana hobbled back to the front door, Chloe pulled on her shoes, and reached for her shoulder purse and her keys. Luciana stood watching on the tiny front porch, while Chloe locked the door behind her.

"You lock your door, now? You no trust your neighbours? Is good street."

"A very good street, Luciana. But it's sensible to be cautious. You should lock your door, too."

"Me? No things to steal. Not like Chlo's picture. By Matisse, no?" She croaked with laughter at Chloe's expression. "I'm no fool," she crowed.

With the little red cocker spaniel in tow, Chloe turned west along St. Clair toward the part of the city where the street signs read Corsa Italia, and where she could smell the aroma of freshly ground coffee and oven-baked bread.

The street was lined with little cafés and coffee bars, but the weather was still too chilly and often too unpredictable for the proprietors to set up their outdoor terraces. In summer, the area would be crowded with tourists and loyal customers, bantering and bartering in Italian, reading Italian newspapers, and sipping thick, black espresso. But in April, summer was still only a promise.

Chloe had long ago decided that Toronto had only three proper seasons, not four. There was the icy clamp of winter, hot, often humid summer, and radiant fall. But spring was just a euphemism. Late March to mid-May was indeterminate and fickle. A single day could bring heavy fog in the mornings, snow showers in the afternoon, and even bizarre electric storms. Then, as if overnight, the long denuded trees would suddenly burst into the raw green of fledgling leaves, and the temperatures would shoot into the high twenties, only to plunge a few days later. Today was a teasing day, with a high sun, clear sky, and a whisper of summer in the breeze.

Chloe was almost too warm in her fisherman's knit sweater and black jeans. She dawdled a bit, letting Amber's short legs rest from the effort of keeping up with her stride, and bought a crusty round loaf of Calabrese bread. Back at the corner of St. Clair and Crang, she stopped at her local variety store to stock up on vegetables and fruit. There were dog biscuits in a plastic bin and she bought two for Amber, her customary treat. The biscuits were a secret from Luciana, who didn't believe in spoiling pets.

Outside, Chloe put them on the sidewalk and was watching Amber gobble them down when she heard her name.

"Hello, Chloe."

She looked up at the face of her father, the usual easy smile replaced by a stern expression. His mouth was like a mail slot in an old wooden door.

"Hi, Dad. What brings you here?" Her tone was a bit too bright as she tried to compensate for the skittish feeling in her stomach.

Sammy Rea shook his head slowly and adjusted his wire rim glasses, his gaze penetrating straight to her false heart. He'd always known when she'd been up to mischief as a child, had caught her in every teenager's lie.

"Ah, Chloe. You don't change. We need to talk."

"Really? What's up?"

"Adam Jensen phoned me."

"Who?"

"Chloe."

Her face flushed and she took his arm with resignation.

Chloe's house was small and simple, sturdy brick with a whitish-gray facade of stone, a tiny porch with a black wrought iron railing, and a dormer roof over the front door. Inside, on the first floor, she had a living room, a poky dining room and a long kitchen, extended in better weather into a small outside deck and backyard. Upstairs was her bedroom that looked out over the garden, a study at the front that she called her studio because it caught the morning light, and a basic bathroom with an old-fashioned claw-foot tub and a hand-held shower attachment. Far from grand, it had its own appeal for Chloe, being entirely hers.

Sammy surveyed everything with a cool, appraising eye as if seeing the house for the first time. No matter how often he visited, the house always seemed to surprise him. Chloe suspected he had to catch himself from saying anything too patronizing like *how cute*, or *how quaint*. Sammy wasn't a snob, but as a prominent surgeon he lived in a different economic universe and felt a bit miffed that Chloe had refused his frequent offers of financial aid.

Chloe led Amber into the backyard, then fussed over coffee in the kitchen. When she returned to the living room, two mugs in hand, she watched Sammy sag into the nearest chair, running a hand through his dark red hair, his eyes fastened on the Matisse still propped against the wall. "So," he said in a soft voice. "You did steal it."

Chloe bristled. "No. I simply took back what's mine. James Jensen stole it years ago when he was helping you move out. Mom tried to tell you that, but you wouldn't listen. You never did."

Sammy refused to be sidetracked. "Chloe, you entered Adam Jensen's house and took this off his wall. I can't believe it. I nearly slugged him when he accused you. Are you crazy? Had it not been for my friendship with his brother, Adam would have called the police."

"But—"

Sammy raised his hand. "No, Chloe. I know it broke your heart when your mother sold this drawing to Jamie. Louise made up those stories about his so-called thievery to placate you."

"That's Jamie's version."

"That's Adam's version too. I want you to see him."

Chloe bolted upright from her chair, spilling coffee across her jeans.

"Sit down, Chloe. I want you to see him for my sake, as much as for yours. You know that Jamie is dead. Your mother wrote Adam an insulting letter demanding the return of the Matisse. But perhaps you already knew that. Did she put you up to this?"

"No. She's still in Arizona with Clarence." Despite herself, Chloe's nose wrinkled slightly when she spoke her stepfather's name. Kind but tedious

Clarence. He had none of the dash, humour, or charming unpredict-ability of her father. She glanced up, caught Sammy grinning.

She sat down, feeling some of the tension drain from the room. "Why should I see him?"

"Because you're a civilized woman, not a sneak thief. Because whatever you thought of him, Jamie was my friend. You and Adam need to work this out. I gave him your number."

"Oh, Dad."

"Oh, Chloe," he mimed. "Be good. Come for dinner sometime."

Sammy rose to leave but stopped in the doorway and stared back at the Matisse. "You know, I'd almost forgotten how beautiful it is. Louise always used to say the woman in the drawing was your grandmother."

Chloe touched a finger to her oval ring with its amethyst stone. "This proves it, doesn't it?"

"Maybe." Sammy leaned in to kiss her cheek.

"Dad? How did Jensen know it was me who took the drawing?"

"He said he'd seen a suspicious-looking woman loitering in the neigh-bourhood several times, one who looked a lot like me. But, of course, I told him you'd never spy on a person."

"Oh … well, bye Dad."

The first two times Adam Jensen called, Chloe panicked and hung up on him. Maybe he'll just give up, she thought, but when the phone rang again she groaned and snatched up the receiver.

"Persistent, aren't you?" she said coldly.

Her rudeness seemed to stun him for a moment, but when he spoke his voice was maddeningly calm. "Ms. Rea, I suggest we meet. Are you free this evening, perhaps?"

"Was it really necessary to involve my father?"

"Necessary? I think prudent would be a better term. This evening?"

"Fine. Where?"

"Well, you do know my house…" He let the sentence trail off.

"Very funny. I shall let my father know where I'll be."

"Of course. I can assure you my house is perfectly safe. Or it *was*. Does seven suit you?"

Suit yourself, Dr. Jensen, Chloe thought, but she swallowed the urge to say so and, in a somewhat strangled voice, placidly agreed.

When she hung up, she paced the room, tried to plan how she would confront him. The fact that he hadn't called the police was a point in her favour, one that suggested that he had no proof that his brother had acquired the drawing legally. She twisted the oval ring on her finger. She would tell him the truth, the stories that her mother had told her of a grandmother who'd travelled in her youth to Nice, who'd met the grand old master himself, and who'd modeled for him. Surely her claim was greater than Jensen's, despite what her mother might have done. Surely he would believe her.

Chloe stretched out on the floor in front of the drawing that she still hadn't hung. She sensed the past held many secrets that it gave up only grudgingly. Yet she believed that the drawing was a window back into time, that by staring into that enigmatic face of a dreamy woman in a blouse she could observe the exact moment, over sixty years ago, when Matisse was in his studio, studying his model, dipping his pen into the ink, lifting it over the page to make the first sweeping line.

She could barely remember a time when the drawing hadn't haunted her. She was maybe four when her mother had first told her the story behind it, twelve when it was snatched away from her by James Jensen. She'd become a painter, had never wanted to be anything else. Her grandmother's legacy had given her the house she was living in and her vocation. She would do anything to keep the drawing.

A sudden plan bloomed in her mind, so brazen as to startle her. She had the means to keep the drawing safe from Jensen. She picked it up, her hands trembling slightly, and climbed the stairs to her studio.

At seven-fifteen, Chloe rang the doorbell of Jensen's house. She'd spent the previous hour carefully grooming to achieve the chic young-professional-look in a belted navy suit. Then she'd scrubbed off the make-up, pulled her hair up into a ponytail, pulled on black jeans and a paint-smeared sweat shirt. Jensen could take her or leave her as she was.

She glimpsed his face in the small window carved into the door and then he was standing before her, smiling graciously.

"Good evening, Ms. Rea. Please, come in."

He was dressed impeccably in gray trousers, a pale-blue cashmere sweater, the crisp collar of a gray shirt around the base of his throat. Does he always dress like this, Chloe wondered, or had he, too, spent the day planning his strategy? She swept past him, not returning his smile. This wasn't a social visit, but a Sammy-commanded performance.

Behind her, Jensen cleared his throat. "I know this is awkward, but let's make the best of it, shall we?" He touched her elbow lightly, and led her into the living room, across a pale thick carpet to an elegant white sofa.

"What can I offer you? Coffee, scotch, wine?"

"White wine, thanks." Chloe smiled for politeness' sake.

"Good, back in a moment."

When he was gone, Chloe surveyed the room, one she had not entered the night she'd reclaimed the drawing. It was a soothing, pleasing space, high, patterned ceilings with subdued crown moldings, soft light from half a dozen table lamps, fresh flowers on the mantle of the fireplace. *Fresh flowers? What single man went to the trouble of fresh flowers?* She felt she had entered a carefully arranged stage set, and tried not to feel too shabby in her stubbornly chosen clothes.

She turned her head to her left where a huge modern tapestry, pure white with black abstract figures, dominated the wall space. The sight of it rattled her. It was unmistakably reminiscent of Matisse, of the playful and exuberant cut-outs and murals he had crafted in the last years of his life. She was still staring at it when Jensen returned, handing her a glass of chilled white wine.

"You seem surprised," he said, with just a trace of sarcasm. "You've not seen the tapestry before?"

"Look, Dr. Jensen—"

"Adam, please."

"Dr. Jensen, I apologize for invading your privacy. But we both know the Matisse belongs to me, and there seemed no other way. I've no excuse, other than I took my cue from your own brother who acquired the drawing in a similar fashion."

He sat down in a chair opposite her, a glass coffee table between them.

"So much for opening pleasantries. Are you always this blunt?"

"I try to be polite, but even when I don't say what I really think, I can seldom hide it."

Jensen laughed. He took a swallow of scotch, his eyes studying her over the rim of his glass. Sky-blue eyes, Chloe noticed, staring back. Deep blue-sea eyes with long, thick lashes. She glanced away.

"Alright, Ms. Rea. Sammy intimated that the drawing holds a special meaning for you. I'm prepared to listen, if you'll tell me."

She held up her right hand, wiggled her ring finger. "Do you recognize this?"

"It's a lovely ring."

"It's the ring in the drawing, the one the model is wearing. I inherited it from my grandmother. She's the dreaming woman."

"You're saying that your grandmother posed for Matisse?"

"Exactly. Her name was Sylvie, Sylvie Brionne, born in Montreal. Very few women traveled in the late nineteen-thirties unless they were very brave or very rich and could afford a chaperone. Sylvie was very brave. She landed up in Nice, working as a maid in a hotel.

"When the war broke out, she was desperate for money to try to get back home. Matisse hired lots of models when he was living in Nice, maids, actresses, and women he would see shopping for vegetables or flowers in the market of the Cours Saleya. He met Sylvie and she agreed to pose for him, wearing the Rumanian blouse. Perhaps for other sketches, too—he did hundreds of them, you know, and some were lost in the war. Sylvie met my grandfather, André, in Nice. The drawing was Matisse's wedding present to them."

Jensen stared into his scotch glass, then stood up abruptly.

"I think I need another," he said. "More wine?"

Chloe shook her head. "Aren't you going to say anything?"

He walked away from her, crossed the room to the liquor cabinet, and poured himself another drink. Then he leaned against the cabinet, looking at Chloe's flushed cheeks, her eyes shining. He raised his glass to her. "It's a wonderful story."

Instantly, her eyes darkened. "You don't believe me."

"I didn't say that. You know, Chloe … may I call you Chloe?"

She shrugged.

"We've met before, Chloe—you don't remember? You were three or four, I was twelve. My brother took me with him to your house and I wandered into the back yard. You were playing in your sand box with a shovel and pail. I tried to take the shovel away from you and you bonked me over the head with the pail. I feel like you've just done it again."

"Serves you right. But I'm not sure I understand."

"I'm not sure I do either, not fully. But let me try to explain. Jamie was a lot older than me, almost eight years. As a youngster, I adored him, trailed after him everywhere. Well, Sammy can tell you that. But as we grew older, our age roles were reversed. Jamie was rebellious, often in trouble."

Chloe smothered a sound that was almost a snort.

Jensen scowled at her. "Do you want to hear this or not?"

"Sorry, go on."

"I was the one who lied to our parents when Jamie needed an alibi, the one who would pick him up at three in the morning when he was too drunk to drive. I excelled at school. Jamie dropped out, drifted. But he was irresistible, people responded easily to him. I could never stay angry with him for long, despite his irresponsibility. It was never dull, having Jamie as a brother. Then, in 1997, he went to Paris. We kept in touch sporadically, I visited him occasionally, but I could never persuade him to come home."

When Adam stopped speaking, Chloe read the sadness in his face. Silence descended upon them and, despite her guard, she felt a twinge of sympathy. "What happened to him?" she prompted.

"An accident. He was on a motorcycle, speeding as usual. He lost control, died instantly—at least that's what the authorities always say, isn't it? Quick painless death is always easier for the survivors to accept. I flew to Paris, brought his broken body home, buried him. But, Chloe, Jamie sent the drawing to me by registered mail days before he died. He sent it with a note that read simply, *Keep her safe. I'll see you soon.*"

"He was finally coming home?"

"He was. I imagined him wandering the tiny art galleries on the Left Bank, flipping through portfolios and finding the Matisse drawing, something simple and beautiful, something that reminded him of his little brother and made him want to come home. I know now that didn't happen. First there was the letter from your mother accusing Jamie of stealing the painting years ago. When she learned of his death, she hoped I would return it. Well, *demanded* I return it actually. I thought the letter was pretty insensitive and dismissed it out of hand. But it seems she wasn't the only one who wanted the drawing."

"Look, I'm sorry for your loss, I really am. But I've already tried to explain—"

"I wasn't referring to you," Adam interrupted. "Jamie's girlfriend in Paris asked me about the drawing almost as soon as I arrived there."

Did Jamie have it when he was killed? Was it destroyed in the accident?

"I thought it strange, but she was in as much shock as I was, and it was clear that Jamie had really cared about the Matisse. When I told her the drawing was safe, she seemed relieved and that was the end of it, I thought. Then a week or so before you ... er, retrieved it from my study, I had a call from George Daniels."

Chloe raised an eyebrow. She knew the name, but not the man. He was a prominent art dealer in Toronto. She'd been to his gallery a half dozen times, had nursed a fantasy that one day one of her paintings might hang on his gallery walls. "You know Daniels?"

"Only professionally. He sold me a couple of paintings. But he has connections in Paris. He wanted to know if Jamie had left me *Woman in a Blouse, Dreaming* and if was I interested in selling it."

"That's an odd coincidence. How would he even know that Jamie had the sketch? I *know* he didn't buy it from Daniels."

"As you say, a very odd coincidence. It makes me wonder if Jamie was trying to tell me something when he wrote I should keep it safe."

"Well I can't blame him, I suppose, for keeping it all these years. But the drawing is part of my history. The woman is Sylvie. She died when I was two. I didn't even know her, just her face in the drawing and her story. Jamie couldn't possibly have cared as much as I do."

"Ah, yes, the story. Look, Chloe, it's obvious that your mother owned the painting before Jamie did. But do you have any proof that the story is true?"

"You're saying that my mother is a liar?"

"I'm suggesting that she told an enchanting tale to her little girl. It's possible, isn't it?"

"No. And she would never have sold the painting to your brother either, if that's where you're heading."

Adam hesitated before responding, and Chloe saw his expression soften. "I'm sorry," he said. "But she did. I have the receipt."

Chloe sat back abruptly, as if she'd been slapped. "I—I don't believe you," she stuttered. "She wouldn't…"

Adam slid a hand under his sweater, took a piece of paper from his shirt pocket and smoothed it out on the coffee table. "Have a look. Is it your mother's signature?"

Chloe stared at the slip of paper until her eyes blurred, and the words danced menacingly in her head. *Woman in a Blouse, Dreaming. Sold to James Jensen for one thousand dollars.* She felt confused, betrayed, angry. She felt bereft. Her world cracked open. All she had believed, all she had become, poisoned by a tiny piece of paper. She pushed it away from her as if it were contaminated.

She stood up blindly, refusing to look at Jensen. She heard him call out after her, but she was already running down the path, running into the night, her face wet with tears, her fists clenched, running away from her mother's signature in blue ink that laid waste to the assumptions on which she had based her life.

What folly to leave Paris to follow a handsome face. Nikolai fed me airy dreams while my stomach grumbled for bread. What did I hope to find? Nice was awash in a tide of émigrés and refugees. Foreigners were shunned. It was illegal for us to work at anything but unskilled labour. My accent was crude, branding me. My clothes grew loose as my body grew thinner.

Sometimes I wandered among the market stalls of the Cours Saleya. I was unused to this press of people, these cries, these smells. A one-eyed man behind a table loaded with glossy aubergines winked and mouthed a bawdy comment as I passed. Customers held their noses at the butcher's stall, purple with flies and black with old blood. A little girl in a shabby coat was selling packets of herbs from the back of a small white goat. She watched me with hard eyes as I snatched up a piece of spotted fruit or a withered vegetable that had dropped to the ground. I felt ashamed.

I clutched the piece of paper with the address in my hand: number one, Place Charles Félix. A chance acquaintance at a bus stop had told me the family was looking for a maid. A maid, when once I might have been so much more. I entered the apartment as timid as a mouse, sniffing the air, ready to scurry away at the first sharp word. The dark brows of Madame made me tremble. She rattled off instructions like a gun shooting bullets.

But when he entered the room, wearing a fine white shirt, black trousers and a waistcoat, the air became still. He spoke to me kindly, with the manners of my father's generation, un vieux monsieur, *a correct old gentleman, white cropped hair and beard. His eyes behind the wire-rimmed glasses were ageless. I called him Patron. Somehow, I sensed he would keep me safe.*

II

CHLOE WOKE EARLY, UNREFRESHED, HER fitful sleep disturbed by uneasy dreams. For a moment she was sure some terrible calamity had happened somewhere, a car wreck, an earthquake, a sudden death. Then her eyes fell on the drawing she had finally hung in her bedroom and the pain of remembrance rushed in. There was no calamity, just a lie that stole the certain ground from under her, just the small death of a childhood trust. Sadness and embarrassment had replaced her anger. She had no claim to the painting now. She was a common thief. She would have to return it to Jensen. She had no doubt he would call soon.

She showered and made coffee, sat on her deck in the pale sunshine. She was sorry that the academic term was over. The life drawing classes she taught part-time at the Ontario College of Art and Design would have preoccupied her, pushed away the questions in her mind. Over the past few weeks, she had neglected her friends and her daily routine with her wild acts and her stubborn certainties. Now she needed her support network, needed some mundane task, something less demanding than her creative work. She decided to go to the college anyway. With any luck, Emily might still be grading papers in her office.

Emily Bryce was her touchstone, the person she turned to when she needed advice and comfort. They'd met when they were Fine Arts students at York University, spending hours together sketching and skipping class, affecting the bohemian look of paint-splattered jeans and loose, flowered smocks that reached to their knees. Chloe hadn't realized how lonely she'd been until she'd met Emmy, the closest thing to a sister she was ever likely to find.

The architecture of the redesigned art college was a point of controversy in Toronto. As Chloe stepped off the Queen Street bus, she tried to decide again whether she loved or hated the polka-dot box that dared to challenge conservative sensibilities. The building certainly made a statement: she just wasn't sure if that statement was ironic given that the building housed a school of design.

She pushed open the glass doors and ran up a flight of stairs to the hallway where Emily's office was located. She cheered up instantly when she saw her door was ajar. She knocked softly.

"Hi Emmy. Still slaving away, I see."

"Well, if it isn't Chloe Rea. The term ends and, whoosh, you disappear. I thought maybe you'd left the country. Or maybe you'd eloped with Paolo. Or maybe you'd been struck on the head and suffered amnesia. You don't answer your phone anymore?"

"Sorry, I—I was working on a project. I'm afraid it turned out rather badly."

"A painting?"

"Not exactly." Chloe blushed.

"Oh dear. What've you done? Wait here. I'll get us some coffee."

Chloe watched Emmy walk down the hall to the administrative office. Her friend had long since given up the bohemian look as economically unsound. Her thick fawn hair, once falling to mid-back, was elegantly cut and styled to shoulder length. Her navy, pin-striped suit was tailored and expensive, the turquoise scarf at her neck intensifying the blue-green of her eyes. She'd cleaned up well, but she was still the same perceptive, slightly cynical Emmy underneath the polished surface.

When she returned, she handed Chloe a mug and listened without comment while her friend blurted out the details of her stalking, her thievery, her confrontations with Sammy and Jensen, and her dramatic retreat from Jensen's house.

"It sounds worse than it actually is," Chloe finished.

"I hardly think that's possible," Emmy countered wryly. "Have you talked to Louise yet?"

"I'm too angry with her. I thought I'd wait a few days until I calm down. But it was definitely her signature on the receipt. The fact that she wrote Jensen that letter when she knew the drawing wasn't stolen, well, it's just outrageous."

"Let's not go there, Chloe. Kettles calling pots black, and all that. But I think you're missing the obvious."

"Which is?"

"How did your mother ever get the drawing in the first place? What's its provenance? Okay, so she sold the painting and lied to you about that. Obviously she regrets it—the letter she sent to Jensen makes that clear. If anything, the letter suggests that the story she told you *was* true. Why would she care if Jensen still had it otherwise? One lie doesn't mean *everything* was a lie."

"I don't know what to believe anymore." Unconsciously, Chloe twisted the amethyst ring. The truth was she wanted to cling to the story, however fictitious it might be. Adam Jensen's insinuations had shaken her, raising doubts about the past in her mind like matches flaring brightly in the darkness, then quickly extinguished. As long as the woman dreaming remained a mystery, she could belong to her. Chloe didn't know how to explain, even to Emmy, the intimacy she felt about the drawing. If it were *proven* that the woman in the drawing had nothing to do with her, that electric connection to the past would be severed forever.

"What's he like, anyway?" Emmy asked, interrupting Chloe's thoughts.

"Jensen? I hardly know. He seemed to care about his brother. And given what's happened, I guess I'd have to say he's patient."

"Do you think he might sell the drawing to you, if he knows what it means to you?"

Chloe shook her head. "He didn't believe me. Even if he did, the drawing must now be worth five or six times what my mother sold it for, maybe more. I could never afford it."

"Sammy could."

"No thanks. He already cajoles his friends into buying my paintings, thinking I don't notice his financial support when it comes through the back door. Besides, that would put me right back in the middle of the Sammy-Louise bickering."

"Dull Clarence then?"

"Never. Besides, Jensen told me that George Daniels wants to purchase the drawing."

Emmy sniffed. "Well, he can't be feeling that sentimental about his brother if he's already approached Daniels."

"That's just it. Daniels approached him, not the other way around." Chloe looked puzzled, remembering the conversation. "He—Jensen I mean, seemed surprised that there was so much interest in the drawing."

"Well, he would, wouldn't he? After all, there was the crazy letter from Louise, and then your burglary. Look, Chloe, I know you have this obsession with the drawing. I think I can even guess why. But your best bet is to do the research, no matter how much you fear what you might find. If the woman is really your grandmother, if you can document it, perhaps Jensen will cut you a deal. And for goodness' sake, call Paolo. He's been pestering me."

"Really?" Chloe grinned.

"Don't look so delighted. He won't be as forgiving as I am."

Paolo DeVito, like Chloe, was an artist. She'd met him when OCAD was being rebuilt, when the construction crew often went shirtless in the summer heat. She couldn't help but notice his shoulder and back muscles, but she liked to tell herself that it was Paolo's grin and his black curls peeking out from under the hard hat that had won her over. She'd since learned that construction work paid his rent and helped to support his carpentry, his art. He designed beautiful chairs, tables, cradles, and sleighs with sweeping lines and wood so polished it was silky to the touch.

Rounding the corner into Crang Avenue, she found him sitting on her neighbour's porch. His Italian heritage made him Luciana's favourite, not least because she could speak to him in her native tongue. As Chloe approached, Paolo said something in Italian that had the old woman shaking with laughter.

"You're a bad one, Chlo," she said, raising an admonishing finger. "You no look after this man, I steal him from you."

Paolo scowled at Chloe and she felt a twinge of guilt for ignoring him over the past few weeks. "You're right, Luciana. I'll feed him. That always cheers him up."

The sound of her voice triggered frantic barking from inside Luciana's house. "That's Amber you hear, poor little dog…" The old woman sighed.

"Later. I'll take her later, okay?" Chloe retreated, with Paolo in tow.

When she'd shut the door behind them, she looked up quickly to see if his scowl was gone. It wasn't.

She hugged him, gave him her best smile. "I'm sorry, Paolo. I should have called. I've just been so caught up."

"Doing what?"

"Oh, it's a long story," Chloe felt reluctant to tell it again.

"I have time. I've had lots of free time lately."

"No, really, it's just a Sammy and Louise problem. I'm caught in the middle again." She turned away to hide her eyes. She'd almost told the truth. "Look, I know it's a bit late for lunch, but if you're hungry—"

Paolo started up the stairs, his scowl gone. He reached back and extended a hand to her.

He has such lovely hands, Chloe thought. She smiled and followed him.

Several hours later, Chloe was in the shower when she heard the doorbell ring. She called out to Paolo, "Will you get that? It'll be Luciana wanting us to take Amber for her walk."

But, ten minutes later, when she entered the living room, wearing a pair of cut-offs and one of Paolo's old shirts, her hair a damp tumble of curls, she saw Paolo and Adam Jensen sitting stiffly in chairs on opposite sides of the room. When she appeared, Jensen rose quickly to his feet.

"I apologize, Ms. Rea, for the interruption. I had something to discuss about the drawing. Perhaps another time?" He turned toward the front door.

"No wait. Paolo, this is Dr. Jensen. He's a friend of my father's. Paolo DeVito."

"We've already introduced ourselves, thanks anyway." There was a slight edge to Paolo's voice that caught Chloe by surprise. Despite their afternoon together, he must still be feeling resentment at her recent desertion. Well, she certainly wasn't going to explain, not in front of Jensen. She glanced from man to man, not a little exasperated with both of them. Jensen caught her eye, biting his lower lip as if trying not to laugh. Clearly, from her appearance, he'd made his own assumptions as to how she'd spent her afternoon.

The doorbell rang again. "That really will be Luciana," Chloe sighed.

"I'll go," Paolo offered, opening the door to a chorus of barks from Amber, and closing it again without another word.

Chloe glared at Jensen.

"Sorry," he shrugged. "Not the best timing."

"No. I suppose you've come for the drawing?"

"Actually, I came to invite you to dinner." He raised his hands as Chloe began to protest. "George Daniels invited me to his home for dinner. I thought you might be curious enough to join me."

"Does he often invite you to dinner?"

"Never."

"In that case, how can I refuse? Obviously he wants the drawing. Will you sell it to him?"

"Right now, I'm more interested in why he wants to buy it, and how he knows Jamie had it. I don't think Jamie's intention was to sell."

Chloe moved reluctantly towards the stairs. "If you'll wait here just a moment, I'll get it for you."

Jensen stopped her with a light touch on her arm. "The drawing means a lot to both of us. I don't mind your borrowing it for a while longer. It's safe here. I'll pick you up at seven, if that's okay?"

Chloe nodded, surprised, grateful, and afraid to speak.

Having spent an hour unruffling Paolo's feathers, Chloe closed the door behind him with a sense of relief. At first, she found his unwarranted jealousy flattering, but ultimately she found it boring. It made her feel slightly claustrophobic.

She went upstairs, flopped on the bed, and stared at the Matisse. Then she rolled over on her stomach and reached for the phone.

Her call was answered in a stolid monotone, unmistakably her stepfather's.

"Hello, Clarence. This is Chloe. Is my mother there?"

"Your mother and I were just talking about you this morning, Chloe. We thought you might like to come for a visit. The golf courses are in excellent shape right now, and there's a spanking new shopping mall, just opened."

Chloe suppressed a shudder but was spared answering by Louise's breathy greeting.

"Darling, how are you?"

"I'm phoning about the Matisse drawing, Mom."

"Splendid. Has Jensen agreed to return it? I made it quite clear in my letter that he has no right to keep it."

"Why ever not? You sold it to Jamie."

"Now, dear, we've been over this before. Has Sammy been talking to you?"

"Sammy has nothing to do with this. I met Adam Jensen. He showed me the receipt you gave to Jamie. How could you do it?"

Chloe listened to the silence with her eyes shut, then took a deep breath. "Mom? It doesn't matter anymore, just tell me the truth. Is the woman dreaming really my grandmother? How did you get the drawing in the first place?"

"I swear it came from Sylvie, and the ring, too. I never sold the ring. You must understand, dear, there were so many expenses—piano lessons, swimming lessons, dance classes. Sammy never gave me enough to cover expenses."

Chloe stopped listening. Of course, selling the drawing would be someone else's fault. Sammy's, or her own for having a middle-class childhood. When she tuned in again, Louise was going on about Jamie.

"…and anyway, why would he keep an old receipt? He never cared about anything but himself. Are you sure this isn't some trick? Perhaps you've been duped."

"Not by Jensen, Mom."

More silence. Then, miraculously, "I'm sorry, Chloe. Really I am. I couldn't face up to telling you the truth. You were only little, and I knew you wouldn't understand."

"But how could you write that letter to Jensen? You knew that if Jamie had kept the drawing, it belonged to Adam now, fair and square."

"I thought it was worth a shot."

Chloe almost laughed. After all, writing the letter wasn't any worse than entering Jensen's house and robbing him. She decided to leave out that detail.

"Fair enough, Mom. Look, aside from the story of the wedding present, did Sylvie ever have any proof that she got the drawing from Matisse, any papers or documents?"

"Papers? Why would she need to document a gift?"

"So there's no proof, nothing to substantiate that the story she told you, and that you told me, is really true. She could have made it all up."

"Really, Chloe. I think that's a bit harsh. After all, she was in Nice. And you have the ring. Perhaps there's something in the letters she kept."

"Letters? What letters?"

"Oh, your grandmother kept all kinds of stuff—postcards, letters, travel souvenirs, even match boxes. She was a bit of a pack rat, our Sylvie."

"Where? Did you keep it all?"

"Heavens, no. I imagine it's all in the cottage in Gatineau unless André cleared it out when she died. When your grandfather died and the cottage passed to me, I never saw anything of Sylvie's, but then I didn't check either. You could always try the attic."

"Thanks, Mom."

"Oh, and Chloe, stay away from Adam Jensen. If he's anything like his brother, you'll be grateful for my advice."

But he isn't, thought Chloe, *not yet.*

Just past seven, Chloe chanced a quick glance at Adam. The car he was driving, a sleek Mercedes, was in a far different class than her rusty Volkswagen. She'd barely noticed Toronto's typical spring obstacle course of potholed roads.

"Nervous?" she asked.

"No, just curious. What about you? After all, you're an artist. If Daniels likes you, this could turn out to be a profitable evening for you."

"I'd rather he liked the paintings."

"Has he seen your work?"

"I hardly think so. I show occasionally in a little gallery in the Distillery

District. That's a long way from the chic galleries in Yorkville."

"You shouldn't be so modest. Quality shines anywhere. I own one of your paintings, you know. *Winter Window*—mostly white with a few streaks of blue, like pieces of sky through a frosted window."

Chloe laughed. "Let me guess. One day, perhaps after a pleasant lunch in the Distillery District, Sammy casually mentions a gallery he knows just around the corner. Am I right?"

"Well, yes. But I wouldn't have bought the painting if I hadn't admired it, Sammy or not."

"Thanks. But I don't recall ever seeing your name on the purchaser lists, and I wouldn't pass over the name Jensen."

"Oh, well. I used Elizabeth's name. She's my fiancée, the painting was for her."

"Was?"

"Just going through a bit of a rough patch. I'm sure it'll work out eventually."

Chloe thought it must be a very long patch indeed. She'd seen no sign of a woman in Adam's life when she was surveying his house, but it was none of her business.

She turned her attention to the Rosedale neighbourhood where Daniels lived. Beautiful old trees, still bare but with a faint sheen of green from timid buds waiting for warmer nights before bursting open. Beautiful old houses, some with high hedges or brick walls to keep the curious at bay. Others were lit up inside, and from the gathering darkness outside, she caught tantalizing glimpses of etched glass doors, crystal chandeliers, even the glint of copper pots in a designer kitchen. She was glad to see there were occasional low-rise apartment buildings, too. They softened the myth that Rosedale was an enclave only for the rich.

"I think this is it," Adam said, pulling into the curb.

Chloe stared. The house gleamed, shimmered in a bath of artificial moonlight from strategically placed floodlights. A huge gray-stone with a wrap-around porch, it loomed over her like something from a Southern Gothic novel—it even had a widow's walk at the very top. Her left hand strayed to her hair as it always did when she was nervous.

Adam opened the car door for her and held out a hand.

"C'mon Chloe. There'll be cocktails. Drink two very fast and you'll be fine."

A butler answered the doorbell—*Jesus*, thought Chloe, *a butler*—and he took from her the same shawl she'd worn on the night she'd crashed Jensen's party. Underneath she wore black silk pants and camisole, topped by a lime green jacket that set off her red hair. She considered herself reasonably stylish, but inside Daniels' opulent lair, she feared she just looked like someone who might steal the towels. She glanced over at Adam in his black suit, black tie, blue shirt, and smiled, feeling less confident than she looked.

They were standing in a kind of outer hall, an orangery with bay trees and plants with trailing leaves in waist-high Chinese jars on a golden-gray marble floor. The sound of a small fountain splashed from a grouping of statuary.

"Adam. I'm so glad you could come."

Chloe followed the voice, and saw a short plump man, slightly balding, with a luxuriant moustache and the keen glance of a collector. His glittering eyes fell on her.

"George, good to see you," Adam replied. "May I present Chloe Rea? She's an artist. By the way, she has a special fondness for the Matisse drawing."

"Excellent. Excellent. Come, my dear, you must tell me all about yourself." Daniels took Chloe's arm and propelled her away, chattering the whole time. She had a vague glimpse of Adam receding into the background and then was dazzled by her entry into a white and lavender room, deep lavender, almost purple.

Dozens of sconce-lamps, each one unique, lined both lengths of the room. Some were clear glass with squared edges in the fashion of Art Nouveau, others were opaque glass in pastel shades of pink and blue and gold, decorated with carved birds or flowers. Some were antique Victorian and some were whirls of coloured Murano hand-blown glass.

"How lovely," Chloe whispered. She looked around for Daniels, but he seemed to have disappeared. In fact, she was quite alone. She began to wander down the line of sconces, stopping to examine each one. She was studying a pale green bird, of a style and quality unmistakably by Lalique, when Adam touched her shoulder.

"Daniels seems a bit obsessive, doesn't he? He has another room like this across the hall filled with ceramics and pottery. Chagall, Picasso, Braque."

"I thought you'd never been here before?"

"I haven't. I've just come from there. You've been looking at these lamps for twenty minutes."

"Really? They're glorious. They should be in a museum though, not a private house."

"I don't think you should share that opinion with our host."

"Where is he, anyway?"

"Just checking on the last minute dinner preparations, apparently. It seems we're the only guests. Very exclusive."

"Hush. And where's my cocktail by the way?"

"Ah, Chloe. I'm pleased you like my little collection of lamps—"

Chloe jumped slightly. Daniels had an uncanny ability, it seemed, to disappear and reappear like a ghost. It must be the thick carpeting, she decided, and turned her attention to him.

"Indeed. The lamps are glorious. Wherever did you find them all?"

"Ah, a question you should never ask a collector. Here and there, my dear, here and there. Venice, Paris, Budapest, some even from here in Rosedale. But dinner is served. Come, come."

They followed Daniels into a soft gray dining room. One end of a long table was laid with crystal, silver, and candles on a field of pure white damask. But Chloe was best pleased to see an ice bucket near the sideboard.

"Shall we begin with a little aperitif?" Daniels offered. "Champagne is my drink of choice."

The butler reappeared to fill their glasses with golden bubbles. Like Daniels, he seemed to move noiselessly, surprising for such a big man. Tall and broad-shouldered, darkly handsome with Slavic features, he reminded Chloe of an extra from the set of *Doctor Zhivago*. She was a bit relieved to learn he had multiple tasks, and downgraded his status from butler to man-about-the-house. When he had left the room, Chloe turned to Daniels, "Does he cook too?" she asked impulsively.

"Peter? Yes, he does a bit of everything. He's Russian, you know, barely speaks English, but cooks like a dream. Tonight, we're having quails and grapes, a French classic in honour of Matisse."

"About the Matisse," Adam began.

"Not yet, dear boy. First we must eat, and Chloe will tell me all about herself. Now, what kind of painting do you do?"

Between mouthfuls of salad and Parmesan flan, Chloe talked about her training as an artist, first in Toronto, then Quebec, New York, and the American Southwest. Over the quails in grape sauce, she talked about her favourite artists—Bonnard, Riopelle, Kandinsky, O'Keefe, Morisot, and, of course, Matisse.

"But you've never been to Paris?" Daniels queried. "That's a shocking oversight for a serious artist. How can you begin to understand Matisse, or even Bonnard, without having been to Paris, or more to the point, the South of France? You must study in the presence of the originals."

"I didn't say I'd never seen the originals. France has no monopoly. Most of Matisse's major paintings are in Russia or America. And I go to exhibitions every chance I get. I've seen the Barnes and the Cole collections, and once," Chloe met Adam's eyes across the table, "I even owned a Matisse drawing, the very one that Adam now owns."

As if they had rehearsed the moment, Adam picked up his cue.

"It seems Jamie bought it years ago from Chloe's mother. I thought he'd found it in Paris," Adam explained. "But that wasn't what happened. Tell me Daniels, how did you know Jamie had the drawing, or even that he'd left it to me in his will?"

"A dealer's secret, dear boy. We've always got an ear to the ground, or a nose in the air, whichever metaphor you prefer."

Adam didn't smile. "Actually, I'd prefer the truth."

For the first time, Daniels looked nonplussed. Chloe noticed that one of his eyelids began twitching like an erratic heartbeat.

"Well, if you really must know, let me see. Yes, well, I believe it was the charming Elizabeth."

The name hung in the air. It was difficult to be certain in the candle-light, but Chloe thought Adam's face darkened.

"Actually, Mr. Daniels," Chloe began.

"George, please."

"Okay, George. *Woman in a Blouse, Dreaming* has a very special meaning for my family. You see my grandmother was in Nice at the time. The drawing was a gift from Matisse when she married, and the story goes that she posed for it."

"Absurd," Daniels spluttered. "Why, all of his favourite models are well known to the art world. Surely you don't believe such a story? To make such a claim publicly, well, dear, I'm sure you wouldn't want to embarrass your family. And I'd be duty bound to debunk such a fairy tale."

He smiled, a condescending, patronizing smile.

It had the opposite effect on Chloe than the one intended.

"You know," she responded brightly, "I've always loved fairy stories, especially those that warn the princess not to open the secret chamber in Bluebeard's castle. When someone tells me not to do something, it only makes what's forbidden more intriguing."

"Why, I don't know what you mean," Daniels replied coldly, though clearly he did. He turned away from her toward Adam.

"So I'm to compete for the drawing, am I? Very well. I'll offer you fifteen thousand."

"That's outrageous," Chloe blurted.

"As you say, my dear. I've a client very fond of anything that shows the Rumanian blouse. Do your homework, you won't get a better offer."

"I'm not certain Jamie would've wanted me to sell." Adam confessed. "He was a man who carried very little baggage through life, people or things. Yet he kept this drawing for a very long time. That intrigues me."

"I'm sure he was only waiting for the right moment to sell," Daniels argued. "And you've a chance to cash in most handsomely. Think it over, my boy. I can't say the client will wait indefinitely."

Beyond this point, conversation dragged. Chloe longed to escape, and Daniels seemed no longer interested in either her or her painting. She swirled her white chocolate mousse into abstract designs with her spoon, while Adam and Daniels talked in a desultory manner about the weather and Gehry's stunning renovations to the Art Gallery of Ontario.

Only once did she listen closely.

"And how is the lovely Elizabeth?" Daniels was asking. "Now there's a model for Matisse, if you ask me. I'd understood from mutual acquaintances that the wedding was to be quite soon."

Chloe read the query as deliberately provocative, a slight against both her presence at the table in place of Adam's fiancée, and the claim of her grandmother.

"Yes, well, Jamie's death has been very difficult for my parents, both quite frail already. We thought we'd let some time pass. Speaking of time, I think Chloe and I must leave."

Daniels' protestations held no sincerity. He rose to his feet as the omnipresent Peter led them to the door, handed Chloe her shawl, and bid them a curt goodnight.

Fresh night air had seldom tasted quite so sweet to Chloe.

"Well, what did you think?" Adam asked, starting the car.

"If I hear one more 'my dear' or 'old boy' I think I'll explode. It's true that most of the models for Matisse's paintings are known, but the drawings are different. Some he named, many others he didn't. I wish I could prove that Sylvie posed for Matisse, if only to wipe that sneer from Daniels' face."

"*Can* you prove it?"

Chloe stared at his profile. "Maybe. I talked to my Mom today. She said that Sylvie kept all kinds of letters in our cottage in the Gatineau Hills. I used to go there often as a child, but it's been years now since I've been. It's possible that there's some record of Sylvie's time in Nice. But why should you care? You don't believe me, either."

"I think it unlikely, not quite the same thing. But stranger things have happened, and it would go some way to explaining Daniels' offer. Suppose Matisse really did have a Canadian model. Surely that would make the drawing more valuable, at least in Canada."

"Sure, and as Daniels said—how did he put it? You could cash in handsomely."

"Shame on you, Chloe."

"Sorry. But *are* you going to sell the drawing? And if you are, won't you please consider selling it to me? I can't offer anything near what

Daniels would give you. But I, at least, care about it. I wouldn't be selling it forward to some anonymous collector."

Adam didn't answer. Chloe watched the night slide by through the car windows, hugged her shawl tighter around her. She felt embarrassed by her plea, faintly ashamed of herself, and irrationally resentful of Adam. She'd not ask again, she vowed to herself. Never again.

The car drew up to the front of her house. She felt Adam touch her shoulder.

He looked straight into her dark eyes. "I won't sell the sketch, Chloe, either to you or Daniels. Jamie never meant me to sell it. I'm as sure about that as I've ever been about anything. But I want to know everything I can about it, perhaps as much as you do. You see, Chloe, I never said a word to Elizabeth about it. She didn't know I had it."

"But why would Daniels lie?"

"Why indeed? Chloe, we need to find out the history of this drawing. It must be important. I'll make you a deal. You can keep the sketch—"

The rest of his words were lost as Chloe scooted across the car seat and hugged him, her arms around his neck.

Adam disentangled himself, more slowly than he'd intended, disconcerted by the smell and softness of her hair. "I hadn't finished yet," he cautioned. "You can keep the Matisse, *if* you can prove that your grandmother really was the model. But I'd like to come with you to search. If there's proof, I want to see it with my own eyes."

"You want to come with me to the cottage in Gatineau?"

"That's the deal."

"Okay, phone me and we'll set it up." Chloe stepped out of the car, but ducked her head back in. "And it's just possible, Adam Jensen, that I misjudged you years ago when I hit you over the head with that pail."

III

THE DAYS SEEM TO MELT, *each into the next. All is hushed when Patron paints, as if the world holds its breath. The entire household bends to his schedule, and suffers in an atmosphere of almost unbearable tension. My task, not an easy one, is to keep little grandson Claude as quiet as possible and run errands for Madame. They have taken me in, even though it is illegal by French law to do so.*

I am ashamed to think of how it began. It was my infatuation with Nikolai, with his dark eyes and sweet words and the long, languorous Mediterranean nights as soft as a lover's caress. I told Nikolai of the kindness of Matisse, how he would find some excuse to keep me longer than necessary so that he could pay me overtime. "Buy a steak for lunch," Patron would urge, shaking his head at my thinness. I told Nikolai how Madame would pretend to go through her trunks looking for costumes for the models, but would suddenly decide, as if on the spur of the moment, that I should have the clothes instead.

"Ask them for money," Nikolai whispered, his head upon my breast. "Ask them."

When my first six months with the family ended, the work period dictated by law for those without citizenship, Matisse drew me aside and asked me what I would do, where I would go. So I told him about Nikolai, about our plans, how we would open a little tea room together for all the Russian exiles in Nice, how happy we would be if only we had the money to get started. It was a coward's way of asking.

He blinked at me once from behind his spectacles and then wrote a cheque, 5oo francs. "I'll pay it all back," I promised. "I swear."

He waved me away, and I danced on air all the way to Nikolai.

He gambled it away in three days.

Desperate, I went to the casino to search for him. I saw a sign advertis-

ing a dance marathon. A prize of one hundred francs for whoever was left standing. I went back to my shabby room, put on my best dress, put away my pride.

My anger kept me upright for forty-two hours. Sailors and gamblers, most of them drunk with roving hands, spun me from partner to partner while customers looked on and laughed. Every touch soiled me. The smell of sweat hung over the dance floor like a foul mist. The beat of the music throbbed inside my head. I tried concentrating on moving my feet, just keeping them moving, but it felt like I was wading through mud.

In that moment, I hated Nikolai, loathed myself. I stumbled forward on bleeding feet, and the crowd roared.

A sturdy hand reached out to catch me. It was André, Matisse's driver. "Come, Mademoiselle. I've been sent to fetch you."

I never asked how Matisse knew where I was, what degradation I had suffered. I stood before him that night, stripped of all dignity. "I'll pay it back, every cent," was all I could manage.

"Go to bed," he said. "You're exhausted."

And so the days melt into each other. I have room and board, a debt to repay, a rescuer, and a wiser heart.

Then, suddenly, one day leaps forward, becomes different from the rest. I am lounging in an armchair, dreaming of the frozen north of my lost home, when he speaks.

"Don't move."

He reaches for his sketchbook, and everything changes.

The forest swallowed Adam's Mercedes as if it were a child's toy. The woods seemed endless, rank upon rank of trees, some of them thirty meters high, their trunks separated like columns, their branches forming an unbroken ceiling so that even the sky seemed to have disappeared. They were only eighty kilometers north of Ottawa, but it felt as if they were on the out-flung fringes of civilization.

"We must be close now," Chloe said.

"You're sure of that?" Adam replied.

"Of course." But Chloe stared out the car window, her nose almost pressing the glass, not at all certain. It had been at least nine years since she'd been to the cottage in the Gatineau Hills. Everything looked different, the woods thicker, more impenetrable. At each bend in the twisty side road, she was certain there must be a break, a thinning of trees, a glimpse of the sandy lane that would lead to the cottage.

At once, Chloe knew why she had missed the lane. Beneath the needled branches of the great firs, snow glistened, wet and deep in patches. The lane would not be sandy. Hers was a summer memory.

"I think I've missed the gate," she confessed. "You'll have to turn around."

"Turn? You must be joking. The road's too narrow."

"We should have brought my car."

"In that case, we wouldn't have made it past Scarborough." Adam scowled, and put the Mercedes in reverse. They crawled backwards.

A painfully silent kilometer later, Chloe's prayers were granted and she spied a crooked gate set back from the road in a pool of shadow.

"Here," she cried. "We're here."

She jumped from the car, keys in hand to unlock the gate, grateful that the snow in the lane was negotiable. While she waited for Adam to maneuver the car off the side road, she tried not to hear the scratch of pine branches along the length of the Mercedes's shiny paint.

Just beyond the gate, Adam stopped the car and she opened his door for him. "We can walk from here," she said. "It's downhill. We might not get the car back up the grade on the way home."

"Great," was his unenthusiastic reply.

While Adam popped the trunk to fetch their backpacks, it occurred to Chloe that he was not having a good time.

"What? You've never been to summer camp?" she teased.

"Soccer camp and science camp. Properly organized activities well within city limits."

"Camping?"

He shuddered.

"Well, c'mon, city boy. Follow me. The cottage isn't far."

Five minutes of walking beyond the gate, they came to a twist in the lane that fell sharply into a little glen. The dark green blocks of firs gave way to deciduous trees—white birches, poplars, and maples that would not begin to leaf for at least another month. There was not even a green haze to mist the trees that flanked the path. In the cold, dry air, all was a bright, vigorous brown, gilding the branches and leaf buds in shades of gleaming copper.

"There," Chloe pointed.

The two-storey cottage of weathered gray shingle, with a screened-in porch, stood at the top of a small lake, too small in a land of lakes to even have a name. In the nearest villages and surveyors' maps, it was known only as André's pond. Its black surface, streaked here and there with bubbled ice, seemed to match Adam's mood. He looked all around him, turning in a small circle before meeting Chloe's eyes.

"Electricity?" he asked.

Chloe shook her head and smiled.

Her key turned smoothly enough in the lock, but the door stuck a little and she had to use her shoulder to push it open. Inside, the light was dim even in mid-afternoon, the still air smelling of dust and pine needles. There was only one long room, fireplace at one end, kitchen at the other, and several tattered armchairs with a braided rug in between.

To Chloe, the plain, simple space was rich in memories. As her glance fell on the fireplace, she remembered curling up on her mother's knee while her grandfather played his fiddle, how handsome he looked with his cheek lying against the silky wood of the instrument, his dark hair falling across his brow. And, of course, he told her stories of Sylvie, how spirited she was, how adventurous. It struck Chloe then, as she looked across time, that she had never done so many of the things her grandmother had done. Never danced on a beach. Never crossed an ocean on a rocking ship, nor waded into the sea at night.

The sound of Adam stamping snow from his hiking boots brought her sharply back to the present. He smiled at her a bit too bravely.

"Oh, don't be such a snob," she chided. "This is what a real cottage is supposed to be. Do you know how to build a fire?"

"Of course. I'm a scientist."

"Does that mean you actually know how to do it, or that you merely understand the principle?"

He laughed and she waved him away in the direction of the wood-pile.

An hour later, Chloe was staring into blue and orange flames, pulled to and fro by curiosity and dread. Adam had helped her drag an old trunk down from the attic, a travelling trunk with hammered tin at each of the four corners. She'd peeked into enough boxes and under enough lids to know this was the right stuff—Sylvie's keepsakes, the flotsam and jetsam of her life. It was why they were here, and still Chloe hesitated.

She reached for the lid of the trunk, then let her hand fall back into her lap. She knew Adam was watching her, trying to read her face.

"Tell me about provenance in the art world. Why's it so important?" he asked, his voice barely above a whisper.

The question surprised Chloe, pulled her from her tangled thoughts. "Provenance is the life history of a painting, a detailed record of its itinerary from the moment it leaves a painter's hands. Sometimes it's used to determine disputed ownership. Sometimes it's used to answer questions of authenticity when the identity of the actual painter is in doubt."

"But surely science can do that—I've read about investigations of paintings that resemble the forensic investigations of a murder. Paintings can be put under a microscope, both literally and figuratively, using x-rays, infrared reflectography, and chemical and gas chromatograph analysis of the paints and canvases."

"Yes, but science can only go so far. Take Caravaggio, for example. Fewer than eighty authentic Caravaggios exist—some would say no more than sixty. We know that several were destroyed in World War II, while still others simply vanished over the centuries. Now suppose a painting is suddenly discovered that appears to be a genuine Caravaggio. Scientific investigation can determine all kinds of things about the age and make-up of the paint, canvas and varnish used, even help the experts examine brushstrokes and typical style.

"But provenance is still important. Researchers would try to determine the life of the painting by tracing it backwards, right back to the moment of its creation, if possible. They'd search the letters and diaries of Caravaggio's patrons and associates, inventory lists of the great Italian houses or churches, anything that might refer to the commission of the painting, or might describe the painting itself."

"But if actual paintings can vanish over time, so must the written evidence of their existence. What happens then?"

Chloe shrugged. "The experts weigh the evidence and decide."

"Million dollar decisions?"

"Absolutely. But let me tell you another story, a contemporary one. An American woman goes to a dollar store and buys a huge, splotchy painting for five bucks as a kind of joke for a friend's birthday. She and her friend have a good laugh together, and the painting ends up in the buyer's garage where it collects dust for a while. She finally decides to have a clearing out and, at her lawn sale, an honest art history professor pulls her aside and tells her he thinks the painting is by Jackson Pollock. What would you do, as a scientist?"

"Easy. I'd do a DNA analysis. Pollack's fingerprints must be all over the painting, if it's genuine. It would be a simple matter of comparing the analysis of the discovered painting with one known to be original."

"So it would seem. But the museums, the collectors, and the art world in general are reluctant to allow DNA analysis. The fear is too great that paintings thought genuine for years might not pass such scrutiny."

"That's appalling."

"Maybe. But that's not art. That's the big business of art. Presumably, the Pollock still lingers in the woman's garage."

"Well, what about paintings by Matisse? Is it difficult to prove their provenance?"

"Not usually, certainly not the major paintings. Matisse was a prolific letter writer, letters to his son in New York and to other painters that often detailed his progress on significant works. There are also studies for the paintings and, in some cases, photographic evidence of Matisse actually working on them. But there were some paintings that disappeared in Soviet Russia and during World War II. And probably a thousand sketches, maybe more, that might not have been so carefully detailed."

Chloe paused, realizing she had come full circle, and was back to staring at the trunk. "I'm feeling a little jittery. I might not find what I'm hoping to find," she confessed.

"This is your best chance, Chloe," Adam advised. "Jump."

She eased herself off her chair and sat cross-legged on the floor before the trunk, flipping open its lid. The first layer of material was a disorganized mess of photographs, some framed, some loose and curling, with a dingy, sepia look around their edges.

Chloe groaned a little when she saw that most of the photos were of her, placed there either by her grandfather or, more surprisingly, her mother.

"C'mon," she motioned to Adam. "You can help sort through this mess." She patted the floor beside her, and he slid into place, mirroring her posture, the knees of their denim jeans almost touching.

He grabbed a handful of photos and began a running commentary. "Chloe on a three-wheeler. Chloe in braces. Chloe as diving champion of the local pool. Chloe with a hideous hairdo…"

"Give me that," Chloe snapped. She glanced at the riot of red curls. "Ouch, that *is* awful. Spare me the reviews, okay?"

Together, in silence, except for the occasional smothered laugh from Adam, they sorted through old report cards, birthday cards, homemade valentines, and a child's drawings. Gradually, the images shifted from Chloe to Louise as a young woman, black hair flying about her face, her arms around a much younger Sammy.

"Wow," Adam exclaimed. "She's quite lovely. Not at all how I remember her."

"Well, you were—what?—twelve when you knew her? You probably thought she was ancient."

"Maybe. But this is not how Jamie described her either."

"No kidding."

"Look, if I promise to stop commenting on your metamorphosis from child to adult, could you lay off my brother for a while?"

"Sorry," Chloe flashed him a smile she knew he would find insincere.

She leaned forward on her knees to reach deeper into the trunk, her hands touching something soft and cottony. She grasped the material in her hands and stood up, unfolding a homemade quilt covered in splashy roses.

"It's Sylvie's," she said quietly. "I've seen pictures of her working on this. She started it when she was first diagnosed with cancer, barely had time to finish it. André must have kept it all these years."

Adam pulled one of the corners of the quilt closer to the light coming from the coal-oil lamps. "It's beautiful," he said, "and quite unusual. Normally quilting patterns are very regular, but these roses are almost free-form, of different shapes and sizes. Look, Chloe, some even overlap the geometry of the patches themselves. Sylvie must have been a bit of an artist herself... Chloe?"

He looked up, saw that she was sitting on the floor again, her head bent forward, her face hidden by the long silky waves of her hair.

"What have you found?" he asked softly.

"It's a photo of Sylvie and André. Look at her hand," she urged.

He took the photo and studied the head-and-shoulders shot. Sylvie wore a simple white blouse with layered frill sleeves that kissed the top of her arms. Her left hand was placed high on André's shoulder. She wore a ring, now Chloe's ring, but what Adam studied was the shape of that young, confident face. Heart-shaped, with rosebud lips, not the square-shaped face and generous mouth of the woman in Matisse's drawing.

"Well, what do you think?" he asked, handing the photo back.

"It's the ring, of course, the ring in the drawing."

"Yes, it very well could be. But, Chloe, look at her face. I've never seen a photo of your grandmother before, but, I'm sorry, I don't think this is the face of the woman in the Matisse."

He watched her as redness washed up her neck and into her cheeks. She leaned closer to the light, eyes riveted on the photo.

"That doesn't mean anything. Matisse's portraits were never duplications. He drew the moment, the feeling between artist and model. He didn't care about replicating exact features."

Adam didn't reply. He walked over to the wide front window. Through the murky glass, the night was already inky. He spoke while looking straight ahead, not looking at Chloe. "Let's go for a walk. We need to clear our heads."

Her response came to him as if it had traveled over a vast distance. "People don't go for walks in the woods when it's dark."

"Well, just down to the dock then."

Chloe pulled her fisherman's knit sweater over her long white shirt. Instead of reaching for her jacket, she wrapped herself in Sylvie's quilt. When she finally looked at Adam, she almost laughed. He'd found one of André's old toques and pulled it so low over his forehead that it covered his eyebrows, making his nose look more prominent than ever. He held up a bottle of red wine, and a Swiss army knife with a corkscrew.

"Why do guys who never go camping always own Swiss army knives?" she laughed.

"To cut the brie," he replied smoothly, tapping his jacket pocket. "And to open the wine."

"I brought a pack of sausages to roast over the fire on sticks."

"Very classy. Perhaps I'll be too drunk by then to notice."

"Then I hope you brought more than one bottle."

He smiled, opened the door and urged her forward. She led him down to the dock where they perched cross-legged at its edge. Together, the lake and the sky melded, black on black. While Adam opened the wine, Chloe dipped her fingers into the still water. Its temperature was freezing, like sinking her hand into a melting glacier. The air smelled of vegetation, evergreens, and smoke from the cottage chimney, a clean, sharp smell.

All around them, the night was silent, and Chloe had no wish to break its spell. She found the thin arc of pale moon, low on the horizon, and stared at it while she and Adam passed the bottle from mouth to mouth. At some point, she realized they had unconsciously huddled together for extra warmth and that they were sitting under a glory of stars.

She had, of course, seen what Adam had seen in the shape of Sylvie's face. But sometime during her childhood, looking at other photos of her grandmother, she'd transposed one face for another, seeing what she wanted to believe. She was not yet ready to let a different truth rush through her body like a river bursting through a dam. She would, for just a while, hold the torrent at bay.

"Tell me more about Jamie," she said.

"Jamie taught me how to ride a bike. He taught me how to drive. When I was seven and had the measles, he sat on the edge of my bed and read book after book of the Hardy Boys series to me. You can imagine my shock several years later when I learned that his versions of the stories were far wilder and much more bone-chilling than the real stories. He'd made up new plots, new details instantaneously. He was my best friend."

"What happened to you? How did you drift apart?"

"There was no single event. He just developed a style of living, a taste for daring that I didn't have the inclination to follow. I lacked his flair, or perhaps more accurately, his courage. As peacemaker between him and my parents, I reluctantly became my brother's keeper, a role that disappointed both of us. It was almost a relief when he went to Paris. I just didn't imagine he would stay there, or die there."

"Why did he stay? Sammy described him as a gypsy, said he never settled in one place or on one passion for long. What did he find in Paris? A job he loved? The girlfriend you mentioned?"

"There were several girlfriends. Jamie was a serial monogamist. Liliane was merely the latest, though she stuck with him longer than most. As for jobs, you name it. At various times he was a waiter, a street musician, a courier, a dog walker, a cab driver. I suspect, at times, he was the escort of very rich women."

"But you visited him in Paris? You were friends at the end?"

"Oh yes. We never quarreled, though he found my choices in life too staid for his liking. He was proud of me, I think, though he despaired of my dullness."

"*Are* you dull?"

Adam rocked back onto his elbows and stared at Chloe. "That's an impertinent question," he laughed.

"Sorry. It's just confusing to me that people who knew Jamie well always seem prepared to forgive him anything. There's even a kind of grudging admiration for his aimless lifestyle, as if those of us with goals, and routines and obligations don't measure up."

"Ah, Chloe. That was his irascible charm. He was a free man, perfectly happy without the shackles of possessions, full of adventure. He could make you believe you were the most special person in his circle with just a single smile. He was generous, not with money because he never had much, but with his time, with his very being. He reminded me that there were dreams to be followed, moments to be savoured, even stars to see on a night such as this."

Chloe followed Adam's gaze up to the spangled sky.

"And yet," she whispered, almost to herself, "he kept one possession." Why, she wondered. Was it possible that he had loved the drawing as much as she did?

Much later, having eaten the sausages and finished the wine, Chloe rose from the bed where she couldn't sleep. She tiptoed past Adam's bedroom and down the stairs, lit the lamp, and peered into the bottom of the trunk. There, underneath a small bundle of hand-knit baby clothes and a loose pile of old postcards from Nice, her fingers grazed a packet of letters tied up in white ribbon. She closed her eyes for a moment, then took a deep breath, and began to read.

Adam found her the next gray morning at the end of the dock again. At first, he could barely decipher her form, but the wind snatched at her long hair and the long black scarf she wore, making fluttering streamers across the silver surface of the lake.

"Chloe?" he called out.

She turned to him, looking tired but clear-eyed, her cheeks reddened from the chill air, her chin lifted. "I've found something," she said, her voice steady.

Silently, she followed Adam back to the cottage, where she handed him a letter on thin paper. At a glance, he could see the script was pale, faded over time, the words written in French and dated June, 1943.

"Can you translate?" Chloe asked

He nodded.

"Read it," she ordered. "Read it aloud."

"*Dear Sylvie,*" he began, then stopped to look at Chloe. She had already turned away. "*Dear Sylvie,*" he began again. "*Our days will be heavier without you. Only follow Louis' instructions and you will be safe. Sell the ring if you must, but keep my image close to you, as I will keep yours. The city heaves around us, but I have taken steps to protect our secret. Rest assured, it shall remain hidden from enemies and lighten the hearts of friends. Was there ever a more precious gift?"*

"The letter is signed *L*, do you see?" Chloe asked, leaning forward and pointing to the curved initial. "Not *M*, for Matisse, but *L*."

"I don't understand," Adam confessed. "Who's *L*?"

"I'm not certain yet, but I think I know. We need to get back to Toronto. At the very least, this gives us more of the provenance of the drawing. Even if it isn't Sylvie's face in the sketch, this proves that it was given to her. This proves she knew Matisse, was perhaps even part of his household as she always claimed."

"Hold on. I don't see any of that in this letter. The only person referred to by name is Louis."

"Yes," Chloe beamed. "Isn't it wonderful? Let's go. I need to get home."

Soon, having negotiated the twists of the side-road, the Mercedes was rushing along the highway. Several times, Adam tried to coax Chloe into telling him what she suspected about the letter, why it had lifted her spirits, but she just shook her head and smiled.

"I want to be sure," she said. "I need to be sure, this time. I've lived my whole life on a story as embroidered as the Rumanian blouse. I don't want to make a mistake. You understand that, right?"

She could sense that Adam didn't want to understand, but that he did.

As barns and cows, fields and villages flashed by, Chloe reread the letter, again and again.

"I think you've memorized it by now," Adam commented.

She spoke as if she hadn't heard him. "The Rumanian blouse. Didn't Daniels say he had a client interested in any sketches of the blouse?"

"He did."

"But, think, Adam. The sketch is called *Woman in a Blouse, Dreaming. Rumanian Blouse* is an alternate title. How did he know it's the *Rumanian Blouse*? Did you show him the drawing?"

"No, of course not. And now that you mention it, he knew its title as well. When he first called me, he didn't ask if Jamie had left me a drawing, he used the exact title. A reproduction must have been published somewhere."

"Yes, that's possible. Still. Daniels seems to know more than he should about it. Have you heard from him since our stilted dinner party?"

"Twice, as a matter of fact."

"And?"

"And nothing. He was cajoling, persistent and insistent, as usual."

"Hmm," was all Chloe murmured.

Ten minutes later she was fast asleep.

When Adam reached the city limits of Toronto, he gave Chloe's shoulder a little shake. It was raining heavily, sheets of water veiling the forest of towering apartment buildings that marked Toronto's north end. Chloe yawned, stretched her arms and legs, and ran her fingers through her hair.

"You look like a cat," Adam remarked, "waking from a day's nap."

"Sorry. I didn't mean to conk out on you. What time is it?"

"Almost five. There was traffic."

"Five? You must be starving."

"I'd kill for a cup of coffee. Do you want to stop?"

Chloe studied him for the first time that day. He was unshaven. His hair was ruffled. She saw that his fair skin was paler than usual. "Thanks, but I'm too excited to eat. I just want to get on with my research. I'll call you in a couple of days, I promise. And, Adam, I know it's a lot to ask after everything you've done, but could you do me a favour? Could you try to remember anyone Jamie might have known in Paris, other than his girlfriend Liliane, whose name begins with an *L*?"

"Okay, but only after I've had something more substantial to eat than brie and burnt sausages."

Chloe stood on her porch with her backpack and waved as Adam pulled away from the curb. She was itching to get to her small library of painting books, to test if her memory was correct. Quickly, she unlocked her door, slipped off her jacket and let it fall to the floor beside her backpack.

She was halfway upstairs when she felt chill air on her face and froze in alarm.

She crept backwards down the stairs and edged her way into the kitchen, her breathing quick and shallow. The sliding glass door onto the deck was open. Water from the driving rain had puddled on the floor tiles and she almost slipped as she reached for the door. She slid it closed, slowly, noiselessly. She was sure it had been locked.

Leaning against the door, she took several deep breaths and bent her head forward, listening intently.

The jarring ring of the telephone made her heart jump. She lunged forward and snatched up the handset.

"Chlo? You okay?"

"Luciana," Chloe breathed weakly.

"I saw you come home. You see your flowers?"

Confused, still a bit shaken, Chloe looked around her aimlessly. There, in a glass vase in the living room, was a splashy bouquet of sharp yellow daffodils and pale pink tulips.

"Luciana, did you come through the back door?"

"No, no. I use my key. We came through the front."

"We?"

"Very nice man. Chlo, you're no good for Paolo. Too many boyfriends," Luciana scolded.

Chloe's heart skipped. "Who was he? What did he look like?"

"You see? You can't keep them straight. This one tall, dark, big shoulders. Very good English, almost as good as mine."

She tightened her grip on the phone, fought to keep her voice calm. "Thanks, Luciana. I'll call you later."

In a moment, she was racing up the stairs. Her neighbour had just given a perfect description of Peter, the butler.

She skidded to a stop in her bedroom, staring at a blank wall. The drawing she had hung there was gone.

Her mind scrambled to piece together what must have happened. Peter bringing flowers, charming Luciana, gaining access to her home. Once in the kitchen, he could easily have released the lock on the glass door without being noticed by the old woman. He could have returned at any time while she was away with Adam, come up here and taken the drawing.

Chloe's mouth was dry. Her hands began to sweat. She had no false modesty about her artistic abilities, and she knew the Matisse by heart. But had she been good enough to fool a thief?

Slowly, she forced her legs to move, crossed the hall into her studio, the dim light turned silvery from the rain lashing against the skylight. She closed her eyes for a moment, praying with all her heart. She moved to the edge of the room, where a stack of her finished canvases leaned against the wall. She began to tip them forward, one after the other, resting them against her knees. There, tucked between the last two paintings, was *Woman in a Blouse, Dreaming*, just where she had hidden it.

She sank to the floor, almost sobbing in relief.

The copy she had made before that first meeting with Adam, the copy she had made to trick him, to keep the original safe from him should he demand its immediate return, had tricked someone else instead. But, though Peter may have been duped, she had little doubt that Daniels would *not* be fooled, even less doubt that he was behind the theft.

Why, she wondered. What would make a respectable art dealer go to such extremes? And how had he known to search her home, and not Adam's? Daniels clearly knew something she didn't, something that pushed him far beyond the boundaries of conventional behaviour or concern for his reputation. His rashness confirmed the suspicions she'd felt ever since reading *L*'s letter. Matisse's simple pen and ink drawing was not the prize. Rather it was a clue, pointing to something else, something worth risking everything for, something that Jamie Jensen and George Daniels knew about, something that Chloe was determined to discover.

She tucked the drawing back into its hiding place, feeling every bit as reckless as she had on the night she'd burgled Adam's house. She walked downstairs, found her keys, put on her jacket. She didn't think about what she would say to Daniels or what she would do when she arrived at his door. She only thought about Sylvie's letter and *L*'s secret and her overpowering need to know. Somehow she would formulate just the right questions to reach Daniels' conscience.

The early evening streets of Rosedale were deserted, all sensible people having been driven inside by the rain. There were no floodlights trained on Daniels' house tonight. It loomed above her draped in shadows, chinks of light visible here and there from behind curtained windows.

Chloe stood beside her car for a minute, her face raised to the pearl-gray sky, welcoming the clean feeling of the rain. Then she climbed up the steps of the porch and approached the massive, carved front door.

It was slightly open. Chloe pushed it gently with her fingertips and it opened further still.

She peered inside. The orangery was only dimly lit, leaving the corners of the room in darkness.

Impulsively, Chloe stepped over the threshold. For a moment, she had a vague sense of trespassing, but her curiosity pushed her forward and across the mirrored surface of the marble floor.

She had almost reached the hallway that led to the room with the sconce lamps, when she heard glass shattering and an unearthly cry, almost the cry of an animal caught in the steel teeth of a trap.

She jerked backwards and turned to run. Halfway across the orangery she heard shouting, running footsteps drawing closer. Instinctively, she ducked into the black corners of the room, shielding herself behind the statuary, not daring to look.

She tried to block out the sounds around her, but the voices were almost on top of her.

"You son of a bitch. You'll pay for this."

"I swear I knew nothing about a switch."

Chloe heard scuffling, panting, a strangled scream. A sickening sound of flesh pounding into flesh, the slow slide of a weight collapsing onto the floor.

Then for a moment, silence. Gradually, almost imperceptibly, she recognized the sound of the rain beyond the open door, the door she could not reach.

Nothing stirred, but she knew someone was in the orangery with her. She held her breath for an interminable time, every muscle in her body rigid.

Footsteps again, this time receding down the hallway.

Chloe crept forward on her hands and knees towards the dark shape on the marble floor that blocked her path to the door.

Daniels' eyes were wide open, crazed with fear, seeming to look right through her. She leaned over him, tugged at his arms, tried to pull him up. She couldn't understand why he wouldn't get up.

She stood up, tried to heave his weight, and her foot slipped.

She looked down the length of his body then, saw the blood seeping from his abdomen, pooling onto the pale marble.

She stared at it, could not pull her eyes away from it. She saw nothing else, heard nothing approaching.

When the blow hit her from behind, she fell forward across Daniels' chest like a small bird shot from the sky.

When Chloe opened her eyes, they would not focus. She blinked once, twice, but the unfamiliar room still swam around her. She lifted her head, felt a wave of nausea, and sank onto the pillow again, a dull throbbing behind her eyes. She was in a bed in a strange room, she decided. She had the sensation of swimming, though her limbs couldn't move without pain. She felt the heavy tug of an undertow and disappeared below the surface again.

Two hours later, her eyes opened onto a face she knew.

"Adam?"

"I'm here, Chloe."

His face moved closer, his lips brushed her cheek.

"Where am I?" she asked.

"Women's College Hospital. You've got a concussion. Try to stay awake for a bit."

"But how—what happened?"

"You don't remember? Somebody knocked you out."

She closed her eyes again, groped through memory. The first thing she found was the rain. She remembered the rain on her face outside Daniels' house. Daniels. There was something dark there, something frightening. Then, as if a flashbulb burst inside her mind, she saw it all. His body, his blood. Her eyes flew open. "Daniels," she whispered. "He's dead, isn't he?"

"Yes. Chloe, there are people here who need to talk to you. Police. Sammy's just outside, stalling them. Did you see what happened to Daniels?"

"N-no. I couldn't look. I heard them, shouting, fighting. I crept forward, saw the blood. Then nothing. How did I get here?"

"I found you. I called the police and an ambulance. Then I called Sammy."

"*You* found me, but how did you know?" She felt the pull of the undertow again and never heard his answer.

The third time Chloe woke up, Sammy's face was like the sun in her sky. He beamed down on her.

"Hello, sleepy girl. Feeling better?"

"Well, at least there's only one of you. No double vision." She smiled.

Tentatively she moved her head. There was no searing pain, but she had a massive headache. "Where's Adam?"

"He's down the hall, being questioned by the police again. He says his house was burgled, then he went to Daniels' house and found you unconscious. Daniels had been stabbed. Chloe, whatever happened, you don't have to talk to the police until you're feeling stronger, okay? Adam told me the police are asking questions about the Matisse drawing."

A shiver ran up Chloe's spine. Her mind replayed the snatch of words she'd overheard, Daniel's desperate protestations that he knew nothing about a switch. Suddenly, the room began to spin again. Had Daniels died because he'd engineered the theft of a copy, a copy she'd made with her own hands? Had her childish, stupid, stubborn copy contributed to his death? This time, Chloe dove for the undertow, desperate to find its sweet oblivion.

A nurse shook her awake. Chloe reached a hand to her tousled hair and winced when her fingertips found the bump, a dinosaur's egg at the back of her head.

"That must hurt," the nurse grimaced. "See if you can keep these down." She handed Chloe two white pills and a glass of orange juice. "So you're Sammy's daughter?" she continued. "We should have known with all that coppery hair of yours. That, and the fact that he's been like a bear since they brought you in."

"How long have I been here?"

"Two nights. This is the beginning of the second day. But you can go home today. Sammy's waiting to take you home."

"Is Adam here too?"

The nurse grinned, and stepped away from Chloe's bed. Behind her, Adam was sprawled across a chair in the corner of the room. He was still in the same clothes he'd worn in the Gatineau Hills. His five o'clock shadow was now a full beard.

The nurse gazed down at him fondly, then woke him up. "Hey," she said as she left the room. "Your girl's awake."

Chloe smiled and held out her hand. "You look dreadful, Adam Jensen."

"Really?" he said as he took her hand. "Must be because I'm a suspect in a murder investigation."

Before Chloe could answer, two men entered the room. She squeezed Adam's hand, hard, suddenly nervous, not wanting him to go.

"Good morning, Miss Rea," said the fat man in the gray raincoat, carrying a briefcase. "I'm Inspector Bradley. This is Sergeant Miles. We'd like a word."

Chloe fastened her gaze on the sergeant who had a mournful, thin face and melancholy eyes. He seemed less threatening than gruff Bradley who spoke with his chin thrust out and slightly raised as if he were trying to see more than his stunted elevation would allow.

"Fine, but I'd like Adam to stay." Chloe said.

"We'd rather talk to you alone, if you don't mind," countered Bradley.

Adam glared at him. "That's ridiculous. Surely Chloe's not a suspect."

"Never mind. There's nothing to worry about." Chloe's grip on Adam's hand had not lessened. "Look, Adam, will you do something for me?"

He glanced down at her and she stared at him, her eyes filled with an urgency that her words belied. "Sammy's taking me home later. There's a blouse I'd like to wear. You know, the one with all the embroidery? It's my favourite. It's in my studio, I think. I draped it over some canvases so I wouldn't get paint on it."

For a moment, Adam looked at her as if she were as crazy as she felt. Then he responded to her request with a squeeze of her hand, just before he turned away. "Sure, Chloe. See you soon."

The door closed behind him, and Bradley cleared his throat, while Miles took out the inevitable notebook and withdrew to the chair in the corner.

"Feeling better now, are we?" Bradley began.

"*I* am, yes. A little."

"Fine, fine. Now can you tell me why you went to George Daniel's house on the evening of April twenty-third?"

"I went to talk to him about my painting."

"You had an appointment?"

"No. It was just a spur of the moment decision. We'd had dinner a few days earlier. He seemed interested in my work."

"I see. So you just turned up. He answered the door?"

"No. The door was ajar when I got there. So I started inside. Then I heard shouting, two men arguing. I heard something break—it sounded like glass splintering and someone, Daniels I think, cried out. I thought I'd better leave so I started across the orangery, but the voices were drawing closer and I couldn't reach the door. I hid. There are some statues there. I hid behind them."

"And what did you see?"

"Nothing. I was terrified. I didn't open my eyes. I heard the men arguing, then I heard fighting, scuffling sounds. I waited a long time, until it was quiet again. Then I crept out and found Daniels. I tried to get him up. Then I saw the blood. Then everything went black."

"I see," Bradley said, though clearly he didn't. "How long did you say you knew Daniels?"

"I didn't say, and I didn't know him. Of course, I knew *of* him. Every painter in Toronto knew him by reputation. We hadn't met until the dinner."

"Ah, yes. And he asked you to dinner because… ?"

"I went as Adam's guest. They had business to discuss."

"What business?"

Chloe had no idea what Adam may have told the police. She glanced over at Miles. His eyes were sadder than ever.

"I'm not sure. Adam is a bit of a collector. I imagine they wanted to discuss a transaction of some kind."

"What is your relationship with Adam Jensen?"

"Excuse me?"

"It's not a difficult question, Miss Rea. What kind of relationship do you have with Mr. Jensen?"

"He's a friend, a friend of the family. My father has known him for years."

"I see. And you spent the night with him on April twenty-second?"

"No, you don't see. He offered to drive me to my grandparents' cottage in the Gatineau Hills. We spent the night in separate bedrooms, not that that's any of your business."

"Did you arrange to meet him at Daniels' house?"

"No. I told you my going there was an impulsive decision."

"So he just happened to show up? Very lucky for you, wouldn't you say?"

"Very."

"And you have no idea why Jensen went to Daniel's house on the very same night as you *spontaneously* decided to visit?"

"You'll have to ask Adam that question."

"We have. He says his house was burgled, even though nothing seems to have been taken. And for some reason, he suspected Daniels of the break-in." Bradley's voice betrayed the fact that he found the excuse untenable.

As Chloe watched him, he reached down for his briefcase, undid the straps and pulled out her sketch of *Woman in a Blouse, Dreaming*. He propped it on the edge of the bed. "Seen this before?" he asked.

She stared at it. A crack in the glass of the frame zigzagged across the serenity of the woman's face. She shook her head, but said nothing.

"Oh, come now, Miss Rea. Jensen says this drawing belongs to him, that Daniels wanted to buy it. The two of them were arguing about it when you arrived, isn't that so?"

"No. No, the other man who spoke—he had an accent. I think it must have been Peter. Peter the butler. I don't know his surname. He's Russian."

Chloe heard a strangled laugh from the corner of the room and glared at Sergeant Miles.

"Sorry," he said gravely. "The Russian butler did it?"

"What did this butler say?" Bradley demanded.

"You son of a bitch."

Chloe almost smiled at Bradley's startled reaction. "He said," she continued, "you son of a bitch. You'll pay for this."

"Ah. Just what a man would say if his house had been burgled and his valuable sketch taken by Daniels, don't you think, Miss Rea?"

Chloe closed her eyes. She felt a groundswell of despair at the mess she'd created. Adam was in terrible trouble. She would have to tell the truth, even though she sensed it would seem only fractionally more credible to Bradley than a Russian butler.

"Inspector Bradley," she said, her voice emphatic, "Adam didn't kill Daniels. The voice I heard was heavily accented. It certainly wasn't Adam who attacked me." The effort exhausted her and her hand sank back onto the pillow.

"I think that's quite enough, Inspector Bradley."

Chloe had never been more grateful to hear her father's voice.

"My daughter's been through an ordeal and I'm taking her home. Now."

"Fine. Fine. We'll be in touch Miss Rea." Bradley nodded brusquely and signaled to Sergeant Miles. At the door, the sad sergeant glanced back at Chloe with a sigh and a conspiratorial smile as if Bradley were a burden they both now shared.

An hour and a half later, Chloe, showered and wrapped in Sylvie's quilt, sat on her couch before her disbelieving father and a very tired Adam.

"Jesus, Chloe, you made a copy?" Sammy queried.

There was no need to reply. Chloe's face felt flushed and hot.

"So this is the original?" Adam spoke slowly, holding the Matisse in his hands.

"I'm sorry," Chloe murmured. "I didn't know you then, Adam. I just thought I would make a copy and try to keep the original drawing safe until you knew my story. I didn't want to admit to anything in front of the police, so I gave you those clues about the blouse hoping you'd come here and find the original sketch. And really, when you think about it, it's a good thing I did make a copy." Her voice trailed off under Sammy's stern gaze.

She felt a stab of guilt, seeing again the grotesque image of Daniels bleeding on the floor of the orangery. "Oh god," she whispered. "Daniels was killed because of the copy. He must have tried to pass on what he thought was the original."

Adam stood up and began pacing the room. "No. Daniels was killed because he was caught up in something far more important and more dangerous than this sketch. What the hell is it?" He turned over the drawing and studied the backing for a moment, then raised his eyes to Chloe's.

"Yes," she nodded. "I think so. There's an exactor knife in my studio."

Sammy watched Adam walk upstairs, his brow furrowed. "What the hell's going on Chloe?"

While they waited for Adam to return, she told Sammy about the letter she'd found in Sylvie's trunk.

"I still don't get it," Sammy confessed.

"I think I do," Adam said, returning to the room. "Tell him Chloe."

"This is all supposition, but I think Sylvie and L's secret is a painting. I think it's a painting *of* Sylvie. Not a drawing, but an unknown Matisse painting. It would be worth a fortune. And *Woman in a Blouse, Dreaming* is a clue to where it is. Go ahead, Adam."

She watched, her heart pounding in her ears, while he placed the drawing flat on the floor and ran the exactor knife slowly along the brown paper backing of the frame. When he had removed it to expose the stiff cardboard backing to the sketch, she heard him gasp.

"There's something here," he said, his voice tight. "PM slash, R slash, 1943 slash, upper studio. And something else, too."

He picked up the drawing carefully and carried it over to Chloe.

In the top right hand corner, she read the inscription printed in block capitals, PM/R/1943/UPPER STUDIO. Then underneath, in script, a message, almost a poem:

Beyond the walls, beneath blue stars,
A tree blossoms and roses veil a virgin bride.

Chloe raised a questioning face to Adam.

"Jamie's handwriting," he confirmed. "But I don't know what it means. A description of the painting, maybe?"

"What?" Sammy stood up and looked down at the handwriting over Adam's shoulder. "You think Jamie wrote this message, that he actually found a missing Matisse? Who the hell is *L*?"

From the folds of Sylvie's quilt, Chloe held up a picture book of Matisse during his stay in Vence, France, at a villa called *Le Rêve*. She turned to a photo of a woman wearing a pair of painter's overalls, seated before an easel. She was looking up and over her shoulder at the photographer, her hair parted in the middle and pulled back.

She was still, almost somber, but her eyes held Chloe. Perhaps, in a crowded room, Chloe thought, when you grew tired of the noise and the social trivialities, perhaps this was the woman you'd seek out. A classic, unselfconscious beauty, a square-shaped face, a generous mouth. The serenity of a woman in a blouse, dreaming.

"Here," Chloe said, tapping her finger to the face. "This is *L*. This is Lydia Delectorskaya."

Part II
Blue Eyes

THE DAY WHEN EVERYTHING CHANGED, *the day when Matisse first drew my face, I was twenty-five years old and he was sixty-five. I had been in his home almost daily for three years, and yet he seemed to see me for the very first time. And I, him.*

I had modeled a bit before, an occupation I found distasteful, but necessary for survival. I remember climbing up creaky steps to squalid rooms where men used painting as a flimsy excuse to disrobe me. Too often in my brief experience, the painters would feel it within their rights to position my arms or legs, twist my torso—just so—to catch the light, and, of course, in so doing, they would inevitably graze a thigh, brush against a breast. The more limited the painter's talent, the more voyeuristic his gaze. I found I disliked becoming an object for money.

*Yet when posing for Matisse, my Patron, I felt an electricity, a vitality I'd scarcely known before. The French expression for thunderbolt—*coup de foudre—*means love at first sight. I think I'd loved the old man, in a gentle, daughterly fashion for some time. But I'd never felt the crash of the thunderclap, or the flaming tongue of lightning that followed it, setting my soul ablaze. Until the day when everything changed, I'd never understood the risk and the passion and the danger of his painting.*

As our eyes met over the sketchbook, I saw at once what a terrible gift his genius was. I saw his desperation, his loneliness. My body rocked from the thunderbolt of that insight. My mind lit up. I knew at once what I must do, how my debts could be repaid. I was young and strong, tired of drifting, hungry for meaning. For Matisse, for love, for my own self, I would become the prow of a ship pointed for land amid plunging seas, a golden beacon in the blackness of storms. I would be his Muse and save us both.

That first sketch led to many more. I would busy myself around the house, performing tasks for Madame or cleaning up the studio, when suddenly I would feel Patron's penetrating stare and the air around me would become still, the activity of the house hushed. Of course, I was flattered. I'd been regularly scorned by the French who called me "Slav" with a curl of the lip. To them, Russian exiles were primitive, uncouth, absurdly temperamental.

"But you are beautiful, Lydia," Matisse would tease. "Why do you scrape your hair away from your face and wear such frowns? Your hair is golden. Your skin is the paleness of pearls. You have the looks of a Siberian ice maiden."

I laughed at his extravagance and grew more confident under his gentle regard, but after that first sketch we both knew it was not my beauty he wanted to capture. It was my strength.

"Shall I tell you what they say in Paris and New York?" he asked one day. "Matisse has become sleek and prosperous, painting harem girls in Arabian pants for rich men's villas. Matisse is finished."

I was not fooled by the self-mocking tone. I knew at once the self-doubt and torment that raged inside him. He had pushed himself to exhaustion working on the huge, semi-abstract figures of The Dance *for an American collector. He was terrified he would go blind. He had not done any easel painting for years.*

I followed him into the studio, picked up a blank canvas, handed him a brush. I voluntarily removed my clothes to achieve a nakedness equal to his own, and sat upon a couch.

He began to paint, to compose spontaneously in colour.

Occasionally, my attention would drift to the studio mirror where we were both reflected. I looked serene and radiantly assured, wearing nothing but a necklace, seated knee to knee with Patron in shirtsleeves and spectacles.

For six months, I posed, while he cursed and stormed and wrested this painting into being. Eventually, he called it The Pink Nude. *In it, my limbs are monumental, yet fluid and graceful. Background and perspective are flattened out so that my body seems to float. I smiled when Matisse showed me: he depicted not my form so much as my will, a formidable will equal to his own. Through it, his painting and my life were renewed.*

IV

IN THE DAYS AFTER HER release from the hospital, Chloe did nothing but think, read, and dream of Lydia Delectorskaya. Art books and biographies of Matisse littered her kitchen and dining tables. Her computer kept her company as she travelled the Internet hour after hour.

The known facts could fit easily onto only a few pages. Born in Siberia and orphaned by twelve, Lydia was raised by an aunt in Manchuria before moving to Paris. Though accepted by the Sorbonne to study medicine, she could not afford the fees. At nineteen, she married Boris Omeltchenko, many years her senior, and less than a year later, she fled to Nice with a young Russian lover. There, she was employed first as an assistant to Madame Matisse and eventually, as her services became more and more indispensable, as a studio assistant to Matisse.

Many people, it seemed, had speculated on the nature of Lydia's relationship to Matisse, despite the fact that he was in his sixties when they met and often infirm. Few doubted that her fierce loyalty and dedication added years to his life and his career. When Matisse's long marriage to Amélie Parayre finally dissolved in 1939, Lydia stayed. When a serious illness in 1941 threatened Matisse's life, Lydia nursed him back to health. She ran his business affairs, managed his studio, hired models, maids, and caregivers, soothed Matisse's night terrors, and lightened his days until his death in 1954. Then she all but vanished from public life until her own death in 1998.

Dissatisfied with this meager sketch of a life, Chloe studied the paintings and drawings of Lydia. Together with her friend, Emmy, Chloe pored over reproductions of the most famous images of the enigmatic Russian. She was sure she would glean more of her character from Matisse's own interpretations of his favourite model and loyal assistant.

"Look at this portrait, Emmy. It's called *Young Woman in a Blue Blouse*. Look at how Lydia's eyes don't quite meet the viewer's. How modest and contemplative she seems."

Emmy stood over Chloe's shoulder. Lydia's head and shoulders filled the frame, the face clean and fresh looking with classic, symmetrical features. "She looks to me like a woman trying to hide her beauty. She looks prim as a librarian in her high-collared blouse with her hair pinned back. Even these colours—pink cheeks, yellow hair, a dove-blue dress—make her seem childlike."

"Really? I just see the clarity of her features, how the straight line of her nose and her long neck seems to suggest presence and strength. No, Emmy, all these different blues—the background, the blouse, and the eyes—suggest calmness. Yet her mouth is so vividly red, so passionate."

"I don't agree, Chloe. I even think she looks a little sad. How old is Lydia in this portrait?"

"Twenty-nine. A fateful time for her. Matisse's marriage ended the same year as this portrait was painted."

"Was she his mistress?"

"No one really knows. Most people at the time assumed so. Most art historians now assume she wasn't. Her motives and her interior private life remain a mystery."

"So just how are you and Adam Jensen going to find out about her relationship with Sylvie? I hope you have a better plan than staring at Lydia's portraits and photographs. In fact, Chloe, are you sure this bump on your head didn't addle your brains? Daniels is dead. The bad butler is still out there and he knows where you live. You should just give up this fantasy of a missing Matisse, ask for police protection, and sit tight until Daniels' killer is behind bars."

"You sound distressingly like Sammy. By the way, I've not been able to get in touch with Paolo. Have you heard from him?"

Emmy's face turned blank. She looked away from Chloe, picked up their empty coffee cups and wandered out to the kitchen. "Can I get you anything?" she called back over her shoulder.

Chloe stayed where she was, cross-legged and silent on the couch. She knew her friend well enough to bide her time.

Eventually, Emmy returned from the kitchen and sat down beside Chloe. "I called him, you know, to let him know you'd been in the hospital. I told him your father was looking after things and I might have let slip that it was Jensen who found you."

"Oh, Em, you didn't tell him about Daniels, did you? The police haven't released my identity, or Adam's, to the media yet."

"No, no. I didn't mention Daniels. I just said you'd had an accident and it was Jensen who found you and called an ambulance. My point is that he reacted rather crudely to Jensen's name."

"How crudely?"

"I think the expression was 'fuck Jensen'."

Chloe laughed, much to her friend's consternation.

"You might want to take this a little more seriously," Emmy said. "I saw Paolo at *Lakes* on Yonge Street two nights ago with a very attractive woman. From their body language, I would say she's neither a sister nor a cousin."

"Good. That's a relief," Chloe announced.

"That's it? I do wish you wouldn't be so sentimental. Seriously, Chloe, you have to try. Not every relationship works out like Sammy and Louise's, you know."

"True. Sometimes they work out like Louise and Clarence's."

"And Adam Jensen…?"

"Is engaged. We are temporarily connected because of his brother and my grandmother. We have a mutual interest in working together. Think of it, Emmy. Not just a sketch of Sylvie, but an actual oil portrait, a painting no one has seen for years."

"Nor is likely to see," Emmy murmured. "Unless you have a better plan than dreaming."

As the days passed, Chloe grew stronger. She resumed her daily walks with Amber, and even slept a few nights at Sammy's posh apartment for his peace of mind as much as for hers. The lugubrious Sergeant Miles came to question her again, asking her to sign a statement about what she had seen and overheard at Daniels' house. Since Inspector Bradley did not trouble himself to accompany the Sergeant, she assumed she was no longer a suspect.

In the midst of this apparent calm, Chloe indulged in fanciful daydreams of what Sylvie's portrait might be like and of how thrilling it would be to find a lost Matisse. The possibility that such a painting might exist seemed too large a thing to believe, yet Chloe felt instinctively that she was right about Lydia's letter. Jamie's cryptic message, even Daniels' death, seemed to confirm it.

As the weak April sun slanted through her studio window, Chloe reached for the Matisse sketch, cradling it in her arms. The discovery that the face was Lydia's, and not Sylvie's, had not lessened its pull on her. Since childhood, the sketch had always stirred a calmness in her, followed by a brief flourish of happiness that stemmed from a sense of belonging, of being connected to the past. She believed, more strongly than ever now, that the past was a living thing, whispering to her, beckoning her forward. Lydia's face seemed stamped across everything she saw, like the afterimage that appears from looking at the sun too long.

The possibility that delving into the past might also be dangerous was a thought she brushed aside. The horror of finding Daniels' body was beginning to subside as quickly as the lump on the back of her head.

She was worried, though, about Adam. The Inspector had questioned him again, this time at police headquarters. She feared that only the disappearance of the Russian named Peter stood between freedom and Adam's arrest. And he seemed preoccupied, drawn into himself, even moody, since he'd read Jamie's message scrawled on the back of the sketch. She wanted to reach out to him, but she didn't know how. She was too blunt, often times too direct. She had so many questions she wanted to ask him, and no clear idea of how to approach him. Uncharacteristically, she chose to wait.

When Adam finally appeared, he did so without warning.

Chloe was already in bed reading when the doorbell rang. She pulled a sweater on over her pajamas and slipped into her studio, peering down at the darkened street. She recognized Adam at once.

When she opened the door, she was already smiling, a smile that slowly faded as she noted his fatigue. His skin seemed to have tightened over his cheekbones; his beard, begun days ago in the Gatineaus, was still unshaven. "You look terrible," she murmured, reaching out a hand to pull him inside. "Sit down. Do you want coffee or scotch?"

"Definitely scotch."

She brought him a glass, sat down in a chair opposite him. While she watched, he took a large swallow and she saw some of the tension drain out of him.

Finally, he spoke. "Did you know that you're being followed?"

"What?" Chloe jumped to her feet and started towards her living room window.

"No, no," Adam cautioned. "Go upstairs. Don't turn on any lights."

Chloe ran up to her studio. She knew she could not be seen by anyone outside, but she dropped to her knees nonetheless and scrutinized the street. As usual, many cars were parked, most of them familiar to her. But for one. A car with two people silhouetted in the pale light of the street lamps. As she watched, she saw a brief flare of light. One of the occupants was smoking.

She walked slowly, thoughtfully, back to the living room, this time pouring herself a scotch. She tipped her glass to Adam in a mock salute. "Okay, why am I being followed?"

"We. Why are we being followed?"

"Is it the police?"

"I don't know. I think, all things considered, I'd prefer it to be the police."

"You're scaring me, Adam. What's going on?"

"You can't be scared, Chloe. We don't have time for that. Have you still got the original drawing?"

"Of course."

"Bring it to me. As long as you have it you're in danger."

Chloe shook her head. "I'm not doing anything until you tell me what's going on."

"Daniels didn't have a butler. Inspector Bradley questioned Daniels' friends and associates. None has ever heard of or seen a butler, let alone a Russian butler."

Chloe stood up immediately and retraced her steps. Upstairs, she picked up the Matisse sketch and looked around for something to wrap it in, finally swathing it in a pillowcase from her bed. She hugged it once.

Adam's voice from the doorway of her bedroom startled her. "Believe me, Chloe. It's safer to give it up."

"So if the people in the car down there aren't the police, who do you think they are?" she asked.

Adam shrugged. "I don't have many answers, Chloe. I just have one question spinning around and around in my head. How did Daniels, or Peter, whoever he is, know that Jamie had hidden something in the sketch? None of it makes sense to me. But given what you overheard when Daniels was killed, Peter, at least, knows that the original sketch is still at large. Sooner or later, he's going to come looking for it again."

"So we should give the sketch to the police, right? Luciana saw Peter, too. We can clear you of suspicion."

"And in the process, give them a stronger case against you? No, Chloe. As ironic as it seems, the more the Inspector knows of the truth, the worse the case looks against us."

"But what choice do we have?"

"Well, he hasn't actually told either of us not to leave town, has he?"

Chloe sank down on the edge of the bed. "You want to run away to Paris?"

"I wouldn't have used those exact words. I think we should try to follow Jamie's lead. You know about Matisse, I know about my brother. Together we have a chance of finding the painting."

"And this?" Chloe asked, holding out the pillowcase.

"I'm going to keep it safe, just as Jamie asked me to do. In the meantime, is your passport in order?"

From her window seat, Chloe stared out at the runway as the plane queued for take-off. She was on her way to Paris. *April in Paris.* Somehow the circumstances were radically different from the romantic idyll the song had always promised. She and Adam had agreed to meet at

Pearson airport and not to take any luggage, apart from what could be inconspicuously carried, just in case they were followed. She had felt ridiculous sneaking over to Luciana's house with nothing but a large purse in hand and slipping out her neighbour's back door. She had felt sweaty going through the tedious security checks and nervous in the lounge, wondering if the police would use handcuffs when she was arrested.

A flight attendant with a sulky red mouth under a fringe of black hair wandered down the aisle on a last minute check. She seemed to look at Chloe much longer than at the other passengers.

"God, I feel paranoid," Chloe whispered to Adam. "Maybe the police are holding up the plane. Did you see that woman? She stared at me. Or you, maybe she was staring at you because at last you've shaved, but in any case—"

"She stared at you because you look rigid."

"Rigid?"

"Rigid, as in tense, strained, stretched and taut. Also jittery, jumpy, and keyed up. She probably thinks you're terrified of flying."

"Oh. Sorry." Chloe leaned her head back against the seat, closed her eyes and tried to assume a more relaxed posture.

"You aren't actually afraid of flying, are you?" Adam asked.

"No, of course not," Chloe opened her eyes and smiled so he would believe her.

His gaze drifted down to her hand clutching his arm. At the same moment, Chloe felt the powerful surge of the engines as the plane gathered speed, the acceleration slamming her against her seat, then, incongruously, the sense of weightlessness as the plane lifted into the sky.

"I have a surprise for you," Adam said, reaching into his suit jacket pocket and handing her a photograph.

Chloe recognized it immediately. She had seen it the night she had rifled Adam's study: Jamie and a woman Chloe now recognized as Lydia standing in front of the Eiffel Tower. The woman leaned against the shoulder of her taller companion, a slight smile on her lips. Her face was lined and softened by age, but still beautiful, imperious, even regal. "She looks like a Russian czarina, don't you think? When was this taken?"

"Jamie went to Paris in January 1997. It was a New Year's resolution to start over, make a big change. But I don't know the date of the photo. Summer, given their clothing."

"Lydia died in 1998 in April so this must have been taken sometime the summer before. I wonder how she and Jamie met. She was a very private person."

"Tell me about her."

Chloe shook her head. "I sometimes think the mystery of Lydia only deepens the longer one looks. She was smart, administratively talented, fiercely loyal. She dedicated herself to Matisse the artist, as much as to Matisse the person. There's a famous quote by Matisse about the temperament of artists, how difficult it is to live with them. People enjoy an artist's paintings, he claimed, much as they might enjoy cow's milk, but they can't put up with the inconvenience, the mud, and the flies. I'd have to say that Lydia put up with the mud and the flies."

"Why did she do it?"

"She was homeless, an exile, a woman alone without qualifications. She had what some might consider the curse of being attractive to men. How many options do you think she had in the 1930s and '40s? Matisse gave her a chance to be part of something important, to contribute to something lasting. He immortalized her as *Blue Eyes,* but she, in turn, gave him fifteen or so more years of life, fifteen more years of glorious drawings, oil canvases, cut-paper compositions. The art world owes her a great deal."

"So why haven't I heard of her?"

Chloe shook her head. "Even I didn't know much until I went hunting, and I've studied art all my life. In all the letters Matisse wrote, in all the books and biographies of him, she only seems to exist between the lines, a vague image as in pentimento. I suppose that's because Madame Matisse and daughter, Marguerite, turned against her."

"What's pentimento?"

"Essentially, it's the reappearance of an older image behind a newer one. You see, painters would sometimes reuse canvases, covering over paintings with a coat of pigment and then composing a fresh picture. With time, as the oils aged, the original image might appear ghostlike behind the new. That's how Lydia seems to me—ghostlike and elusive."

"Were Lydia and Matisse lovers?"

"Poor Lydia. That seems to be the one question she couldn't, and still can't escape. Why is sex so important?"

Adam raised an eyebrow at her question, but didn't respond directly. "Matisse certainly draws her with tenderness in the Rumanian blouse. Was she a favourite subject?"

Chloe reached down for her oversize purse, wriggling it from underneath the seat where it was wedged. "Here, see for yourself." She handed Adam a book of Matisse drawings. "Many of these are of Lydia. Later in their relationship, Matisse commented that he knew her face and body by heart, like the alphabet. This one," she added, turning a page, "is one of my favourites. It's called *Nymph and Faun*. It's an enormous charcoal drawing that took years to complete, but it looks so spontaneous."

Adam shook his head. "I can't believe this. You've only a purse to pack clothes in for Paris and you bring an art book?"

"I also have a hairbrush, a toothbrush and Sammy's credit card. Do you want to look at this drawing or not?"

Adam took the book and studied the double-paged sketch for some time.

"Well, what do you think?" Chloe prompted.

"I think that Matisse and Lydia made love on the page, regardless of what they may or may not have done beyond the page. The faun is seducing the nymph with his music, his passion evident in the blurring of his fingers as they fly over the pipe. The nymph is responding energetically with every sensual curve of her body. This is a powerfully erotic image." Adam closed the book and offered it back to Chloe with a smile.

She frowned, thinking him just a little too smug. "You know, Matisse also said that the mutual relationship between model and painter was like a shared language, a *platonic* love."

He shrugged. Chloe thought it a typical final gesture, a man's gesture, a kind of challenge. She refused to rise to his expectations and changed the subject. "Did you pack *Woman in a Blouse, Dreaming* in your briefcase?"

"No. I brought practical things like underwear and toiletries. Even a clean shirt. I left the drawing at home."

"Why did you do that? You said you would protect it."

"It's okay, Chloe. I took it to my bank and put it in safe storage and I made sure the guys following me saw the whole transaction. If they're police, they can get a warrant. If not, well at least the sketch is safe."

"But the clue—"

"Is written on my heart as clearly as Lydia's face was written on Matisse's."

Chloe was sure he was teasing her, but his face was perfectly serious. "Please, tell me the clue again."

"*Beyond the walls, beneath blue stars, a tree blossoms and roses veil a virgin bride*. I wish I knew what Jamie was trying to tell me. I can't even decide if the words are a description of the painting, or a guide to finding the painting."

"Let's go over the story again. We agree that Lydia hid a painting, probably of Sylvie. She wrote the letter in 1943, so there would be good reasons for her actions given that the Germans seized a number of paintings during the war. We have a photograph to prove that Jamie and Lydia met in 1997. He must have told her that he owned *Woman in a Blouse, Dreaming*. Perhaps she confided in him and told him where the painting was hidden before she died."

"I don't think so. Jamie was impulsive. He certainly wouldn't wait all this time before announcing to the world that he'd found a missing Matisse. Lydia may have told him there *was* a painting, but died before telling him *where* it was."

"Oh, Lord. I've just thought of something else that doesn't make sense. Matisse's art became the core of Lydia's life. If she knew of a painting, she would never have kept it hidden so long. She would have wanted to share it with the world. To do anything else would have seemed to her a betrayal of Matisse. And if it took Jamie over ten years to find it, what hope do we have?"

"One step at a time, Chloe. First, we'll try to find Liliane, Jamie's girlfriend. We just need to be logical and methodical."

"Adam?"

"Yes?"

"Would you go back to the galley and see if you can find me something strong to drink? I think I'd like to get a little drunk and fall asleep."

A few hours later, a jolt of turbulence shook Chloe awake. The cabin was dark, slumbering. She felt groggy and slightly nauseous from the lingering after-effects of some disturbing dreams and several miniature bottles of vodka. She thought she might go to the washroom to freshen up, but Adam was snoring softly beside her and she didn't want to wake him.

In the dim light, a man walked down the aisle, passing her quickly, his face no more than a blur above his upturned jacket collar.

Chloe felt a flash of fear, a sudden conviction that the man had been looking for her. Instinctively, she began to twist the amethyst ring on her finger, her link to Sylvie and Lydia. She leaned her head against her hand and closed her eyes, willing herself back to sleep.

In the end, I had no choice but to go.

For years, Madame has been close to an invalid, tormented with back pains, increasingly unable to keep up the demands of overseeing Patron's business affairs. She has placed more and more trust in me, once even sending me to Paris with Matisse since she was too weak to accompany him.

Then, one day, Madame received a long letter from Paris from her daughter, Marguerite. Her body sagged as she read the news: Marguerite's marriage was in tatters. Immediately, Madame retreated to her bed and commanded the curtains and shutters closed, though it was midday. I brought her a glass of water and helped her undress, unpinning her long black hair.

"Lydia, you think me a fool?"

"Indeed, no, Madame. But these days, a failed marriage is not so uncommon. Apart from protecting little Claude, you should not be overly concerned." I might have added that she was surely no stranger to scandal: Marguerite was Madame's adopted daughter, the child of Matisse's liaison with a bohemian shopkeeper, and Matisse himself had been publicly and variously branded a beast, a dilettante, and a madman.

"Well, if that is all you think then you've not been paying attention," Madame replied. "Marguerite is invaluable to the business. She's our eyes and ears in Paris. She contacts galleries and sends us news about prices, sales, and collectors. She scans reviews, goes to all the important expositions, keeps

up with other painters. Who is to do that now? This marriage business will distract her and I'll be left to piece things together."

With a small moan, she turned her back to me and I crept out of the room. I resolved to pay better attention.

In the months that followed I learned more about painting and painters than I had thought possible. I learned about weights of paper for watercolours and sketches; I learned about kinds of paints and where to order them; I learned about brushes and palettes and the priming of canvases for oils. Once I had dreamed of becoming a doctor. Now Patron teased me that I ran his studio as if it were an operating theatre.

I began to take notes on the progress of paintings, documenting their journey from preliminary studies to final composition. I filed reviews, paid bills, corresponded with galleries.

In short, I learned the business without ever losing sight of the mystery and the agony of Matisse at work. He taught me that there is a certain shade of blue that enters the soul. When the evidence of brushstrokes has been painted out, the blueness becomes velvety, coating the canvas like sea water. I learned that emerald green was a royal colour in his palette: pure, it was transparent, almost like a glaze; tempered with white and a touch of red, it could yield beautiful grays; mixed with alizarin crimson, it was transformed into the most sensuous purple.

Madame watched my apprenticeship from the sidelines and seemed pleased. No one knew more than she the total dedication Matisse demanded. I gave it willingly, knowing that I had found the purpose that would give shape and definition to my life.

But there were storm clouds all around me, if I had only looked up from my apprenticeship long enough to notice. Mussolini and his Fascist Blackshirts crowed loudly in Italy, and looked greedily in the direction of Nice. Many people feared Il Duce would seize the city in the name of Italian annexation. Madame fled to the Roussillon, to Beauzelle and the home of her sister, Berthe. Though I had travelled there with her many times before to enjoy the clear air and cool nights, Madame did not invite me to come.

Instead I stayed with Patron who was facing an exhausting move from his studio at Place Charles Félix to two adjacent apartments in the Regina, a stucco and glass wedding cake of a building, once a grand and imperial hotel in Queen Victoria's day and now a private residence. He was in a foul temper. Sylvie, both maid and cook, usually able to coax him into laughter, took to creeping about on tiptoe to avoid his notice. Even his closest friends laughed at his decision to leave the seashore and move up into the hills of Cimiez. With war being whispered everywhere, the Regina apartments were white elephants. For a long time, Patron was the only purchaser even at sharply reduced prices.

He was too proud to admit that he was abandoning his proximity to the sea on doctor's orders, and that he had chosen the Cimiez district chiefly because its elevation allowed him to look over the shimmering red roofs of Nice to the Mediterranean he loved so dearly.

I had never seen him so vulnerable. It seemed no one wanted paintings to express joy or beauty any longer. Picasso was painting the harshness and cruelty of the times—no one could make a flower look more vicious. Meantime, an old friend, Clive Bell, wrote that Matisse was painting rapturously as a bird sings. It was not meant as a compliment. It was meant to say that Patron was passé, out of touch with the cataclysmic changes in Europe.

One night, I heard him crying and I rose from my bed and went to him. While I held his hand, he confessed to recurring nightmares of his paintings disintegrating, shot through with light and shadow like leaves eaten into lace by insects.

Of course, I engineered the move. With Sylvie's help, I rolled the canvases and crated the furniture and packed the linens and china. When we arrived at the Regina, we saw that the builders had abandoned it in the general panic of impending war. I picked up a hammer and finished laying the floor in the studio. I picked up a brush and finished painting the walls. I tried to make Patron as comfortable as possible.

The summer finally ended, and with the autumn, Madame returned. She wore a black dress and a stormy expression, eyes glowering beneath her dark brows. She looked like a beautiful thundercloud. She walked into the studio without warning and pointed a finger at me.

"Choose, Henri," she demanded. "Lydia or me."

Everything stopped. Matisse's brush stopped in mid-air. Sylvie, carrying a tea tray, stopped moving. I stopped breathing.

I felt myself in the grip of a sudden frost. I felt Madame's coldness to the bone.

I must have made some noise then. Perhaps I shifted the pose I'd been holding for one of the figures of Le Chant. *Perhaps I sighed.*

Patron looked toward me. I had expected to see surprise in his expression, a sense of shock to match my own. Instead, I saw only sadness in his eyes, the drag of time and loss in his features. It was a moment of such naked desperation that I could not hold his gaze. I slipped on a robe and left the studio.

The household battle raged all through the autumn and into the winter, while outside the world slid helplessly toward war. Madame had risen from her sick bed with a terrifying energy, all of it hurled against Matisse in a pitiless struggle to have me dismissed. He pleaded with her to relent. Marguerite, his youngest son, Jean, his friends, and even his doctor tried to intervene. They argued the fragility of Matisse's health, the risk of a stroke, the dwindling amount of time left to him, all to no avail. Madame was intransigent.

I moved into a crumbling boarding house in a narrow street by the port. My days were aimless, my nights feverish. Sylvie was my only friend. We were natural allies, she used to say, by virtue of geography: her country, Canada, was at least as cold as Russia. She would convince André to drive her to the market in the Cours Saleya, then slip away to meet me.

"Matisse wants you back," she told me. "He says he cannot work without you. The night nurse says he doesn't sleep and that he suffers violent nose bleeds. Madame's sister, Berthe, has come from Beauzelle."

I smiled, remembering the kindness of Berthe. "And has she, too, turned against me?"

"She speaks only of your virtues, but Madame insists you have betrayed her. The scandal has even reached Paris. I don't believe the rumours, Lydia. I don't believe you've slept with Matisse."

I reached out, took Sylvie's hand in mine. I could see, through her example, how easily Madame's anger would be misread by others. "Oh, Sylvie. Madame is not concerned by anything as fleeting as sex. If I were the mistress of the bedroom, she wouldn't care. But I am the mistress of the studio. Do you understand?"

"Not yet."

I shook my head. How could I explain that Matisse knew how to take possession of people and make them believe they were indispensable? It was like that for me, and I knew instinctively that it had been like that for Madame. My crime was that I had made her unnecessary to his work. She was no longer vital to his art. Since, for Matisse, there was no distinction between art and life, she was no longer vital to his well-being. Her part in the unfolding of his genius was over.

In struggling to explain this to Sylvie, I understood the depth of Madame's pain. She had nursed it, perhaps for years, sharpened it into a cutting blade and aimed it at my heart. She wanted most to take away from me what I had taken from her. I couldn't blame her, but I couldn't let the battle continue.

I held Sylvie's face in my hands, looked into her dark eyes, so trusting, so guileless. "You must take a message to Patron for me. Tell him he must do whatever Madame wants, agree to whatever it takes to save himself, for he has more to give, much more."

After Sylvie had gone, I wandered down to the port. It was a rough area, filled with dark alleys, the briny scent of the sea and the pungent odours of the fish market. Almost anything illegal could be purchased there.

Back in my room, I waited until the day had faded away and the sky was halfway between black and indigo, like ink spreading across a page. I wrote a letter to Berthe because I thought she might understand.

For some reason, I thought of Russia, of my mother's dark, chewy bread and my father's folktales of brave maidens who drew their swords to battle Death. I remembered the carved wooden house where I grew up in Tomsk, and the great stove that warmed it. I remembered holding my father's hand when I was eight years old while we walked between the lines of the Bolsheviks and the anti-Bolsheviks. The enemies had called a ceasefire so that Dr. Delectorskaya could visit the sick. "Be brave, my chick," he'd whispered.

I wedged the single chair with its broken wicker seat under the door handle. Then I picked up the gun and aimed it at my chest.

The impact of the bullet slammed me backwards onto the bed, but I felt very little pain. I stared down at my chest. My wound seemed slight. I could see nothing but a small circle of spreading crimson.

My first thought was that the gun must be faulty, that it had somehow malfunctioned. I tested it by firing out of an open window. The gun worked *perfectly, the shot destroying a nearby flower pot. I did not have the courage to aim the gun at myself a second time.*

I pressed a towel to my chest and stumbled down to the streets where a fisherman, a young boy really, found me and took me to a doctor. Few questions were asked, and even those I refused to answer.

"I have no alternative but to send for the gendarmes," the doctor warned.

I begged him not to and confessed the wound was self-inflicted. I stood up quickly to run away and felt the room swing and sway under my feet.

When I regained consciousness, I saw that my wound had been dressed. The doctor called me a mad woman and told me I was lucky that the bullet had lodged against my breastbone. "An inch here, an inch there," he growled. "You might easily have been killed."

Precisely, I thought.

I slunk back to my boarding house to brood and contemplate my future. My world had shrunk. The air in my room was damp and the mattress on my bed was lumpy. Across from the bed was a chest of drawers covered with chipped white paint and a rickety washstand with a cracked marble top. A mirror, foggy with age, hung crookedly on the wall. I stared into it for a long time. It struck me as curious that my reflection should look so normal, so unaware that it belonged to somebody quite different now.

A little after midnight, I fell asleep.

A day, perhaps two days later, I woke to find Sylvie leaning over me. As a good Catholic, she must have thought my actions wicked, but she had the kindness not to say so. She had discreetly removed the letter to Berthe and disposed of the gun. She fed me a thick bean soup she'd bought in a nearby bistro. Before she left, she kissed me on the forehead, and pressed a letter from the pocket of her coat into my hands.

It was from Matisse, of course. I smiled to see that he'd not been able to keep himself from decorating the envelope. In black ink, he had drawn a spill of roses that tumbled diagonally across the heavy white paper. He had addressed the note simply to Mme. Lydia.

I did not open the letter for several days. I loved him, but I was afraid, too. For the sake of his art, he could be horribly selfish. He never hesitated to demand as much from others as he demanded of himself. If he spoke of his sadness or his own terror that he would not paint again, I knew I would be helpless, yet I wanted to navigate by my own instincts. I wanted to choose freely to go or to stay.

Finally, I broke the seal and read the enigmatic message: "You must know, Lydia, that I paint beauty in self-defense. I do not paint the dark agonized cry of the world that is plain enough for all to see. Perhaps the whole point of life is just to rest in its moments of beauty, to contemplate and eventually disappear into its beauty."

I reread the sentences several times, tried to make what sense I could from them. I believed, perhaps because I wanted to, that he understood the darkness I was trying to move through and that he was guiding me toward the light I was hoping to find.

The next day was wild and windy, typical of wet February. I walked across the Promenade des Anglais to the curving line of Nice's great bay and contemplated the pitch and tumble of the sea, the endless percussion of its waves hitting the pebbled shore. The surface of the sea was a hundred shades of gray and silver, luminous, as if lit from underneath. I found myself imagining how Matisse would paint it, how he would distill from the motion and sound before me strange, abstract shafts of beauty.

Two weeks later, I left Nice and travelled alone, north to Paris.

V

T HE PLANE LANDED A LITTLE before eight in the morning, Paris time, and the air terminal was chilly. Anxious to stretch her legs, Chloe was glad of the long walk through echoing and deserted halls to customs, and the even longer trek to the public transportation area. She was heading to the queue for buses into the city when Adam hailed a taxi. He opened the door for her and she climbed in, promising herself she would talk to him later about finances. For now, she was too excited, anticipating her first glimpse of fabled and romantic Paris.

The taxi driver was a woman, maybe mid-thirties, with long straight brown hair, impeccably cut. Adam gave her an address, in rapid and polished French, and the cab lurched into gear.

"Where are we going?" Chloe asked.

"I've made reservations for us—a little hotel I always stay in on the Île Saint-Louis." When it seemed as if Chloe was about to object, Adam held up a hand and talked over her. "Please don't be difficult about this, Chloe. We have different areas of expertise. This is mine."

Chloe sat back abruptly, but not before she saw the small grin on the driver's face.

"Ees your first time in Paree, yes?" the woman asked.

Chloe nodded.

"You will not be disappointed," she promised, hurtling the cab into a small space between cars in the morning traffic headed for the city.

But Chloe was disappointed. The long, tedious drive from the airport resembled the approach to any large North American city: multi-laned highways and lots of ugly industrial parks separated by the occasional cluster of sterile high-rise buildings.

She was beginning to feel her morale sinking when Adam tugged at her sleeve and nodded his head toward the driver. At eighty kilometers an hour and with one hand, she was pouring mineral water from a large bottle into a little saucer set on the seat beside her. She didn't spill a drop. A black and tan puppy, some kind of miniature terrier not much larger than a squirrel, began to lap from the dish. The driver laughed at Chloe's amazement. The next moment she was leaning on the horn and cursing at another taxi cutting into the lane in front of her.

Finally, after some chilling lane changes, more cursing and sudden turns, the cab entered Paris and Chloe caught her breath. The Seine flowed beside her, silvery and serpentine, a mesmerizing force pulling her into the heart of the city. From her cab window, she could see tree-lined *quais* at the river's edge and ancient buildings, their stone facades tinted pink by the morning sun. She thought of the great artists who had walked on these bridges and over these cobblestones, silently whispering their names like a kind of chant: David, Delacroix, Courbet, Degas, Manet, Monet, Renoir, Cézanne, Gaugin, Chagall, Picasso, Bonnard, Matisse. The list was glorious and seemed endless. Chloe relaxed and felt herself drawn into the net of beauty and history that hung like a bridal veil over Paris.

With one last turn, the taxi stopped in front of an elegant seventeenth-century building that looked more like a home than a hotel. As Adam counted out euros, the driver peeked around his shoulder and waved to Chloe. "I know always," she laughed, "from first sight. Those who love Paree."

When the cab was gone, Chloe and Adam stood side by side on the sidewalk in front of the *Hôtel des Deux-Iles*.

"The rooms won't be ready until noon or thereabouts," Adam said. "There's a courtyard where we could wait if you're very tired. Or we could walk."

Chloe simply smiled and took his arm. They walked and walked, over the Pont Saint-Louis and past the magnificent Nôtre-Dame, the cradle of Paris, through the narrow streets of the Left Bank, past markets and churches, bookstores and antique shops, finally collapsing at a café. By this time, the sun had burned through the early mist, leaving the air fresh and damp, and perfumed from chestnuts in bloom. Chloe felt exhilarated, all her doubts of the previous night banished with her first whiff of adventure.

She took a long, slow taste of French coffee and watched a cat the colour of apricots grooming itself on a stack of *Le Monde* newspapers. Someone in a nearby flat was playing the piano, the notes spilling onto the street from an open window. This moment, she thought, was perfect.

Adam, too, seemed lost in his own reverie. She found it restful that the frequent silences between them did not make either of them anxious. He seemed content to let her drink in Paris on her own terms.

His hair, she noted, was beginning to curl in the dampness. It made him look less serious, despite his suit and tie.

"Do you always travel in a suit?" she asked.

Adam looked a little startled by the suddenness of the question, but answered agreeably enough. "It's practical. Suits are difficult to pack."

"Yes, but are you going to need a suit at all?"

"Maybe. Liliane, as I remember, is very chic." He glanced casually, but not unkindly, at Chloe's crumpled linen jacket and black jeans.

"It was good of you to make the hotel reservations, Adam. I shouldn't have objected. I'm just not used to spending Sammy's money. In fact, you and Dad have made things very easy for me, so unlike what it must've been like for Sylvie all those years ago. And, don't worry, I'll get some clothes. After all, I'm in Paris."

Paris, I thought, is always a good idea. I had found refuge there before. But the city I returned to was different from the city I had left. It struck me that people who loved Paris always remembered it the same way: the Seine brilliant in the sunlight, boulevards lined with chestnuts in bloom, flower markets and fountains and little sun-soaked cafés. And always, somewhere in the distance, music.

But this Paris was a dull metallic gray. This Paris was jumpy and surly, a heady mix of bravado and dread. The German threat hung over the streets and the parks and the monuments like a thick mist.

Nonetheless, I felt safe and anonymous here. The streets were dark and I could walk them for hours, invisible, head down like all the world these days, moving quickly, just one more shadow in the twilight.

After a little searching, I found my aunt had moved to the outskirts of the city, to the unfashionable northern fringes of the Bois de Boulogne. She was not overjoyed to see me. In her eyes, I was a disgrace. I had divorced my husband, an elderly and, more importantly, wealthy Russian. It did no good to explain to her that his hands were the coldest I had ever known. Worse, I had allowed scandalous pictures of myself to be shown in public. The glorious canvases that took months for Matisse to paint and the sensual and flowing lines of his drawings were just "nudie" pictures to my aunt. Models were prostitutes. Her accusations were directed at me like sniper fire, unforgiving and unrelenting.

Still, she took me in as I knew she must. We were both Russian, after all, born of the same bitter past. As children, wrapped head to toe in thick, scratchy wool, we had walked to school between high, hard-packed walls of snow. We knew how the sky could disappear among sheets of fast-moving clouds, and how the winds could howl. We remembered larders outside kitchen windows filled with dead rabbits stacked stiff and straight like rifles in a gun-case. We remembered dead bodies, alabaster skin punctured with bullet holes like black moons, and the cholera and typhus epidemics that swept away first my mother and then my father.

I found work modeling in a furrier's showroom. I spent my days draped in luxury—champagne-coloured minks, white and black-spotted snow leopards, thick, midnight sables—and my nights trying to stay warm in my aunt's drafty apartment, with its leaky roof and slanting floors. I read a good deal, and thought about training as a nurse. I knew what kind of damage war would bring. Once, when I'd been kneeling beside Madame's bedside, Matisse had teased that I was undeniably a doctor's daughter, a stretcher-bearer, with first-aid written on my heart.

Sylvie was my lifeline, my one friend. Her letters to me were not always comforting, but they were honest, somehow more real than the glittery nervousness of Paris. In them, she spoke of her growing love for André, and her growing fear of the Fascist rallies in Nice. She described a terrible row that broke out in one of the many restaurants that lined the Cours Saleya. Two opposing groups of men shouted at each other. Tables were knocked over and a tray of glasses smashed. An innocent woman passing by was cut on the cheek by the flying shards of glass. Sylvie worried that both of us, both foreigners, might soon be at risk.

Most of all she worried about Matisse. Madame had left the apartment in the Regina for an unknown destination in Paris in early March, but only after her lawyer had drawn up a detailed deed of separation. Her trunks were jam-packed with etchings, drawings, sculptures, and paintings.

"Matisse," Sylvie wrote, "is utterly alone, except for me and André. Marguerite and Berthe have left. Even the cook has departed. Since he can't paint, he pours his energy into long, long letters to his son, Pierre. He's the only occupant of this whole, vast, empty, echoing building. He does not ask me about you, except to inquire after your health."

Finally, in August, the distracting chatter of Parisian existence came to an end. The French government declared war. It seemed as if all of Europe let out a long pent-up breath and suddenly started to move. The desire to act, to do something, anything, was contagious.

I put on some lipstick and climbed all the way up to the Montmartre in search of red wine, smoky jazz and tall, handsome men convinced they would soon be fodder for German guns. I felt a fierce need for sex, for skin against my skin, for stripping away clothes with passionate speed. It was not difficult to find a partner in a generation adrift. He bought me pink roses from one of those tired women who carry them around in wicker baskets from one café table to another. In the hotel room, with its scratchy blanket, he undressed me with appropriate hurriedness. "Lovely," he said. Between the two of us, I hoped we had enough art to get to pleasure.

His kiss in so much loneliness was like a hand pulling me up out of the water, lifting me up from a place of drowning and into the reckless air.

In the end, we managed to achieve something that felt good and physically exhausting. Then we lay without talking in each other's arms for several hours, which, I suspected, is what we both came for. In the morning, we smiled too much to hide our embarrassment and wished each other good luck. I can't remember his name. I remember waking up once, seeing pink roses in the dark night.

ADAM AND CHLOE HAD BEEN in Paris for three days before they finally arranged a date with Liliane. In the meantime, Chloe had fallen in love with the tall French windows in her room that looked out over a tiny green courtyard. She had fallen in love with the statues in the Luxembourg Gardens, the boisterous street markets, the Art Deco metro signs, the Pont Neuf, and fresh croissants for breakfast.

Best of all, the rhythm of the city seemed to suit her. During the day, it might be all business, cell phones, and the ear-splitting roar of motor bikes with their blue-gray stench of diesel exhaust. But by five in the afternoon, as she and Adam strolled to the Café de Flore, the ambience was relaxed. People laughed a lot, leaning towards each other and touching shoulders, and seemed not in a hurry to go anywhere else or do anything other than sip an aperitif and watch the lowering sun stain the sky a pale rose.

It was a mild evening so Adam chose a table on the terrace and ordered *café noir*. Chloe sank into the past imagining Sartre and Simone de Beauvoir in one corner, Gertrude Stein and Hemingway in another. Now the terrace, less crowded than at lunch when people came to see and be seen, was the meeting place of suntanned Italians wearing expensive gold jewelry, chattering Americans in clothes either too casual or too formal, and the French who looked elegant no matter what they wore. Adam, Chloe noted, fit in rather well, wearing a black T-shirt under his black suit jacket and jeans. She wasn't the only one who'd shopped. As she watched him, he turned to her and smiled.

"This is an amazing place," Chloe said. "Legend has it that Gertrude Stein introduced Matisse to Picasso here. She was a great fan of Matisse during his Fauvist 'wild beast' phase, but later dumped him for Picasso."

"You seem at home here, Chloe. Gertrude Stein also said that America was her country, but Paris was her hometown. Do you feel that way?"

"Paris is like a dream, but I think it must be difficult to live here. Everything's so expensive, for one thing." She smoothed her fingers over the silky turquoise shawl she'd bought in a little boutique on the Rue du Bac. "Sammy will be shocked and it'll take years to pay him back, but I'll think about tomorrow, tomorrow. You're more relaxed here, too. Except tonight, you seem a little distracted. Are you missing Elizabeth?"

"Elizabeth?" Adam seemed genuinely surprised for just a moment. "Oh, well, it would be lovely to share Paris with her. But it's Jamie I'm remembering."

Chloe immediately felt embarrassed by her blunder. Of course Adam would be thinking of his brother and of his loss. "I'm sorry," she blurted out. "I didn't think." She placed a hand on his arm, then pulled it away and ran it nervously through her hair.

Adam turned away from her, signaling the waiter. "I don't think Liliane would mind if we ordered some wine while we're waiting. White or red, Chloe?"

"Er, red," Chloe mumbled. While Adam perused the wine list with the waiter, Chloe watched one of Paris' ubiquitous mopeds roar past the café. The female driver parked the bike illegally between two cars and pulled off her helmet, releasing a wave of dark hair that fell across her shoulders.

Mesmerized, Chloe stared as the woman began walking, hips swaying, toward the Flore. She wore a black leather jacket with big lapels and silver chains looped over the pockets. Underneath was a short, white dress with a flounced skirt and underneath that, denims and killer black heels. It was an outlandish outfit, one that Chloe knew would look ridiculous on her. Yet this woman, Liliane beyond a doubt, looked stunning. She tugged on Adam's sleeve, nodded slightly in Liliane's direction, and whispered hurriedly, "I thought you said she was a quiet, shy girl."

"Adam, *mon ami, ça va?*"

Adam jumped to his feet in time to take both of Liliane's outstretched hands in his, and to deliver the obligatory three kisses.

"It's good to see you again, Lil. You look wonderful."

Liliane, taking her cue from Adam, immediately switched from French to English. "Ah, you and your big brother, always good with the flattery. And this must be Chloe. Tell me, how do you like Paris?"

"Very much."

"I'm glad. Perhaps you'll be able to persuade Adam to come a little more often. Jamie loved it here. Now tell me all the places you've been so far."

As Adam poured the wine, Chloe listed the sights and thought how exquisite Liliane was, dark eyes under perfectly arched brows, full lips, flawless skin. No wonder Jamie had stayed in Paris, she thought. Adam must be blind.

"Yes, yes," Liliane was saying, "these are lovely places, but for the tourists. Adam, I'm disappointed in you. You must show Chloe off-beat Paris."

"We've only been here three days," Adam said in self-defense. "And Chloe slept for half of one day."

"Don't listen to him, Liliane. Please tell me what I'm missing."

"He must take you to a Moroccan restaurant off the Place Blanche in Pigalle where you'll sit on carpets that have been strewn with rose petals. On a misty evening, he must take you to the *quai d'Anjou*. This is where Baudelaire and the Hashish-Eaters Club used to meet, and some say his ghost wanders there. And then there are the Catacombs—don't go if you're squeamish—filled with skeletons from the French Revolution. There are secret hiding places there used by the Resistance during the Occupation." Liliane sighed, and ruffled Adam's hair. Picking up her wine glass, she tilted it slightly in the air. "A toast, yes? To Jamie. Later, we'll speak of sad things. For now, the omelettes here are very good."

When the evening became cooler and the Café de Flore more crowded, the trio decided to retire to a quiet bar several blocks away. As she peered through the door, Chloe thought the dim interior looked slightly mysterious, slightly dangerous. Smoke floated up to the ceiling in lazy arabesques and the smell of beer hung pleasantly in the air. As her group made its way through the shadows to a candle-lit table, Chloe heard the sound of an accordion, the voice of a woman singing, spilling from an old-fashioned juke-box. *I love Paris in the spring time.*

They ordered more wine and Liliane immediately focused on Jamie. "I miss him. We would have drifted apart eventually, but with the accident, well, our time ended too soon. You have questions, Adam. I will answer what I can."

"Do you remember, Lil, the sketch that Jamie sent me through the mail before he died?"

"Of course. The drawing of Lydia. I was afraid it had been destroyed in the accident. It was very important to him."

"How long had he known Lydia Delectorskaya?" Chloe asked.

"He met her when he first came to Paris. This was before I knew him, you understand, but he talked of her often. To him, she was a *grande dame*. You know this phrase?"

Chloe shook her head, and leaned closer to Liliane. Her French accent became stronger with each sip of wine, her voice mesmerizing. Adam, too, seemed enthralled.

"Jamie saw Lydia as a kind of romantic heroine, beautiful and abandoned. But more than this, he admired her courage, the heroine who defied the odds, defied conventions. Not for Lydia, the traps of memory or the fragility of the elderly."

"Did she talk to Jamie about her relationship with Matisse?" Adam asked.

Liliane laughed. "Your brother used to say that Lydia was very reluctant to speak of her life with Matisse. But about his art, she could talk you under the table. She knew all the paintings, every sculpture and sketch. Jamie said that she documented everything she could, that each line was drawn on her heart. So, of course, he believed her when she told him about the painting she lost."

Chloe and Adam stared at her, watched her mouth curve into a sly smile as she noted their intent stillness.

"Oh, yes," she laughed. "Jamie told me that story, too. It was during the war. Lydia was being pressured by a German soldier, threatened with deportation. There was a painting he admired … well, you can guess the rest: Lydia hid the painting. When the war was over, she returned to the hiding place, but the painting was gone. *C'est finis.*"

"But what if it wasn't finished?" Chloe murmured.

Liliane, in the act of drinking her wine, suddenly froze, her chin still tilted upward. Slowly, she brought down her glass, lowered her head. When she looked up again, looking right at Adam, her beautiful dark eyes were filled with tears. "So, it is true. What I feared most about your coming here."

"What—?" Adam leaned toward her.

She pressed a finger to his lips. "Just tell me. Are you here because you believe this painting exists?"

"Yes."

Liliane took a deep breath and her voice trembled. "Did Jamie find it? Did he tell you where it is?"

"Not exactly." Adam gave her a brief summary of his initial suspicions regarding *Woman in a Blouse, Dreaming*, Daniels' murder, and the discovery of Jamie's message written on the back of the sketch. "Chloe and I were both being followed when we were in Toronto, perhaps by Inspector Bradley and the police, perhaps not," he concluded. "We hoped you could help us figure out what was going on."

"Go home," Liliane whispered, tears now falling freely down her cheeks. She brushed them away angrily, and rose to her feet.

Chloe reached for Liliane's hand and coaxed her back down to her chair. "Please help us, Liliane. I need to stay here for my grandmother's sake. To trace what happened to her all those years ago. Look," she pulled the amethyst ring from her finger. "This came from Lydia, to Sylvie, to me. There's a connection—I don't know how to explain it. I feel I'm *supposed* to do this."

Liliane stared quietly at the ring, then slowly shook her head, her hair swinging across her shoulders. "I've feared for a long time now that Jamie was not in a motorcycle accident. He was murdered. It is too dangerous for you to stay."

"Please, Lil." Adam's voice was flat and even. In a rush of certainty, Chloe realized that Liliane's comments about Jamie's death had not surprised him in the least.

"This much only I know. Soon after we met, maybe eighteen months or so ago, Jamie found something, some message he thought from

Lydia. He started telling me wild stories of a missing Matisse. He spent hours researching Matisse. Then last summer, we went together to Nice. It was supposed to be a vacation, but he left me alone for hours at a time. There were people he had to talk to, he said. When we returned to Paris, he wasn't the same. He was obsessed. He even visited some dealers here and asked all kinds of questions about Matisse paintings at auction, private sales, museum bidding. Two weeks before he died, he went back to the Côte d'Azur. He called me. He was excited, wild. Two days later, he was dead."

"But why do you think he was killed?" Chloe asked.

Liliane gave her a slightly pitying look, as if she were a child. "Because Jamie was born on a motorcycle. And because he too was being followed."

"Liliane," Adam said. "Jamie gave us a message. Listen: *Beyond the walls, beneath blue stars, a tree blossoms and roses veil a virgin bride.* Does it mean anything to you?"

"No. I've never heard this before. It doesn't sound like Jamie."

"Did he leave any notes, any papers in the apartment that might explain what he meant?"

Liliane glanced away and Chloe sensed that Adam's question had made her uncomfortable.

She waited, and when Liliane's eyes next met hers, Chloe guessed the cause of her new friend's unease.

"Jamie had already left you, hadn't he?"

Chloe put her hand gently on Liliane's arm, but the expression she saw on Liliane's face surprised her. It was not anger, or even the sadness so recently evident. It was longing. Chloe recognized it because she'd felt it too. All her life, she'd felt the longing to be safe, to belong.

"I'm sorry," she whispered.

Liliane shrugged. "I knew it wouldn't last. But I blame the painting, his obsession with finding it. He moved to a flat in the Marais—number five, rue des Blancs Manteaux."

A half-hour later, Adam and Chloe were strolling back to their hotel.

"How did you know," Adam asked, "about Jamie leaving Liliane?"

"Just a feeling I had."

"Something, some understanding seemed to pass between you."

Chloe nodded in agreement, but didn't offer any fuller explanation. Her bond with Liliane had to do with women's lives, how entangled they became with fathers and husbands and brothers and lovers. She'd first sensed this vulnerability as a child when Sammy had left. She'd learned the stunning ease with which a life can be changed, in a minute, on any ordinary day. She'd learned she had to adapt to the future on her own, to reinvent her relationship with her father, to reinvent herself. She'd learned the flexibility of women, their suppleness.

Adam interrupted her thoughts: "Paolo, wasn't it? Are you missing Paolo?"

Chloe couldn't help but laugh. "No, Adam. I assure you I'm quite safe from Paolo and from the perils of romantic love. It's too dangerous, driven by hormones and dizzying illusions."

"That's a sad thing to say."

"Really? And you call yourself a scientist? I'm always reading that love is reducible to some kind of chemical reaction, just a fizzing in the brain."

"And you call yourself an artist? Look," he said, pointing to the *quais* just beside and below the bridge they were crossing to the Île Saint-Louis.

A young couple was dancing beside the river, arms wrapped around each other, music rising up like smoke from a portable CD player they'd set on the ground. As Chloe and Adam watched, the lovers swayed back and forth, cheeks touching, oblivious to all but the moon on the Seine, the music and each other.

"Now that's romantic," Adam sighed. "You must remember your first love at moments like this."

"I do," Chloe admitted. He was like a song she had memorized and then forgotten, though unexpectedly hearing a bit of the tune or catching a phrase could bring him back to her in a rush. "He was handsome and clever, and he tossed me away as carelessly as a coin. Your turn now."

"My grade three teacher, Miss Fitzgerald. Sadly, unrequited."

Chloe laughed and impulsively reached for Adam's hand. Head down, she watched the way their strides matched as they neared the pools of light in front of their hotel.

"Chloe, I think we should try to find Jamie's last apartment. It may be rented out by now, but it's the only lead we have."

"Of course. And I've asked Liliane to write down a list of all the places Jamie visited in Nice, at least the ones she knows about. Do you really believe your brother may have been murdered?"

"I can't know for sure. An accident wouldn't be out of the question. But if he were being followed... Suppose Jamie really did find the painting on that last trip to the South of France and he mailed the sketch with its clue to me as insurance. Perhaps he knew his life was at risk. Perhaps that's why he moved out of Liliane's flat, to protect her. I'm doing my best to think well of him. I've done that most of my life."

As they walked across the small lobby and climbed the stairs, Chloe struggled to find comforting words. Tried, but failed. They said goodnight in tight voices in the hallway before their respective doors. But before she fell asleep, she could not dispel the notion that Adam had wanted to tell her something, and that the inclination had ebbed away.

The Marais was a medley of the best and worst of Paris—elegant seventeenth-century buildings lining the Place des Vosges with its fountains and symmetrical gardens, and the twisting narrow streets of the old Jewish quarter. There were street plaques that marked centres of the Resistance in World War II, and street plaques that marked schools where Jewish children had been rounded up for deportation to death camps. There was a museum devoted to the history of Paris that housed a statue of the Sun King, Louis XIV, the only public statue of a king not destroyed in the French Revolution. And there was a museum devoted to Picasso in a splendid seventeenth-century house built by a salt tax collector. The entire area was undergoing a slow process of gentrification, Adam explained, and some of the Marais's oldest treasures, like Goldenberg's delicatessen, were paying the price.

Jamie's apartment was in a low-rise, slightly grubby building probably erected in the 1920s. Chloe and Adam had walked by it several times during the day, trying to decide if they, or the building itself, were being watched. Eventually, they'd entered the small hallway that served as a lobby and found Jamie's name still posted beside the flat numbers. Two glass double-doors barred their access to an old-fashioned staircase that spiraled up the centre of the building.

"What now?" Chloe asked.

"I think dinner's a good plan. Aren't you hungry?"

They found a cave-like bistro with vaulted ceilings and a table near the window. Chloe ordered French onion soup for both of them and rested her chin on her hand. "We don't actually know that the apartment is vacant," she said. "Even though Jamie's name is still listed, the flat might have been leased to someone else."

"Right. Let's assume it *has* been re-let. I'll introduce myself as Jamie's brother and we'll find out if he left anything behind. Or we'll find out where his stuff has been moved."

"Adam, didn't you ask about any of Jamie's things when he died? I mean, you were here in Paris. Didn't you wonder about his stuff? Clothes or books or photographs? I wonder why Liliane didn't tell you about this apartment then. Surely you had a right to sort through what he'd left behind."

"Jamie didn't accumulate much in the way of material stuff. Liliane gave me a box with some of his personal effects. I already had the sketch. Frankly, I don't expect we'll find much more."

A steamy, fragrant bowl of soup was plunked onto the table under Chloe's nose: caramelized onions in a rich, beefy broth, a round of baguette smothered in a thick gooey cheese. For a while, food trumped conversation.

"But what about a cell phone, a computer, an address book?" Chloe finally added.

"A cell phone maybe, though it was probably lost in the accident. He'd have had it with him if he owned one. A computer sounds unlikely to me and a date book would be totally out of character."

"But if he really was doing research on Matisse, he must have had some way to keep notes or to keep track of appointments. Liliane said he'd been meeting with gallery owners, maybe even potential buyers. There must be some kind of paper trail."

Adam wound a string of cheese around his spoon like a spaghetti strand

and shook his head. "You overestimate Jamie's powers of organization. Also, if you imagine the worst case scenario, the chance of finding a paper trail becomes remote."

"What worst case?"

Adam just raised an eyebrow.

"Oh," Chloe continued. "You mean the one where there are murderers out there following him—and us. So naturally Jamie would have deliberately covered his tracks and destroyed any notes."

Chloe put down her spoon and shivered slightly.

Adam watched her closely but said nothing, waiting.

"I think the danger must be over," she said finally. "I mean, no one seems to be following us in Paris and no one seems to be watching Jamie's apartment. So let's check out this place before I lose my nerve and you succeed in convincing me that we're completely wasting our time."

The night was damp and cool when they left the bistro. Something less than rain and more than mist hung woolly and gray over the city. The lights of the shops and the bars flashed neon pink and green across the puddles forming on the sidewalks.

In the end, they relied on cliché to get through the barrier of the lobby doors. When Jamie's bell went unanswered, Adam simply pushed all sixteen buzzers simultaneously. True to human nature, someone released the lock and Chloe and Adam slowly began climbing the winding staircase.

"This is creepy," Chloe whispered. "Did you ever see a movie called *The Spiral Staircase*? It's about a madman who strangles women and the camera zooms in on his eyes and then closer and closer until one eye fills the—"

Suddenly there was no light. Blackness fell across the stairs like the crashing descent of a steel gate. Chloe jumped, made a clipped squealing sound. Almost unbelievably, she heard Adam laugh.

"Sorry," he choked, trying to pull himself together. "It's an automatic switch. The lights go out automatically. We can reset the timer on the next landing."

When the lights came on again, she glared at him to very little effect.

They climbed another flight of stairs, finally reaching the third floor and followed the numbers around to Jamie's door. Adam knocked gently at first, then louder.

The lights went out again.

"Damn," Adam swore. He reached into a pocket and handed Chloe a pencil-thin flashlight. "Could you hold this please?"

"What are you going to do?"

She watched as he dipped his hand into his jeans pocket again and brought out a metal tool of some kind. Then he crouched down to the level of the doorknob.

"Are you actually going to try to pick the lock?" she gasped.

"Please be quiet, Chloe. This is a lock pick for a standard five-pin lock. I'm hopeful it might work."

"I can't believe this."

"Is this really the time to remind you that breaking and entering is not an activity with which you are unfamiliar?"

"I didn't break. I only entered. Besides, I thought you didn't like taking risks."

"I've thought this through and weighed the possible outcomes. I'm a scientist. This is a calculated risk."

"You're a researcher, a theory man."

"I'm very resourceful. Now if you'd just be quiet."

"It won't work. And what if someone's in there?"

Adam stood up and turned the doorknob, pushing the door open. Together on the threshold, he and Chloe listened for the faintest sound, the slightest suggestion of movement. Adam crossed into the room first, beckoning to Chloe and shutting the door behind her. His finger to his lips, he switched on a second flashlight and began to survey the room.

Chloe felt her shoulders relax. The musty smell that filled her nostrils told her that the shutters had not been opened, and likely the room had not been lived in for some time. The flashlight beams cut across a dead gray interior, a bit dusty and almost vacant. A lone divan, probably a cheap variation of a Futon, hunkered like a gray beast in the corner. A stack of books leaned crookedly against a wall.

She heard Adam flick on a light switch, but nothing happened. The electricity had been shut off.

Chloe began to move quietly into what appeared to be a kitchen, realizing as she did so that the floor was gently slanted. She felt off-balance, as if she were slightly drunk. There was nothing in the cupboards or in the small fridge resting on the counter. A couple of plates and some cutlery, bone-dry by now, were still propped up in a drainer beside the sink. A table pushed into a corner was bare and slightly chipped.

She knelt to check the kitchen drawers and found that one of the two top drawers had jammed. She rattled the top drawer ineffectually, then eased the drawer below it off its runners, dislodging a folded piece of heavy paper. From its size and shape, Chloe guessed it was a business card of some kind and slipped it into her pocket.

When she re-entered the main room, she saw that Adam was going through the stack of books one by one.

"Find anything?" she whispered.

He held up a photo. It was an image of Liliane, her black hair held back with a red band, her lovely mouth almost smiling. For Adam's sake, Chloe was glad Jamie had kept the picture. It seemed to suggest that he'd still cared for Liliane.

She left him with the books and moved on to the bedroom. The door stuck, as if the hinges needed oiling. Lowering her shoulder, she gave the door a push, almost tumbling into the room.

She stared at the floor. Immediately, she felt the groundswell of fear, the tilting of the room, the ripple of nausea.

She spun around, slammed into Adam's chest and felt his arms enfold her like a vice. She closed her eyes, but could still see the body face down on the floor, the knife protruding from between the shoulder blades, the head twisted awkwardly to one side.

"Jesus," she heard Adam say. "It's Peter, the Russian butler."

Without moving, Chloe mumbled into Adam's chest: "What do we do now?"

Adam backed out of the room, pulling Chloe along with him, and shut the bedroom door. "It's okay. You can breathe," he said quietly, releasing her.

She lifted her head, saw a thin line of light seeping under the front door to the apartment. She grabbed Adam's arm and pointed to the light even as she heard the first scratchings at the lock.

She dove for the kitchen and slid under the table, feeling Adam right behind her. Slowly she turned her head, followed the beam of a flashlight as it swooped across the living room wall.

Her heart was stuttering in her chest. The rush of her blood made a roar in her ears. The table was no protection. They would be discovered in an instant.

She heard footsteps, strained to hear more. Two pairs of footsteps, something that made a faint clicking sound low to the ground. The sounds ebbed towards the bedroom door. She braced herself for a scream, an exclamation, the shock of a person stumbling across a corpse.

Nothing happened.

For a minute, perhaps more, she stared into Adam's eyes that were just inches from her own.

Nothing happened. No reaction. Whoever had entered Jamie's flat knew the body was there.

She could see the pulse in Adam's throat as his heart quickened its rhythm. She felt an overpowering need to move, an instinct to run, but when she stirred he put an arm around her and held her still.

Soon the sounds coming from the other room telegraphed their own unmistakable message. *They had come to remove the body.*

Chloe found the tension unbearable. Time seemed cruelly stretched, every second an ordeal. She pictured the knife in Peter's back in exquisite detail. She began to shake and Adam held her closer.

Finally, she heard a voice. Low, almost indistinct, words she couldn't understand. The light swung around again. She heard the clicking again. Then the front door opened, more clicking. She held her breath. The door closed and she exhaled.

They lay in each other's arms a moment, feeling a rush of relief. Then Adam disentangled himself and stood up, reaching out a hand to help her up.

"Stay here," he cautioned. "I'm going to follow them."

Chloe didn't answer him. She was not going to stay alone in the apartment for all the world.

Adam eased the door open and edged into the hallway, hugging the wall. The darkness was complete but Chloe could hear something heavy bumping down the stairs. She crept out of the apartment on her hands and knees and peered downwards through the stairwell.

The sudden flooding of light was like the flash of a camera. At once Chloe saw the spiral of the stairs, the upturned faces of two men, a large crate balanced on a dolly. The men looked straight at her. She had the briefest impression of weightlifter bodies and razored haircuts.

She pulled her head back, but it was too late. One of them shouted. She heard his feet pounding on the stairs.

She ran like a wild thing. No thought, no plan, just running up and up, trying to put distance between herself and the pounding feet of the man who was chasing her.

Then she skidded to a stop. She had left Adam alone.

She began to move down the first hallway she came to, banging on doors, screaming. "*Aidez-moi, aidez-moi. Appelez les gendarmes.*"

"Chloe."

His voice cut through her panic.

"Chloe. Come down. Hurry."

This time she heard the urgency in his voice and she rushed down the stairs. "What happened? Where are they?"

"Later, Chloe. I've called an ambulance. We need to get out of here."

She followed him, hardly pausing when she passed a man sprawled on his back on the stairs, one leg bent awkwardly. Of the other man and the crate on the dolly with the wheels that made a clicking sound, there were no signs.

They emerged, breathless and heaving into the clamour of the street. The mist had turned to pounding, drenching rain that blurred the night. Maybe it was just adrenaline or the desperate joy of being alive, but Chloe suddenly saw Paris with fresh eyes as she ran through the streets with Adam: it was a city of warrens, of escape routes, passageways and shortcuts. She found it exhilarating.

The next morning, Chloe could barely raise her head from the pillows on her bed. She'd been up half the night, waiting for her heartbeat to slow and trying to decide with Adam what they should do next. In the end, they'd called the French police. Chloe's high school French couldn't cope with official bureaucratese, so she'd left the final negotiations to Adam. They were meeting with a certain Commissaire Lejeune at ten in the courtyard of their hotel.

Reluctantly, Chloe threw back the duvet and groped her way to the shower. She needed lots of hot water and then food, lots of food. She was ravenous.

Forty minutes later, Chloe pushed open the French doors into the courtyard. She could see Adam deeply engaged in conversation with a man whose back was towards her.

"Adam?" she said, stepping out from the shadowed doorway into the brightness of the morning.

The stranger stood at the sound of her voice and turned to face her. He was impressive, tall and broad-shouldered, in his mid-thirties. He had a smooth shaven head, intense green eyes. Chloe found herself staring. A part of her realized that Adam was introducing him, but she was temporarily incapable of forming words.

Commissaire Lejeune reached for her hand. "*Enchanté*," he said with a smile and a gaze that held hers for much longer than was necessary to establish a professional relationship.

Even his voice is beautiful, Chloe thought, deep and resonant. He pulled out a chair for her and she sank into it.

"Coffee, Chloe?" Adam asked.

She looked at the used plates and empty cups and crumpled napkins on the table. "Oh, you started without me, I see."

"It's forty minutes past ten, Chloe. Coffee?"

She glanced at Lejeune and saw that he was grinning at her. She would have felt self-conscious except that his smile was so welcoming and the expression in his eyes so unabashedly admiring.

"What have I missed?" she asked, smiling back.

"Breakfast," Adam replied. "We saved you some croissants."

"Thanks, but I'm not hungry. Just coffee's fine."

"Allow me." Lejeune reached for the coffee pot and poured for Chloe. He lifted up the milk jug and she nodded. He leaned back in his chair:

"Sugar?" The word sounded like an invitation or perhaps a promise.

That was when Chloe knew there'd be trouble. The hint of seduction in his voice, the thudding of her pulse, the quick image of the disaster to come. It was all right there, laid out in front of her across the table: plates, cutlery, coffee, and heartbreak. She had a breathless, giddy feeling, as though she were about to dive off a high board into a pool.

With an effort, she pulled herself back from the edge, focusing her mind on the reason for Lejeune's presence. "So Adam has told you what happened to us last night?"

"He has. Peter Fyodorov was probably killed a few hours before you found him. Stabbed, as you no doubt noticed, with a carbon-steel Henckels butcher's knife."

"You've found his body already? And the knife?"

"The unfortunate gentleman with the broken leg has been singing like the proverbial canary."

"So Adam and I are free of suspicion. That's a relief." She smiled at Adam, saw the look of concern on his face, and added hurriedly, "Isn't it?"

"The police haven't yet found the other man, Chloe," Adam responded.

"But you know who he is?" Chloe directed her question to Lejeune. "Surely, you can find and arrest him."

"Yes, of course." The Commissaire regarded her intently. "But it's not quite that simple. You must ask yourself why Peter Fyodorov was killed and why he was in the apartment of Dr. Jensen's brother in the first place. An Inspector Bradley has been in touch with me. He used information from airport security to trace Fyodorov from Toronto to Paris. The Inspector believes Fyodorov killed George Daniels."

Chloe was astounded. "We didn't think Bradley believed us."

The Commissaire shrugged. "He found your story too ridiculous to be a lie. In any case, Fyodorov was already well known to us. We suspected he'd been involved in several recent art thefts from private homes and we'd been following him since his return to Paris. Yesterday he eluded my men." Lejeune spread his hands, eloquently expressing the dire consequences of evading the police.

"If I've understood Inspector Bradley correctly," he continued, "Fyodorov was looking for a Matisse sketch that belongs to Dr. Jensen. In fact, there are two of these sketches, aren't there, mademoiselle?"

Lejeune barely blinked when he talked to her. His gaze seemed to take in every detail of her face, as if she were some kind of wonderful surprise. Chloe found it disconcerting.

"Mademoiselle?" he prompted.

To Chloe's relief, Adam intervened. "It seems Bradley *was* very curious about what I'd deposited with my bank. Chloe made a copy of the original sketch for sentimental reasons, not for any fraudulent purpose. Fyodorov must've returned to Paris hoping to find the original. He probably assumed it was Jamie who'd made the copy."

Lejeune nodded. "That scenario seems most likely. But what, I wonder, makes the original so valuable? Not, I suspect, the talent of Matisse alone. Fyodorov did not concern himself with beauty, you understand. To him, art was merely a commodity."

Chloe turned to Lejeune eagerly. She wondered if the French were taught as children to love Matisse in the same way they were taught to learn the alphabet, or if Lejeune's admiration was particular to him. "You admire Matisse?" she asked.

"Anyone who doesn't admire Matisse must have a very low opinion of joy, don't you think?"

Chloe thought this a wonderful answer. Really, Lejeune was ridiculously handsome. She forced herself to look away from him, kept her eyes downcast. She thought she heard Adam sigh.

"Commissaire Lejeune," Adam began, "I'm sure you know that my brother believed there was an undiscovered Matisse painting. That's why Chloe and I came to Paris, to try to follow in his footsteps. But there's nothing about the original sketch that tells us where to find it. After all, my brother had owned it for years."

Chloe noted Adam's lie and kept her head down.

"A most dangerous decision," Lejeune cautioned.

Chloe bit her lower lip. Did Lejeune mean only that following Jamie was dangerous, or had he also just implied that lying about the message hidden in the original sketch was equally dangerous?

"There's no question that Fyodorov was working for someone else," Lejeune finally continued. "He may have been killed by his own people for the same reason Daniels was—failing to deliver the goods. Or he may have been killed by rivals. I'm afraid your brother, Dr. Jensen, approached a number of people in Paris with this fabulous story of a Matisse. There could be others determined to find it, at any cost."

A piece of the puzzle slipped into place for Chloe. She glanced at Adam. "You wondered how Daniels knew you had the Matisse. Someone here in Paris must have tipped him off, someone Jamie had approached."

Lejeune sighed. "It's a shame we haven't yet found the singing canary's partner. He may have led us someplace interesting. In the meantime, he has most certainly revealed your presence at the apartment to whoever hired him. And he's no doubt anxious that you not remember his face."

"I saw the men on the stairs for a split second only. I can't even describe them clearly, which means their glimpse of me must be equally vague—"

"Ah," Lejeune nodded. "I see you've worked things out for yourself. Chances are you've indeed been followed and these people already know who you are. Dr. Jensen is, after all, the strongest link to his brother."

"Yes," Adam added. "And as long as they thought we might lead them to the painting, we could be assured of being reasonably safe. Now they'll wonder what we were looking for in the apartment. If they suspect we know as little as they do, we're much more expendable. Am I right, Commissaire?"

Lejeune tilted his head toward Adam in acknowledgement.

"But you'll protect us, right?" Chloe asked.

"As you wish, mademoiselle. But we can do much more than that…"

Chloe wondered if it was lust or just a lack of sleep that made her read a double-entendre in Lejeune's words. She waited for him to finish his sentence.

"…We can help you find the painting, if it exists."

"How?" Adam demanded bluntly.

"We could ask some questions of the people following you. Perhaps arrange, discreetly of course, for you to meet some gallery people. You could find out if your brother told them more than a fantasy. I have resources and contacts here in France that could prove valuable."

"And you would do this because?"

"Dr. Jensen, I understand your wish to defend your brother. But he stirred up trouble among the art world in Paris and it is my responsibility to investigate. We're in a position to help each other. That is all."

"And just exactly how would we be helping you?"

Lejeune shrugged. "It wouldn't hurt to discover the identity of the people in the hunt. I'd like to know who Fyodorov was working for. Hundreds of pieces of art go missing every year from Paris. Statues, ceramics, drawings, sculptures, and paintings. I'd like to know the names of some of the people who pay for stolen—or found—art."

"My brother didn't steal anything."

Chloe could hear the anger in Adam's voice and, instinctively, she leaned closer to him.

Lejeune caught her slight movement. She suspected he rarely missed anything.

"Please, Dr. Jensen," he said. "I have no wish to offend. But you must realize that if a Matisse painting is hidden somewhere in France, I would do everything in my power to keep it in France. I think your brother knew that."

Once again, Chloe could hear the edge of warning in Lejeune's words.

"So you don't believe in finders-keepers?" Adam responded.

"A child's game. A strong legal case could be made that an undiscovered Matisse may well be the property of the state or, at the very least, of the Matisse heirs."

"Unless, of course, the painting had already been given to someone else by Matisse himself," Chloe said. "And documentation existed to prove it."

Lejeune stared at her, and this time she had no trouble reading his expression. He was astonished. Part of her thought she should explain about Sylvie and Lydia and the letter, but it was too much fun having the upper hand for once.

"Still, it's all speculation, isn't it?" she continued. "Unless we can find out more about Jamie's movements. In the meantime, Adam and I are cleared of any suspicion in Daniels' death. I'm sure we'd be glad to co-operate with the police, wouldn't we Adam?"

The silence stretched out a moment too long, and Chloe gave Adam a little kick under the table. "Adam?" she repeated.

"Right. Certainly. I'd very much like to meet some of the people Jamie talked to about the painting."

"Very well." The Commissaire rose to his feet. "I'll be in touch. It has been a pleasure."

His words included both Adam and Chloe, but his eyes rested on her alone. As she watched him cross the courtyard and disappear into the hotel, she felt a surge of desire.

"Be careful, Chloe," Adam murmured.

She reached for the leftover croissants, but avoided meeting Adam's eyes. "What did you think of the Commissaire?" she asked.

"I think he's an outrageous flirt and a very dangerous man. He certainly thought Jamie was running some kind of scam. C'mon, Chloe. Don't pretend you didn't notice. Is that a French thing? Naked admiration?"

"I found it flattering."

"You were supposed to."

"I'm sorry, though, for what he implied about Jamie. Is that why you lied to him about the message hidden in the original sketch?"

Adam shook his head. "I'm not sure. I'm hoping it will give us some kind of advantage. Besides, strictly speaking, I didn't lie."

"Who's pretending now?"

"Well, we don't know what the message means, do we?" Adam put his head in his hands. "I just wish, for once, Jamie could've confided in me, played things straight. Think about it, Chloe. Jamie didn't know anything about your grandmother or the possibility that the painting was intended as a gift to her. He probably *was* planning to sell the Matisse to some private collector, someone shady, with enough resources to get it safely out of France. You know, Jamie could have done anything, but he wanted a bigger life, something spectacular. In the end, that prob-ably killed him."

"I'm sorry."

"Will you please stop saying that?"

"Fine. We both know your brother wasn't a saint. But Lydia might have told him about Sylvie. Liliane also said he was doing tons of research on Matisse. Remember what a prolific letter writer Matisse was? Maybe he referred to the painting somewhere, maybe even to Sylvie somewhere. You can't know for certain that Jamie was doing anything illegal."

Adam stood up, leaned over her and kissed the top of her head.

"Where are you going?" Chloe called after him, as he strode away.

"The Bibliothèque Nationale."

Chloe reached for another croissant. Lejeune's mesmerizing effect on her was fading: she was starving again. When she was finally full, she left the crumbs for the small birds that visited the courtyard and returned to her room.

Crumpled on the floor by her bed were the black jeans she'd worn the night before, still slightly damp from the rain. At once she remembered finding something in Jamie's apartment. She slipped her fingers into one of the back pockets, and fished out a creased business card.

It advertised a picture framing shop on the rue de Cluny.

Chloe found her map of Paris and then grabbed her purse. It seemed she also had a plan for the afternoon.

Rue de Cluny was a little curving street on the Left Bank lined with shops selling a wide range of antiques at a wide range of prices. Chloe peered through the windows marveling at Second Empire *objets d'art,* antique musical instruments, Japanese prints, and even ancient medical instruments and astrolabes suitable for an old apothecary shop. On the corner, she stopped to admire a display of Art Nouveau and Art Deco glass, spying a wall sconce fashioned by Lalique. She thought of poor Daniels and wondered if he, too, had stood where she was standing now.

When she pushed open the door of the framing shop, a little bell sounded in a back room. The front of the shop was fairly small, its walls hung with drab-looking lithographs and maps. She waited, patiently she thought, for about five minutes, but no one appeared.

"*Bonjour*," she called tentatively.

She was answered by a rough, deep voice: "*Entrez, entrez!*"

Chloe walked across the shop floor and pulled back a thick black curtain. She saw a man, a very fat man, hunched over a worktable. He looked up, waved her over.

"Are you a tourist?" he asked abruptly.

Chloe noted his large nose, no doubt broken more than once. One eyeball skittered off to the side. His thin hair lifted like smoke off his scalp. "I confess I'm a tourist, but one on a mission," she replied.

"There are too many tourists in Paris," he grumbled. "If you're not buying, don't waste my time. Go look in one of the pretty shops."

"I have just one question," Chloe took the business card from her purse and placed it on the table directly under the man's once-broken nose. "I found this in Jamie Jensen's apartment. He was tall, good-looking, a Canadian ex-patriot, very friendly. Do you remember him?"

He took the card in his thick fingers and peered closely at Chloe. "You know Jamie?"

Chloe caught her breath. "I'm here with his brother, Adam. We're trying to trace his last movements in Paris."

The man frowned and handed back the card. "You'd do better to leave things alone. Chasing a dream. That's what got my friend killed."

Chloe turned to leave, but stopped at the curtain and looked back. "But it wasn't a dream, was it? Jamie sent *Woman in a Blouse, Dreaming* to his brother before he died. If you were really his friend, you'd help us."

The framer seemed to tense at the name of the sketch, but shook his head again. "I don't know anything. And I don't know you, mademoiselle. I get all sorts in my shop. You could be anyone."

Chloe took a deep breath and decided to gamble. "Really?" she asked, retracing her steps. She placed her hand, palm down, on the picture he was framing on the worktable. The purple amethyst shone on her finger. "Do you recognize it, monsieur? It came to me from my grandmother, and to her from Lydia Delectorskaya."

The man made a sound in his throat like a strangled squawk and Chloe snatched back her hand. Wide-eyed, she watched as he rose from his workbench, crossed the room in a quick, rolling gait, and placed a sign that read *Fermé* in the shop door. He pulled out a chair for Chloe in the workroom and sat down opposite her.

"My name is Alain Reynaud," he said, extending a giant hand.

Chloe introduced herself and smiled, looking into his good eye. When she took his hand, her own was swallowed whole.

"Tell me, please, about the ring." Alain leaned back in his chair, and folded his arms over his large stomach, as if preparing for a long tale.

"My grandmother, Sylvie Brionne, knew Lydia. I think she may have worked as a maid for Matisse, perhaps even posed for him. When she left France, Lydia gave her this ring and also the Matisse sketch. Jamie later bought it from my mother."

"Sylvie, yes, I remember the name. Lydia spoke of her fondly. And you're her granddaughter?"

Chloe felt exhilarated. "You knew her?"

"Not Sylvie. I knew Lydia. She was beautiful, and with my face, I don't meet many beautiful women. I tell you, she had a summer dress, pale blue with white flowers, cinched at the waist. That dress could break a man's heart. It was Lydia who introduced me to Jamie."

"Do you know how they met?"

Alain's laugh sounded more like a guffaw. "Now there's a crazy story. Only someone like Jamie would ever get away with it. Apparently he was walking in Luxembourg Gardens when he saw Lydia sitting on a bench by one of the fountains, just staring into space. He stopped and tapped her on the shoulder and said 'Woman in a blouse, dreaming?' Well that got her attention, alright. She was very close-mouthed about those days with Matisse, but Jamie made her laugh. And he treated her like a queen."

"I wish I knew more about her," Chloe sighed.

"Don't we all. There was a sadness about her, as though something was broken inside her, something that never healed. Didn't your grandmother have any stories?"

"She died when I was very young. But she kept a letter from Lydia. I think Lydia must have helped Sylvie and her husband escape from France during the war."

Alain shook his head. "Like I said, Lydia didn't talk about those days, especially the war. *Les années noires*, we French say. The black years. There's plenty who don't like to recall what they were doing then. But she counted Sylvie among the few people in her life who were true friends. I even think that's why she took to Jamie initially, because of the link to Sylvie through the drawing."

"And you, too, monsieur. You were a true friend, I think."

Alain nodded, a wistful smile on his lips. "I saw her as she was, not as something framed on a wall. Journalists always wanted to interview her, but none of them were really interested in her life. Only in Matisse's. She was tired of their curiosity and their judgements. She told me once she picked out my shop because it was the shabbiest on the street. She hoped I wouldn't know her. I didn't judge her, that's all. Nor did Jamie."

"Monsieur, do you believe Jamie was killed?"

Alain scratched his head, but remained silent. His bad eye seemed to circle wildly about the room. He lumbered over to a cupboard and brought out a bottle and two glasses. "This is a fine Scotch, mademoiselle, one of the few things worth importing from Britain."

He offered her a glass, but Chloe waved it away. "Suit yourself," he said. "Me? I drink when I talk about dead friends. But first, how much do you know?"

"We know Lydia told Jamie about a Matisse painting, one that went missing during the war. And Liliane said he called her just a few days before his death. We're fairly certain he found it, or at least discovered what had happened to it. We also know that Jamie was not particularly discreet and that some of the people he told about the painting might also have been looking for it."

"Liliane?"

"Jamie's girlfriend. You wouldn't have forgotten her had you seen her. Did Lydia talk to you about the painting?"

"No, she never did. But I saw it once."

Chloe stared at Alain, too stunned to speak. She pushed her glass towards him and he poured a neat inch of Scotch.

"It all started with an accident," Alain explained. "Just over a year ago, Jamie dropped the Matisse sketch one day and the glass broke. Such a simple thing to happen, *non*? He brought the drawing here to be reframed. And there it was. A photograph. And some letters written on the back."

"The initials *P, M,* and *R*. The year, 1943. And 'upper studio'. Lydia's inscription. But Adam and I didn't find a photograph. We should have realized there'd be one somewhere. Lydia documented so many of Matisse's paintings. But why didn't Lydia tell Jamie what was hidden in the sketch? He might never have found the photograph."

Alain tipped the Scotch bottle over his glass again. "Why look for something she believed was lost forever? I think she was haunted by that painting. She hid it, but could never find it again. In the end, she felt responsible for its loss. That guilt went round and round in her head like a barrel of wasps all buzzing at once."

"Please, Alain. Tell me about the photograph. Tell me what you saw."

"The initials, *P. M. Portraite de la Mariée*. I saw a portrait of a bride."

"Sylvie," Chloe whispered. "I know it was Sylvie."

"Indeed, mademoiselle. She is wearing the ring."

Chloe lowered her head and blinked back tears. Matisse had actually painted her grandmother. It wasn't just a little girl's fancy. It had been real, and it was marvellous. She closed her eyes and tried to imagine what the image of the bride might have looked like, but all she could conjure up was a swirl of colour around a blur of white. She steadied herself, forced herself to return to the present.

"So Jamie knew exactly what he was looking for and he had proof that the Matisse existed or had once existed." Chloe reached up a hand and pushed some hair that had fallen across her face back in place behind her ear. "What happened to the photograph?"

Alain nodded his head so vigorously his upper body seemed to rock back and forth.

"You think he showed it to someone? And that person killed him?" Chloe continued. "Why?"

Alain shrugged. "Jamie wanted the money a missing Matisse would fetch, sure. But mostly he wanted the fame, the kick of finding it. He believed so much in its existence he didn't see the obvious."

"Which is?"

"That the original is long gone, stolen, or destroyed during the war. But the photograph could be used to forge a Matisse and the original need never be found. Of course, the photograph was in black and white, but that wouldn't be a problem for a student of Matisse. It would tell the forger what to paint, you see. At the same time, the photo would seem to give the forgery provenance, especially if the sketch of Lydia with her inscription on the back accompanied it. The swindle's almost foolproof. Lydia's dead. And now, most conveniently, Jamie's dead."

"Have you told this to the police?" Chloe asked.

"The *flics*?" Alain sniffed. "Not likely. No one even knows I saw that photograph. And you'd do well not to mention it either, if you value your safety. I'd be very careful about wearing that ring, too."

"Thank you, Alain. Thank you for trusting me." Chloe reached out her hand and touched his shoulder.

As big and gruff as Alain was, he blushed like a boy at her touch. "Least I could do for Jamie," he mumbled.

"Can I ask you one last question? Is there anything else you remember about the painting in the photograph? Walls, starry skies, trees in blossom?"

"No trees. No stars."

Chloe thanked him again and left the shop. The ringing of the little bell above the door filled her with melancholy for a reason she couldn't name. Paris was filled with ghosts, she thought.

I was in a gallery on the Left Bank when I heard two men talking.

"Matisse is back in Paris."

"Really, have you seen him?"

I was sitting in a small room adjacent to the show room, looking through a portfolio of drawings. I knew I should cough or make some noise to warn the men of my presence, but my sense of curiosity was greater than my sense of propriety.

"He was with his dealer. Man named Rosenberg. I'm surprised he still employs a Jew."

"Matisse never cared about politics. How did the old man look?"

"*Frankly, he looks like he's been hit by a cyclone. Of course, you've heard that his wife and family have virtually deserted him? Imagine a man his age still screwing his models. I don't think he'll be here long.*"

"*Bit risky of him to come to Paris at all, I'd say. The Germans have already branded him a decadent painter. God knows what'll happen if they ever get to Paris.*"

"*No, you've misunderstood. I meant to say I don't think he'll live much longer. His wife will be the end of him, and if she needs a little help, the Nazis are waiting in the wings.*"

"*Well, he must be in his seventies by now. I dare say the best of his painting is behind him.*"

I'd heard enough. I'd always known what the gossip was. What disturbed me was the casual meanness of the gossipers, the ease with which they dismissed a man's genuine pain and a genius' painting. I left the gallery without a word, though the men jumped a little when I revealed my presence. There was no point in trying to explain how wrong they were about so much. I felt outraged on Matisse's behalf.

I knew where he'd be staying, the apartment on the Boulevard du Montparnasse. I longed to visit him there, to sit with him in the window, perhaps, and share some tea, while he talked about his cats or the shape of a fern leaf. But I knew I could not go there uninvited.

I walked to the Luxembourg Gardens and found a bench where I could eat my bread roll and bit of cheese. It was hot and I missed the sea breezes. I had dressed too warmly and the cotton top I wore clung to my skin. I pulled at the material and a small cry caught in my throat. I was wearing the striped sweater Matisse had given me when he painted Blue Eyes. *In the portrait, my head rests on my forearms, and my eyes are fastened on the painter: the strange thing is that, despite the title and the nickname Matisse had given me, my eyes do not look blue. They are dark in the painting, of an almost indeterminate colour.*

"*But why?*" *I had asked.*

"*That's what I saw.*" *Matisse answered.* "*Perhaps that's what you were seeing too, or how you were looking. Who knows? It's better to risk ruining a likeness than compromising a painting. You have to move beyond surfaces and the shackles of convention.*"

Suddenly, the words I remembered meant something entirely different to me. I'd had months to think since returning to Paris. I'd had months to walk the bridges and stare down at the Seine and listen to the sly gossip of Parisians and the narrow-minded jabs of my disappointed aunt. Without the habit of self-examination, I'd relied on others to define me, to paint me an existence. But by walking away, I'd become free. I felt calm and certain of myself. I'd become free enough to choose my future on my own terms, live by my own rules.

When his letter finally came, as I knew it must, begging me to return, I did not reply by mail. Instead I walked all the way from the outskirts of Paris to the apartment on the Boulevard du Montparnasse. I brought him a bouquet of pure white daisies and blue cornflowers.

He painted them in Fleurs pour le St. Henri—*sharp, bright, full of light.*

There was a message waiting for Chloe at the hotel desk, a note from Adam urging her to meet him later for dinner at *Le Bilboquet*. She hoped the restaurant would be quiet, but when she asked for directions from the concierge, he assured her that *Le Bilbo* was the best place on the Left Bank for live jazz and dancing. Chloe couldn't think of anything that reminded her less of Adam. Classic Miles Davis, or Oscar Peterson, maybe. Dancing, never.

It was just past nine-thirty when she stepped into the cool night air. She snuggled into her turquoise shawl, glad that the black sweater she'd chosen to wear had long sleeves and a high turtleneck. Even she was growing tired of her black jeans by now, but she felt guilty about the hotel bill mounting up on Sammy's credit card. Besides, the cost of the high-heels she'd bought, though not nearly so glamorous as Liliane's, was shocking.

Crossing the Pont St-Louis, she stopped to consult the little hand-drawn map the concierge had given her. A gust of wind snatched it from her hand and she whirled around trying to catch it before it sank into the Seine.

That was when she saw him. He seemed a perfectly ordinary man carrying an attaché case, probably on his way home after work, except that her sudden change of direction had caused a stutter in his movement, a momentary awkwardness that caught Chloe's attention.

She stamped her foot down on the fluttering map, and knelt to pick it up, sneaking another look at the man from behind the curtain of her hair. He had stopped walking now and was sorting through his case as if looking for something. Chloe didn't believe the ruse for a minute. She was being followed.

As she began walking again, she thought she ought to be alarmed, but seeing the man, seeing how ordinary he looked, made her feel relieved. He wasn't sinister enough to seem threatening. In fact, he was probably one of the Commissaire's men, sent to keep her safe. She was rather proud of herself for having spotted him.

When she reached *Le Bilboquet*, however, her good spirits vanished. The place was smaller than she'd imagined, but crowded, loud and bright. There was no sign of Adam. The place was filled with affluent looking men dressed in expensive casual clothes and *bon chic* women wearing little Chanel jackets over their Levis. Abandoned instruments on a small stage suggested there was a band that either hadn't started to play yet or was between sets. In the meantime, there was no music of any kind, just the high-pitched sound of slightly drunken conversation. Chloe crossed the room to a staircase and hoped for better luck on an upper floor.

She spotted Liliane sitting with a man who was slouched over the table, his head resting on his arms. He appeared to be sleeping.

Chloe hesitated for a moment, feeling a bit like an intruder, before she recognized the sandy curls. At the same time, Liliane waved her over.

"Adam?" Chloe raised her eyebrows as she sat down, relieved to see that Liliane looked more amused than upset. "What's happened?"

"The bartender said it was four double tequilas."

"So much for the completely logical scientific man I knew. What drove him to tequila?"

"Someone named Elizabeth I think. Wasn't he engaged to an Elizabeth once?"

"So he said, but I never saw her even when I was watching—um, I never met her. Poor Adam. How did you find him here?"

"I used to come to this place all the time with Jamie. It was one of his favourite spots. So when I saw Adam, I thought he'd come to reminisce. I know the bartender pretty well. We brought him up here to wait for you. Adam told Jean—that's the bartender—that you were coming. Shall I help you get him back to your hotel?"

Chloe leaned back in her chair, looking down affectionately at the tousled head. "He seems very comfortable. And I'm hungry. Have you eaten yet?"

Liliane smiled. "The *cassoulet* is very good here."

"Sounds perfect. As long as he doesn't start to snore, he's no bother. If he wakes up, we'll feed him."

Chloe wondered about the dynamics between Jamie and Liliane. She was so exquisite, it was difficult to imagine her as a jilted lover. Several men seated at other tables, escorted and unescorted alike, were openly admiring her. Tonight, she wore her hair swept up into a long ponytail; her dress was lime green silk with long sleeves made of crisscrossed black silk ribbons.

Liliane caught Chloe's wistful sigh. "It's not what you think. I know a second-hand store. Last year's couturier clothes with the labels cut out."

"Really?"

Liliane laughed. "Sure, I'll take you there."

When the *cassoulet* arrived—a savory mixture of white beans, duck confit and sausage in a wine sauce—the two women ate with relish, Adam passive between them. He didn't stir, not even when a woman with a voice like thick honey began to sing *De Temps en Temps* to the syncopated accompaniment of a bluesy piano and a bass guitar. Chloe ruffled his hair and he turned his face towards her, but didn't open his eyes.

"Adam was crazy about his brother," Chloe said. "If he finds out Jamie was running some kind of scam with the Matisse painting, it's going to break his heart."

"What kind of scam?"

Chloe realized how much had happened since she'd last seen Liliane. She told her about the body in Jamie's apartment and about the visit from the Commissaire that morning. "It sounds like Jamie was offering the painting to more than one buyer. That is, if he ever found the painting at all."

"He must have. He had to have something more than air to lure the buyers."

Chloe realized that Jamie could have offered them a glimpse of the photograph but she didn't want to talk about that yet, not until she'd had a chance to share the information with Adam. "It'd be nice to stay and listen to this dreamy music," she said, changing the subject, "but I think I should get Adam back to the hotel."

"Of course. We'll find you a taxi. I think I'll go downstairs, for the dancing. But first, a very large espresso?"

She signaled to the waiter while Chloe roused Adam. For a moment he seemed bewildered, blinking his eyes several times and rubbing his face. Then he seemed to take in the evidence of the empty dishes on the table and the grins on the faces of his companions.

"Please," he pleaded. "No ridicule. How bad was it?"

"So bad you have to pay for our dinner," Chloe teased. "After that, we'll not speak again of this night. It will be our dark secret."

She heard Liliane stifle a giggle, while she guided Adam's hands to the coffee cup.

"I see you need a minute to find your sea legs," Chloe said. "I'll just go and freshen up."

The singer had moved on to a Billie Holiday classic, *God Bless the Child*, the honey in her voice giving way to a sandpaper rasp. The song made Chloe think of Lydia and Liliane at the same time, but she couldn't have said exactly why. As she skirted tables on the way to the women's washroom, she noted again that several men were watching Liliane, some of them looking a bit dismayed now that Adam seemed a contender for her attention.

Chloe splashed water on her face and was brushing her hair when another woman entered the room and stood beside her. Chloe's eyes met the stranger's eyes in the mirror, worried eyes that clearly had a message. Slowly, Chloe put down her brush and turned to face the woman. "What is it?" she asked.

"I am coming from the Commissaire, *vous comprenez?*" The woman reached into her bag, flashed her identification. She was young, younger than Chloe and taller, with short, gelled hair combed back behind her ears. She wore almost no make-up, but managed to look striking in her simple red trench coat and black pants. Chloe wondered where she'd come from and why she hadn't noticed her before.

"Your friend," the woman continued, "he is not drinking so much."

"Four double tequilas, I'm told." Chloe replied.

"*Non, non.* I am telling you. The bartender is giving more." The woman mimed the action of pouring liquid into a glass. "I see this, but your friend is not seeing. He was followed today. Maybe the bartender is paid by someone else, yes? So you are being careful now."

Chloe felt her throat tighten. She nodded and the woman left as quickly and quietly as she had come. Why would someone want to make Adam drunk? In *vino veritas* ?

When she returned to the table, Adam stood up and gave her a hang-dog smile. Chloe smiled back and put her arm around his waist to offer support. Gently, he removed her arm: "I'm perfectly capable of walking," he insisted in words that were only slightly slurred.

Chloe rolled her eyes at Liliane, and waved goodnight. She surveyed the room to see who might be watching, but there was no splash of red, no eyes following that she could see.

Adam managed his balance, but couldn't muster conversation so the ride back to the hotel was short and uneventful. Chloe kept turning around to peer out the back of the cab, but no one paid her any mind. She pressed some euros into the cabby's hand and maneuvered Adam up the stairs and down the hall to his room.

He watched while she opened the door for him, the synchronized timing of the electronic key and the turning of the door handle temporarily beyond him.

"Good night, Adam," Chloe sighed. "You'll feel better in the morning."

He reached out, tucked a stray curl behind her ear. "Your hair is the colour of cinnamon bark."

"And you're drunk, Adam Joseph Jensen."

"Hold on. How do you know my middle name?"

"I know everything," she whispered, giving him a push over the threshold. "Good night."

Much to Chloe's delight, Liliane called late the next morning. There was neither sight nor sound from Adam, so Chloe slipped a note under his door and jumped into a cab. She felt like a schoolgirl playing hooky.

Liliane took her to her special dress shop in the sixteenth arrondissement, looking on with pleasure as Chloe grew almost dizzy with longing amid beautifully cut clothes, jeweled hair combs, and tiny satin evening bags shaped to look like peonies. Then the pair bought bread and cheese, and two pieces of bitter chocolate cake, and strolled through the Bois de Boulogne. When they stopped by one of the lakes for their picnic, Chloe told Liliane about the swan, now immortalized, that had once attacked Matisse when he was sketching here, and Liliane gave her the list of places she and Jamie had stayed on their trip to the South. Chloe almost asked if Liliane had noticed anything suspicious about the bartender feeding Adam drinks, but it had been a perfect day, and she was reluctant to break the mood. Chloe returned to the hotel exhilarated, exhausted, and laden with packages.

After a long shower, she called Sammy and confessed her uncharacteristic extravagance. She remembered all the times she'd curled up on the stairs as a little girl, listening to Sammy and Louise snipe at each other in the living room over her mother's uncontrolled spending, wondering if this would be the night their arguments would become so fierce that her father would leave and her world would unravel.

But Sammy was not angry; he was delighted. "You're in Paris, Chloe. Think of this as spending the allowance you've refused for years. How's Adam? I hope he's taking care of you."

Chloe hesitated. Should she tell her father about the dead butler, the handsome policeman, the woman in the red trench coat? Absolutely not. He'd be on the next plane. Quickly, she changed the subject.

"Actually, I'm taking care of Adam. It seems he's broken off his engagement with Elizabeth."

"Elizabeth Graham?"

"I don't know. Is there more than one Elizabeth in his life?"

"Elizabeth is on the hospital board, Chloe. She and Adam broke up months ago. In fact, it was just around the time that Jamie died. She told me they were keeping news of the break-up quiet because of Jamie's parents. They already had enough bad news to cope with."

Chloe was more puzzled than angry. She couldn't think of a reason why Adam would lie to her about Elizabeth, or why he would lie to Liliane.

She said goodbye to Sammy, promising to call again, and eyed the packages she'd piled up on a chair in her room. In one of them was an inky blue silk dress that swayed like a soft breeze when she moved. She picked up her phone and invited Adam to dinner. Then she put on the dress. Remembering her conversation with Alain, she hoped the dress would break Adam's heart.

She waited for him in the hotel lobby and was gratified by his expression as he crossed the floor towards her.

"You look stunning, Chloe. Should I change?"

"No, not at all. You look very French, in fact, in your jeans and suit jacket. I'm just glad you don't own a beret. I'm not sure my scruples could stand up to a beret."

Adam looked at her suspiciously, but ignored her comment. "Where shall we go? I know some places close by that we haven't tried yet."

"No, tonight's my turn to be the travel guide. We've a lot to catch up on and I've found the perfect place."

"Is it far? You don't look like you could walk far in those high-heeled shoes."

This time it was Chloe who ignored his comment. She took his arm, smiled confidently, and led him into the twilight. As they strolled along, she stopped occasionally to admire the light glancing off the Seine or to point out something in a shop window, but, if they were being followed, she could not detect anyone, let alone a tall woman in a red trench coat.

The *Bistro de la Gare* was on the Boulevard du Montparnasse in the sixth arrondissement. "It's a bit early for dinner, but I've heard the place is quite popular," Chloe said. "This way we'll get a table. Besides, Matisse had an apartment once on this very street."

She was delighted with her choice. The bistro had a lively, friendly atmosphere and Art Nouveau décor: tiled walls, exotic mirrors, an intriguing glass ceiling, and ornate light fixtures. There was even a young blonde wearing a black velvet choker and black low-cut jacket serving behind a bar, her long hair reflected in the mirror behind her. Chloe felt she'd walked into Manet's painting of the bar at the Folies-Bergère.

When they were seated, Chloe waved to a waiter and ordered a bottle of the house red. "Oh," she said, turning to Adam. "I forgot. Maybe you don't want to drink tonight."

"Okay, okay, Chloe. I get it." He made a lazy gesture of defeat. "I'm sorry. I don't blame you for being angry."

"I'm not angry, Adam. After all, you must be heartbroken. Liliane told me about Elizabeth."

In the ensuing silence as she and Adam stared at each other, Chloe was vaguely aware of the waiter approaching, reading their expressions, setting down the bottle of wine and slipping away again without a word. Contrary to the myth that all Parisian waiters are rude, Chloe found them superbly efficient and, above all, sensitive to any tête-à-tête.

Adam poured the wine, lifted his glass and tilted it towards her. "So you know I lied. How did you find out?"

"A lot of little things, such as never seeing her and you never talking about her."

"Never seeing her when you were stalking me, you mean?"

"Don't change the subject. You lied to me and to Liliane. Why?"

"I wanted to tell you, Chloe. I almost did a couple of nights ago, but the right moment just didn't come up. I had a quite different reason for lying to Liliane." He hesitated a moment, then continued, "I know you like her, but you shouldn't be so trusting. She followed me to the jazz club. She didn't think I'd noticed her, pretended to be surprised when she found me at the bar. But she'd followed me for blocks, ever since I left the Bibliothèque Nationale."

"Oh, Adam. You're wrong. She told me she often went to that club with Jamie. It's just a coincidence. Jamie's apartment isn't that far from the library, is it? She was probably wandering around the neighbourhood, missing him. After all, we've stirred up all those memories. And she gave me the list of places around Nice that she and Jamie visited. She's trying to help us. But why were you drinking in the first place?"

"Six hours trying to read Matisse's handwritten French? I felt like I'd just crawled across the desert. Besides I didn't think I was drinking that much. Liliane asked me about Elizabeth, and I just ran with it."

"Actually, you weren't drinking that much. And you *were* followed, but not by Liliane."

Adam's eyes widened. "Tell me," he said, pouring more wine.

So Chloe told him everything that had happened with Alain in the framer's shop, and the Commissaire's agent in the red trench coat in the jazz club.

"Did the bartender ask you questions? Did anyone ask you questions about Jamie and the Matisse?"

"No, nothing like that," Adam replied. "But then Liliane came to sit by me. Maybe she spoiled the opportunity."

"There. You see? I knew Liliane was on our side."

By the time they'd finished talking, the tables around them had filled, the candles were lit, and a crackly recording of old French songs sobbed away in the background. The waiter made a tentative approach and this time Adam and Chloe ordered dinner.

"Did you find anything in Matisse's letters?" Chloe asked.

"I only scratched the surface in the time that I had. I'd no idea Matisse kept up such correspondence. Even restricting my focus to the Lydia years didn't narrow things down much. You know he wrote almost every day to his friend André Rouveyre and he lived just a few miles away. I found no mention of Sylvie, barely any of Lydia. He doesn't seem to pay them any particular regard. I hate to say it, but it seems obvious that he treated his models badly, probably chauvinistically."

"So obvious that no evidence has ever been produced to back up that statement. C'mon, Adam. All the women around him—Madame Matisse, Marguerite, Lydia—were formidable, independent, strong-willed. Even Camille, Marguerite's birth mother, was a fiery, bohemian type. She refused to marry him. There's not a single milk sop among them. They were hardly victims. What's more, Matisse couldn't do without them. There's no question that he needed Lydia more than she needed him, at least by the end of his life. What angers me is not the way Matisse treated her, but the way her contribution has been all but expunged from history. She's just his snow princess, the beautiful Russian slave, Saint Lydia. She's not flesh and bone at all."

"Well, you may be right," Adam glanced at Chloe's face and altered his sentence. "I'm sure you're right. But I don't see how defending Lydia's character gets us any further."

The waiter reappeared, placing their dinners before them with a flourish and an emphatic *bon appétit.*

Chloe stared at her plate, at the butterflied duckling with crisp roasted skin floating atop a raspberry sauce. She took a bite and moaned, closing her eyes.

Adam laughed. "The French call it *joie de manger*, Chloe. Your face is an advertisement for the chef."

"Laugh if you like, but I'll remember this duck the rest of my life."

They ate with appropriate abandon until their plates were clean. Finally, Chloe laid down her fork. "Sometimes you just have to trust, Adam. Lydia's character is important. She seemed to trust Jamie. And we need to find out which galleries he might have approached. I'll try to get some names from the Commissaire, and I think you should talk to Alain. He really cared about your brother."

"Do me one favour?"

"Of course."

"Don't wear that dress when you meet the Commissaire."

Chloe reached for her napkin, hoping to hide her smile behind it.

They left the restaurant an hour or so later, walking shoulder to shoulder through the luminous night. As they entered the hotel, they were watched by a striped cat with ragged ears and wide, inquisitive eyes. The cat was not the only watcher.

Commissaire Julien Lejeune watched Chloe cross the terrace and approach his table as if she had not a care in the world. About thirty metres behind her and on the opposite side of the street, the man following her turned into a bookstore and disappeared. The Commissaire rose and pulled out a chair.

"*Bonjour, mademoiselle.* Thank you for meeting me here. It is not too cold, I trust?"

"I'm fine, Commissaire," Chloe replied, knotting her shawl over her jacket. "I'd really rather not know what the inside of a French police station looks like."

"Gray and institutional, I assure you. Please, call me Julien."

Chloe thought she could hardly refuse him anything. She looked for a waiter, ordered a café au lait, and tried not to think about how green Julien's eyes were. "Tell me," she queried. "Did you ever find the second man from Jamie's apartment?"

"We did. Unfortunately, he too was a small fish. We still don't know for certain who was giving the orders."

"For certain?"

The Commissaire smiled at Chloe as if she were a particularly quick student. "There are rumours. There are always rumours in Paris, you understand. The men you saw are both Russian, Fyodorov was Russian. There's always the possibility that two and two do add up to four."

"The Russian mafia? Here in Paris?"

"*Mais oui.* The Russians have a history of fleeing to France in uncertain times. There's a man named Yevgeny Kirov we've been suspicious of for some time, but he's careful to stand in the shadows." Lejeune slipped his hand into his jacket pocket and held out a photograph.

Chloe stared at a man's face, a composite of sharp angles and flat planes that somehow managed to convey hostility. It was not a face she ever wanted to meet. "I'm relieved you've caught Fyodorov's killers," she said. "I feel safer."

"Chloe—may I call you Chloe?—you're at greater risk than you imagine. You've been followed here this morning, did you know? You take this matter too casually."

"I spotted someone following me once, an ordinary man with an attaché case who looked like a banker. He didn't seem too threatening."

The Commissaire flicked his hand in the air as if batting away a fly. "That's because he probably *was* a banker. The people following you, so far as we know, are Kirov's men—petty criminals for the most part, but they wouldn't hesitate to tip you into the Seine if ordered to do so."

"Why don't you arrest Kirov?"

"He has a perfect alibi for Fyodorov's murder. He also hires clever lawyers for his team of thugs to ensure their loyalty. And perhaps, most significantly, he provides security services to one Kamal Ashkar. Ashkar was born in Saudi Arabia. He owns a villa on Cap Ferrat, cruises the Mediterranean in his yacht, and collects art."

"I see," Chloe commented faintly.

"Do you, Chloe? Because if you really did, you'd be scared. So far two men are dead."

"But that's just it. Peter the butler could have killed me when I found Daniels, but didn't. So far, the worst that's been done to us is that someone paid a bartender to get Adam drunk."

"Kirov is biding his time. He thinks you have something he wants. What is it, Chloe?"

"I—I don't know. It must be the sketch. They don't know that Adam left that in Toronto." Her voice trailed off. She cupped her hands around her coffee and put her head down.

After a few moments of silence, Lejeune leaned towards her, his voice low, almost caressing. "You're not, I think, a very good liar. Very well, I will talk a little and you can listen. Not so long ago in Paris, Yves Saint-Laurent auctioned off some of his art collection. It was a glittering event, many beautiful paintings, many beautiful people. The painting that sold for the highest amount that night was a still life by Matisse. Thirty-two million euros, roughly forty-one million dollars, Chloe. The fact that the painting once belonged to Yves Saint-Laurent added to its cachet, no doubt, but the year before a Matisse sold in London for thirty-three million dollars."

"*Good lord,*" Chloe murmured.

"Exactly. The longer a painter's absence from the market, the more attractive collectors find the painting. Museums can't compete. Most of these paintings disappear into private collections. Now, think of it: a lost Matisse. Just think of the romance of it. With certain obvious requirements, like proof of authenticity and the good condition of the painting, I'd have to estimate, conservatively, a price of fifty million. Do you still feel safe, Chloe?"

She stared at him, finding nothing to say.

He reached over the table, placed a hand over hers. "The art business is an international village inhabited by gossips. Someone always knows something. Jamie Jensen started a rumor in this village. He met with some legitimate gallery owners. I've interviewed them. Each one assured Jensen he would be glad to do business with him, would have no trouble finding a buyer. Had Jensen approached only one gallery, the story might have stayed secret. But three?"

"Ashkar undoubtedly has heard the rumours. I believe he is actively going after the painting and is determined to have it. He can afford to pay for it, but so much the better if he can find it himself. But the rumours began months ago, and now the trail seems to be growing cold. Kirov's men have already failed to retrieve the Matisse sketch. Kirov may be content to follow you in the hope that you'll lead him to the painting, or he may become more aggressive."

"You can stop now," Chloe murmured. "You've managed to terrify me."

But Lejeune was relentless. "I've been thinking a great deal about our conversation at your hotel. You claimed you had documentation that could prove Matisse gave the painting to someone. Such a document would be a mixed blessing. On the one hand, it would lend authenticity to any Matisse that might suddenly appear. Rumours of the kind Jensen started often precede the 'discovery' of a painting that is, in fact, a forgery. On the other hand, if the documentation could be used to establish legitimate ownership, Ashkar would be very displeased. You must see the danger."

"But Jamie didn't know about the letter," Chloe protested. "He couldn't have told anyone. It was from Lydia to my grandmother."

"I see." Lejeune folded his hands and smiled at her. He had a way of looking at her that was at once flattering and alarming. "Lydia Delectorskaya knew your grandmother. That's very interesting."

"I think you must be a very good policeman," Chloe said. "Do people often tell you what you want to know so easily?"

"Tell me this. Do you have this letter with you in Paris?"

"No, I don't."

"And it is quite safe?" Lejeune leaned towards her, his face now quite close to hers, his shoulders almost touching hers.

As a painter, Chloe had an excellent visual memory. She could see the letter now, tucked between the pages of a Matisse art book on her living room floor. Still, her house had been burgled once. Perhaps she should find a safer place for her treasure. She glanced at the Commissaire, felt a flutter in her stomach at the intensity of his gaze. "Yes, of course," she said, no longer sure what question she was answering, distracted by the shape of his mouth.

He handed her his card. "This number will reach me directly. Promise me you'll contact me if you hear anything from Kirov or Ashkar. Promise me you'll be more careful."

Chloe nodded, but she felt reckless. She was tempted to run her fingers over his extravagantly bald head and lay her head on his shoulder and let her mind shimmer into blankness without a thought for Adam or Lydia or Sylvia or Matisse. In a flash, she saw her hotel room, a tangle of sheets, a twining of limbs. A flush of desire left her breathless. It was tempting to believe that Julien was everything she wanted and she was everything he wanted and that it would all turn out perfectly if only she would take that first jump into the unknown.

She hadn't felt this ridiculous for a long time.

When Sammy had left, Chloe's mother had frightened her. At first, Louise was dizzy with fear and grief. Later, her heart became so filled up with blame and revenge, there was no space left for her daughter. Louise's breakdown was like a hurricane in Chloe's memory, a huge swirling wind into which everything was sucked. The child had made up her mind that she would never fall so hard, never come so close to the edge of ruin.

Chloe stood up from the table and offered her hand to Julien, so beautiful, so potentially ruinous. "I'll be careful," she promised and walked away, certain that the moment was an illusion, a spell cast by Paris and a pair of green eyes.

Hours later, she was lying on her bed fully clothed, just waking from a long nap, when she heard a light tapping at her door. She sat up, realized her head was pounding and wished the tapping would go away, but instead it became more insistent.

She opened the door, saw Adam's earnest, anxious face, and behind him the looming bulk that was the old framer, Alain.

"What on earth—"

The two men barged into the room, almost knocking her aside as they crossed the threshold in a rush. Alain flopped dramatically into the nearest chair, one hand pressed to his heart. Adam gripped both of her hands in his.

"We need to leave Paris, tonight," he announced. "Alain's shop was ransacked last night."

Chloe pulled away her hands and rubbed her eyes. "You're serious, aren't you?"

"I am. And so are the people looking for this painting. They must have followed you to Alain's shop and this is the result. C'mon Chloe, pack. We need to disappear."

VII

SOMETIMES EVEN PARIS IS TOO small a town. With Madame somewhere in residence, Patron and I decided to leave almost immediately. It was not as if I had much to pack.

We traveled south and west by train. Halfway along the route to Chartres, Matisse felt ill and we were obliged to disembark at Rochefort and book rooms at a village inn. There was a beautiful courtyard there, with a stream sheltered by feathery willows. We sat under the trees and watched the day fade. At five in the afternoon, the water was cool and magically pale, its surface almost silky. It seemed to us that we had found a little pocket of space that existed outside of time, far away from the rush and clamour of a country at war.

Always prone to chills, Matisse asked me to bring him a blanket for his lap so that he could linger outside a bit longer. When I returned to the courtyard, I could see he had placed a package wrapped in silver and black striped paper on the table beside him. He cocked his head towards it: "For you, Lydia."

My eyes stung briefly. In the past, Patron had often given me gifts indirectly, as if I might not notice the extra pay or the special pastries and fruits at mealtimes. But he had never been so bold as to announce a gift with coloured wrappings. I smiled at him tenderly.

"Open it, open it," he urged impatiently, his eyes dancing.

It was a travelling cape and hood, ultramarine blue, woven from fine wool as soft and light as a lover's breath. I bunched the material in my hands, rubbed it across my cheeks.

"The rich colour complements your eyes," he said, already reaching into his canvas bag for pencil and sketchpad.

I put the cape around my shoulders, bringing the hood up to cover my hair and frame my face.

"If Jesus had been Russian, you, Lydia, would be the Madonna of the North. Do you like it? Is it comfortable?"

"I like it very much," I replied. I understood that the gift was symbolic. He must have bought it days ago in Paris, long before he sent the letter that had brought me back to him. In the giving and the accepting of the gift, we made a conscious pact and reached a point from which there would be no turning back. In more ways than the obvious, our journey had just begun.

They left at midnight, Alain and Chloe in one cab, Adam in another, each car travelling in different directions.

"Whoever's following us will have to decide," Alain declared. "And since my shop came up empty, my guess is that Adam will be the target. Still, can't be too careful."

Chloe stared out the window chasing shadows. The concierge who'd whistled up the cabs was now on his cell phone. Across the street, a young man lit up a cigarette. She stared at the back of the cabbie's head. Had she seen him before? How was she to know if she were being followed? So far, she'd failed miserably, and the vandalizing of Alain's shop was the result. She looked at his clothes, the faded overalls, a checked shirt with fraying cuffs, scuffed shoes worn down at the heels. He could scarcely afford to lose even the meager income of his framing business.

She studied him silently as he directed the cabbie into a maze of tiny streets requiring multiple turns. At the end of a cul-de-sac, he asked the driver to wait, assuring Chloe he'd be right back.

She twisted around in her seat and watched him lumber back up the sidewalk, checking in both directions at the corner. He reminded her of a bear standing on its hind legs, his head nodding on a thick neck above wide shoulders, his gait rolling slightly from side to side.

Alain returned in less than five minutes with an open shopping bag stuffed with some clothes and a few toiletries. Chloe felt another pang of guilt. It seemed he couldn't even afford a proper suitcase. She wanted to make reparations for the damages he'd suffered, but she knew instinctively that she would embarrass him if she offered.

The taxi crossed the black ribbon of the Seine, sped across quiet black bridges and their watchful statues, circled around the Place de la Bastille several times, and then shot down the Rue de Lyon to the train station.

The Gare de Lyon was brightly lit. As the cab pulled up to the entrance, Adam suddenly emerged from behind glass doors and leapt in beside the driver. When the cab squealed away, Chloe saw a man spring forward, his mouth opening and closing like a beached fish. Just a few blocks later, the cabbie pulled to the curb and the three passengers tumbled out.

"Did it work?" Alain prodded.

"I think so," Adam replied. "I bought a ticket to Marseille, put it on my credit card so that it could be traced."

"I'm up," said Chloe. She pulled a voluminous black scarf from her shoulder bag. With a few clever folds and knots, she managed to hide her coppery hair. Quickly, the three friends returned to the train station, Alain and Adam keeping watch from a distance while Chloe went to the ticket booth and paid in cash for three seats to Aix-en-Provence.

Twenty minutes later, Chloe was speeding through the darkness. She tried to glimpse the landscape through the train window, but could see only her own startling and strangely unfamiliar reflection. Beside her, Adam's head nodded in sleep, his legs sprawled in front of him. Across from her, Alain seemed to be studying a map.

Chloe felt too keyed up to sleep. Her mood swung like a pendulum from excitement to despair. She wished they had a better plan. She wished she felt braver. Perhaps she should have insisted that Alain report the break-in of his shop to Julien Lejeune, but the old man had a stubborn suspicion of the police, and Adam had taken an unreasonable dislike to the Commissaire. So, here she was, fleeing Paris like a thief in the night.

She glanced up again at Alain, her eyes worried, her brow creased.

He grinned back at her as if he were having the time of his life. One eye fixed on her, while the other swiveled to the left.

With so much behind them, and so much before them that could go wrong, Chloe could not fathom why he should look so cheerful.

"I'm glad someone's happy with the plan," she grumbled.

Alain only smiled more widely. "Do you have a better idea?"

"Any idea would be a better idea."

He laughed, a deep rumbling sound that came from his belly and shook his shoulders. "You'll see," he said consolingly. "All we need is a month's quiet, and time to make all the arrangements without any dodgy strangers around."

"Why should you care about the missing painting? I mean, after what happened to your shop, I'm surprised you want anything more to do with us. We've brought you nothing but trouble."

Alain nodded his head in the direction of Adam. "Don't much care about the painting, 'cept for Lydia's sake. But Jamie talked a lot about his brother. It wouldn't sit right with me to let him track Jamie's killer alone."

"What was Jamie like?" Chloe asked.

"Like someone flinging open a window to let in the fresh air."

Chloe sighed. Here was yet another person willing to forgive all of Jamie's flaws.

"Of course," Alain continued, interrupting her thought, "Drafts can sometimes be damned uncomfortable."

This time, it was Chloe who laughed.

Morning was only a faint yellow streak on the horizon when the train pulled into the Aix station. Chloe's head scarf had long ago unraveled, her hair was tangled and her eyes stung from lack of sleep. She felt herself swept along by Adam's determination and Alain's bulk, too tired even to quibble with their arrangements. She would wait and see what happened for the time being. But she had Julien Lejeune's phone number in the pocket of her jeans and few qualms about using it if she felt the need.

She watched as Alain crossed the platform, greeting a man dressed as a farmer with great *bonhomie.* Then he turned back, waving at her and Adam to follow.

"My friend, Jean Guillot," Alain said proudly.

Chloe smiled and shook a hand rough from labour, but surprisingly gentle.

She climbed into the open back of the farmer's truck while Alain and Jean jumped into the cab. Adam settled in beside her as the truck pulled away from the station. Chloe watched it shrinking gradually from her vision with a sinking heart. Above her, the circle of moon began to fade from the sky. Beside her, avenues of plane trees bursting with spring-green leaves flashed by. Eventually, the truck turned into a bumpy country lane and Chloe bounced against Adam's shoulder.

"Tell me again why we agreed to this," she grumbled.

Adam's smile vanished when he saw how serious her expression was. "Okay. Point one, Alain is sure that whoever killed Jamie found the photograph of the Matisse. Point two, since all attempts to find the sketch have failed, it is likely the bad guys will soon give up the hunt for the real Matisse and produce their own forgery. Ergo, that puts anyone who knows about either the photo or the sketch in increased danger. Point three, you didn't see the damage done to Alain's shop. Whoever trashed it was in a terrible rage."

"No one actually uses the word 'ergo' anymore. And who *are* the bad guys?"

"Commissaire Lejeune's guesses are good enough for me. Kirov has Russian ties to Peter. He sounds like a perfect candidate for the KGB alumni association. Kamal Ashkar is rich enough to hire him, rich enough to have a yacht, and the means of smuggling a Matisse out of France."

"But that's a contradiction," Chloe exclaimed. "I agree that Kirov might well want to produce a forgery and try to pass it off as the real thing—he's in it for the money presumably. But someone like Ashkar wouldn't be satisfied with anything less than an original. Kirov and Ashkar seem to be working at cross purposes."

"Maybe Kirov is in trouble with an impatient boss. Maybe he needs to pass off a forgery to Ashkar, not for the money, but to save his own skin."

Chloe shook her head, but remained doubtful.

"In any case," Adam continued, "Our best chance of finding the killer is to come up with the Matisse ourselves. One way or another."

"It's the other way that worries me."

"Don't fret," Adam soothed. "I suspect Alain has hidden talents. And in the meantime, we've won some time to catch our breaths."

Suddenly, the truck lurched to the side. Chloe rolled with it, banging her head before Adam could catch her.

"I think I'll send a postcard to Sammy before I disappear," she said while rubbing her temple. "I'll be sure to tell him I'm having a wonderful time."

As it turned out, Adam was right. Provence in May was a langorous procession of delights: the clarity of the light, the subtle taste of lavender in the wine, the sharp scent of rosemary and thyme in the air. Jean handed Alain the keys to a hundred year old farmhouse, wished them luck and waved goodbye. The block-shaped house of rough gray stone with pale green shutters looked out over rows of vines and an orchard of flowering almond trees. Chloe's favourite room was the big kitchen with its stone oven. During the day, she always found a bowl of olives and a stoppered wine-bottle on the long table of cider-coloured wood. During the evening, she savoured Alain's surprisingly excellent food: glasses of *pastis* and crisp mouthfuls of salty anchovies wrapped in puff pastry; onion confit and roasted duckling; leg of lamb in a wild grape sauce.

Chloe began to understand the man's bulk. In self-defence, she and Adam went for runs in the morning, past the curious eyes of goats and their keepers. They talked about Alain's cooking, Adam's extended leave from his work, Lydia and Sylvie and the weather—everything except what Chloe did every afternoon.

Every afternoon in an upstairs room, where light spilled through tall windows, Chloe painted. During long conversations with Alain, she'd plundered his memory and drawn a sketch, her best approximation of a black and white photograph of *Portrait of a Bride.* She kept the dimensions small, roughly sixty by forty centimetres. She had to guess at the colours, a creamy white for the dress, red and pink for the roses, black for Sylvie's hair. She took care with Sylvie's head tilted slightly to one side, spent long hours over the line of the chin. Some days, she just sat and stared at the canvas, paralyzed by all the ways she could ruin it. Other days, she prayed to Sylvie.

Towards the end of May, Chloe, Alain and Adam were sitting on the terrace at dusk, drinking rosé, surrounded by the smell of acres of grape vines. A tangle of roses spilled from terra-cotta vases. Sunset was deepening the blue of the sky into streaks of purple.

"It's finished," Chloe said.

Adam, who had been rocking gently back and forth in an old wicker chair, suddenly became motionless.

Alain cleared his throat and poured more wine. "*Salut, chèrie.*"

The two men resumed their silence. Somewhere in the distance, Chloe could hear cars passing on a highway, and nearer to the farmhouse, the rush of a stream, a chorus of frogs.

"Well," she said. "Would you like to see it?"

Adam stood up so quickly, he knocked over his wine. Alain didn't stop to help pick up the broken glass. By the time Chloe and Adam joined him, he was tapping a foot outside the studio.

Chloe pushed past him and opened the door, turned on the light. The painting was propped up on an easel. The colours gleamed, the brush strokes lovingly worked into a matte-like surface reminiscent of frescoes.

"It's beautiful," Adam said.

"It's good work," Chloe added. "But it has none of the exuberance of a Matisse."

"Should you varnish it? To protect it?"

"No. Matisse never used varnish. He thought it dulled the colour."

Alain, staring silently until now, gave her a resounding pat on the back, enough to make her take a quick step forward to keep her balance. "It's splendid. It's just what we need. But where's the signature?"

Chloe hesitated, turned to look first at Adam, then at Alain. "Are you sure you want to go ahead with this? Ashkar will know this is a fraud."

"Of course, he will," Alain insisted. "That's the point."

Chloe picked up a brush, dipped it in black paint. She couldn't bring herself to forge the full name, so she settled for the initials, *HM*.

When she was finished, Alain winked at her with his good eye and Adam took her hand.

They closed the door of the studio and returned to the terrace.

They made their final plans under the moonlight and then went upstairs to bed, where each of them lay awake until morning, each disturbed by different ghosts.

Their month in the Provence countryside was over.

I often looked back with longing at the oasis of that courtyard in the months that followed. We traveled on to Bordeaux where Paul Rosenberg, Matisse's dealer and an art collector in his own right, was expecting us at his chateau outside the city. At least he was expecting Matisse. He seemed startled to see me. I'd communicated with him often in a professional capacity and our encounters had always been civil and respectful. Yet I could tell that he was struggling to keep his aplomb and he actually stumbled over the syllables of my name when introducing me to his wife. She bestowed upon me a thin, joyless smile and then excluded me completely from both her welcome and her conversation.

Matisse understood more than I imagined and tried to protect me by keeping me close. Of course, that only made things worse. I was on edge, as unstable as dynamite. A young beauty with a rich and famous old man, or a manipulative schemer with a doddering fool—whichever way our relation-ship was interpreted by outsiders, it seldom rose above the level of cliché. I was disappointed that Madame Rosenberg should be so unimaginative, but not surprised. I had lived a lifetime on the fringes of respectability.

I trailed behind as she led Matisse to a large and sunny guest room, where care had obviously been taken to make him comfortable. There were plenty of pillows, some books of poetry on the nightstand, a splashy arrangement of anemones, Matisse's favourite flowers, in a cut-glass vase. I helped to settle him in while Madame stood sentry in the open doorway. She was like a prudish chaperone from a Balzac novel, fearful and disappointed by turns that we might leap upon each other in some uncontrollable act of passion. We dared not look at each other for fear of dissolving into laughter.

Patron devilishly gave me a kiss on the cheek and sent me straight into the glare of his hostess. She did not take me to my room, but pointed to the staircase. "Two floors up," she hissed. "There's a small room at the end of the hall."

The bed had not been made-up, but there were linens. There was a wash basin and a pitcher of fresh water. And, perhaps by accident, a dormer window that looked out over miles of glorious vineyards. I put my suitcase down in a corner, but didn't unpack it. I was a woman who'd learned the wisdom of being ready to leave at a moment's notice.

For the most part, I tried to be as unobtrusive as possible during our stay in Bordeaux so as to lessen the social embarrassment of Madame Rosenberg. As a model, I had mastered the art of stillness and so could easily blend into the corners of rooms. Mealtimes were most awkward, for a place had to be set for me at the table.

Then our world erupted. Less than a year after our departure from Paris, bombs burst in its gray skies, triggering a chaotic, almost hysterical exodus from the capital. Days after the Germans marched into Paris, the government fled to Bordeaux and was even now attempting to negotiate an armistice.

"You must leave France, Henri," Rosenberg urged. "My wife and I have friends in America. We leave in two days."

"But what of your home, your art collection?" Matisse replied. "You know what efficient removal men the Germans are."

"It can't be helped. Friends will hide some of the paintings. They are building a false wall in their wine cellar to protect their most valuable possessions. We must risk the rest. The choice is between art and our very lives. Surely your son, Pierre, will help you from his gallery in New York."

"But what of my family here?" Matisse looked at me, then back at Rosenberg. "Don't worry. Pierre has already been at work. I have a visa to Brazil in my luggage should I need it. Godspeed on your journey, mon ami."

We packed that very morning and caught a train south, just ahead of a surge of people following us, scurrying like two water bugs riding the edge of a huge wave.

We were lucky to get tickets. With much of the population in flux and the Germans pouring into the north, train service stuttered and finally shut down completely. We managed to make it to the coast, to St-Jean-de-Luz near the border with Spain.

"Now's your chance, Lydia," Patron smiled. "Take the visa. One of those little fishing boats out there can slip you into Spain."

I didn't bother to answer him. Later, once we had found a room for the *night in the suddenly crowded town, he became irritable and querulous, pushing me away when I tried to help him, calling me a damned Bolshevik. It was the stratagem of a child.*

"I'm not leaving, Patron," I assured him.

He squared his shoulders and faced me, throwing his last weak excuse at me like a handful of sand. "I don't need you. You'll be more trouble than you're worth."

"As you already are?" I replied.

The next day, we traveled as far as St-Gaudens where we were trapped for a month at the Hotel Ferrière because there were no trains in July.

Finally, we were able to book passage on a train to Marseilles leaving at two in the morning. For once, Patron's insomnia was a blessing. By the end of August, 1940, it seemed a kind of miracle to us that we were standing once again at the windows of the Regina apartment in the liquid light of Nice.

Matisse's hair and beard had grown whiter, his features more gaunt, his neck scrawnier. He took my hand, and spoke in a low voice, almost a whisper. "Look at France, Lydia, still asleep in the sun, so humiliated, so dishonoured. I would have felt like a deserter had I left."

Having been orphaned by my own wretched country years ago, I felt considerably less sentimental. Or perhaps I just lacked the Gallic genius for evading unpleasant practicalities. There was a great deal of work to be done.

Together, Matisse and I turned the Cimiez apartments into a luminous, sensual retreat, as different from the grim reality outside as it was possible to be. The walls, which had been stripped of drawings and paintings by Madame Matisse's careful packing, once again sang with colour, draped in tapestries and embroidered cloth from Morocco and Algiers. We flung rugs around the floors like splashes of paint and left the windows wide open to the lemon Mediterranean sky. The air was filled with the scent of flowers, lilies and carnations in huge bouquets spread out on tables in the studio. From the aviary came the chirping and cooing of doves. Patron loved to leave the huge cages open and the birds would often fly about. Each time I found a feather floating in the air, I thought of the presence of angels.

We were, of course, perfectly conscious of living in an illusion. It was no surprise to me that when the studio was finally ready and Matisse began to paint, he created a variation on The Dream. *I wore the Rumanian blouse again and laid my head on a pillow. "Think of a story," Patron urged, "Follow it through to its end."*

When The Dream *was finished many months later, it was an interpretation of my life at the very moment I was living it. All the love and longing my body could contain was spun into the alphabet of colour: pink for the tenderness of my heart, the clash of violet and red for its depth and passion, strident yellow for all the wishes under the sun. My hair was just three wavy lines, no more than an extension of the pattern of the blouse. Best of all, my right arm, unnaturally elongated, curved about my head, suggesting an embrace, a circle of inviolate tranquility.*

But the world would not leave us alone. The war was too urgent. Matisse was too famous and too driven. Behind the closed door of my bedroom, in a small closet, I kept my suitcase packed.

September turned hot and sour, with thunderstorms every other day, the sky purple-gray over the swelling sea. Matisse often suffered from tension headaches and would lay in darkness with a lavender-soaked handkerchief across his face and his pills at hand beside him. Some of those pills were morphine.

I set out to find Sylvie. I asked about her in the Cours Saleya where I knew her easy smiles would be remembered. But instead of the welcome and open-handed guidance I expected, I was met with suspicious eyes and shut faces. Finally, an old vegetable farmer I remembered from my days at Charles Félix pulled me aside.

"Fool," he hissed. "Do you want to put your friend in danger? She's got no papers, and Pétain's toadies come sniffing every day looking for foreigners. She's not got a rich man to protect her, like some I could name. If you want to find her, look for André. And be discreet about it."

After that, it was easy. Patron placed a notice for a driver in the Nice-Matin and we waited for André to respond. He was hiding Sylvie in a boarding house near the Port where questions were seldom asked and never answered truthfully.

"You must bring her here, at once," Matisse ordered. "She'll be much safer with me and I need a nurse. Vichy would not dare raise its hand against me or those in my household."

André and I exchanged glances. Matisse found Pétain and his collabo-
rationist government headquartered in Vichy loathsome. But the armistice
the old Maréchal had signed with Hitler meant that at least Nice was not
occupied. For the time being, the French need only fear the French.

So Sylvie returned to us with her black hair and eyes the colour of dark
honey and her cheeky, lopsided grin. "We are allied by geography, once again,"
she whispered to me. "We can both be arrested and deported."

Even in risky times, Sylvie was seldom solemn for long. She loved to sing
and her voice was rich and pure. Her voice could make your hips swing when
it hummed American jazz. Or it could break your heart when it trembled
over the minor keys of French-Canadian folk songs, mournful ballads of lost
and wandering voyageurs. In exchange for her shelter, she nursed Matisse,
often teasing as she helped dress him in the morning that he looked more
like a banker than a painter. "Your fine linen shirts come from Charvet in
Paris? You wear a tie and a waistcoat every day. No one would believe you
are an artist."

More than once, her stories of her homeland, her journey across the Atlantic,
or her exploits as a pretty girl in Nice cheered Patron and saved him from
the bleakness of his insomnia. He called her his Scheherazade and never
suspected, as I did, that most of her stories were pure fiction.

Encouraged by the comfort of Sylvie's company, I wrote a letter to Berthe
assuring her of a welcome in Cimiez. I hoped the sun and the warmer air
would convince her to pay us a visit. A month or so went by with no response,
yet I was not alarmed since the mail was often unreliable. I sat down to
write again and this time Sylvie stayed my hand.

"She cannot come, Lydia. Nor can she reply to your letters."

"But I only want to extend my friendship," I protested, "to thank her for
her past kindnesses."

"That kindness has cost her dearly."

"What? What do you mean?"

"Madame Matisse has sworn never to speak to her again."

"Her own sister? But why? Berthe has always been loyal to Madame."

"Not loyal enough. Berthe refused to condemn you completely, and for that
she's been ostracized. As far as the rest of Madame's family is concerned, you
don't exist. None of them will acknowledge you. I'm sorry, Lydia. The entire

family believes you are living here as Matisse's mistress."

I stopped listening. Sylvie's words became a deep buzz, the droning sound of hornets scouring the nest.

Plenty of other people were happy to visit. Matisse lived among a group of old friends: André Rouveyre in Cannes and Pierre Bonnard at Le Cannet, to name two. There were constant requests from magazines, feature writers, photographers, and collectors. But chief among the visitors was Picasso.

He was thin and quick, with dark eyes that missed nothing. I didn't consider him handsome, but his was a face you could look at more than once. It was his energy that I found most compelling. I would greet him at the door and lead him to Matisse. "What is he working on?" was always Picasso's first question to me. When I showed him Still Life with Magnolia, mauvy pinks and livid greens on a carmine background, he furrowed his brow and cursed.

"Matisse is a magician," he grumbled. "His colours are uncanny."

I loved to listen to Matisse and Picasso argue, for arguing was what they did best. Both men had very little experience in being deferential. They were fiercely competitive. They reminded me of two icebergs grinding away at each other, the surge and thunder of their emotions hidden under a surface of clever conversation. But they were enemies who needed each other and who, in their later years, stumbled into a deep, if often uneasy friendship.

Though I had often heard that Picasso went out of his way for no one, he offered to stand in as Matisse's authorized key-holder at the Banque de France where many of Matisse's paintings were kept in storage. The strongrooms of the bank were designed to be proof against theft, fire, or bombardment, but not official confiscation of the contents by German authorities. Picasso's repeated reassurances that the paintings were still safe meant Patron would sleep those nights, and I blessed Picasso for those visits.

As winter approached, Patron began suffering from stomach pains so wrenching as to make him stagger. Soon he could eat nothing but a boiled egg or a little vegetable soup and a glass of wine. André fetched the doctors, but they could do little. Matisse was seventy-one, after all, they said. They would shake their heads and prescribe useless medicines.

Matisse refused to stop painting. He refused to acknowledge the pain when *holding a brush. Under his steady hand, steady by sheer force of will,* Still Life with Oysters *breathed life: the tablecloth a series of vivid, abstract planes of crimson, peach, and velvety navy; the table set with oysters on a white plate, an acid pink tankard, a knife with a handle of throbbing yellow.*

I watched and could not help him. His mouth was perpetually set in a thin white line, his eyes holes. The level of pills in the jars in his bedroom diminished more rapidly than ever.

Finally, I had to say it. I knew he didn't want me to, saw his fixed gaze deliberately avoiding me, concentrating on the painting, the painting, the painting and wishing I'd keep my mouth shut:

"Listen to me, Patron. You are gravely ill. You must allow me to get help from Paris."

He turned away furiously, afraid of my words and my terrible patience.

Many hours later, he called out for me. I could find my way to him in the dark. Some nights I closed my eyes as I walked along rather than strain them trying to see. I felt the corners of walls with my fingertips, avoided the stairs that creaked, could turn a doorknob as silently as a leaf falls. The colours of his face were very wrong, yellow around the eyes, a pale lavender near the lips.

I placed the palm of my hand, quite tenderly, to the side of his cheek and whispered into his ear: "Promise me you will fight this sickness."

His fear was iridescent in the dark, shining from his eyes. He nodded, covered my hand with his own.

The next morning, I was waiting outside the doctor's office with André. I remembered this particular doctor well for he used to give me instructions for the care of Madame Matisse.

"Please," I began. "You must give Monsieur Matisse a referral. I'll take him to Paris, or if that's not possible, perhaps Lyon. He needs surgery."

The doctor raised his eyebrows and looked me up and down. "Tell me, Mademoiselle, are you acting on behalf of the family?"

I stared back at him without blinking. "Of course."

"Are you really?" he asked in a silky voice. "I wonder. You must see I can't take the word of a servant, and a foreigner at that."

He turned away from me insolently and I had to restrain André from making things worse.

On Christmas Day, 1940, I sent a telegram to Marguerite:

Father dying STOP Urgently needs surgery STOP *Lydia.*

I couldn't see the patient behind the bed curtain, just a stream of light filtering through the fabric. When I pulled it aside, Matisse's body was limp, as though his muscles were no longer connected.

I'm not frightened by illness. My father often took me with him to visit the sick. There was one old hunting lodge just beyond my village with a stone fireplace and exposed beams in the high ceiling. I loved its rich, loamy smell of earth and cedar. But most of the places we went were little more than sheds, with wood stoves and crooked pine plank floors, gloomy and damp, choked with smoke and smelling of unwashed clothes and chamber pots. I'd seen some things a young girl should probably not have seen. I'd seen the Angel of Death with his black wings curled up on the chests of old and young alike.

Matisse fought to live like an old lion, every breath a struggle. The operation to remove the cancer was arduous, his recovery complicated by blood clots. I didn't believe in God, but the impulse to pray was still there. So I thought of my father and it seemed fitting to pray to a doctor to allay my fears.

Marguerite had arranged everything: the travelling to Lyon, the hospital, the surgeon. I had braced myself for her anger, but her first words, flung at me like poison darts, stung me nonetheless.

"Well, there you are," Marguerite said scornfully. "The Muse. Did you ever stop to think he might be tired? That he might want to die?"

Her accusation startled and dismayed me. Self-doubt gnawed at me like a rat trapped in a box. Was it true? Did I want Matisse to live so that my own life could continue? I'd had nothing. He'd given me a home, work I loved. I lived my days surrounded by beauty. I felt like the selfish monster Marguerite and Madame always believed me to be.

I was shaken enough that I almost didn't follow Matisse to Lyon. It was Sylvie who convinced me.

"You'll always be evil in their version of the story," she said. "But you know Matisse, perhaps better than anyone. If he ever opens his eyes again after this operation, it will be your face he looks for."

I left for Lyon the next morning.

"I hoped you wouldn't come," Marguerite said.

"I don't care," I replied.

From then on, for the sake of her father, Marguerite and I managed a precarious, icy politeness. She sat with him during the day. I stayed with him during the long, restless nights, staring at the fragile blue veins on his scalp.

One night, the surgeon visited while Matisse was sleeping, a drugged, far away sleep. A thread of drool glistened at his lips. From time to time he shook his head, as if plagued by wasps.

"He has amazing strength," the doctor said. "He's hung on beyond the bonds of what anyone would think humanly possible."

"Yes," I replied. "I know his strength."

"You've nursed him before?"

"More than that, I've watched him paint."

We returned to Nice at the end of March, though Matisse still battled pain. Sometimes he would squeeze my hand so tightly, my skin would turn white. My bones felt crushed. But he was jubilant, his spirits soaring. He felt reborn. He had cheated death.

He was far too weak to paint, so I devised a kind of revolving bookshelf for him with dozens of compartments. It stood by his bed and held everything Patron was likely to need: a sketchpad, charcoal crayons, pens, ink, books of poetry, graphite pencils, pills and handkerchiefs. He began a series of drawings, Thèmes et Variations *he called them, each one more beautiful, more delicate than the last. For the first time since I'd known him, he seemed almost content while working. He began to tease me again, calling me Saint Lydia. One night he smiled and said: "I've perfected my drawing. It's like a flowering. And it's one of the things I wanted to live for, so you see, my dear, Marguerite was quite wrong."*

Sometimes a single sentence can dispel months of self-doubt. I stood up straighter after that and vowed to trust my own instincts.

I had need of my quick wits, for Nice was a nest of collaborators. There were Fascist demonstrations in the streets. The newspapers wallowed in a steady stream of racist muck. Two Vichy officials came to visit Matisse—two loathsome little clerks who'd once been invisible and were now puffed up by their titles. They bowed and scraped before the great man, but out of his earshot, they threatened Sylvie and me.

"Keep your heads down," they leered, their eyes on our breasts, not our faces. "Or you may disappear. You can model for the Germans in Nice's whore houses or dance naked for Il Duce." They roared with laughter at their own joke and snapped their fingers to demonstrate how easily things could be arranged.

In July, when Hitler invaded Russia, I turned to Sylvie, hugging her. "He's made a mistake. We may yet survive," I said.

She didn't believe me, but I knew my country. I knew how cheap human life was there. I knew how long my people had suffered. I knew the cruelty of their leaders and their winters. One blast of that breath could freeze the flames of Hitler's hell.

In the short run, though, the invasion fanned resentment against Russian émigrés and made things worse for me. Patron even stopped calling me the damned Bolshevik, one of his favourite taunts, for fear of being overheard and misunderstood.

And then Louis came into our lives. Beautiful, reckless, Louis Aragon, with mischievous eyes and black hair that he combed back with his fingers when it fell down on his forehead. He wore a white collar and a long tie: a lean, angular man who looked as if he'd just stepped out of a canvas by Modigliani. He could talk for hours about almost anything in a voice so mesmerizing you forgot about the time it wasted. He was a publisher and a poet, a founding member of Surrealism and, most dangerously, a Communist. Vichy tracked his every move, and hated him.

Always blind to politics, Matisse invited him into our home without a moment's hesitation. He wanted his drawings to be published in book form and he wanted Louis to write an introduction. What was politics compared to art? I shook my head in frustration. I couldn't decide if Matisse was self-consciously thumbing his nose at Vichy or merely being naïve.

"Don't you see that having him here is risky?" I demanded.

But he didn't see, or refused to see. The problem with geniuses is that they're so often right, they're unable to fathom the possibility of being wrong.

So Louis came and sometimes stayed for days. He was married to a Russian woman, Elsa Triolet, and he had learned to speak a little Russian. My native language, my island in France, sounded wonderful coming from his mouth, all sharp consonants and drumming syllables. I was nearly undone by my longing for him.

Louis was enchanted by the studio at Cimiez. The bright red stripes of the bergère chair that so inspired Matisse seemed to pulse in the light. The sun poured in through the tall windows, casting the shadows of palm leaves across the floor. The tapestries were gold and green and blue, every shade a jewel. Who would not want to be in these rooms?

"How magical," Louis murmured in his dreamy voice. "However do you manage?"

"It's all Lydia," Matisse replied. "Without her, there would be no studio, and no household. I call her Saint Lydia. There's nothing she can't do. It wouldn't surprise me if she could ride a horse bare-back or fly a plane."

Louis stared at me and I felt the flush of desire creep up my neck and across my cheeks. "She is, indeed, many things," he said to Matisse. "But not, I think, a saint."

All those years of nursing Patron left me a light sleeper. When Aragon slipped out of the apartment one night, I followed him. I felt crazy, but I didn't care. The moonlight was bright, gleaming off the edges of things, turning the night to silver. Louis entered the gardens across from the Regina. The upper garden was planted with a grove of olive trees leading to an old monastery, while the lower garden had been excavated to reveal Roman ruins, walls and archways of white stone, ghostly under the moon. Louis strode through the olive grove towards the monastery. He knocked on its heavy door and glanced over his shoulder while I slipped behind a tree.

I waited under the tree until my limbs were stiff and cold. I had plenty of time to think about my own rashness, and just enough time to realize I was lonely. All Louis had done was remind me I was young and that the night was filled with stars.

When I heard the soft tread of his steps in the grass, I stepped out from behind the tree. "Where have you been? What've you done?" I asked. "You mustn't put Matisse at greater risk than his own foolishness already has."

"Sweet Lydia," he smiled. "No daughter could be kinder."

"I'm no daughter. He has one of his own and she despises me."

"Then she's a fool. But come, we mustn't be found out here."

We hurried back to the apartment and sat in the kitchen drinking tea. Louis explained that hundreds of Italian intellectuals had fled Mussolini's fascist government and found uncertain refuge in France. There was a clandestine press in Nice that smuggled news and encouragement back to Italy. "This is what I'm sworn to do, Lydia. Fight fascism with my words and my typewriter. Tomorrow I'm to meet one of these journalists in Place St-François. Do you know it?"

"It's in the old town. There's a fish market there."

"Will you come with me? A woman with a basket for shopping would be ideal cover. I promise to keep you safe."

I laughed at him. "You can't make such a promise."

"Will you come anyway?"

"Yes."

We set out together the next morning at dawn. It was a very long walk from the fragrant orange and olive groves of Cimiez down to the busy, briny sea. Louis talked to me about Russia the whole way and it was like listening to birdsong. When we reached the narrow streets of the old town, however, their dark pools of shadow seemed to warn us to be silent. I led him along streets no wider than alleys, following my nose and the smell of fish.

Tall narrow buildings in pastel shades enclosed the square, the façade of the Palais Communal opposite it. We sidled along a pink wall, scanning the shoppers. Fish was one of the few items that had escaped the rationing system. Already there must have been over a hundred people milling around the stalls. Above, seagulls swirled in the air, diving low with open beaks for scraps.

"There he is," Louis whispered into my ear. "At the stall with the yellow awning. Head that way."

We were in the thick of the crowd when we heard whistles and shouting. Half a dozen Blackshirts were pushing their way across the square. We heard one yell, "Stop. Stop him."

For an instant, everything felt timeless and still. Nothing moved.

Then everything exploded. The seagulls shrieked, wings fluttering. People were cursing and shouting, shoving and running to get away. Others were fighting the Blackshirts, fists and feet swinging wildly. A smash against my shoulder sent me sideways into a stall. Blood poured into my mouth from a cut on my lip and strong hands under my arms dragged me out of the melee.

A young man with old eyes, a fishmonger by his apron, pressed a piece of ice into my hand. I looked at him with gratitude, then scrambled to my feet to search for Louis.

A thin piercing scream cut across the emptying square.

The press of onlookers exhaled a kind of communal gasp and fell back.

There, in a small heap, lay a child, a little girl with long black ringlets, wearing a dirty flowered smock. Her feet were bare.

A woman sank to her knees beside the child and touched her gently, but she did not stir. Frantic, the mother pressed the girl's head to her breast and it was then I saw the pool of blood on the ground.

The mother began rocking the body slowly back and forth, her keening as sharp as the cruelest blade.

Louis was nowhere to be seen. I watched as the Blackshirts began to retreat like a slick oily tide. They were all boots and braid, not a single individual face among them.

The young fishmonger stepped alone into the square. He walked in front of the Blackshirts, looking each one in the eye, his back perfectly straight. He walked to the grieving mother and knelt by her side. Then, in one fluid motion, he picked up the child as if she were a fallen feather and carried her into the church.

Louis found me ten minutes later, still standing by the vacated fish stall.

"Did you see?" I asked. "A child was trampled."

I felt so angry I wanted to slap him. I didn't care about his Leftist cause, or his secret meetings, or his political poetry.

I think he understood because he hung his head. "Come away, Lydia. I shouldn't have brought you."

I read the newspapers diligently over the next few days, but the child's death was no more than a line or two of empty phrases—dreadful accident, such a terrible shame. The Blackshirts were not mentioned. There'd been no panic in the square.

Her name was Bella. I watched as they buried her in a churchyard beneath a little plaster cross and an angel.

Beloved Daughter, 1936-1941.

As I turned to leave the graveside, I saw the fishmonger, a cloth hat crushed in his hands, his sad eyes following me.

In Chloe's imagination, Nice was a dream city bathed in pastel shades of dusk like Sylvie's old tinted postcards. In reality, she was dazed by the sun, dazzled by the clarity of the light. Poor old Daniels had been right after all—Matisse, Picasso, Bonnard, Chagall—it was Mediterranean light that had soaked into their souls and lit up their palettes. It filtered through the palm trees along the Boulevard des Anglais, and brightened the pastel facades of the grand old hotels. Most of all, it turned the sea into swirling shades of green and blue and turquoise. Chloe could hardly believe she was here, in the Côte d'Azur, where Sylvie had come before her, where Sylvie had fallen in love with André, and lived with Lydia and Matisse.

Chloe stirred her tall glass of *citron pressé* and gazed at the tall golden-yellow building that faced the Cours Saleya, the building where Lydia had first met Matisse. She almost believed that if she turned away, and then turned back again quickly, she would see the blonde Russian gazing out a window, or perhaps Sylvie, crossing the market with a bouquet of flowers tucked under her arm. Instead it was Adam who approached her café table.

"What is that?" Adam asked, interrupting her visions of the past. He was staring at her glass, as he pulled up a chair to join her.

"This? This is pure lemon juice, freshly squeezed. The cold pitcher of water and the sugar jug that come with it allow you to make your own lemonade." Chloe poured in a lot of sugar and a little water and held the concoction out to Adam. "Want some?"

He shook his head and raised a hand for a waiter.

Chloe delighted in the market with its bunches of lavender, heaps of fruit and vegetables, throngs of people with dogs or baskets or cameras, and thought that everything was different since they'd come to the South. The coffee was stronger, the air smelled different and tasted saltier. She felt more relaxed. Even Adam was different, she decided, as she watched him with the waiter. When he spoke French, his body became more fluid, his eyes more expressive, his hands in constant motion.

He caught her watching and smiled. "What's on your mind, Chloe?"

She opened her arms. "All of this," she said. "It's like dreams melting into reality. All the great painters were here. Sylvie and Lydia were here. I wonder, do memories have a life of their own? Can the memories of a person so passionately connected to one place speak across time to a stranger?"

"I don't know," Adam confessed. "But I think Jamie thought so. I think we were right to follow him here."

A couple of tables over, two long-limbed girls sat chatting with a trio of young men. The girls posed dramatically for photos, then pushed the camera away. Chloe found herself staring at them.

"I wish I could do that," she said.

Adam was mystified. "Do what?"

"Do you see that woman, that pout? She has a brave-orphan smile that makes you want to fetch her a shawl."

"Do you want a shawl?" Adam asked.

Chloe rolled her eyes. "Never mind. Did you call Liliane this morning?"

"I did. I've a list of places to visit. What do you want to see first?"

"Everything. Was Liliane upset that we hadn't said goodbye?"

"She said she'd guessed where we'd gone. Commissaire Lejeune came to see her though, and *he* seemed annoyed."

"Oh well, we're out of hiding now. What is Alain up to today?"

Adam shrugged. "He was very mysterious. He said he had some final arrangements to take care of and that he'd meet us at the Matisse Museum at four this afternoon."

Chloe shook her head. "I don't believe he's a simple framer from Paris."

"What?"

"Really, a man who can cook like that? He could make a fortune. And he carried his clothes from Paris in a paper bag, yet he checked us into the Hotel Négresco. That makes no sense at all."

The Négresco, a pink-and-white domed confection, was the flagship hotel of Nice. Chloe had been almost as awestruck by the Baccarat chandelier in its royal salon as she had been by the cost of the rooms.

"I think we both underestimated him," Adam agreed. "But he says the glitter is part of the plan. In any case, we're checking out tonight."

"Good. The Négresco's unlucky, I think. Romantic, but unlucky. It was built for a man who was once a gypsy violinist. He went bankrupt. And Isadora Duncan died just outside the hotel when her trailing scarf got caught in the steering wheel of her Bugatti."

"How do you know stuff like this?"

"C'mon, Adam. It's the Riviera. Russian aristocracy, British royalty, Coco Chanel, Scott and Zelda Fitzgerald, Brigitte Bardot? Don't you ever go to the movies?"

"Sometimes. The only title that seems to fit is *To Catch a Thief.*"

"Touché. Let's go."

They spent the rest of the morning and the early afternoon trying to retrace Jamie's steps, hoping to see something in what he'd seen or learn something from where he'd been. Adam introduced himself as Jamie's brother at both the hotels on Liliane's list, but no one there remembered him and he'd left nothing behind.

They took a bus to Cimiez, the wealthy enclave in the hills above old Nice, and lingered outside the Regina where Matisse had once lived. It looked like a palace with its multiple domes and huge glassed-in foyer with marble floors and giant, feathery ferns in pottery urns. Chloe took photographs of the intricately carved balconies and the Art Nouveau canopy fashioned from glass and curving lengths of wrought iron. Matisse, she knew, had bought two of these apartments, and opened up the space to make a studio with high ceilings. She'd seen pictures of him there, a grandfatherly figure in a wheelchair with perhaps a dove perched on his shoulder.

She turned to Adam, excited and disappointed both. "This is where the painting was done, or at least stored for a while. Remember the inscription, PM/R/1943/UPPER STUDIO? The letter R is for the Regina."

But the Regina was a private residence now, more a monument to wealth than to a fabled past. For a moment, Chloe indulged herself with fantasies of a painting stashed under the floor boards or behind a false brick wall. But the fantasy disintegrated under the certain knowledge that if Lydia had hidden it in such a place, she would surely have returned for it years ago.

They wandered past the Roman ruins and the ancient stone amphitheatre now used to host jazz concerts, and into the olive grove outside the Venetian red Matisse Museum. It was a cheerful, even playful building, a seventeenth-century Genoese villa, famous for its trompe l'oeil façades.

But Chloe found herself drawn to the olive grove, to the weathered, twisted trunks and the sunlight filtering through silvery leaves. To her, the park was the sweetest, greenest part of Cimiez. She felt the trees would still be here even when the Regina and the museum itself were ruins.

Adam seemed to sense her contemplative mood and made no objections when she asked to see Matisse's grave before entering the museum. It was somewhere across the park, in the grounds of the rose-coloured Franciscan monastery. They found the old gated cemetery, its graveled paths twisting through a labyrinth of marble headstones and stone angels. It was much larger than Chloe had supposed, full of surprising turns and hidden niches. Finally, Adam found a small sign, indicating the path to Matisse's grave. It led away from the other graves, away from the community of the dead, and down a set of steps that curved around a little green meadow.

Apart from the impressive size of the stone slab that marked Matisse's final resting place, the monument was very plain. It was set in a peaceful place, certainly, but to Chloe, it seemed lonely, even a touch forlorn. Matisse's son, Jean, had carved only the names of his parents and the dates of their births and deaths. No details of their lives, no sentimental verses. The real monuments, Chloe supposed, the ones that people would flock to see, were the paintings. She wondered how Matisse would have felt about spending eternity with Amélie Parayre and her stormy temper.

As they climbed back up to the monastery graveyard, Adam put a hand under her elbow. "Are you all right, Chloe?"

"Hmm. I was just thinking how sad Matisse's funeral would have been. Apart from his children and grandchildren, the people he loved best were not there. The nun who inspired him to build the Vence chapel was forbidden by her Mother Superior to attend. Picasso didn't show. When Matisse died, Lydia rose from his bedside and left immediately with a suitcase she'd kept packed for fifteen years."

"But surely his wife attended?"

"Oh yes. She descended from Paris at once to become the guardian of the temple."

"What temple?"

Chloe pointed to the red villa, as much a landmark in Nice now as the sea itself. "It's ironic, don't you think? Madame Matisse lived only a few months in Cimiez, and those were months filled with her rage. This was Lydia's place. She walked in this garden, I'm sure of it. I've read that the museum is full of Matisse's personal possessions—objects he liked to paint over and over again. The silver Venetian chair, the Tahitian cloths, countless vases and jars and jugs. It was Lydia's hands that filled them with flowers, Lydia's eyes that composed arrangements for still life paintings. Yet it's as if her name has been air brushed from history."

"Not entirely," Adam replied. "You haven't forgotten."

Chloe looked down at Sylvie's ring, without replying. She didn't know how to tell him that her link to Lydia felt personal, electric. Sometimes, she almost believed she could feel what Lydia might have felt and hear what Lydia might have said. She felt she was close enough to hear Lydia's voice, a voice that tried so hard to hide its true nature, the passionate woman behind the ice maiden's façade.

"C'mon," Adam urged. "Let's go in. You can teach me."

They walked past the villa to a modern, unfortunately designed entrance that led to the museum's newest wing, built when the collection was expanded.

"Don't be disappointed," Chloe said. "The great paintings are not here. This is a humbler place, even domestic."

But Adam was not listening to her. His attention was riveted on the huge wall mural, *Fleurs et Fruits*, one of the famous cut-outs that Matisse fashioned only a year or two before his death. It was joyful; an interior garden of hot yellows, cool greens, pinks that shouted and blues that rippled. No matter his frailty or the pains of old age, Matisse continued to delight and surprise to the very end.

Chloe smiled to see Adam so entranced and wandered away to explore on her own. She saw dozens of sketches, Matisse's lines fluid and quick, springing across the page. But, just as she had expected, Lydia was invisible. She might never have existed, though Chloe estimated that roughly half of the artwork on display would never have existed without her. Then, just as she was passing through a small hallway that led from the new wing to an interior staircase of the old villa, her eye caught a small glass display case.

One of Matisse's delicately illustrated books, Baudelaire's *Les Fleurs du Mal* was laid open, showing two exquisite drawings of Lydia, one on each leaf. The model was unnamed, unidentified, but Chloe would have recognized the classic features anywhere by now, the smooth brow, the pensive expression. Though most of the museum's holdings had been donated by the Matisse family, Chloe felt a surge of joy to see that this particular book was a gift from Louis Aragon.

This was the Louis referred to by Lydia in Sylvie's letter, the Louis who had surely helped Sylvie and André escape from France during the war. As Chloe examined the book more closely, she saw that the edges were slightly worn. She imagined that Louis must have loved this book, perhaps even these two particular pages, very much.

Her musing was interrupted by the noisy arrival of a group of French school children, running on the stairs and giggling, much to the horror of their teachers. Chloe followed them, partly drawn to the energy of a pack of seven-year-olds, and partly curious to overhear what they would learn about Matisse.

But there were no lectures, no pedantic drills. Instead, the group headed for the empty floor space in front of *Fleurs et Fruits,* the mural where Chloe had left Adam. The children opened their satchels and pulled out papers and crayons and markers. They sat cross-legged or lay on their stomachs, limbs sprawled every which way, heads propped up on their hands. And they began to draw, anything they wanted, with abandon.

Adam found Chloe down on the floor with the children a half-hour later. "Time to move on," Adam said, laughing. He offered a hand to help her up. "Alain has already checked us out of the hotel."

Chloe waved goodbye to the children, then looked around for Alain.

"He's waiting for us outside," Adam said. "You won't recognize him. He's wearing a light tan suit. Very smart-looking. He's rented a car."

When they'd climbed back up the museum steps to the park, Chloe was surprised to see the same two girls from the breakfast café, the pretty girls with the French pouts. Once again, they were teasing their boyfriends and posing for pictures. The photographer was shooting with a very expensive looking digital camera. When he lifted it to focus, Chloe caught a glimpse of a solid gold wristwatch.

At the same moment, she heard Alain's booming voice. "Here, let me borrow your camera, young man. I'll get a shot of all four of you. *Pas de problème.*"

The startled boyfriend handed over his camera. Alain took his time focusing and framing the shot, fiddling with buttons—*Smile! One more!* At last he handed back the camera.

"No need to thank me. My pleasure," Alain said.

He turned towards Chloe and Adam, hurrying them away, across the park to a small, sporty Peugeot.

"There were a dozen shots of the two of you in the camera," he said. "Most in a café, a couple in the olive grove, one of Chloe sitting with children. You just looked like tourists so I didn't erase them. I don't think they got close enough to hear or record much."

Chloe and Adam looked at each other, flabbergasted.

They climbed into the car, Chloe volunteering for the back seat for the sake of Adam's longer legs, Alain confidently behind the wheel.

Before pulling away from the curb, he turned to look back at her, then at Adam. "Look, you two. I don't mind being the leg man of this operation. I've got the broken nose for it. But you have to start using your brains."

Properly chastised, Chloe remained quiet for several blocks. "I thought the car would be flashier," she finally said.

"Keep up," Adam teased. "The bad guys will have big black cars, maybe Mercedes. The Peugeot is sneakier, small enough to zip down the narrow medieval streets of old Nice and into impossibly tight French parking spaces. The bad guys won't be able to chase us in their cars. Am I right, Alain?"

"Getting warmer," he chuckled. "Though we won't be staying in Nice."

"Where then?" Chloe asked. She was dismayed to be leaving Nice when she'd only just arrived.

"Don't worry," Alain consoled. "We'll be close enough that you can come into the city any time you like. We're going to stay on Cap Ferrat."

Adam whistled. "How can we possibly afford—"

Alain raised his hands to silence all questions, an action which startled Chloe since they were now speeding along the sweeping bends of Princess Grace Boulevard, seemingly suspended in air above the sea.

"I've a small surprise," Alain said, his hands now firmly back on the wheel.

Here we go again, Chloe thought.

"I haven't always run a framing shop in Paris," Alain continued.

Chloe leaned forward in her seat.

"I have a brother who happens to be quite well off, and for a while I lived with him."

"How well off?" Adam asked.

"Let the man talk," Chloe urged.

"My brother was very handsome as a young man, though you may doubt it, looking at me. Quite the ladies' man. Some might even have called him a gigolo, in fact. He married an Italian countess. I think the English word that best describes her is shrewish. Anyway, an ill-tempered, spoiled lady. She spends a good deal of her time at spas, I believe, submerged in mud."

Chloe laughed out loud.

"She has a standing account at the Négresco. I charged our rooms to it, but don't worry, she'll never notice. Eventually, the Countess drove my brother straight into the arms of another man. I believe they travel together a great deal. My point, *mes amis*, is that their villa is vacant."

Chloe met Adam's eyes, then they both looked away quickly. *Who is Alain Reynaud?* She didn't believe his outrageous story for a minute, yet here they were, turning into the road to Cap Ferrat.

Alain was clearly not interested in the leisurely delights of sight-seeing. He accelerated up a steep hill, cut sharply in front of a startled motorcyclist, ignored the colourful French idioms that followed, and began winding his way through the quiet, curvy streets of the Cap.

Chloe's first impression was of an extended garden, impeccably maintained, surrounded by the serenity of a deep blue sea where white sailboats in the distance were added decoration. The peninsula had none of the boisterousness or brashness of Nice. Also none of its noise, street litter, or graffiti. Villas of the famous and notorious were hidden behind high walls and thick hedges, guarded by iron gates, insulated by palm trees and towering pines.

Alain followed the Boulevard General de Gaulle past a lighthouse, turning off down a narrow private road, a cul-de-sac that led to the tip of the Cap. He stopped the car in front of an ornate set of double gates. Beyond them, Chloe saw a drive perhaps seventy metres long, lined in the typical French way with palm trees, ending in a turning circle before the low-slung, white house that seemed to undulate across the contours of the landscape. She had a fleeting impression of glass, archways, and a red-tiled roof, before Alain cut across her thoughts.

"Welcome home. Just the place, don't you think, for a grand party? A Matisse hanging on the wall won't look out of place here."

He hefted himself out of the car and fiddled with the digital security pad embedded into the gates. They swung open majestically.

Later that night, Chloe, Adam and Alain were sitting on the terrace of a restaurant in the port village of St. Jean Cap Ferrat. An empty bottle of champagne was turned upside down in the ice-bucket beside their table. From behind a small mountain of empty mussel shells, Chloe admired the paper lanterns strung along the edges of the mooring docks. The water in the harbour shimmered, giving off a pale light, like a mirror shining in a darkening room.

"Is it always this beautiful?" she asked. "Does it never rain here? Does the food always taste this good?"

"Steady," Alain warned. "This is the stronghold of the far-right politician, Jean-Marie Le Pen. He and his disciples hate Jews, Arabs, and blacks. They also hate the English and the Germans and the Americans who buy up French real estate. They want France for the French, whatever that means, but they also want to be paid in cash so they can cheat on their taxes."

Chloe sighed. There was always a snake in paradise.

She looked at Adam across the wreckage of their meal. He was gazing out to sea, seemingly a million miles away. She studied his profile, the line of his jaw, the way his hair curled slightly at the base of his neck. While her own pale skin had freckled slightly under the Provencal sun, Adam's had tanned to a golden brown.

Suddenly, without shifting his gaze from the sea, he began speaking, in a low conspiratorial tone: "Do you two see that yacht out there? Beyond the port, just where the bay begins to widen out?"

Chloe nodded. She could hardly miss it. It was a triple-decked, white and silver floating hotel. She heard Alain make a small grunting noise.

"Well, unless I'm mistaken, it has its own helicopter. Bit over the top, don't you think? Anyway, I talked to the waiter on the way in. It belongs to Kamal Ashkar."

Alain tapped his fingers rhythmically on the table, his own version of a drum roll. "Positions, please. Show time."

"I'd like to go to Vence first," Adam said. "Back to the site of the accident."

"I'd like to go with Adam," Chloe said. When she spoke, Adam turned to look at her, an intense blue-eyed gaze.

"Fine, fine," Alain shrugged. "Just be careful. I believe those big, overfed dogs you see sleeping on the deck of the yacht are actually Ashkar's bodyguards."

That night, Chloe found it difficult to sleep. She felt she'd stumbled into a dream. The villa felt more like an illusion than an actual building. It was open and airy, with high ceilings and curved archways, one room flowing into the next. The foyer had a stained glass ceiling that let in shafts of blue and rose light. The floors were marble, the faucets in the bathroom were gold, the furniture mostly Louis the 16th. She was afraid to touch anything. She swung her legs out of the canopy bed, and walked to the balcony window.

It was a glorious night. The moon was full, the sea luminous.

Below her, the silhouette of a man slid across the edge of the terrace, disappearing into a gap between trees.

Chloe stood rooted and still, her breath locked in her chest.

For a long time, she didn't move, saw nothing move outside, save the rippling surface of the sea. She turned away and climbed back into bed, a sense of menace swirling up through the darkness.

But the next morning, sitting in the sun, soaking up the pleasure of the warm air, the company, and Alain's breakfast, she thought she was seeing monsters under the bed. Her nerves were jittery, that's all.

"Are you sure you have enough time and enough help to arrange the party for tomorrow night?" she asked.

Alain gave her a baleful look. "Not to quibble, dear Chloe, but that's the third time you've asked, and that's just counting this morning. I've hired people, the guests are being invited as we speak."

"Who exactly is coming?" Adam asked.

"A motley collection of jackals, guttersnipes, thugs, scoundrels, and parasites."

Chloe stiffened.

Alain reached for her hand, patting it reassuringly. "Let me rephrase that. Only the most indiscreet people, friends of the Countess."

"And of your brother, too?"

"My brother? *Bien sûr.*"

As the Peugeot left the seaside and began to climb the foothills of the Alps, Chloe felt invigorated. She breathed in lungfuls of pine-scented air, marvelling that just twenty kilometres from the coast, she could find herself in the midst of forest and windswept outcrops of rock. Away from the exclusivity of Cap Ferrat, where most of the noise was made by white curtains snapping in salty breezes, or by cocktail glasses clinking on terraces, Chloe felt free enough to shout. She felt some of her confidence returning, some of her certainty that following the clues of the past would lead her to Sylvie's painting.

Adam, however, seemed to be feeling the opposite. He sat beside her, his face often turned away from her, watching the woods slide by. He spoke only to give her directions according to the map spread out on his lap.

Chloe knew why.

"Is this where it happened?" she asked, gently.

"Yes. Somewhere along this road, Jamie lost control of his motorcycle. Plunged over the edge into the ravine. But he was going the other direction. Downhill, I mean. Away from Vence, not towards it. There's no marker. I could pass by and never know exactly where he died."

Chloe suppressed a shudder. The road was difficult. Downhill, if a person were speeding—she could easily imagine losing control. Was Jamie's death an accident, after all? Or was someone chasing him, pushing him to take breathtaking risks, or worse, bumping a back tire, deliberately forcing him over the edge?

The road was narrow. There were no banks or verges, no places to pull over and be safe from traffic. "I can't stop," Chloe said.

"No. I remember. There's a gas station just on the outskirts of Vence. Stop there. I'd like to walk back a bit."

When she'd finally parked the car at the gas station, Adam strode away alone. She knew, without asking, that he'd want to be alone. She knew he'd learn nothing, but understood completely why he felt compelled to walk along the road, and even climb into the ravine.

The past was a living thing. It was always present. You couldn't just sweep it away.

She felt the sun beating down on the roof of the car, and wandered into the shop for a cold drink.

The girl behind the counter was slight, short brown hair, warm eyes. She looked about seventeen, wearing a man's shirt over a pair of faded jeans.

When Chloe paid for her soda, the girl's eyes fastened on Sylvie's ring.

"*Très belle*," she said shyly.

"*Merci. C'est un cadeau de ma grand-mère.*"

Quickly, the girl switched to English. "You are American?"

"No," Chloe replied. "Canadian. Is my accent that bad?"

"No, no," the girl hurried to reassure her. "I take the chances to practice my English. I am seeing your friend on the road. Is very dangerous, you know. Many accidents there."

"We *do* know, sadly," Chloe replied. "My friend lost his brother there sometime last fall."

"*Mais, c'est tragique.* I lost a cousin."

Chloe smiled sympathetically, then turned to leave.

The girl's voice called her back. "The brother of your friend, he was Canadian also?"

"Yes. Though he'd lived in France for some time."

"Jamie? Jamie Jensen?"

Chloe's breath caught in her throat. "You knew Jamie?"

"He was very handsome. He was taking me for a ride one day on his bike. He came here for gas."

"Did he come here often?"

"Oh no, maybe three times. He was staying in Vence, *en vacance.* He left something here, you know, before—"

"You mean just before the accident?"

The girl nodded. "Only a map. But when he died, I thought I am keeping it. He was writing on it. I liked him. It did not seem the right thing, to put it in the trash."

"That was kind of you," Chloe said. "Did the police, the gendarmes, did they ever come to ask you questions about that day?"

The girl seemed surprised. "What for? The newspapers said Jamie was too fast, racing."

"Speeding?"

"Yes, speeding. But I have the map. You would like it for his brother?"

"Very much."

Chloe watched as the girl left the counter and walked to a storage room at the back of the shop. She was gone only a minute or two, but long enough for Chloe to feel elation, certain the riddle would be solved, that she would soon hold in her hands the map to the missing Matisse.

When the girl returned, she handed Chloe a folded map of Nice. Chloe thanked her profusely, promised to send in Adam to meet her as soon as he returned, and rushed back to the car.

The heat, as she slid into the seat, smothered her like a steamy blanket, but she scarcely noticed.

She unfolded the map, scanned it quickly for Jamie's handwriting.

Her eyes followed a thick red line that started in the Nice port, passed through the old town to Cimiez, then to the edge of the city in the direction towards Vence. Place St. Francois in the old town was circled. Beside it, Jamie had written Matteo and St. Jeannet.

She turned the map over, looked again. She found Adam's telephone number.

Nothing else.

Chloe felt so frustrated, she thought she might cry. Who the hell was Matteo?

It was early September in 1942 and summer was drawing to an end. Still hot, there was a new ripeness in the air, something rich and fragrant.

I found myself drawn again and again to the fish market in Place St-François. Patron swore that he was eating so much fish, grilled, baked, fried and stewed, that he would never again paint one.

Matteo was unusual. It was the quiet way he talked, the way he looked people in the eyes, the way he held his head up. He was half-Italian on his mother's side, dark like most Mediterranean men. Though not handsome, his face was memorable, lit by curiosity and intelligence. He had only a half-smile, half amused, half discouraged by the absurdities of life. He brought with him the sharp, invigorating smell of the sea. His skin tasted like salt.

With few preliminaries and little conversation, we became lovers. I felt free when I was with him, untethered, as if I could float on air, or skim across the surface of the sea like the gulls that dipped and soared through blue and gold skies. We met each other without expectations, and left each other without recriminations. We touched each other gently, and did no damage.

Despite the curfew, we often met at night. We had little choice. Patron's schedule had once been unvarying: work from nine to twelve, then a little lunch and a short nap or perhaps a garden stroll, pick up the brush or pen again at two and work until the evening. Now pain made him less predictable. He found his wheelchair confining, and raged against his immobility. Sometimes he would begin drawing at three in the morning, and fall asleep finally at dawn. With Sylvie's help, and the models I hired who would only agree to sit during the day, I managed to stay one step ahead of Matisse's needs. An hour or two either side of midnight were mine.

When I could not go to the market during the day, Matteo and I had a simple signal. From the upper studio in the Regina, I could look down into the monastery gardens. At night, if the household was quiet, I would light a candle and walk the flame to the window. Then I would snuff out the candle, count to one hundred and light the candle again. If, when I stared into the darkness, I saw an answering petal of fire bloom in the garden, I would run to meet it.

Sometimes we would speak only through touch. Other times, we would sneak into the cemetery behind the monastery, hide among the tombstones and talk for hours. The graveyard did not seem macabre to us. It was filled with lost love and loneliness, which both of us knew well. Matteo was an orphan too, his father lost to the treachery of the Mediterranean and his mother to the fevers of influenza. We leaned against marble crosses and angels' wings and compared childhoods, memories worn thin from use, like pieces of shiny cloth rubbed too vigorously and too often.

Matteo had a younger sister and an aunt, much kinder than mine, who made them a home, but he missed his father and never had a doubt that he would earn his living from the sea. He told me once he'd attended the same school as André when they were young boys and that he'd teased him unmercifully when he became Matisse's driver. Matteo and the other village toughs, as they liked to think of themselves, used to pester André for scandalous tales of the Matisse household, but André would just shake his head and turn away. Until one day one of the boys saw Sylvie at the market, made a lewd suggestion about her and found himself on the ground with a bleeding nose.

"That's how we knew André was in love," Matteo told me.

"Did you believe all that nonsense about Matisse?" I asked.

"Of course," Matteo laughed. "I was nineteen. Nude women danced in my head at all hours of the day and night. I would've been bitterly disappointed to think about an elderly gentleman playing with his cats and bouncing his grandson on his knee."

"And now? Do the fishermen of Nice make lewd suggestions about me?"

Matteo squeezed my hand. "The ice princess? Not any more."

He whispered my name over and over, his lips brushing my hair. His fingers trailed across my cheek and down my neck. I felt a sweet, sensual warmth spread through my body, a rushing of blood, not at all like a woman made of ice and snow.

After I left him, slipping noiselessly back into the apartment, the memory of his kiss was perfumed by the violets that filled the little stone vases affixed to the gravestones.

Of course, we could not have met at all without Sylvie who noticed everything, hid my absences as best she could and told no one. Soon after I began meeting Matteo in the garden, she warned me that Matisse was not sleeping, that he was enraged by the slightest disturbance and becoming increasingly moody. She believed that my secret life cast a shadow, however faintly, and that Matisse could see it in the corner of his eye. I believed the only thing Matisse knew for sure was how much he needed me.

I went to his bedroom, sat on the edge of his bed, and kissed his forehead: "Sylvie says you've not eaten your lunch or your supper."

"You know I can't eat when I'm upset."

Silence.

He was waiting for me to tell him something I'd decided not to tell. I sighed and shook my head.

It frightened him a little because I'd never refused him anything before.

Lying in bed, without his glasses, he seemed so vulnerable. The white stubble of his beard suddenly looked to me like a killing frost. Then, without warning, he did something very brave and I remembered why I loved him.

"Go," he ordered. "Go and don't feel guilty."

"And where should I go? Back to my homeland to serve as cannon fodder on the Russian front?"

"I'm a selfish old crank."

"Yes, I know."

"Leave if you know what's good for you."

"I think I'll stay a while longer."

"Saint Lydia," he whispered.

"Please stop that. The lives of saints usually end in martyrdom. I have different plans."

He tried to laugh, but instead made a sound in his throat that went right through me in some deep, wrenching way.

The next day, with the help of Sylvie and André, I wrapped Patron in a blanket and put him in the car, put a panama hat on his head, twisted a wool scarf around his throat and, eventually, settled him on a bench in front of the sea where he could watch the light skate across the waves. It was one of those perfect days with most of the tourists gone and everyone else out for a stroll under the palm trees on the Promenade des Anglais. In the background, we could hear calliope music played from the staticky loudspeaker of an old-fashioned carousel, white horses with painted reins of cotton-candy pink, prancing golden hooves and curling manes.

Sylvie brought an orange out of her pocket and dramatically presented it to Matisse. He clapped his hands, but refused to eat it. Oranges were scarce and he loved to paint them: fat Spanish oranges with their thick dimpled rinds and finer grained blood oranges from the South with their ruby flesh. He was already painting that orange in his mind. He looked at me watching him and we both laughed aloud at how easily I could read his thoughts.

I was glad of that gentle day for months to come.

In November, the Germans swallowed up Vichy, occupying the whole of France. Their Italian allies sailed into the Nice port, newsreel cameras grinding and flashbulbs popping. The world seemed dark in every direction.

The pulse of evil and the unending flight from it eventually turned my life upside down.

The Italians stirred up everything. They were unpredictable. On the one hand, they were content to let the sly little Vichy men continue to run the bureaucracy and do the paper work. On the other hand, they wanted to be seen to be in charge, patrolling the streets, arresting people, reclaiming Nice for Italy. Some of the soldiers, veterans from Mussolini's cruel war in Ethiopia, were hard and arrogant and liked to push people around. Others were boys snatched from farms, small villages, and the slums of Rome. They liked to play football in the streets and take siestas. It was difficult to take them seriously and so easy to make mistakes.

One thing was clear: Nice was becoming a war zone. Along the Mediterranean, Germany was defending three thousand kilometers of coastline. Shells burst in the skies above Cimiez, air sirens shattered the nights. Some mornings we woke to see the tops of palm trees blown off, leaving behind charred and splintered stumps.

Varian Fry, founder of the Emergency Rescue Committee based in New York, wrote letters and sent telegrams from his office in Marseilles. Eventu-

ally he came to the Regina in person and begged Matisse to leave France. Fry was a fair-haired, fair-skinned American with an open American face. He had connections to Eleanor Roosevelt and was responsible for saving many artists, writers, and scientists from the persecution of the Nazis. I liked him. I liked his freckles and his optimism, but eventually he gave up and stopped coming.

I never forgot his last day at the studio in the Regina. The drawings for Thèmes et Variations *were pinned up on the walls in five rows from floor to ceiling. There were over a hundred of them: sketches of flowers spilling from vases, sketches of faces, dreamy and pensive, with sensuous lines of spiraling hair. Some of the faces were mine. Fry stared at them for a long time and then bowed his head. As I walked him back to the train station, he was very quiet.*

"Mademoiselle," he finally said. "I have come to accept that your old friend will not leave Nice. I have done my best for him. But those drawings I saw—they are the only human consolation we have in the life of horror that surrounds us. It saddens me to think of them turned to ashes. Perhaps you will do your best for them." He tugged the brim of his hat, stepped up into the train and was gone.

He was right, of course. It was too dangerous to stay in the Regina any longer. It was up to me to find a safer place for Matisse. It was up to me to leave Matteo.

We met in a little restaurant off the port. With its arched stone walls and dim pools of light, it made me think of a secret cavern, perhaps the hiding place of saints or thieves. I told Matteo what Varian Fry had said. I told him I would write to Matisse's old friend, André Rouveyre, and ask him to find us a house in the countryside.

"When will you go?" Matteo asked, no emotion evident in his voice.

"As soon as we can. As soon as the summer, perhaps. Matisse is too frail to risk a winter move."

"Then we must make the best of the time left to us."

I was hurt, disappointed that he would do so little to try to keep me from going.

"Lydia," he whispered, leaning across the table and stroking my hair. "Why are you sad? You know you must leave. I've known this too, for a long time."

"How did you know? How could you know before me?" I asked.

He shrugged. "In time, Mussolini and his Blackshirts will falter and fall to bigger wolves. In the meantime, the Italians are not all fools. Matisse has already been linked to Louis Aragon. They watch him, and the watchers are moving closer. In the meantime, the most urgent threat comes from those who share the Matisse name."

"I don't know what you mean. What are you saying, Matteo?"

His voice was so low, I had to strain to hear him.

"Jean Matisse. We know he is liaising with British Intelligence. Some say he travels around the South with a suitcase of dynamite for blowing up bridges. He hides explosives in his statues."

I was shocked, shocked and frightened. I scarcely knew Matisse's youngest son. He was a sculptor, I'd been told, with a studio in Antibes. I trembled to think what the authorities could do with such knowledge. They would have Matisse at their mercy. They would be able to make him do anything, say anything, give them anything. I couldn't believe Jean's carelessness. "How do you know these things?" I murmured.

Matteo didn't answer, just gave me his half-smile.

I felt a moment of dreadful foreboding. I felt old, suddenly ancient, though I was barely thirty. I wanted to slap Matteo. I wanted to tell him that since I was twelve years old I'd known there was no romance in war, just bodies cut in half by bullets, bones snapped, hearts ripped open. I'd watched my beloved father try to sew together those fragments of bodies until he was so exhausted that disease swept him away.

"What you and your friends are doing, Matteo, will it really change anything?"

"Maybe, maybe not. But if I don't do anything, it will change me."

I searched for words that might shake some sense into him, but found none. One look in his eyes and I knew he couldn't be persuaded. He wouldn't run from danger.

"Meet me in the garden later tonight?" I asked.

"I'll try," he answered.

Hours later, I lit my candle and looked out the window of the upper studio, but there was no answering flame. I let the blackout curtain fall back into place and put out the candle. Smoke from the snuffed wick *lingered in the air. It carried the scent of sorrow.*

In the morning, I wrote my letter to André Rouveyre asking him to find a new home for his old friend.

I also wrote a letter to Marguerite.

She'd been staying in Cannes, close enough to reach Matisse quickly if his health failed, far enough away to avoid seeing me. She'd sent her son, little Claude, to her brother Pierre and his family in America to be safe. I guessed she was probably lonely. She would be too curious not to come.

Her reply was as stiff as the notepaper she wrote it on. She would not be summoned. Instead she named a day of her own choosing to visit her father. If there was time at the end of her visit, if she were not too tired, she would speak with me for a moment or two.

All that anger still smoldering away. All that pride. It just made me feel tired.

Patron, of course, was delighted. Of all his children, I suspect he loved Marguerite the best. He wore his finest tailored waistcoat and a tie for her visit.

When she stepped into the studio, I heard her exclaim from my hiding place in the hallway. She had never seen how magical the studio looked with the sunlight pouring in, the colours alive, the lacy shadows on the floor cast by the Moroccan curtains. She'd always been an honest critic, sometimes as brutal as any Paris lampooner, but Sylvie told me she had only praise for the fluid beauty of the drawings. When she and Matisse finished their tea, she stepped into the hallway and motioned me to her side.

"You wanted to speak to me? Very well, what is it you wish to say?" She held her head up, her black hair curled around her pale face, and even though I was taller, she managed to convey the impression of looking down at me.

I wasted no time on the niceties of conversation. Neither of us cared, and formality was a waste of time. I blurted out everything I'd learned about Jean and his dangerous statuary. I begged her to speak to him, to try to intercede for her father's sake.

Her eyes took sharp little bites at me the whole time I was talking, but she said nothing until I was finished.

"You are a far greater danger to my father than Jean. You and your Communist friends."

"I suppose you mean Louis Aragon. He was summoned here by Matisse himself to write a preface for the book of drawings, but if you truly believe I'm a threat, I will leave. My suitcase is already packed."

Her eyes widened, and she looked away from me quickly. She needed me. I represented her freedom. Without me, the care and the succor of the frail, moody genius that was her father would fall to her.

"I'll ask Jean to be more careful," she conceded, "for his own sake."

"Thank you."

We walked together to the front door without talking, then she turned to me. "The drawings are magnificent. They surprised me. Perhaps I was wrong about him being tired. But you do too much for him. The studio, the way you anticipate his every need, it's all unhealthy. You overindulge him."

I smiled at her, the first truly felt smile I'd given her in a long time. I knew this was the best she could do, the closest she could come to accepting me.

I had one more task before I could sleep at night. I had to get the drawings safely to Louis for publication. Then he would have no further need to visit Cimiez. I wrote the note in Russian so only Louis would know what it said and set out early the next morning for the Cours Saleya.

The dawn was chilly and crisp and I pulled my shawl tightly around me. By the time I reached the market, people were already milling about. Food was becoming scarce and shoppers lined up early for meat, butter, and cheese. I strolled about for a while, edging closer and closer to one particular stall. Louis had given me careful instructions to follow should I ever need him.

Two Italian soldiers, rifles over their shoulders, were strolling up and down the length of the market street. One of them caught my eye and winked.

I panicked, veered away from him and walked off in the opposite direction. This was exactly the wrong way to behave, I knew. My sudden movement would only draw the soldier's attention to me.

My note felt like a grenade in my empty basket. I wondered whatever possessed me to write it in Russian. I would be arrested as a spy.

I went around the stalls and began filling up my basket. A big floury loaf from the baker's stall, aubergines with their purple-black skins, a couple of melons. When I had enough courage, I looked around for the soldiers and breathed again. They seemed to be gone.

I approached the stall with the blue and white striped awning, pretending to look at some potatoes.

"Bonjour, mademoiselle," the farmer said. His voice was pleasant, his eyes bright behind a scrawl of cigarette smoke.

I observed him warily, not daring to move, unsure whether or not he was the right contact. "The ... the harvest is spare," I stammered.

"Better in years to come," the man replied. His eyes narrowed and he gave me a slight but encouraging nod.

I groped around in the basket until my fingers found the message. I pulled it out and buried it among the potatoes.

"Come back in two days." The farmer's voice was low, his face turned away from mine. "Go now."

So easy. My heart was beating hard, but it had been so easy to pass the message. I felt exhilarated. I turned away from the stall, very casually, my basket swinging from my arm.

Then I froze. From across the square, one of the Italians was watching me. He was standing by a fountain, slouching a little, a cigarette cupped into his palm. The market goers skirted around him, not wanting to come too close, like children at the zoo watching some dangerous animal. He stood in a circle of stillness, his eyes fixed upon me. He must have seen me pass the message. He could hardly have missed it.

For a moment I stared at him, unable to move. I felt the blood drain from my face as my mind skirted off in several directions at once. Marguerite was right, I'd put Matisse in terrible jeopardy. I'd be sent to prison. The soldiers would search the studio. Perhaps they'd even arrest Sylvie. Oh God, Sylvie.

He was watching me still. Then he flicked his cigarette to the ground and smiled at me, shaking his head. As he walked away, I could see his shoulders moving up and down as if he were laughing.

My legs were trembling so badly I was sure people would notice, but they were preoccupied with their own business. I dared not look back at the farmer.

As soon as I felt able, I fled the market square and almost ran through the narrow streets of Vieux Nice to Place St-François. Matteo was still there, packing up his fish stall, throwing scraps to a dozen ragged eared cats twisting themselves sinuously around his legs. He glanced up at the sound of my footsteps and with his usual acuity read my expression and my flushed complexion in a moment.

"Come," he said. "I know a little café where old fishermen meet. A pretty face will brighten their day."

It was a tiny place, squeezed between two other buildings, facing the port. An Italian warship was moored there. Italian flags flew from the masts of a dozen fishing boats. There was no proper door, just row upon row of stringed beads suspended vertically from the top of the door frame to the wooden floor.

Even at eleven in the morning, it was shadowy and smoky inside. There was a small bar, a row of bottles and glasses hanging on hooks, an abandoned and weathered fish net nailed up on one wall. A man in an apron waved to Matteo and gave me a smile.

A trio of men who'd been playing cards at a corner table looked up to study me. They had faces leathered by the sun, and two of them wore caps pulled down over hairy ears, while the third had a stub of a pipe jammed between his lips. I could smell the tobacco smoke, heavily laced with dandelion leaves these days, and the smell of chicory coffee. They ducked their heads at me. I was okay. I was with Matteo.

I was introduced to the bar man, Jean-Marie Dupré, another of Matteo's old school chums who brought me a little glass of pastis and a carafe of water. I picked up the glass and swallowed, fire blazing down my throat. After thoroughly enjoying my sputtering, the two friends poured water into the clear liquid pastis that instantly rendered it opaque and slightly less lethal. I felt warmed, my limbs weightless.

Around noon, Jean-Marie brought us omelettes, fragrant with herbs and thick with potato slices, slightly crisped around the edges.

In that moment, everything about Matteo seemed perfect, the way his collarbone rose above the rounded neck of his sweater. The way he held his glass, his fingers long and thin. The way he chewed his food and tossed off jokes with his friends. The way he took me as I was without a single question about where I'd been or what I'd done.

But we were learning, all of us, that happiness was meted out in moments only. The beads rattled, yanked back roughly. An Italian soldier stepped into the bar. Backlit by the sun, he stood in the doorway like a block of darkness.

I heard grumbling from the corner table where the three men had been playing cards. They'd drunk rather a lot at this stage. There was little else for them to do. The hours and the places they were allowed to fish were severely restricted. The grumbling rose to a low snarl.

The soldier turned in their direction, squeezing his eyes to focus better. He may not have understood the French swear words, but he recognized the tone. He was heavy, a veteran soldier. He looked coolly at the card players for a moment before turning to Jean-Marie. He ordered a glass of wine.

It happened again, a second later. The man with the pipe swore at the soldier. Maudit bâtard. And this time, Matteo and I saw the hand of the soldier going to the belt where he kept his pistol. The old man glowered back at the Italian, his pipe jutting out between his yellow teeth like the barrel of a gun.

For a moment, the tension between them was paralyzing. I saw Matteo make a movement towards Jean-Marie and a silent exchange passed across their faces. Then Matteo stepped forward, almost casually, started speaking Italian to the soldier, while Jean-Marie maneuvered the old fisherman out of harm's way. I don't know what Matteo said, but he and his friend saved two lives that day. The soldier would have shot the fisherman, or arrested him, and if he had, he would never have left the bar alive. I knew this as surely as if it were a set of facts written down in black and white for me to read.

When the Italian soldier got to the doorway, he flung Matteo's arm off his shoulder and yelled towards the group at the back: "Fottiti. Fottiti." He thundered off into the street, leaving the beads shaking crazily behind him.

There was a moment of utter stillness, a moment to think about what might have happened.

Finally, Jean-Marie said, "So what does that mean, Matteo? Fottiti?"

"It's an old Italian saying," he replied, the half-smile back. "It means 'Fuck you'."

We collapsed with laughter.

I returned to the potato farmer's stall with the blue and white striped awning two days later to collect a message from Louis. He would come personally to collect the sketches, they were far too precious to leave to the precarious mails, and, yes, he understood it was too risky to approach Matisse directly. I was to meet him at the train station to deliver the package of drawings.

Matteo was furious. "This is madness," he seethed. "The worst communists are the intelligentsia, living in the skies, philosophizing. He'll get you arrested yet. At least let me come. Jean-Marie, maybe André too. We can distract the guards."

But I trusted Louis. I wanted to believe that he could ride a train in Occupied France anywhere he liked, whenever he wished, a dark romantic hero outwitting the enemy. I hoped that Matteo's overreaction was jealousy.

In the end, I went to the station alone at one-thirty in the afternoon with a thick package of drawings wrapped in brown paper under my arm. I could see Matteo pretending to read Nice-Matin at a café table, but I ignored him. I bought a return ticket to Cannes that I would never use and lingered on the platform.

Two French thugs, Milice, were patrolling the far end of the platform. The Milice were Pétain's paramilitary police and most people feared them more than the Italian soldiers. They began stopping people, inspecting their papers. I walked a little further away from them. Every step I took felt like a step further out onto a sheet of ice.

A local train pulled in. Passengers began disembarking from the right side of the train. All the passengers remaining on board also moved to the right side of the train, leaning out through the open windows to buy drinks and sandwiches from merchants with push carts who suddenly materialized on the platform. Arms reached out with money, arms reached up with cups of tea or glasses of water or oily sardines slapped between bread. People shouted, "bonjour!" "Ça va?" "Combien?" "Une baguette, s'il vous plait."

The train groaned and hissed. The Milice were swallowed up in the bustle and confusion.

Louis didn't even need to show his face. I heard his low whistle through the cacophony of voices and looked for his elegant hands jutting out from his fine black coat. I placed the package in his hands, watched it disappear as if by some clever magic trick. Then he was gone, no doubt back to some hiding place, some secret compartment on the train where neither the Milice nor the Italians would find him.

When I returned to the square outside the train station, André was waiting in Matisse's old coupe sedan. Driving the car was an extravagance—if not for Matisse's name and frailty, the household would not have been allowed to keep the car. As it was, gas was severely rationed. My face showed my surprise, but André just shrugged and opened the door for me.

Matteo was waiting in the back seat. "We thought we might need a quick getaway," he explained. He wrapped his arms around me as tight as I had ever wanted to be held.

I was so happy, I pretended not to see the Luger pistol he'd shoved underneath a cushion.

When we arrived back in Cimiez—André had chosen a deliberately circuitous route and I was very late—Sylvie met me at the door, her eyes dancing. "You're missing all the fun," she whispered, and without telling me any more, put a tea tray in my hands and pushed me in the direction of the sitting room.

It was old Rouveyre, Matisse's friend since their student days together at Gustave Moreau's studio in Paris. He was old and bent now, but in his youth he had a scandalous reputation as a womanizer, much of it, I suspected, spun from his imagination. He rose when I entered the room and bowed dramatically. Matisse's laugh was like a bass rumbling inside a bear.

"Lydia, Lydia. Leave this old curmudgeon and come live with me," Rouveyre teased. "He has nothing to give you but paint. But I can give you poetry."

"Then you must need someone to type it for you," I replied shrewdly. It was well known that Rouveyre had spent years on a trilogy of autobiographical novels that he freely admitted were almost unreadable. Poetry was beyond him.

"Ah, you wound. I shall remain a solitary recluse brooding at the back of dark caverns while you languish in the brilliance of this studio."

"I don't languish, Rouveyre. I clean the paintbrushes."

"Matisse tells me you do much more," he paused here and wiggled his eyebrows like a lecher in a farce. "He tells me this to make me jealous. You can't possibly be so beautiful and so accomplished at the same time."

I glanced over at Patron who was enjoying himself hugely. "She's very handy, Rouveyre. I'd be reluctant to part with her."

"Please," I said, glaring at Matisse. "Don't praise me so much. I'll be ruined." Then I turned my attention back to Rouveyre. "Very well, I accept your challenge. Set me a task and we'll see how good a teacher Patron has been."

Rouveyre thought for a moment, wisps of his gray hair spilling over his collar. He looked every inch a hermit or a monk, dressed entirely in black. "I have it," he announced, fixing me in a schoolmaster's gaze. "Recite the colour theory of Goethe."

"In German, French, or Russian?" I replied.

My bluff left Rouveyre speechless for once. I poured the two friends their tea and left them to their memories of their younger, simpler student days. It was a healing nostalgia. It papered over the cracks of old age—infirmities, ailments, despondency, and fear.

An hour or so later, I helped Rouveyre into his coat.

"It was kind of you to come," I said. "Travel, even a short distance, isn't pleasant these days. He's just finished a project. Soon he'll be restless."

Rouveyre often acted the fool, but was far from foolish. "I got your letter. I'm having some agents look for houses higher up in the hills behind Nice, somewhere he might still be able to glimpse the Med. I'll be in touch. In the meantime, I've put it into his head that he should read some love poetry. I meant it as a bit of a joke, but, who knows, something may come of it."

December was bitter. Snow dusted the higher reaches of Cimiez. But roses bloomed in Matisse's studio. Every day I read aloud the love verses of Charles d'Orleans and Pierre de Ronsard, my tongue tracing their voluptuous imagery, my voice lifting and falling to their rhythms. I dreamed of Matteo, while Matisse sketched me, naked but for the flowers that spilled across my torso and down one leg to my knee. One of my breasts became a rose.

Perhaps it was the poetry, but one day Sylvie came in to sit with us.

"André and I are getting married," she announced.

Matisse celebrated New Year's Day, 1943, by phoning his doctors to say he had been free from pain and fever for almost two months. However, he was still not strong enough to get up for more than a couple of hours a day, and by the spring, he had developed a cough so violent I thought his ribs would shatter.

He was too frail to be left alone and soon Sylvie and I were exhausted. I *put an ad in the* Nice-Matin *and hired two nurses, one for day and one for night. Sylvie and I could breathe again.*

"You treat him like a crystal vase," Matteo grumbled on the few occasions I could arrange to see him.

"Yes," I agreed. "He's very breakable. But he wants to do something special for Sylvie and André for their wedding present. He wants to paint her portrait, and for that he must get stronger."

Matteo forgot his resentment in a moment, impressed by Matisse's generosity. I laughed and laid my head on his shoulder: "Patron's like that," I said. "Just when you think you'd like to poison his tea or send him crashing down the stairs, he does something remarkable."

We were snuggling under a blanket in the Cimiez cemetery, for despite the warm days of May, the nights were still cool.

"Do you really think about pushing him down the stairs?" Matteo wondered.

"Of course. Sometimes I'm enraged at how much he asks of me. Get this, stand here, be quicker, be smarter. Endless orders, barely a word of thanks for days on end. But my anger never lasts beyond a walk in the garden, or the time it takes to smoke a cigarette. He always wins me back."

"How, Lydia? How does he win you?"

I counted off the ways on my fingers: "He is a gentleman. He has a sweet smile. I can't bear to see him suffer. And I always remember in time that he must hate me a little because I've seen him at his weakest, his most vulnerable. I keep a packed suitcase in my bedroom just in case he pushes me too far. I can leave at a moment's notice."

"Then leave." Matteo turned to face me, our foreheads touching under the blanket. His fingers traced the shape of my lips. "Marry me and unpack your suitcase for good."

I could feel his breath on my skin. The love I felt for him rose up into my throat and blocked the air. For what seemed a long time but could not have been a whole minute, we neither moved nor spoke.

I felt as if anything could happen. As if I could open a door and step into a normal life. Or plunge off a cliff.

"I have to go back now," I whispered.

Matteo walked me to the edge of the garden. The darkness of the blackout night was so impenetrable I could barely see his face. "I won't ask you to choose," he promised. "I'll wait if I have to."

I wrapped his words around me like a cloak. I heard them again and again, as if in a dream.

When I entered Matisse's bedroom, I found him asleep, one hand flung out over the bedclothes as if in silent entreaty. I sat down quietly in a chair by his bedside and felt the dream recede like a slow, whispering tide.

The old women of Cimiez walked their dogs every day. They wore black coats, regardless of the weather, though on very hot summer days I had sometimes caught them going about with only sweaters on. They disapproved of me heartily and muttered to their pets as I passed by.

I was just returning from posting a packet of Matisse's letters when I saw Sylvie running toward me.

"Lydia!" Sylvie panted, her cheeks flushed. "Come quickly."

Immediately, I thought of Patron and my heart flipped over.

"Come," Sylvie repeated, grabbing a hand and pulling me. "It's Matteo. Something dreadful has happened to his sister. He's waiting for you in the olive grove."

I thought of a dozen different things at once. It was just after midday, dangerous to run, dangerous for Matteo to travel all the way from the port to Cimiez. In February, the puppet Vichy government had passed a law to send able-bodied French men to Germany to work in the enemy's factories. Matteo and most of his mates, including André, were trying to keep a low profile. I forced Sylvie to slow down.

I thought about Matteo's sister, Lucie. Apart from his aging aunt, she was his whole family. She was one half of his childhood, one half of his memory of his father and mother. He didn't need to think or talk about loving her. Her face was imprinted on his soul.

I said goodbye to Sylvie and walked into the Cimiez garden. The silvery-green leaves of the olive trees twisted slowly in the soft May wind. Matteo was sitting on a bench, his head bent over his knees as if he were ill with sadness.

He jumped to his feet when he heard my approach. "Lydia," he said, his voice overflowing with relief. "I thought you'd never get here."

His fingers brushed my shoulder as I sat down, and even in that slight touch I could feel his desperation. I let my shawl slide down my arms and held his hand tightly underneath it. "Lucie has been injured?" I asked.

"No. Yes. Worse."

I waited and looked straight ahead. I knew the news would be terrible if Matteo had to search for words, struggle to make sense.

Finally, he began again, his voice tight, his tone bitter. "Lucie was attacked. Three soldiers. It was just past dawn and she was on her way to mass. I was fishing. It is my duty to protect her, yet she was all alone. Neighbours found her in an alley and carried her home to my aunt."

I closed my eyes, but I could not stop the sound of his voice, the agony in it.

"They were drunk, probably had been drinking all night. They threw her down on the pavement, held her down. They passed her around. They—"

"Stop it," I interrupted. "Don't think of them. Think of Lucie. What does she need from you right now?"

"She needs me to kill them."

"No, you need to kill them. Lucie needs you to love her just as you did before. Be her brother. Have you taken her to see a doctor? Have you reported these soldiers to the Italian authorities?"

Matteo held up a hand to silence me. "My aunt revealed all of this to me this morning. Lucie is too ashamed to talk to me. I see the attack over and over in my mind as if it were happening now and I've told you the story this way. But, Lydia, the attack happened nine weeks ago. Lucie is pregnant."

I turned to look at him then, saw his eyes filled with fear. He knew what the pregnancy would do, was already doing to Lucie. She would relive the rape with every breath until her soul was corroded. She would probably never marry, her future ruined at seventeen. But what were the alternatives?

Under Vichy law, abortion was punishable by death.

"Take me with you," I said. "Down to the port. There's someone I need to find."

Some people have a quality that marks them as clearly as a scar or a birthmark. I found my old boarding house, unchanged down to its sheets, and from there a few guarded questions led me to a doctor who'd once dug a bullet out of a desperate woman. Michel Clairmont. I recognized in him the quality of kindness. He recognized my face. He agreed to meet me later that day at Jean-Marie's café.

Matteo and I both rose from our chairs when the doctor entered. His face registered no surprise that I wasn't alone. He waved aside the offer of a drink and sat down, his hands folded on the table before him.

"Tell me," Clairmont said.

Matteo's voice was barely above a whisper. It went on and on as I watched the doctor's face pale, his shoulders droop.

I realized as I studied him that Clairmont could not be much older than me. Exhaustion had aged him prematurely, just as it had aged my father. Wartime is a bad time to be a doctor. Only the alertness of his blue eyes, surprising under his black hair, betrayed his true age.

"I can't help you," he sighed. "You know the punishment should we be caught. How can you even ask such a thing?"

"How can we not?" I replied. "She's seventeen. She's been torn apart. She wishes she were dead. Without you, she'll be driven to find some old woman with a pair of rusty spoons."

Clairmont blanched. The knuckles on his hands grew white. Matteo leaned forward as if to speak and I kicked him under the table to stop his words. I knew that in those moments of silence the doctor was already imagining some dingy room, an innocent girl writhing in pain, bloody sheets. I knew that once he had looked upon Lucie's pitiable fate, he would not be able to turn us away.

"Bring her tomorrow, mid-afternoon," he said, looking straight at me. He reached into his jacket pocket for paper and pencil, scribbled an address, pushed it toward me. "You know where this is?"

I read the words quickly and nodded. A street just off Place Masséna.

Clairmont screwed up the paper, lit a cigarette, used the match to burn the paper in an ashtray. "Just you and the girl."

Matteo protested and the doctor cut off his words. "These are my terms. Vichy's pact with the devil makes a young man on the street suspect—the Milice are looking for workers to send to Germany and I don't want you catching their attention, understood?"

Matteo had no choice but to agree, but I could see his frustration. He blamed himself for not being able to protect Lucie, and guilt lay like lead in his chest. Like most men, he sought a cure in action.

When the doctor left, I took Matteo's hand and promised him I would let no harm come to Lucie while she was in my care. He nodded and squeezed my hand, but I could tell he was elsewhere. His sense of helplessness was eating him alive.

We ordered pastis from Jean-Marie and sat staring into our glasses. We were both shaken. I could guess what horror was replaying itself in Matteo's mind. For my own part, I wondered if France still used the guillotine for state executions. We finished our drinks and walked like ghosts out into the still bright afternoon.

When I returned to the Regina, Sylvie was waiting anxiously. I made a sign to reassure her and she left me to prepare Patron's dinner. He was sitting by the window, a cat in his lap. I was surprised that he didn't greet me when I entered the room—his manners were usually impeccable. I took a chair beside him, thinking perhaps he was dozing, but he began to talk to me almost at once. His voice sounded old and wavery and he had to repeat his words several times. I leaned my ear almost to his lips.

"Marguerite and Jean," he managed to say. "They've joined the fight."

Nobody knew more about Matisse than me. I knew every mood he had and how long it would last. I knew how he moved, what he feared, and who he loved. He was frightened for his children.

The Resistance, no more than a whisper at the beginning of the war, was growing into a shout. People were weary of the Occupation. They were weary of living so meanly, everything broken down, worn-out, used up. Black soap that abraded the skin. Bitter chicory instead of rich coffee. Never quite enough food. And the cynical view? Well, the Resistance was more romantic than withering away in the munitions factories of Germany.

I put my hand on Patron's arm, but remained silent. I'd done my best. I'd asked Marguerite to warn Jean to be cautious for the old man's sake and she'd responded by returning to Paris and joining the Resistance herself. I knew what would be next. Madame, never one to be left in the rear guard, would soon join her children. Perhaps it was uncharitable of me, but I couldn't help thinking that Madame, ever astute, saw that the Germans were not as invincible as once feared and wished to jump to the winning side before it was too late.

"Did you know, Lydia, that Marguerite was quite ill as a child? A problem with her breathing, but she fought back. She's quite strong now."

Yes, I thought, strong and as terrifyingly single-minded as her father. Yet I couldn't condemn her without condemning myself. The next day, I would risk my life for Matteo and his sister, and in so doing I would knowingly put Matisse in danger. The authorities would surely seek to manipulate my arrest to their advantage. Would they demand paintings? Would they demand some kind of public support for Vichy's shameful collaboration? Even if they left the old man alone, who would care for him as I could?

I felt Patron's hand patting mine. "You look quite shaken, Lydia. I'm sure Marguerite will survive this, too."

I smiled at him to cover my shame. I was more concerned about my own survival than Marguerite's.

Later, after Matisse had settled in for the night, Sylvie and I took a walk. The Cimiez gardens were fragrant and dark green, almost black in the shadows.

Sylvie was appalled by Lucie's story and wept when she heard it. "So much cruelty," she sighed. "I don't think the world will ever heal from it. I'm coming with you, tomorrow. I can keep watch."

She turned to me, her eyes looking deeply into mine, silently communicating words that women have said to each other for centuries, words about violation and survival and healing. Any objection I might have made died on my lips.

Lucie was a dark-haired Madonna with a Renaissance face, pensive eyes, a rosebud mouth, a cross on a chain at the hollow of her throat. She met me in the doorway of her home, a set of humble rooms on the ground floor of an older building that might once have housed administrative offices. Over her shoulder, I caught a glimpse of a white-haired woman, Matteo's aunt, whose profile was of chiseled stone like the sad angels in the Cimiez cemetery. I saw no trace of Matteo.

Sylvie met us at the end of the narrow street. She gave Lucie an encouraging smile and took her hand. For all the danger she was facing, Sylvie's step was light and confident, the confidence of a woman who'd never faltered, never failed anyone who needed her.

We walked along the seafront towards the Hotel Négresco, flamboyantly pink and white and gold, the undisputed queen of the Promenade des Anglais. But Lucie hardly glanced at it, her face turned to the sea. Thunder rumbled in the distance. Flashes of heat lightning lit up the horizon far out over the purple bay.

A few blocks behind the Négresco, the Place Masséna was quiet in the heavy, sleepy stillness of mid-afternoon. The open square was lined with stately arcaded buildings rendered in startling, deepest red. I remembered how Masséna had looked before the war: bustling, thick with traffic, outdoor cafes, and shoppers. Now the cars had disappeared. A few late shoppers bicycled by the café tables where Italian soldiers sat writing postcards home to Turin or Padua. They looked hot and itchy in their uniforms.

We crossed the square to a small street that slanted off to the north. I'd looked it up on a street map the night before. No hesitation. No asking directions of strangers. It was a plain wooden door, painted yellow, squeezed between a hairdresser's on the right and a patisserie on the left, both closed for the midday siesta.

Above us, laundry was strung across the narrow gap between buildings, casting the street in shade.

"I'll stay here," Sylvie said. "I'll watch the square."

I nodded and tried the door. It opened easily. We climbed up a staircase, steps that dipped a little and creaked with age. Apartment 2B. The room was cramped, but had a tall window letting in plenty of light. The sheets on the bed were pristine, and someone—the doctor?—had left out clean towels. While Lucie went into the bathroom to undress, I looked back down at the street, saw Sylvie speaking with the doctor.

"He's here, Lucie," I said, turning back to the young woman. "It will soon be over."

Lucie's eyes, staring back, were enormous. Her skin was whiter than the sheet she'd wrapped around herself. Her hands trembled, she tried to hold them down in her lap.

I went to her, sat with her on the bed. She put her arms around my neck and buried her face in my hair crying like a rainstorm. I held her. She was so thin, it was like holding a bird fallen from its nest.

When Clairmont entered the room, she pulled away from me, one hand clutching the cross around her throat.

She was Catholic. I felt a flash of anger at myself for overlooking something so obvious. I'd thought she was dreading pain. I realized she was dreading the damnation of a mortal sin.

I gripped her hand, shook it free from the cross. "There's only forgiveness, Lucie. Not punishment."

She looked bewildered at first, then seemed to understand what I was trying to say. "I can't not," she whispered. "I can't not do it."

"I know."

Behind me, the doctor had washed his hands and prepared his instruments. He stepped toward Lucie, his eyes filled with compassion, a hypodermic needle in his hand. "This will relax you. You understand I can't use an anesthetic? Those drugs are scarce and can easily be traced."

"I understand," Lucie replied.

Clairmont looked at me. "Give her that towel, please. She can bite down on it." Then he turned back to Lucie. "I'll be as quick as I can. I'm sorry. You mustn't scream."

He placed his hand gently on her forehead, brushing back her dark hair, then gave her the injection. She smiled up at him with the trust of a child.

We waited for ten minutes in utter silence, locked together in the same purpose, the same agonizing tension. Then, almost imperceptibly, Lucie nodded.

I took Clairmont's place at the head of the bed, squeezed Lucie's hand tightly while he lifted the sheet.

A moment later, her face contorted with a pain so pure it made me want to cry out, but Lucie made not the slightest sound.

I pressed my free hand to the side of her cheek, wiped away the sweat that had broken out on her forehead, stared into her wide gray eyes.

The pain went on and on in relentless waves. It seemed to last forever.

Finally I heard the doctor whisper as he stepped away from the bed, "It's over."

Lucie's body relaxed, her head rolled to one side. She reached up to her throat and pulled off the cross, letting it fall onto the bed sheet.

I drifted over to the window, shaken by Lucie's ordeal, and leaned my forehead on the window frame.

Sylvie was standing at the very top of the street we'd entered. She was quite motionless, transfixed, staring ahead into the square. I could not follow her gaze, but there was no mistaking her absolute intentness even at this distance.

My heart began pounding. I looked back at Lucie. Her eyes were still closed, her breathing deep.

Clairmont was cleaning his instruments, replacing them in his bag. I took his hand, held my finger to my lips as his head jerked up in surprise. I led him to the window just in time to see Sylvie spin around and race towards us. An instant later, we heard her steps on the stairs.

And an instant after that, heavier steps behind her.

I was paralyzed, unable to move, to think, to breathe.

"Get her dressed," the doctor hissed. "There's a way out, through the courtyard to an adjacent street. Hurry."

The door burst open. Sylvie tumbled into the room. "Milice!" she panted.

Immediately behind her was a shapeless woman with a kerchief around her head, swathed in shawls and a patched skirt that fell to her ankles. She called out, "Lucie!"

I recognized the voice. It was Matteo. Matteo dressed as a woman.

He crossed the room in two long strides and picked up Lucie in his arms. "Help me, Lydia!"

The urgency in his voice was the slap I needed. I rushed forward, stuffed the sheet around Lucie's body. Her eyes were wide with terror.

Matteo was already moving out the door. I looked back at Sylvie. She thrust the doctor's bag and Lucie's clothes into my hands and pushed me away. "Go," she snapped and shut the door in my face.

I stumbled after Matteo and Lucie in a daze. At the bottom of the stairs we found the hallway that led to the back entrance and the courtyard. We ran across it, grass and flowers nothing but a greenish blur. Then through a high gate, and finally the pavement of a parallel street.

An old man in a shiny black suit, faded medals pinned to his lapel, skidded to a stop beside us. His mouth fell open.

"Please," I begged.

He turned away. Matteo set Lucie on the ground and I helped her dress. She was bleeding, but not too badly. It was shock and pain that made her weak.

Matteo folded up the sheet and tucked it under his skirt. We set out for the port, deliberately avoiding Place Masséna, one of us on each side of Lucie, willing her to walk, lifting her when we could, dragging her when we couldn't, step after painful step.

When we reached the Promenade des Anglais, we had to stop. Even the tourists were staring at us. We were a mad-looking trio: a woman with a pronounced Adam's apple wearing a head scarf in May weather, a dark-haired girl with eyes that stared out of dark hollows, a blonde foreigner carrying what looked like a doctor's bag. We found a cheap fish restaurant and ordered a meal, though none of us could eat a bite.

I opened the doctor's bag and looked for something to ease Lucie's pain, finally recognizing a bottle of the sort that used to stand in Matisse's bathroom cupboard. Morphine. I pressed a pill into her hand and she swallowed it hungrily. A few minutes later, Matteo rose and wandered off to the toilets. If anyone noticed that he returned to the table as a man, they didn't seem to care. We stayed for a long time with barely a word spoken among us.

At one point, Lucie began to cry silently. Matteo put an arm around her and kissed her forehead. Everywhere I looked I saw Sylvie's face. Sylvie arrested, Sylvie shot. When I closed my eyes, I saw Clairmont's gentle hands and the compassion in his eyes.

When we finally left, the moon was coming up and the sky was mother-of-pearl like the inside of a shell. The sea for once was quiet, with silvery ripples barely moving.

Matteo's aunt helped me put Lucie to bed. I gave her another pill. Let her have one good long sleep, I thought, before she has to wake up and remember everything for the rest of her life.

Matteo pressed me to stay, but I would not. "The curfew," he said. "Please don't be foolish."

"Matisse is alone," I replied, though I knew in my heart he was just an *excuse. There were nurses to care for him. I could have stayed, but I needed to go, to think about Sylvie and, if she were still alive, what might be done to save her.*

I was surprised to see anger flare in Matteo's eyes. "It's always Matisse, isn't it?"

"Not always. Not today." I was sorry the moment the words fell from my mouth.

Matteo turned and left the room, left me with a feeling of hollowness around my heart.

I began the long climb back to Cimiez, skirting lights, clinging to shadows. My body felt heavy and clumsy. I dragged along with me a sense of ruin, my mouth tasted of ashes.

When I opened the door to the apartment, I was tempted to simply lie down on the smooth, cool floor of the hallway and go to sleep, perhaps forever. But instead, when I closed the door behind me, I felt wide awake, very alert as if the silence of the still half-empty building had cleared my head. There was a charged atmosphere in spite of the stillness, like something was waiting to happen.

Did I hear her step before I heard her voice? I can't remember. Confusion, relief, elation rushed over me like the waters of a flood. Sylvie's voice, resonant, as if in a dream. "Are you alright, Lydia? Is Lucie safe?"

I hugged her. I tried to tell her half a dozen things at once and broke off, coughing, but laughing at the same time. "How on earth? How did you get away?"

Having found each other, we felt reckless, delirious with relief. We giggled down the hall like school girls, locked ourselves in my room, lit Gauloises, and poured vodka.

I made her tell me the story again and again. How she had stripped down to her slip, tugging at the same time at the doctor's pants. How they had hopped and lurched their way across the room, finally collapsing on the bed. The shock of the Milice as they smashed through the door to find two half-naked people in a passionate embrace.

It all seemed wildly comic in the retelling, but it was terror that made the performance so convincing while it was unfolding. "We were acting for our lives," Sylvie told me. "Clairmont rented the apartment several months ago, and he's been using it to patch up men from the underground. He thinks someone in the building grew suspicious and reported him. I was hardly what the Milice were expecting."

"So Clairmont is safe? No longer suspected?" I asked.

Sylvie nodded. "They think Clairmont was merely using the apartment for secret assignations with women. If anything, they rather envied him. They didn't even ask to see my papers. Apparently, they'd seen enough of me."

Laughing again, we flopped down together on the bed and stared at the ceiling. Then Sylvie flipped onto her stomach, propped herself up on her elbows and looked into my face. "Lucie?"

"She has a chance to heal now, a chance to live."

We lay quietly, side by side. Neither of us spoke. We both knew that Lucie would never be a girl again, a carefree seventeen. Her innocence had ended abruptly, brutally. From now on, whenever she opened up the past to find herself there, it would be like finding the stone in a bitter fruit.

I reached for Sylvie's hand, glad of her friendship, grateful for her life and mine. Tomorrow I would love Matteo with such fierceness, he would be certain to forgive me.

I had to work harder to win Matisse's forgiveness. He was astonished that I had left him alone with the nurses, without even Sylvie to keep him company over his tea.

"I agree it was quite wrong of me not to warn you I'd be busy," I confessed. "But I'm not an appendage, you know. I sometimes need to deal with private matters."

"Don't be ridiculous," he huffed.

"About the appendage? Or the privacy?"

Usually, I could cajole him into a better humour. Not today. He sulked. He threw me black looks. He even snapped at Sylvie.

In the end, the postman rescued us from Patron's gloom.

The old fox, Rouveyre, kept his promise to me. He found a villa, a refuge for Matisse just outside a town called Vence. "It's a charming village," Rouveyre wrote. "The walls of the old town are still intact."

Matisse was cheered by the news. Nice had grown strange to him. Too much of the old civilized life was vanishing. He couldn't go for drives any longer in the car. He'd felt shut in, cut off from many of his friends. The paintings helped him to remember better times, but when the paintings were sold, all he had left was a fleeting impression of beauty, a burst of colour like fireworks in his mind.

We could move in as early as June.

I saw the sparkle in the blue eyes behind the steel-rimmed glasses, recognized the spurt of vitality that came with the promise of a fresh start. He'd always thrived on a shift of scenery, a shift in the light. The move wouldn't be nearly as exotic as his past travels to Italy or Spain, Tahiti or Tangiers. But for an old man who'd cheated death, Vence sounded like an enchanted place.

I thought it a shame not to capitalize on all that anticipatory energy. I found Sylvie and told her my plan. She agreed at once.

We unearthed the old costume trunks Madame had once kept for the hired models, trunks that had been packed away ever since we'd first moved to Cimiez. Underneath the shimmering satins, I found a white muslin dress: a square neck, billowing sleeves, a long floaty skirt.

The dress was a bit big for Sylvie—the war had shrunk all of us—but I found a sash, the colour of black currant liqueur, which served to tighten the waistband.

"Give me a head start," I said. "Then come into the studio."

Matisse was humming to himself, idly sketching a lemon on a china plate. I tiptoed into the room behind him, then motioned to Sylvie.

"What are you doing, Lydia?" he called out.

At that moment, Sylvie drifted into the studio, looking like an angel with the white dress slipping off one shoulder. She'd tied a white velvet ribbon around her throat, slipped Lydia's amethyst ring on one finger, and let down her black hair.

Matisse suddenly became very still. He was mesmerized, as if he'd never seen Sylvie before. He flipped a page in his sketchbook and the lemon was forgotten.

As rugs were packed, pictures lowered from the walls, furniture hoisted and leases signed, the Americans and the British landed in Sicily, Allied ships patrolled the Mediterranean, and the arresting image of Sylvie as a bride slowly took shape on a gleaming canvas.

It was time to say good-bye.

I spent the night before we left for Vence cradled in Matteo's arms. I wanted life to be simple. I wanted to stay with him forever.

I followed him to the water's edge, saw his fishing boat join a flotilla of others and disappear eventually behind a jutting arm of green land.

This would be my last morning in Nice for some time. I strolled along the curving shoreline because the light was beautiful, smoked a cigarette with a young Italian soldier whose job it was to be suspicious of anyone so close to the sea.

"Can you speak French?" I asked.

He nodded, his eyes veiled, guarded.

"You must be sick of all this," I said.

"The sea? No, not ever," he replied, surprised a civilian would speak so frankly to him.

"I meant Nice, the Occupation, your uniform."

"Oh. Now that you mention it, I'd quite like to go home."

"Where is home?"

He closed his eyes to see it better. "A valley, filled with poppies and the sound of church bells, near Assisi. And you, mademoiselle? You were not born to the French language. Where is your home?"

"I'm not sure," I confessed. "I'm trying to decide."

Part III
Le Rêve, The Dream

WHAT ROUVEYRE HAD NOT WRITTEN in his letter was that beyond the walls of Vence, the countryside was wild and beautiful. Villa Rêve itself was a plain, two-storey house: a pale yellow box with brown shutters, standing at the foot of the Baou mountain, covered in olive trees and wild holm oaks. It had thick walls and glass doors and windows reaching right up to the ceiling. Best of all, light spilled through those windows and everything it touched seemed glazed, varnished with gold.

Three huge hundred-year-old palm trees framed the villa and there was a garden at the front, lush with rosy-pink laurels, yuccas, cypresses, orange trees, purple irises, fire-red geraniums. The heat and the foliage seemed to press against the windows, the air laced with pine, thyme, rosemary, the perfume of grass and wild flowers.

I wanted everything to be perfect for Matisse's arrival. I hung the red, openwork Moroccan curtains in the sitting room to filter the light and cast elaborate and lacy patterns on the floor. I hung the walls of his bedroom with Polynesian tapa cloths and Kasai textiles from the Belgian Congo. In his studio, I scraped and sanded his palette, rubbed it with linseed oil. I even set up a still life for him: half a dozen apricots, pinky-orange streaked with bronze, on a cloth so blue it might have been carved from the sky.

On one of his last days with us, André drove Patron, Sylvie and me along the coast, then north, up and up the curving roads and through pine and oak forests, past the pretty town of Saint-Paul-de-Vence perched on its hill, and finally to the walls of Vence. The gray stone walls seemed almost forbidding, hiding the town's pleasant courtyards, seeming to discourage visitors. Matisse frowned and wriggled impatiently in his seat.

"Just around the corner," I promised. "From the balcony you can see the town."

He was not disappointed. As André and Sylvie carried in the last of our *luggage and began unpacking, I handed Matisse his cane and walked him around his new home. He was delighted with everything, the curtains, the tapestries, all of his favourite objects—jugs and vases and china—that he painted again and again. A shallow spurt of a laugh came from his throat when he saw the easel I'd set up, the cleaned palette, an array of brushes and paints to hand.*

"I see them, too," he said, holding out his hand to me. "I see the paintings all at once, all that they can be."

We stood together for a moment on the balcony, listening to the church bells rolling across the valley. On the horizon, just to the left of the panorama where the land met the sky, there was a small triangle visible of the now distant sea.

VIII

THE NIGHT OF THE PARTY, the villa on Cap Ferrat was transformed. Strings of tiny white lights twisted up the trunks of the palm trees and outlined starbursts of leaves. There were plants everywhere: red and orange hibiscus the size of small trees, snowball viburnums with ruffled flowers the size of plates, trellises of roses with a fragrance straight from heaven.

The Matisse gleamed down from the dining room wall, well-lit from above.

Below it, on long tables with white damask cloths, were pyramids of cakes and champagne glasses. Outside, from the terrace, a violinist could be heard tuning his instrument.

Chloe and Adam had grilled Alain when they'd returned from Vence, but he could tell them little. Lydia had never spoken to him of Place St. Francois or of Saint-Jeannet. He thought she'd mentioned the name Matteo once or twice, someone she'd known during the war.

"What was his last name? Was she close to him?" Chloe had prodded.

Alain shrugged. "I've told you before. She didn't like to speak about the war."

Chloe was deeply disappointed. She'd allowed herself to believe the map would lead them to somewhere other than another dead end.

Adam tried to cheer her up. "Jamie'd written down my number. I'm sure he was trying to call. We must be close."

Alain had immediately taken Adam's side and stuck there. "You can drive back to Vence tomorrow, check all the hotels there. Visit Saint-Jeannet. But first, the party."

All day, Alain had been ordering about the caterers, the florists, and the musicians as if he were directing a stage play.

Chloe owed him her best performance. She finished dressing, fiddled with her hair. She had rehearsed her part over and over, but now that the time was here, she couldn't stop herself from shaking.

She wandered downstairs, eventually found Alain in the kitchen, giving last minute instructions. He'd tucked a flower into the lapel of his tan suit. It looked remarkably small against the bulky landscape of his chest. His thin hair floated around his ears like feathers.

He turned, beaming at her. "You look dangerous, Chloe."

"Liliane helped me find this dress in Paris."

"Ah, yes, the beautiful Liliane. Such a flair for style."

"I thought you'd never met her?"

"That's right. Jamie must have mentioned her." He looked away quickly, fussed, unnecessarily Chloe thought, with a tray of cheeses.

His manner, more than his words, felt momentarily artificial, awkward. Suddenly, Chloe felt a flutter of panic in her stomach. She'd known for weeks that Alain couldn't be what he said he was—a framer in a shabby Paris store. But she trusted him. The fake Matisse, the party designed to flush out Jamie's killer, it was all Alain's plan. What if she and Adam had been duped? What if Alain couldn't be trusted at all? She felt the room spin slightly.

She lifted her head slowly. Alain was staring at her intently, his brow creased. "Are you all right, Chloe? You look quite pale. You're not having second thoughts, are you?"

She smiled grimly. "Oh, I'm well beyond second. Maybe fourth or fifth. You know, Alain, Adam trusts you. It would be very cruel to let him down now."

Alain searched her expression, his large body momentarily still. But he shook off the tension. "I'm sure our plan will work. The whole world is connected by email and cell phones and twittering. The party begins in a half-hour. By ten, Ashkar will know there's a Matisse in our dining room."

He gave her a conspiratorial smile and began to leave the room.

She stepped in front of him. She was determined, brazen.

"Look," she whispered. "Maybe you're a fence or a con man. I don't really care. I just need to know you're totally on our side."

"Totally," he vowed. "Now isn't the time to worry. Just be bright and positive this evening, sure of everything you say."

"Lie, in other words."

"Yes, but confidently. Remember that truthful men sometimes lie, and liars sometimes tell the truth."

A little stunned, Chloe watched his broad back disappear. She needed fresh air, a glimpse of the sea, something authentic.

Adam found her on the terrace, in the soft violet shadows cast by the strings of blue light in the palm trees. Her hair hung in waves around her shoulders.

"Dance with me tonight?" he asked, leaning into her line of vision.

"Look at us," she laughed. "You in your black suit, me in my dangerous dress. James Bond and Mata Hari. What would Jamie say about his little brother now?"

"Something like 'let the dance begin.' But it wouldn't sound so corny coming from him. Shall we?"

Chloe took his hand and together they left the terrace to greet the early arrivals.

The party was a swirling mass of images. Nothing would stay still for Chloe. She remembered a movie, *Arabesque* maybe, in which Gregory Peck is kidnapped and blindfolded. Using only his sense of sound, Peck tries to memorize the route the kidnappers take as they drive him away. When the car passes a flock of honking geese, he mistakes them for a crowd of people talking, incessantly and noisily.

For forty minutes, Chloe was trapped by a reed-thin, beaky man with a silver moustache—Monsieur Pierre something?—who drilled her about the Matisse. His eyes, hidden behind the thick lenses of his glasses, scrutinized everything around him, apparently with distaste. He aimed his words at a place just above her head and spoke to her as if she were a trifle stupid.

Over the man's shoulder, she caught glimpses of Adam looking slim and elegant and composed. Monsieur Pierre droned on. In between his words, she caught snatches of Alain's booming laughter.

Finally, she could stand it no longer. She simply walked away from

Monsieur Pierre. In a minute or two, he might realize she'd gone.

People were draped along the walls and the furniture. Some were drinking champagne. The terrace was a whirl of music and lights streaming through the night.

She felt a tap on her shoulder, arms whirling her around.

"My dance," Adam smiled, catching her at the waist. "How many people have asked you about the Matisse?"

"Three," Chloe responded, breathlessly. "The last told me point-blank it was a fake. I don't think he's noticed yet that I'm no longer listening to him."

"Really? My five ladies told me it was a treasure. Three of them asked me if we wanted to sell it. I wonder how many of them are spying for Ashkar."

"Where did you learn how to dance like this? No, wait. Let me guess. Jamie, right?"

"I was his partner, ages nine through twelve. After that, I had to learn how to lead on my own."

Chloe felt his hand on her back, guiding her gently. She leaned into him, her head on his shoulder. Her body swayed to the music. She let her mind drift, relaxed in his arms. She felt the couples around them recede.

An image of Sylvie came to her, her black hair loose, blowing across her face in the wind from the sea. She'd crossed the ocean and fallen in love here, here in the place where every spray of roses, every candlelit terrace conspired to spark romance.

Chloe felt Adam's arms tighten around her. When she opened her eyes, she saw that the music had stopped and the dancing had stopped and still he held her. A second stretched into two, into ten. She felt a momentary sensation of floating, of becoming unmoored from her life.

She searched his face. His eyes fell to her lips.

And she panicked. Bolted.

She scanned the rooms for a place to hide and nearly blundered into a waiter. He offered her a glass of champagne, and she drank two, very quickly. She drifted aimlessly from one knot of people to the next and avoided the dance floor.

Finally, gradually, the conversations grew quieter and more sporadic. The music slowed and the candles burned down.

Au revoir. Merci bien. A lovely party.

Chloe thought she heard Adam whisper goodnight, though it might have been the breeze rustling the palm leaves.

Safe in her room, she tried to make her mind empty, as blank as an unpainted canvas, a perfect vacancy. But images kept rushing in—yachts and bodyguards, glasses of champagne, Adam's eyes.

She opened a drawer in the small table beside her bed and took out the Commissaire's card. Then impulsively she picked up the phone.

On the fourth ring, she heard his voice, gravelly with sleep.

"Lejeune," he said.

"This is Chloe Rea."

"Chloe? Where are you?"

"Cap Ferrat. The thing is Julien, we're expecting a robbery in the next few days, and I wonder if you could send someone."

She talked on the phone for some time, then lay awake most of the night staring at the painted ceiling above her bed.

When Chloe woke, she could smell something baking, a yeasty, comforting smell that called to her like a siren's song. She followed the aroma down the stairs, past the wreckage of the living room. Someone had dropped a blueberry tart, fruit side down, onto one of the white sofas; someone else had spilled red wine. A vase of flowers had toppled over, dripping pale green water into a pool on the marble tiles.

The kitchen, however, where she found Alain, was spotless. He wore a bibbed apron over a pair of oversized shorts and a pair of flip-flops. So much for the formality of Cap Ferrat. He looked almost comical, certainly harmless.

"Coffee?" he asked as she sat down.

She nodded, cradled the bowl of café au lait he offered her in both hands. "Mmm. What's that smell?"

"Croissants."

"You're making croissants? My god, why are you wasting your time framing pictures?"

He winked at her with his good eye. "I've put your Matisse in the safe. I think we have a day or two before we hear from Ashkar or Kirov."

"Adam told me at least three people offered to buy our painting last night."

"Four. I also was approached once. By the way, what happened between you two last night?" Alain glanced at Chloe's face. "Feel free not to tell me."

"Don't start, Alain," Chloe warned. "Adam and I are very different. Too different."

"You think so? I'd say you're kindred spirits. Your heads trump your hearts. He's too rational and you're too scared. There's sparks between you, if only you'd notice."

He shuffled across the room before she had a chance to reply and opened the oven, removing a tray of golden croissants. Chloe felt her irritation with him evaporating.

"There's a safe in the villa? Of course, I should've worked that out for myself. And the Countess, or your—er, brother, is it?—shared the combination with you?"

Alain was whistling, removing the pastry from the baking tray to a cooling rack, and seemed not to have heard her.

Chloe finished her coffee, yearned for more, and wandered over to the French doors leading onto a patio and the kitchen gardens. From where she was standing, she had a clear view across sloping lawn to a sliver of beach, and the lapping edge of the sea.

It was a perfect, shining morning, blue and gold and tropical green. Chloe thought again how seductive the villa by the sea was, the soothing quality of the heat and the air, the feeling that the rest of the world was a very long way away.

The unmistakable sound of helicopter blades cutting through the air shattered Chloe's reverie. She stiffened as the illusion of tranquil, somnolent wealth vanished. There must be a half-dozen helicopters swinging over the Côte d'Azur at any given time, but only one that mattered. What had Ashkar been doing last night? Watching from a distance, waiting, sending out his minions, gathering information? Was he angry?

"Good morning, Chloe."

Adam was leaning against the kitchen counter, coffee already in hand. She hadn't heard him come in. He looked rested, composed. He was wearing a collarless, linen short-sleeved shirt and navy slacks.

She felt a bit miffed by his composure, knew perfectly well why she felt miffed, and resented him a little for it. "Good morning," she said brightly. "Alain bakes, too."

A plate of croissants passed under Chloe's nose as Alain ushered her and Adam out to the patio. For a moment, life came down to layers of buttery pastry, crisp at both tips of its crescent shape, soft and slightly warm inside.

"*Ah, bon,*" Alain said. "Now we compare notes. How many people knew the Matisse was a fake last night?"

"Monsieur Pierre, for sure. There may have been others who thought it was fake but were too polite to say so," Chloe replied.

Alain looked astonished, even his bad eye seemed to widen. "The French? Discreet? No, no Chloe. They wouldn't hesitate to express an opinion about anything, especially art."

"Most of the people who spoke to me wanted to buy it," Adam added. "They thought it was authentic, I'm sure."

"Then Monsieur Pierre Villiers is our man," Alain declared. "What did he say, Chloe?"

"The colours were not properly balanced, not enough tension, the brushstrokes were not quite fluid enough, blah, blah, blah."

"Did he seem indignant?"

"Yes."

"Do you think he'll be able to describe the image in detail."

"Absolutely."

"Were you rude to him?"

"Very."

Alain rubbed his hands together. "Excellent. He'll be lunching today on all the details of our pretty picture. Our reputations are in for a thorough drubbing, I'm afraid. Ashkar will hear everything."

Chloe went over the plan again in her mind. The key assumption was that Kirov, either acting alone or under Ashkar's orders, was responsible for Jamie's death. If Ashkar was in possession of the missing photograph of *Portrait of a Bride*, he would know exactly what the original Matisse should look like. The morning after the party, the Cap would be buzzing with conflicting descriptions of her forgery. And Ashkar couldn't be sure, could he? He'd have to see the painting for himself. He'd never trust anyone like Monsieur Pierre to authenticate the painting for him, would he?

Alain settled back in his chair, looking very pleased with himself, resting his hands on his belly. "I think, Adam, you should take Chloe to lunch today. I know just the place."

"I'd love to, ordinarily, but I was hoping to strike out on my own today, follow up on Place St-François. I think Jamie was trying to lead me there, perhaps to this Matteo fellow."

There was a small, awkward silence. Chloe and Adam took pains not to look at each other. Alain sighed heavily.

Chloe, annoyed and surprised, rushed to make things worse. "Fine. You do that, Adam." She turned away from him and concentrated on Alain. "Do you really think Ashkar will try to steal the painting? When?"

Alain rolled his eyes at her before answering. "Well, I don't think he'll come himself. Of course, we hope he sends Kirov. But, yes, someone will try to steal the painting. When? Ashkar won't take unnecessary risks. He's a calculator, I'm told. We just have to make certain that when he acts, we're ready. We have, I'd guess, two or three days to wait. In the meantime, if Adam's busy, perhaps you'll lunch with me, Chloe?"

"Delighted," she replied. She searched Adam's impassive features. Nothing.

"Excuse me," Adam said a few long, heavy minutes later. "I hope you both enjoy your lunch."

"Wait," Chloe blurted.

Adam looked at her then, his face serious, his blue eyes inquisitive.

"We can drop you off in Nice, can't we Alain?" Chloe offered, her gaze icy.

"That's very thoughtful of you," Adam replied without the slightest bit of sincerity.

He strode away.

Chloe glared at his back.

"Calm down," Alain cautioned. "You'll wear yourself out. The poor man's baffled enough."

A few hours later, Chloe and Alain were ensconced on the terrace of the Colombe d'Or in the hill village of Saint-Paul-de-Vence. Their table, snug against one of the ancient walls that ringed the town, looked out over a valley of terraced slopes, red-tiled roofs, and neat farmyards. Beyond cultivated bands of green, Chloe could see the purple snow-capped Alps in one direction and the blue shimmer of the sea in the other. A tree with blossoms the colour of pomegranate juice grew next to their table. The scent of the flowers was spicy and rich. Across from them, on the other side of the outdoor restaurant, was a wall mural designed by Fernand Léger.

Chloe scanned the menu. The caviar was three hundred euros.

"Okay," she confessed to Alain. "I'm impressed. Does the Countess have an account here?"

He looked like Carroll's very smug cat. "I do believe she does. I can recommend the grilled sole."

The waiters fussed. The food was ordered. Drinks were poured.

Chloe ran her fingers over her dewy glass of Sancerre and grinned at Alain. "First," she demanded. "Tell me about this place. Then tell me why we're here. Not that I'm complaining."

"The Colombe d'Or, the golden dove," he began. "The hotel and restaurant was founded by Paul Roux just after World War I. He used to be a farmer in the valley, but he had an eye for beauty and a generous nature. When artists needed feeding and a place to stay for a few weeks, Roux invited them to stay here. In return, the artists—Chagall, Braque, Picasso, Bonnard, just to name a few—repaid him with their work.

"Roux had a good eye. Soon he began to collect in earnest. After forty years or so, he had assembled one of the finest private collections of twentieth-century art in France. We'll take a peek after dessert."

"You mean it's here?"

"Oh yes. I told you Roux was generous. He's not one of those collectors who lock their treasures away to gloat on them privately. The paintings hang in the indoor restaurant and even in the rooms for let. There's a

Calder mobile by the outdoor pool."

"I think I like Monsieur Roux. Now, we're here because—?"

"Look around you."

"I have. It's a beautiful spot."

Alain gave her one of his reprimanding looks, and she tried again.

The clientele was a lovely mix. The tourists, like her, were flushed with delight. The French were very chic and looked as if nothing less would possibly do. One long table had been set up for a small wedding party, rose petals scattered among the heavy silver. The bride wore a simple cream dress and smiled radiantly at Chloe.

Only two diners looked hunched over their food, refusing the sun-soaked, *laissez-faire* ambience. Two men.

At that moment, one raised his nose from his plate to peer at Chloe suspiciously. His eyes narrowed pointedly at her casual dress.

"What a vile little man," she scowled. "Monsieur Pierre is here."

"I thought he might be," Alain said quietly. "And his companion?"

"Hard to tell. He's wearing dark wraparound sunglasses. The bottom half of his face looks rather grim. Unsmiling, I mean. Dark hair. Big shoulders."

A waiter appeared announcing the arrival of their lunch with a flourish. Chloe abandoned herself to the full enjoyment of every mouthful, knowing that Alain would have no time for conversation while there was grilled sole in a dijonnaisse sauce before him. She thought of an evening in Paris when Adam had told her about *joie de manger*.

"I think I was a little unfair to Adam this morning," she ventured.

A small snort came from the other side of the table.

"Was it that obvious?" she asked.

"It couldn't be missed. Even by a person with just one eye. Now enjoy your food."

A contented silence reigned over their table until Alain had scraped up the last crumbs of his *tarte tatin*. Then he led Chloe away from the terrace and its honeyed light into the cool, shadowy interior of the hotel.

The paintings were well spaced around the room, softly lit from above. A Bonnard portrait of a young, dark-haired woman in a dark-purple dress took Chloe's breath away. She admired the trumpeting reds of a

Nicholas de Stael abstract and the quizzical swirls of a Miro. She thought it would be strange to see the paintings in a dining room rather than in the hushed formality of a museum, but they looked quite at home, consummate hosts presiding over the feast.

She turned a corner and bumped into a Picasso, smiled to see how many other diners had followed her and Alain inside.

She looked around for Alain, but he seemed to have disappeared.

A man was crossing the room towards her. Without the dark sunglasses, she knew exactly who he was. She'd seen his image once before in a photograph shown to her by Julien Lejeune, the sharply angled face, the mouth a thin wire.

Quickly she crossed to the other side of the room, ducked into a hallway, pushed open a door. She found herself at the foot of a staircase. She stood still for a minute, her hands gripping the railing, trying to slow her breathing.

One glimpse of Kirov and she was a wreck.

It had all seemed so easy in theory, so easy to trick Ashkar and Kirov. But the expression on Kirov's face had terrified her. He looked angry, his eyes burned like cinders.

Slowly, the door began to swing open.

She was halfway up the stairs when Alain called after her. "Chloe? What are you doing?"

"It's Kirov. He's here."

"Yes, I know. He's registered at the hotel."

"You *knew*? Then why are we here?"

Alain shrugged. "A show of bravado. A little scene in the drama, perhaps. Two friends having lunch, carefree, a little careless of their Matisse. It's good to be underestimated."

"Thanks for telling me," Chloe snapped.

"But, *chèrie*, you are perfectly safe here," Alain sputtered. "So many people, so many witnesses. Kirov is not such an idiot. Come now. I've a surprise for you. The real reason I brought you here."

He held out his arm, beckoned to her with his head.

Reluctantly she walked down the stairs. "Your surprises are too much for me, Alain Reynaud." She took his arm and whispered into his ear.

"When are you going to tell me who you really are?"

He smiled down at her like a doting grandfather. "You know, Chloe, I'm really quite proud of you. Apart from the rash conclusions you sometimes jump to, you're quite clever. That's good. Adam needs a smart woman."

"Okay, okay," Chloe laughed. "No more personal questions. Lead on."

"Close your eyes."

She leaned against his arm, excited in spite of herself, as he guided her back to the dining room.

"Now," he said.

She opened her eyes, looked straight into the eyes of Lydia Delectorskaya. Wide, candid eyes, perfect cheek bones.

But there was more than the symmetry of physical beauty: Matisse's sketch had captured more than that. There was something about her beyond mere harmony, something unique. She had the dignity of an empress and, at the same time, the exoticism of a cat. She embodied strength. Her vulnerability was almost palpable.

"I would have done anything for her," Alain sighed. "She had a kind of grace, a stillness about her. Sometimes I used to think it was sorrow, a kind of bittersweet view of the world. Never a sad face or a tear, but something always there. Accepted. Her fate, maybe."

Chloe said nothing. She felt that if she turned away, and then turned back again quickly, Lydia's expression would be different. She felt a connection to her across time as tangible as an electric current.

We had not been settled at Villa Rêve for more than two months before the world heaved around us once again. In September, Italy surrendered to Allied forces. Mussolini was deposed, then rescued by German commandos and set up as a puppet leader in the north of Italy. Chaos reigned in Nice.

I thought of the Italian soldier I'd talked to the last time I'd seen Matteo. He and a hundred homesick others simply put down their guns and headed for their farms, villages, and valleys. Some disappeared into the underground Resistance. But many others stayed, cruel and unpredictable as the wounded often are.

At night, the bombers roaring overhead made vibrations I could feel in my stomach. We often fell asleep to the muttering thunder of guns in the distance. Sometimes, even during the day, shells burst high above the trees, sudden puffs of black smoke that floated off on the wind.

Transportation was very difficult, train service erratic. The car could only be used for medical emergencies; we couldn't waste precious gas for daily errands. Once or twice a month, I bicycled to the village of St. Jeannet a dozen kilometers away and, if I was lucky, caught a local train from there to Nice. I had supplies to get for the studio, packages to mail to publishers and dealers, and a thousand and one things I wanted to say to Matteo.

Which is why I was with him when the Germans entered Nice.

Their gray-green uniforms looked like the pelts of wolves, the larger wolves that Matteo had once warned me would swallow up Mussolini and the Italians. The soldiers seemed to be made of helmets and guns, small guns holstered at their waists, larger guns cradled like infants or brandished like sticks. No one saw their faces, only their guns. They were disciplined, straight as arrows and just as sharp.

A sense of danger hung in the air like smoke. People became quieter, their movements smaller, their posture guarded. No one wanted to draw the Germans' attention. Even the boisterous, gaudy market of the Cours Saleya became more subdued.

Matteo still took his boat out to sea in the dawn light, but the patrols were stricter than ever. We didn't speak of his involvement in the Resistance, but I guessed that sometimes he had passengers hidden below deck. Once, in Jean-Marie's café, I saw a woman and two children wearing yellow stars on their chests slip through the beaded doorway and disappear down the back stairs.

Alarms went off in my head. I wanted to shout "Be careful. Don't do it. Keep your head down."

I said nothing. Just loved him a little more, while at the same time feeling transfixed by fear.

Most days we tried to pretend that our lives were carrying on like trains still on schedule. Until someone blew up the train tracks. Or a man was shot down in one of the public squares.

To my dismay, I discovered that Lucie was acting as a courier for Dr. Clairmont, carrying messages in her clothing and hiding medicines in the false bottom of her market basket. We were sitting on the pebble beach, waiting for Matteo to return, our vision of the sea now marred by looping coils of barbed wire strung along the shoreline.

"Why do you do it, Lucie? You know the punishments are terrible."

She took a long time to answer my question. I had time to study the fine arch of her brows, the sharp angles of her cheekbones, barely grazed with colour by the sun. She was no longer pretty like the other young girls of the port; rather she had a grave, quiet beauty.

"I think," she began, "that the best way to fix a life is to save someone else's. You think so too, Lydia, or else you'd have left Matisse by now to marry my brother."

"I love Matteo," I replied. "Perhaps, when the war is over..."

She smiled a little then and nodded. "Yes, when the war is over."

It was a comforting phrase, spoken again and again in those troubled days like a kind of prayer. It conjured up a future sugared with promise. It seemed to shelter us from darkness.

That night, back at Villa Rêve, Sylvie and I saw the sky over Cannes burst into an angry, fiery orange. A bomb fell on the gasworks there, turning it into an inferno.

Within days of their arrival in Vence, the Germans impounded Matisse's car. It was so old it couldn't have been of much use to them. The point, I suppose, was simply to take it. André found work as a labourer on one of the neighbouring farms, a war widow who needed help, and we saw him far less than we would have liked. I remembered Patron's series of odalisque paintings from the 1920s—women in gauze trousers, sprawled on improvised divans—and teased him that he finally had his harem. He was the centre of a household that consisted of models, nurses, Sylvie and me. The Germans grumbled and threatened and glared at us, but like the Italians and the Milice before them, tolerated our existence. As far as they were concerned, Matisse was a sleeping lion, best left undisturbed.

While I helped in the studio, or wrote letters, or cut out reviews, or read about gallery openings in Paris, Sylvie fed us. She combed the woods for mushrooms and berries, even braved wild bees to steal their honey. She planted a small vegetable patch with tomatoes, carrots, potatoes, and garlic, an herb garden for basil, tarragon, and mint. Fences and stone walls couldn't deter her: she'd steal anyone's ground fruit to make fig, sour cherry, and raspberry jams. She charmed all the farmers around Vence, who were soon saving bits of cheese for her, or maybe a rabbit or a stewing hen.

When she wasn't scavenging for food, she posed for Patron. I loved to lean against the frame of the studio door and study her. She looked enchanting. Patron had her hold a bouquet of roses that had just begun to swell and bud, a cascade of half-opened flowers against the white muslin dress. I could almost smell their heady scent.

But there was nothing of the sentimental bride in the portrait that emerged. Matisse painted Sylvie's courage, her quick energy, the cadence of her voice. Deep pinks and reds the colour of crushed raspberries splashed across the canvas and resolved into images—here a spill of flowers, there the sensual line of the lips. The whites glowed, the blues healed. Her song was a zigzag of orange. The greens rippled like leaves and grass in the wind, all of the movement of the painting anchored by her face, skin like white roses brushed in pink, the black spiral of her hair. It took my breath away.

When she came to my room one night to tell me that the Germans planned to ship André east to work in one of their wretched factories, and that she and André had decided to flee, it broke my heart.

We hid André among the sheet-draped furniture and packing cases stored in the old studio in the Regina. Most of the building was still empty and every few days I brought him food. It was not unusual for people to see me come and go there, but there were few enough to watch. It was November, gloomy and cold, and people shut themselves away from the rain and the Germans.

Under cover of night, Matteo came to plan an escape. It wouldn't be easy. The fishermen usually transferred escapees from boat to boat, beginning the journey in Nice, finally landing somewhere on the Liguria shoreline riddled by dozens of rocky coves. But Italy was too dangerous now, a third front in the war.

"I won't risk taking Sylvie there," André vowed. "I'd sooner give myself up."

"*There must be another way, then.*" *Matteo put a hand on his friend's shoulder. "I've been listening to the radio. The Allies are bombing Germany regularly, especially the factories. You'd be buried under the rubble within months. No, we have to get you out. We need help, a bigger operation than our little fishing fleet."*

"*It's too dangerous," I pleaded. "You can keep hiding here. You needn't try to escape at all."*

But we all knew that nowhere would be safe once André failed to report to the labour centre and the Germans began actively looking for him. His past would lead them directly to Matisse and Sylvie.

I felt sick with apprehension for the people I loved. And I felt a rush of anger that almost flattened me. We'd retreated to Vence to be safe, we'd started over again and again, I'd started over again, and now my world was going to be torn apart once more. I looked around the ghostly studio, its crated paintings and empty easels, and my hands itched. I wanted to hammer my fists against the window, kick over the easels, and break all the paintbrushes, snap them like bones.

Instead I volunteered to send a message to Louis Aragon.

By December, Villa Rêve seemed timeless, wrapped in winter and woodsmoke as if nothing that happened in the rest of the world could change it. While Sylvie and I waited to hear news from Louis, Matteo moved André to Dr. Clairmont's apartment where it was warmer and where Matteo or Lucie could more easily smuggle in food.

Snow lay thick on the hillsides around Vence. I heated the studio with a wood-burning stove and hung heavy rugs at doors and windows to block the icy wind from the mountains. Sometimes the only sounds were the soft meows of Matisse's cats, Minouche and Coussi, or the fluttering wings of his pale, delicate doves. The days blurred into each other. The snow drifted down. There were no visitors. We learned that Bonnard had broken his leg and was holed up in Cannet. Picasso was busy falling in love in Antibes.

A week or so before Christmas, I wrapped up Portrait of a Bride *in brown paper and hired a local merchant with a van to take me to the Regina where the painting could be properly crated and stored. There was no chance that Sylvie would be able to take it with her. It would wait for her, we said, someday it would bring us together again.*

I felt excited as the van crawled through the wet streets of Cimiez, where the snow had melted into rain. I was meeting Matteo and I felt like celebrating. I'd brought some long-saved cheese, a loaf of Sylvie's nut bread, a bottle of wine and some candles. We would have two precious hours before the merchant would return to take me back to Vence.

I pushed open the door of the abandoned apartment and ran down the hallway to the studio. Around me, the air was absolutely still. The buzz of energy that once permeated the space had vanished, but the faint scents of turpentine and linseed oil remained. I propped the painting up on an easel, but left it wrapped. Later, as a surprise, I would show Matteo.

The wintry light of early afternoon seeping in from the edges of the blackout curtains was pale green. I pulled back one curtain about six inches, my signal to Matteo that I was waiting for him inside. I took a dust sheet off one of the tables, and brought out two brass candlesticks from my basket. As I fixed a pair of candles into the sockets, I thought how pleased Matteo would be to eat by candlelight.

I settled down to wait. Five minutes, ten. Twenty minutes that stretched into forty.

I was so intent on my own disappointment that the soldiers were almost upon me before I could react. Their boots seemed to kick the building apart, smashing through every entrance. I snatched up one of the candlesticks and held it in front of me. I had no wish to be shot for a phantom in the shadows.

Two soldiers burst through the door. Seeing me, they halted abruptly, their faces slack with surprise, and their guns aimed at my heart. One of them shouted out a name over his shoulder. I could hear other soldiers in the background, pounding up stairs, hammering on doors.

A tall man in civilian clothes entered the room. There was something subtly aggressive in the way he occupied space, in the way he moved. A thin, joyless smile spread across his face. "Papers, mademoiselle," he said softly.

My hands trembled as I put down the candlestick and rummaged in my basket for my identity card and work permit. I handed him the papers, hiding my fear as best I could, keeping my eyes downcast.

"Here," he snapped. "Look up, look at me." His French was correct, but *heavily accented. I could hear in it the undertones of the harsher German tongue.*

His eyes were a dull matte gray. He looked me up and down contemptuously. "So, a Russian," he sneered.

My mind was blank, my mouth dry as chalk.

With a nod of his head, he sent the two soldiers into the corners of the room, overturning furniture and opening cupboards. He walked around me, blew out the candles and picked up the candlesticks. He studied them for a moment, then tossed them to the floor. "Cheap brass," he said. "Perhaps there's something better in your basket."

He picked it up, began methodically unpacking its contents, probing each package with greedy, delicate fingers. The wine bottle disappeared into his coat pocket, the cheese and bread he crumbled and left strewn across the table. Perhaps he was looking for messages hidden in the food, perhaps he was merely delighting in destruction.

I tried to tell myself it didn't matter, but I could feel my eyes stinging, as if the tears gathering there were made of molten lead. I struggled to keep them from spilling over onto my cheeks, but nothing could stop the bleak, hateful feeling of helplessness.

Then I thought of the blackout curtain yawning open at one edge of the window, and my spine stiffened. Better he should arrest me, I thought, than Matteo. Anger saved me.

The German was looking at me with a curious expression, his eyes cool and assessing as if to say, What now? What next?

He moved toward the painting, one step, and I moved with him.

"Ah!" he exclaimed. "There is something you don't wish me to see. Open it."

I shook my head. "It belongs to Matisse."

Our eyes met in front of the painting. My gaze never wavered, but I was perfectly aware that he'd eased a gun out of his suit pocket. He pressed it against my chest.

"Open it," he commanded.

My movements were slow and deliberate. I undid the twine, watched the brown paper slide slowly to the ground.

The painting was achingly beautiful. Even in the dim light, the colours seemed to shine forth with exceptional clarity.

The German stiffened. From across the room, the other two soldiers were watching with hostile curiosity. For a long moment, we stared at the painting. None of us moved.

"Cover it up," the German suddenly growled.

I was stunned by the venom in his voice. I couldn't believe his reaction. My eyes flew to his face.

He prodded me with his gun, "Cover it. It's disgusting."

My hands were clumsy, slippery with sweat, but I wrapped the portrait as carefully as I could. I was dismayed, disoriented, terrified. For in the instant I'd glanced at his face, I'd seen the truth.

Avarice. Longing. No matter what the German might say, the glittery brightness in his eyes betrayed how much he wanted the painting of Sylvie.

I waited for the gunshot that would silence the witness to his greed, but it didn't come. Instead he shouted orders to the two soldiers. They receded from the room like a rank tide.

When we were alone, he leaned towards me. I could feel his breath on my face when he spoke. "You're lucky we're looking for Jews today instead of Bolsheviks. Don't be here when I come back."

So that was it, I thought. He'd come back, take the painting later when there were no soldiers to remember. I wasn't even a threat. He could dispose of me anytime.

When I inhaled, I felt a small, piercing ache in my chest where the point of his gun had been.

My knees buckled and I sank to the floor where Matteo eventually found me. He kissed my cheeks and brushed back my hair and breathed courage back into me while I told him everything.

"Take it, Matteo," I pleaded, lifting the painting up from the easel and thrusting it into his arms. "Please take it and hide it. I'd rather die than see it stolen. The German will be back, maybe even tonight. Please keep it safe."

"I promise," he said. "I promise. But now you must think of Sylvie. She and André must be ready to leave in two days."

I wished I could have seen Louis' face once more but he lived in the shadows, always on the move, slipping from one train to the next, almost invisible.

He planned everything down to the last detail, but none of us, not even André knew the full plan. Louis Aragon might have the heart of a poet and the soul of a pirate, but he also had the head of a master plotter. He knew how to hide people in a dizzying maze of false papers and false trails. His arrangements were meticulous.

Except for one detail.

On the second day of January, 1944, an hour before their secret journey began, I saw my dear friends married in the Chapelle de la Miséricorde, just off the Cours Saleya where they'd first met. There was no white muslin dress, no cascade of roses. Sylvie wore travelling clothes and the warmest coat she had, a white kerchief covering her hair for a veil. But still, she shone, André at her side, tall and straight-backed as a sword, dressed in a dark blue suit and overcoat. Lucie had found a willing priest, Matteo stood as witness, and I provided the feast. I even managed a small cake with layers of almond marzipan that filled the chapel with a delicious aroma of sugar and vanilla.

Matisse's health was too delicate to risk the winter air and, in any case, his presence would have drawn far too much attention to the wedding party. I promised to be his eyes and ears, but it was very hard on him not to attend. He'd known André longer than he'd known me, and Sylvie had always been a favourite. On the morning of the wedding, he'd opened his arms to her and she'd walked forward, blinded by tears, until she bumped into his chest, burying her face there and breathing in his familiar scent of cigarette smoke, soap, and paint.

Now, suddenly, it was my turn to say goodbye. I gave her one of the first sketches Matisse had ever made of me in the embroidered Rumanian blouse and I gave her the purple amethyst ring that she'd worn when he was painting her. The sketch captured a dreamy kind of serenity, but more than that it told a part of my story when the river of love between Matisse and me was overflowing. I knew she would understand.

I found I couldn't speak. I pressed a letter into her hands, hugged her once, almost brusquely, and then André was pulling her away.

She looked back once, one last grave, sweet smile, and then she was gone.

I felt dazed by my loss. Matteo dragged me along to Jean-Marie's café, settled me at a table and ordered me a brandy.

"I'm taking Lucie home," he said. "Wait for me."

I nodded and sipped the brandy, felt its heat crawl down my throat and into my body. My head swam with memories, an interminable series of endings. My father pulling a blanket up over my mother's face while I backed into a corner. My father drenched with fever, limp in my arms. My aunt's scorn, Madame Matisse's stony face, Nikolai stealing my money and mocking me from the shadows.

I waited in the café until Matteo returned and lifted the burden of my memories. He led me downstairs and we made love with abandon, until neither of us knew where we were or who we were or where one ended and the other began. Finally we fell apart and I laid my head on his chest and listened to him breathe.

"Clairmont will take you home," Matteo said. "The Germans have allowed him a car for medical emergencies, but you must go while it's still light."

When I rose to dress, Matteo caught my hand.

"I'll never leave you, Lydia," he said.

There was such a tightness in my throat I couldn't reply.

Later, I sat in the doctor's car while he chatted amiably and felt Matteo's words imprinted upon me. I couldn't hear or think of any other words. Just his.

Matisse spent most of the winter in bed fighting a constant battle against bronchitis and pleurisy with an array of ointments, pills, and herbal concoctions. Weak though his body might be, he was not idle.

Under his direction and critical eye, I painted sheets of paper of different sizes with apple-green, damson black, all the ripe fruits of his palette. Then I watched, spellbound, as he perfected a technique he'd experimented with years earlier when designing the huge figures for The Dance. He was cutting into pure colour, like a sculptor carving into stone. Flowers, leaves, stars, birds, bathers, dancers, starfish and shells—a complete world fell from his scissors, a world full of strength and vitality. Because he could not go outside, he brought nature inside and I pinned it up on the walls. Some days, when the sun was strong, I would walk into the studio and imagine myself in a garden in Tahiti amid tropical greens that looked as if they would be wet if I touched them.

"I want the colours to sing, Lydia," he would say. "I want them to shout and vibrate."

I smiled. We were both missing the sound of Sylvie's voice.

I hired a cook, a pleasant woman named Josette who lived just down the road near a nursing home run by Dominican nuns. It was not her fault that she couldn't make a stew to match Sylvie's.

We encouraged visitors to fill up our loneliness. A young Dutch painter, Annelies Nelck, somehow found her way to our doorstep. She was malnourished and destitute, having left everything behind when she fled Amsterdam. Her husband was in the Dutch Resistance and she feared for his life. She was so thin by the time she found us, her cheeks so bright with fever that it would have been impossible to turn her away. Matisse gave her food and paint, and in return she would sometimes model for him. Later she told me that when she first saw the studio she thought she had wandered into a hallucination and feared that she would suddenly wake up.

A cousin I thought I had lost to the war and my aunt's displeasure also found us. Hélène studied photography in Paris and set about documenting our lives at Villa Rêve. She took pictures of Matisse's favourite chair, a Venetian baroque chair in varnished silver. She took pictures of the fabric on the walls, the still life arrangements that I set up and varied every day, pictures of Matisse drawing, Matisse with his models, Matisse with his cats. She nearly drove us mad. Finally, at Patron's urging, I would hide her camera and we would have a few hours of peace.

Picasso finally surfaced from Antibes with his new lover. The first time I saw Françoise Gilot, I thought her the most beautiful woman I'd ever seen, creosote black hair that reflected the sun like glass, luminous skin, limbs impossibly long. She greeted me like a sister and the understanding between us was whole and completely silent.

She sat with her head tilted to the side staring at the paintings and the paper cutouts that covered the walls.

"Well," Matisse prodded. "What do you think?"

"They're beautiful," she said simply, and I could tell from the catch in her voice that she was sincere.

I smiled to myself, and waited for the counter attack, knowing Picasso would resent Françoise's admiration.

"Really, Matisse," he began, his hands cutting like quick knives through the air. "You can't continue painting this way. Life is ugly. There's no beauty, no mercy."

"As you say, my friend. I've seen Guernica, and it, too, is without mercy, a masterpiece."

Picasso sat back, feeling pleased.

I looked at Françoise and she grinned back, both of us waiting for the punch line.

"But if life is as grim as you say it is, Picasso," Matisse continued, "my paintings would be more necessary than ever."

Françoise laughed out loud. Picasso scowled.

I poured tea and commented on the weather, the slow coming of spring.

Meanwhile, beyond the interior of the villa, the Allied bombardment intensified. One day, I read in the Nice-Matin that the Germans planned to evacuate the sea front, eastwards from Matisse's old apartment overlooking the market all the way round to the port on the far side of the headland. I worried for Matteo and his family, fearing that they would be forced out of their home. Without André to act as a messenger, I felt cut off, anxious. Dread sometimes swept over me like a recurring fever whenever I remembered my encounter with the German in the Cimiez apartment.

Despite the danger, I had to see Matteo again. I bicycled into Vence, to the kind merchant with the van and begged him to take me to Nice.

"You don't want to go there, mademoiselle," he shook his head. "There have been arrests, reprisals."

"I must go," I cried.

He shook his head again and turned away from me.

It was early in the day, just past eight, but already hot. I got back on my bicycle and began pedaling. I felt an irresistible urge to go to Nice, a blind push forward that couldn't be denied.

I was five kilometres down the road, when the van pulled alongside me.

"Get in," the merchant said.

I climbed into the front seat while he stowed my bicycle.

"Where?" he demanded.

"The port."

"Jesus. I'll wait at the flower market a half hour, no more, understand? Find who you're looking for and then get out."

We rode the rest of the distance in tense silence.

I ran to Jean-Marie's café first.

The streets were strangely empty. I saw two little boys hunched over the sidewalk, gathering up brightly coloured beads.

Then I saw why.

Where the curtain of beads had once hung, someone had blocked the entry to the café with a few scrap boards. Inside, shelves of broken bottles rose above the bar, in front of a charred wall. The ceiling was black. Tables and chairs were overturned amid puddles of black water. The acrid smell of burnt-out fire, burnt plaster and paint, hung in the air on the street.

Fear swept through me like a tornado, sudden, unstoppable and violent. I backed away slowly from the wreckage, almost tripping over one of the little boys.

I turned towards the harbour, searching for Matteo's boat, but all I saw was battleship gray, none of the bright colours of the Nice fisherman.

"Where are the boats?" I cried aloud.

I felt a tug on my sleeve, looked down into the solemn face of one of the small boys. "The Germans got them," he said. "They're closing down the port."

I knelt down to be eye-level with the boy. "And the fishermen?" I asked, my voice trembling. "Where are the fishermen?"

He shook his head, wide-eyed, frightened by my fear.

"I'm sorry," I managed. "I'm looking for a friend and I can't seem to find him. He lives near here."

Again the boy shook his head. "Soldiers came to move the people," he said, pointing over my shoulder.

I stood up then, looked around properly. I saw that the buildings on all three sides of the port were boarded up, their windows blackened. Matteo's home and his family were gone.

As I walked numbly back to the flower market, there was hardly a soul to be seen and no sound but the wind rustling the fronds of the palm trees.

The stalls of the Cours Saleya were empty. There was no one waiting by the white van.

Something—instinct or memory or dread—turned me in the direction of the fish market.

As I approached Place St-François, I met a priest, his broad hat hiding his face, the skirts of his long robes sweeping over the cobblestones. He held up his hand, palm open before my face.

"Don't look, mademoiselle. Turn back, I beg of you."

I pushed him aside and entered the square.

I leaned against the wall of the nearest building to keep from sliding to the ground. Something out of control was spinning towards me, something from the underside of the world.

The air was rank with the stench of death.

The bodies of the men hung limply from the nooses fastened to the black wrought-iron balconies of the apartments lining the square.

The men wore no shoes.

Their hands were tied behind their backs.

Their faces were swollen, purple from being beaten.

As I stared, paralyzed with anguish, the hanged man closest to me turned slowly on the cord that had snapped his neck. His eyes were blank, his lips stretched back in death's grimace.

Jean-Marie, Matteo's friend, the bartender of the ruined café.

Then, suddenly, I couldn't quite see him anymore. His face rippled and shifted like a face seen underwater. My eyes couldn't focus properly. My mind wouldn't let them. There was a screaming sound in my ears.

My knees sagged, ratcheting sobs shook my body.

I felt hands on my shoulders, pulling me roughly to my feet.

It was the priest. "Quiet," he hissed. "Don't give them the satisfaction."

I looked over his shoulder, saw for the first time the line of soldiers guarding the square, guarding the bodies. The sight of them filled my bones with ice.

The priest pulled insistently on my arm, dragging me from the square.

"How long?" I cried. "How long have the bodies been there?"

"Two days now," the priest replied, his voice tight with anger. "The Germans won't let us cut them down. They won't let us bury them."

"But why?"

"So that we will never forget."

I struggled against the grip the priest had on my arm. "I have to go back,"

I pleaded. "I have to look for my friend. If he's there, I have to see him."

If anything, the priest's grip tightened. He pulled me closer, looked into my face, his expression suddenly tender. "No, mademoiselle. If your friend is among those doomed souls, you don't want to see him. You don't want to remember him that way."

Suddenly my mind made sense of the constant screaming in my ears, the screaming at the edge of my consciousness. It was the seagulls. They soared high above the square, wings open, flat and stiff, riding currents in the air. Then they dove, shrieking, wings beating against skin, their hungry beaks open.

I stopped resisting then.

As the priest led me back to the Cours Saleya, darkness seemed to press against me like a weight, though the sky was cloudless and the sun must have been bright.

The merchant rushed forward to meet us, and helped me into the van. He'd ripped a poster from one of the trees lining the marketplace. It listed the names of the seven men, executed by hanging for the crime of resisting, the crime of refusing to run with the pack or look away from cruelty.

As we drove away from Nice, I touched my fingers to the broadsheet, tracing Matteo's name over and over, as if by touching the paper I were touching his face.

A part of me knew that his strength had not failed him, nor his heart, not ever. He'd just seen one cruelty too many.

In the weeks and months that followed Matteo's death, I rarely left the villa. At the same time, I had never left Matisse so alone. I was there at his side, and not there, withdrawn, huddled over my pain.

He could not fathom my sadness. Sometimes, while I was reading to him, or doing up a button, or pinning up a gouache cutout, he would stroke my hand in the same way that he stroked the satiny feathers of his doves, tentatively, as if afraid I would fly away.

But my memories rooted me. I knew the images of that day in Nice would never leave me. For a while, I could block them out, bury them under the list of tasks to be done or drown them in an amber sea of whiskey, but they always seeped back into my mind like smoke under a door.

I tried to find Lucie and Matteo's aunt, but they seemed to have faded into thin air. The doctor, Clairmont, had also disappeared. I hoped that he was still protecting Lucie, that perhaps they were hiding somewhere together.

My own despair was soon matched by Matisse's: he received terrible news of Madame and Marguerite. In the months leading up to the long-anticipated assault of the Allies on the French Channel coast, the Germans had become almost fanatical about security. Madame was arrested, found typing out reports with two fingers on a battered typewriter for the FTP to pass on to British Intelligence in London. Marguerite, who carried messages hidden in her gloves from Paris to Bordeaux to Brittany, was imprisoned at Rennes.

Matisse staggered under the shock. He complained of blood pounding at his temples, his heart kicking against his chest. For two days, he took to his bed and barely moved, barely spoke.

I reminded him of his fierce battles with Madame that had left him exhausted, his nerves screaming. "She'll not give up," I said. "Nor should you."

Together we wrote a hurricane of letters to Paris, begging friends and officials to help intercede on Madame and Marguerite's behalf, but there was little that could be done.

When the Allies finally landed in Normandy, our spirits rose, but lines of communication were either sporadic or cut off completely. We were left to hope in silence.

Matisse and I shared a melancholy summer that year, tormented by our ghosts. The current of passion that had once run between us had resolved itself into a quieter, generous love. We could communicate perfectly with a glance, a sigh, a tilt of the head. Whenever he closed his eyes, I knew he was seeing Marguerite, the daughter of his first love, the daughter of his youth, with her black eyes and intelligent face. Whenever I turned my face towards the sea, he knew I was lifting up the burden of my lost lover whose name I'd never revealed. Sometimes, we would just sit together in the garden in the gathering twilight and let the memories tear through us until our strength dissolved like salt in water.

I coaxed his old friend, Rouveyre, to visit as often as possible, and Annelies and Hélène distracted and comforted us.

As October faded along with the sunlight into November, the days grew despairingly short and the temperature in the evenings fell below freezing. The German lines were collapsing in so many spots, there were so many breaches on so many fronts, that an end to the war seemed only months or even weeks away.

Matisse was sketching again, illustrations for Baudelaire's Fleurs du mal. *Annelies was posing for him when she saw a troop of Germans march past the window, so close she could see their breath in the cold air. She cried out in alarm, but Matisse did not even turn his head.*

"Never let it be said," he growled, "that I stopped work to watch the Germans depart."

One day, driven by guilt and curiosity, I took out the bicycle that had lain neglected for so long, put on my warmest jacket and gloves, and pedalled all the way to Nice. The wind felt fresh on my face. Running my tongue across my lips, I could almost taste the salt of the sea.

I entered the Regina tentatively, a hammer gripped in one hand, ready to defend myself if necessary.

The studio was deep in shadow, just as I had left it. The easel where Sylvie's painting once rested, stood empty and forlorn. It seemed to mock me for acting so impetuously. I might have hidden the painting myself, I might have carried it all the way back to Vence. Instead, I'd panicked and given it to Matteo, afraid that the German who'd threatened me would hunt me down.

I inspected the room, inch by inch. Whatever crumbs the German had scattered from my doomed picnic had long since been eaten by vermin. I straightened up the furniture that had been toppled over by the soldiers, readjusted the white drop sheets. Most of Matisse's paintings were safe in the Bank of France, but some had been necessarily left behind. I opened the cupboard where they were stored like entombed saints in a sealed crypt. When I counted the number of crated paintings, I learned, with no surprise, that several were missing.

The thieving German had come back, but at least he hadn't gotten Portrait of a Bride. *I used my hammer to break up the easel and nailed the wood across the cupboard door.*

Perhaps Sylvie's painting was still safe, I thought. Perhaps it wasn't taken or destroyed when the Germans evacuated the port. Perhaps I would one day find Lucie or Clairmont and they would know where Matteo had hidden it. I had these thoughts many times. They gradually became prayers and then wishes.

But in my most secret nightmares, the paint in Sylvie's portrait dissolved and ran down the canvas like rain down a window-pane, or tears down my face.

IX

THE ENDING WAS MORE SAVAGE than the beginning. The Allies pushed from the West and the South, the Russians marched like a juggernaut from the East. The German counterattacks were mostly launched by old men and boys, most of whom were slaughtered. Dresden burned to the ground. Berlin became a city of ruin and rubble.

There were atrocities everywhere, but the worst had nothing to do with the front lines. The worst happened behind barbed wire. When Allied soldiers reached the first of the death camps and saw what the Nazis had done to the Jews, the civilized world cracked open, sickened and stunned.

Soon the roads were clogged with displaced persons trying to get back home after having been kidnapped by the Nazis. German civilians and deserting German soldiers pressed westwards, fleeing the Russians and retribution. Papers were passed around like germs, identities morphed, no one knew for certain where anyone was, or who they'd once been. Collaborators in Vichy scurried back into the dark corners from where they'd come.

But in the midst of this chaos, there were a few miracles.

Sylvie and André had found their way from France to Spain to Portugal to Venezuela and finally to Quebec. She was pregnant with her first child, Louis if it was a boy, Louise if a girl, in honour of the hero of their story.

Madame was released unharmed from prison in October. Rumour had it that even the guards had been alarmed by her temper. A few days later, a postcard reached us in Vence announcing that Marguerite was also free.

Matisse was jubilant. He would have rushed to Paris to see his daughter again had either his health or the train service allowed. She wrote to him several times over the next few weeks, gradually revealing all that had happened to her during the five months of her captivity.

They were terrible letters to read. She had been tortured, so severely that she had tried to kill herself by slitting her wrists with a splinter of broken *glass. The train she was put on, the train that would have taken her eastward to Germany and certain death, was strafed by Allied bombers, held up by impassable bridges, and finally halted just before the German border. She was released almost at random. Without food or water, she stumbled into a nearby town, but no one would help her. The townspeople had locked their doors and windows against an influx of fleeing collaborators who were desperate to get out of France. She was found crouching in the woods by members of the local Resistance, who'd looked after her until the liberation.*

When at last Marguerite was able to travel to Vence, and father and daughter were reunited, I thought she had changed. She would never accept me, but she was kinder to me, her voice less harsh when she spoke to me. Perhaps she saw in my eyes, as I saw in hers, that the war had taken something from both of us.

She would not sleep under the same roof as me, but her daily visits would often stretch into the early evening. Once I passed the studio door and saw her head to head with Matisse, looking through a portfolio of drawings. The glow of the lamp edged her with light so that she looked translucent, a woman in a stained glass window, dappled with sparks of gold.

In the spring of 1946, the garden at the Villa Rêve could not have been more beautiful or more exuberant, as if trying to rub out all traces of the war. The lavender was still green, but already pungent. There was thyme and cologne mint and lemon balm and rosemary and great drifts of basil. The scents alone made me dizzy. There were dozens of rosebushes just beginning to bud along a high stone wall, and majolica pots filled with ferns. But no flowers or vines could cover over my memories. Not even Matisse's colours had that much depth.

Annelies stayed with us. When word reached her that her husband had been killed, she was stoic. She said she'd known it for months in her heart. Friends wrote her letters, urging her to come home and describing the liberation of Amsterdam by Canadian soldiers. But the liberation had come too late for many. Thousands had died of hunger in the previous winter. Annelies had lost too much to go home too soon.

Matisse, generous as ever, took charge of her education as a painter, gave her employment as a model, even found buyers for her work. Now and again, he gave her drawings of his own. "For your old age," he would say with a wink. "In case you can't work forever, like me."

And it was true. Outfaced by incredible odds, Matisse began to paint again. In part, it was the rush of love and relief he felt for Marguerite's survival that inspired him. But more than that, more than me, it was a country girl named Monique Bourgeois.

Sylvie had hired her to help with Matisse's nursing several years earlier when we were still living in Cimiez. Monique was silent and shy, with masses of ebony hair and a long neck, serious eyes and a sober expression. Little by little, in the long nights of his suffering, Matisse coaxed out her story.

She was the child of a strict and deeply conventional French family. Her education consisted of saying the rosary and embroidering because her father believed that ignorance guaranteed the submission of women. The war changed his mind. When the family was starving, Monique began training as a student nurse and was sent out to find work.

Patron found her combination of innocence and sensuality irresistible. She was so unworldly she had never read a book without first asking her mother's permission. At all costs, she was to be protected from the fantasies of love and the traps of men. Yet, somehow, when her nursing duties were completed and Matisse had recovered enough to paint, he persuaded her to pose for him.

When he was finished the painting, Monique in a Gray Dress, *Monique's figure outlined in a vivid yellow-gold, he showed it to her proudly. She practically recoiled.*

"It's nothing but a meaningless series of blobs of colour," she said incredulously.

I held my breath from my corner of the studio, but Matisse just laughed. After a few more canvases, she drifted away.

In 1943, chance and tuberculosis brought Monique back into our lives, to the nursing home run by nuns, Foyer Lacordaire, just down the road from the Villa Rêve. This time, I paid more attention. I knew she was going to be important. Her return meant something.

She came for tea when she was well enough, settling in with the languor of a relaxed cat. She enjoyed Matisse's teasing. They shared long, rambling conversations and mischievous smiles. Then one day, she startled us all with an announcement. "I've decided to become a nun. I leave tomorrow to begin my novitiate," she said calmly.

Matisse was horrified. He saw her as a prisoner, trapped in a thicket of dogmas and prejudices. He raged and argued and then begged her to reconsider, but she would not be moved.

Though I hadn't chosen the same path as Monique, I believe I understood her. Given her upbringing, she had two choices: marriage or the convent. Since her father had proven himself to be intolerant, I guessed that Monique was putting her faith in Jesus as a kinder task-master.

Matisse, however, dismissed my argument. He wrote her dozens of letters. Eventually, he convinced himself that Monique's life of austere discipline and dedication paralleled his own. While she had taken the veil, he had taken up the paintbrush.

In 1946, against all customs of the Catholic Church that forbade a nun to be assigned to a convent in a place she had once lived, Monique, reborn as Sister Jacques-Marie, returned to Foyer Lacordaire in Vence as if it were fated. In his old age, Matisse found in her a muse that spoke to his indefatigable spirit. He reinvented himself one last time, gathered up his strength for one last starburst of creativity.

The paintings that poured from his hands were breathtaking, a series of interrelated canvasses that became known as the Vence Interiors: Interior in Yellow and Blue, Interior in Venetian Red, Interior with Egyptian Curtain. The gouache cut-outs, collected for a book called Jazz, were even more daring, a triumphant negation of old age and pain. There were kings and clowns, Creole dancers and circus ponies, all vibrating with energy: prancing pinks and yellows, the rich blues of Byzantine enamels, velvety purples, brilliant whites against midnight blacks.

I felt my own spirit renewed. The entire household buzzed and hummed with energy. One day, with Patron's paintings orbiting around me, and the light streaming through the windows of the studio, I surprised myself by feeling completely happy.

"Don't move," Patron said.

I wanted to laugh aloud, to sweep him into my arms, to dance on air, to swim in my unbridled love for him. Instead I held still.

Sometimes, when everyone else is asleep, I stare at the portrait that Ma-

tisse began painting of me that day. It hangs on the wall of my bedroom beside the first portrait, Girl in a Blue Blouse. *In the first, I see the straight nose, pink cheeks, and yellow hair of an ingenuous young girl, a promise of strength but a little hesitancy, too. In the second, painted eight years later, my hair is bright green on one side, dark green on the other. My face is divided into geometrical zones of blue and yellow. The colours are those of our life together, the colours of spring, the sea, the sun. I look confident, bold, moving forward, in motion.*

I see also that Matisse always understood my divided self, the part I chose to give to him and the part I chose to give to Matteo.

Patron called the painting Bicoloured Portrait: Lydia Delectorskaya. *He gave history my name.*

Chloe found the waiting almost intolerable. Two nights had passed since the party and still Ashkar and Kirov had not responded. The hours itched and fretted at her like a bad case of poison ivy. At times, the villa felt like a prison and she would run outside and sit by the edge of the sea, letting the waves soothe her. Then she would see a yacht, imagine a pair of binoculars trained on her, and rush back indoors, feeling exposed and vulnerable.

She was assaulted by doubts. Her forgery wasn't nearly good enough, a child could see it was a poor, pale copy. The Commissaire had called their plan foolhardy and arrogant and a lot of other French words that sounded insulting. He was probably right.

Adam was taciturn, not speaking, not needing to speak, just waiting. He'd been quite happy when he'd returned from his trip into Nice and Place St. François. Chloe had seen it in his face, but he'd told her nothing.

"What?" she'd finally snapped. "What did you find out?"

But he just shook his head and smiled. "Not yet. Let's just wait for Kirov first. Let's just get this part done."

She wanted to strangle him.

Alain was intolerable. He walked about the villa whistling. He took naps. He clattered about in the kitchen preparing impossible food: whole grilled fish on a bed of fennel stalks, saffron gnocchi, lavender ice cream.

Occasionally, he and Adam would put their heads together over the architectural drawings of the villa, studying entrances and exits.

"Surely you're not planning on catching the thief on your own," Chloe nagged. She hadn't told them yet about her phone call to the Commissaire. She sensed they wouldn't feel grateful.

"No, no. We've discussed all this, Chloe. I've friends in Nice." Alain smiled at her benevolently.

Chloe began to wonder seriously if he was a French version of Professor Moriarty, head of a shadowy criminal underworld.

Finally, she gave up on the two men and retreated to her room. Curled up by the window, she watched the sky flare red and golden as the sun slid below the horizon. She watched the surface of the sea slowly darken and then turn silver as mercury as the moon rose.

Her head nodded forward. Her eyes closed.

When she woke, she saw that the moonlight had made everything silvery and sharp.

Sharp as the sound that had roused her, the sharp urgent sound of footsteps on the pavement of the terrace below her. She leaned forward and craned her neck to get a better view. The terrace was deserted except for the shadows in the corners and along the edges of the trees.

She drew back from the window, counted slowly to ten.

She looked again. The terrace seemed still, the night eerily empty, save for the whispering palms. But she couldn't shake the feeling that she'd heard something.

She strained her ears but found only her own quickened breathing.

Then, a flash of light, a thin flicker of light, crossed her vision. She knew at once it had come from inside the villa.

Suddenly a cacophony of sounds ripped open the night—firecrackers exploding in her ears, shouting, pounding footsteps.

She whirled away from the window, adrenaline pulsing through her veins. She raced down the hallway, skidded to a stop at the top of the stairs.

Halfway down, a large figure slumped sideways on the steps.

"Alain," she gasped, rushing forward.

His face was slick with sweat. With his right hand, he was clutching his heart. In his left, he was fumbling with a bottle. He lifted it to his mouth, sprayed something under his tongue. He was breathing hard.

"Go, go," he urged. "Take this."

Chloe registered the gun and recoiled. Fear was rising like a wave inside her, lapping at her throat. If she opened her mouth, the fear would spill out in a scream.

Alain shook her. "Adam. Through the kitchen," he mumbled, his head lolling backwards.

Chloe ran, skidding to a stop at the flung-open door to the patio. She crept outside, around the corner of the house, pressing her body against the white wall.

A red-yellow muzzle-flash tore across her vision. She dove away from the explosion that followed it, her ears ringing. Bullets ricocheted from the wall to the roof and from the roof to the ground, drawing fiery lines across the patio stones and filling the air with the smell of burnt gunpowder. The noise was deafening.

She raced away from it, moving swiftly, silently, wet grass suddenly beneath her bare feet, her eyes sweeping the lawn.

The flashlight blinded her before she heard the voices commanding her to stop. Bright, blue-white light as searing as a flare, white neon in the space behind her eyes.

She dropped to her knees.

When she opened her eyes, the sight of Adam slammed into her. He was lying on the grass, covered in blood. Blood running from his head into his eyes. Blood from his side leaking through his shirt and over his fingers. She crawled towards him, calling his name. Her chest felt as though it were being crushed.

Beyond the blazing light that pinned her to the ground, she heard more shouting, more pyrotechnics, and then a voice she recognized.

"Quite a mess," the Commissaire said. "Call an ambulance for this man."

Adam stirred. He reached for Chloe, grabbed her shoulder and pulled himself up to a sitting position. "No, wait. Kirov's out there."

"Not any longer," Lejeune said. "Kirov's dead."

Chloe sagged with relief.

From a distance, far out over the shining expanse of sea, came the distinctive whir of helicopter blades.

X

WHEN MATISSE BEGAN HIS LAST *great work,* The Chapel of the Rosary in Vence, *he was seventy-eight years old, with a body that had been rocked many times by illness and storms of anxiety.*

It all began with a design for a stained glass window shown to him by Sister Jacques-Marie. She had a dream of turning the leaking garage beside Foyer Lacordaire into a chapel for the nuns. Her drawing was crude and poorly executed. Naturally, Matisse could not resist taking over the design.

Soon he was imagining the interior of the chapel, white tile walls and marble floors that would reflect the light and colour from the windows in the same way that the surface of the sea reflected the sun. He imagined a roof of blue starbursts, an ornate black spire spiking the sky. He saw huge figures outlined in black on the white walls, a Dominican monk, a Madonna and child. The Moroccan curtains, which turned light and shadow into lace patterns, became the model for the exquisitely carved confessional doors.

It was madness to undertake such a huge project.

Almost everyone was against him. I bit my tongue and trembled for his health, even finding, briefly, an ally in Marguerite. The Mother Superior of the convent was scandalized by Matisse's reputation and fiercely objected. Picasso was equally scandalized for entirely opposite reasons. He detested anything to do with religion. "Better to design bullfighter's capes than vestments," he declared.

But Patron had always wanted the chance to create some public piece of art, some monument or mural. The fact that no one had ever asked was a hurt that he carried deep inside himself. He wouldn't let go of this chance. All resistance was swept away by his implacable will.

I was witness to his extraordinary effort.

He used gouache cutouts to design huge sheets of radiantly coloured win-

dows. We traveled to Paris, to the best glassmakers, to find the exact shades of bottle green, cobalt blue, and lemon yellow. He called the double window behind the altar, The Tree of Life, and illustrated it with a cactus in bloom, a plant that thrives even in the most arid deserts.

The scale of the figures was so large, we were forced to leave our secluded Villa Rêve and move back to the Regina where the two floors of the studio could accommodate Matisse's ambition. He climbed a stepladder and drew a Madonna with a nine-foot pole with a rag attached to the end that he would dip directly into black paint. In the end, he had to draw a bit of his Madonna on each ceramic tile and then fit her figure together like a jigsaw puzzle.

All the while, he fought the treachery of his body, fevers and chills, pain that bit his stomach and hands mercilessly.

In June of 1951, the chapel was finally completed. Four years of slavery to its beauty had drained Matisse of his remaining strength. He was too weak to attend the consecration ceremony.

Since Patron was unable on most days to rise from his bed, I put his bed on wheels and organized the household around him. When he put out his hand, my hand was there with a glass of water or a cup of tea before he even knew he wanted it. I brought him photographs and magazines of the latest gallery shows. I read to him, typed his letters, surrounded him with flowers. On rare days, we'd take a taxi down to the sea and he'd slumber in the back seat like a child coming home from a day at the beach.

He ended up sketching in his pajamas, quite literally sleeping with the work that had always consumed his life and had always been at the centre of our enduring love.

"What part of your head hurts?" Chloe asked, staring at the bandages that swathed Adam's brow.

"The part above my shoulders."

"Oh. The doctor says you were lucky. A cut on the forehead and a nasty gash in your side. Besides, you didn't have to answer all of Julien's questions. He was livid."

"You call him Julien now?"

Chloe raised her chin defiantly. "That's hardly the point. You might have been killed. You *and* Alain."

"How is the old boy?"

"Cross with me for calling in Julien."

"It was a bit disloyal of you."

Chloe threw him a bitter look. "Not you, too. You might be a touch grateful that the gendarmes saved your life. Alain's unbelievable. He says his friends could have handled Kirov by themselves, but the *flics* mucked everything up. Did you know I thought he was having a heart attack on the stairs?"

Adam nodded. "He takes nitroglycerin for his angina."

"So why didn't either of you tell me?"

"It must have slipped our minds," Adam lied. "Where is he? I thought he'd have driven you to the hospital."

"He told me he was going to the police station. A date with Julien."

"Would you please stop calling him Julien?"

"Alain's with the Commissaire. They're tying up loose ends with the local gendarmes. He said to tell you he'd be along later to take us back to the villa. The doctor's releasing you, on the condition that you'll promise to rest."

"What loose ends?"

"Ashkar's gone. With Kirov dead, there's no way to make a case against him. I'm sorry, Adam. I know you wanted to be sure about what happened to Jamie."

Adam closed his eyes, turned his face away. Chloe noticed the bruised hollows beneath his eyes, the tightness in his jaw. She knew he was in more pain than he was admitting. She wanted to touch him, but suddenly felt shy.

"I've done my best for Jamie," he said. "Proof or not, I believe Kirov, or one of Kirov's men, killed him. And I've found out who Matteo was, though not why Jamie thought he was important."

Chloe snapped to attention, hungry for information.

"I went to Place St-François, remember?" Adam continued. "I talked to an old man there, a fisherman at one of the stalls. He didn't know Matteo, but he told me there was a terrible massacre in the Place during the war. The Nazis executed seven men, hung them from the balconies. So I went to the war memorial on the hill beside the port. There's a list there: *Martyrs of the Resistance*. One of the names is Matteo Laurion."

Chloe shuddered. She could never think of the cruelty of those times without feeling a sense of vertigo, of teetering on the edge of an abyss. She never forgot that Sylvie had blundered into the path of that savagery, yet had still managed to find love and escape with her husband. Had she known the unlucky Matteo?

Adam's voice dragged her back to the present. "The tragedy is that the war was almost over. It happened in the summer of 1944."

"At least Sylvie wouldn't have witnessed the killings then. She and André were married in January, just before fleeing the country."

"Your grandmother was married here, in Nice?"

Chloe stared at him, surprised by the urgency in his voice. Slowly, she nodded her head.

Adam tried to sit up, winced, and sagged back onto his pillows.

"What? What did I say?" Chloe demanded. She stood up and leaned over him.

"French bureaucracy, Chloe. All French marriages have to be registered with the civil authorities. The records are kept in the local *mairies*, town halls. You could look up Sylvie's marriage."

"But what would that tell me that I don't already know?"

"Witnesses. The couple would need witnesses. French records are very thorough. The full names of the witnesses will be listed together with their occupation and place of birth. You might find the link to Saint-Jeannet."

All the exhaustion and fear of the previous evening that had frayed Chloe's nerves seemed to vanish at once. She felt energized again. She felt optimistic. Kirov and Ashkar were no longer lurking in the shadows behind her, following and watching and threatening. She was free to hunt for Sylvie's painting in earnest.

She reached for her purse and whirled toward the door, calling back over her shoulder. "Tell Alain I took the Peugeot."

"Hey, wait! That's all the thanks I get?" Adam complained.

Chloe stopped in the doorway, turned around, crossed the room in a flash, and kissed him. Softly, on the lips, her hair brushing his cheek as she leaned over him.

When he opened his eyes, she was gone.

There was a map of Nice in the glove compartment of the Peugeot, standard tourist issue in all rental cars. The *mairie* was not difficult to find, located at five rue de l'Hôtel de Ville, *l'hotel de ville* being a French synonym for the town hall. It was only a few blocks from the western end of the Cours Saleya.

As usual, there was no place to park on the Promenade des Anglais. Chloe crossed her fingers and maneuvered the car down the steep ramp of a cavernous, subterranean parking lot beneath the market square. It was like entering Dante's inferno, each labyrinthine turn leading to a lower level of darkness and dank, exhaust-heavy air. She managed to park without scraping the paint off the passenger door and struggled up several flights of concrete stairs.

Stepping into the open air was like stepping into another world, the damp grey stench of the garage instantly dispelled by bursts of colour, wafts of perfume. She was standing in the middle of Nice's flower market, knee-deep in bouquets of daylilies, pansies, azaleas, and anemones. Roses climbed up trellises in curving lines of red, peach, pink, and yellow. She took in a deep lungful of the deliciously scented air, knowing that Sylvie must also have stood here, maybe on this very spot.

She reached the *mairie* at ten, giving thanks that it had Saturday hours. Like most government buildings she had ever been in, it was characterized by an air of icy formality, hushed but for the hum of air conditioners and ringing phones. She located the right sign, *registres d'etat-civil*, took her place at the end of the queue and waited.

At eleven o'clock, Chloe finally found herself looking into the face of a man with dark, silver-streaked hair, a silver moustache, and eyes like black olives. She gave him her best smile and made her request in her most grammatically correct French.

The man immediately switched to English. "Date of the marriage?" he asked.

"January second, 1944."

He raised both hands to shoulder level, palms up, fingers spread. "Only records over a hundred years old can be viewed by the public. *Desolé.* Next."

"No, wait! I'm the granddaughter of Sylvie Brionne and André Denoyer. They were married here in Nice, then moved to Canada."

The olive eyes swept over her, softened a little. "Can you prove direct descent?" the man asked.

"I have my passport, but my surname isn't the same. They were my maternal grandparents."

"I'm afraid I need to see a birth certificate. The rules, you understand?" He watched the light go out in Chloe's eyes and hesitated before moving on to the next person in line. "Mademoiselle," he relented, "since you have come all the way from Canada, I would accept a facsimile. Perhaps you have someone at home who could fax a copy of your birth certificate here?"

The sparkle came back, as if he had lit a fuse inside her.

Chloe rummaged in her bag for her cell phone and prayed that it might be raining in Toronto so that Sammy would not be playing golf.

An hour and forty-five minutes later, Chloe held in her hands a copy of the record of the marriage of her grandparents in the Chapelle de la Miséricorde, just off the Cours Saleya.

Her fingers traced the loops of the signatures as if she could glean secrets from them. There was Sylvie's name, small and slanting to the right. Bride. Born in Montreal, Canada. Occupation, cook and part-time caregiver. There was Lydia's signature as witness, bold and slanting to the left. Friend of the bride. Born in Tomsk, Russia. Occupation, artist's assistant and secretary.

Both women seemed to Chloe so modest, so humble, neither mentioning their attachment to Matisse, nor his to them.

Besides André's name and information, there were two other signatures. Matteo Laurion, fisherman, and Lucie Laurion, nurse in training. Both were born in Nice. Man and wife, maybe, or brother and sister?

Why was Matteo so important to Jamie? Chloe held the proof in her hands that Matteo must have been close to both Sylvie and Lydia.

But no matter how often she ran her hands over the signatures, her imagination galloping, she could find no link to Saint-Jeannet. Except for the red arrow on Jamie's map and her intuition that told her she must go there.

Chloe followed the route she'd travelled earlier in the week with Adam, this time passing through Vence high above the coastline. Just beyond Vence, the pine forest disappeared and the massive rock face of the Baou de Saint-Jeannet dominated the skyline. The view from the rocky mountain, across undulating valleys to the distant sea was breathtaking, but Chloe kept her eyes trained on the twisting, narrow road, trying to convince herself that she was not afraid of heights even as the Peugeot laboured up a seemingly vertical grade.

The hamlet of Saint-Jeannet sat on a ledge beneath the towering Baou, a haven for climbers and hikers. Chloe gratefully parked the car and walked into the village, its streets winding back among ancient stone houses and artisan's shops. The afternoon was sleepy, still but for a chorus of cicadas. She wandered by an ancient church, read the names of the dead carved onto the war memorial. There was no one named Laurion.

She passed through a beautiful low-arched passageway and found herself on a terrace with a panoramic view sweeping across fields and farms, orchards and vines, villas and perched villages, all the way down to Nice. Beyond Nice, the sea travelled on forever. She found a bench, grateful for a breeze under the hot, white sky.

She didn't know what she'd expected by coming here, but she felt happy being on her own, taking the time to drink in the peacefulness of Saint-Jeannet. Maybe Alain was right, maybe *Portrait of a Bride* had been destroyed or stolen years ago. She realized it was enough for her that it *had* existed, more than enough that she had followed the memories of her grandmother across time to the places she'd once loved. Despite its dangers and frustrations, the trip had been good for her, as if somehow it had been meant to happen. Maybe, she thought, it wasn't the painting she was intended to find, but her own self.

Chloe sat on the bench for a long time, until the village around her began to wake up from its afternoon siesta. She heard voices raised in greeting, dogs barking, chairs scraping across a terrace. She followed the sounds to a little outdoor café just around the corner from the panoramic view. The menu, scrawled in chalk on a blackboard, was promising enough to tempt her to take a table. She knew it was too late for lunch and too early for dinner, but at the very least she could order something to drink, maybe some bread and cheese.

A bored-looking young waitress in a white sun dress sauntered across the terrace, hips swaying. She had fine brown hair escaping from a braid that hung down her back. As she neared Chloe, a group of male hikers who'd gathered to drink and jostle with each other began whistling and hooting. Casually, the young woman flicked them her middle finger, then turned and grinned at Chloe. "The village idiots," she shrugged, nodding her head in the direction of the teenaged boys.

The smile transformed her. It was a sunny grin, all the more charming for its suddenness. Her teeth were very white against her honey-tanned skin. Her eyelashes were impossibly long. "Don't worry," she added. "They're harmless."

Chloe smiled back at her. "I think I'll have a *citron pressé* and whatever scraps of bread and cheese you can find in the kitchen. Join me, if you're not too busy. I'll buy you a drink."

The grin flashed again.

The girl returned five minutes later with a laden tray. She placed a generous basket of baguette slices, a bowl of black and green olives, a circle of goat cheese and a thick slice of country pâté on the table. She handed Chloe her lemon drink, then settled down across from her with a glass of *pastis*.

"My name's Rosa," she said. "Rosa Clairmont. Thanks for the drink."

Chloe introduced herself, asked a few polite questions about Saint-Jeannet, and settled into her late lunch and an amusing account of Rosa's much more sophisticated life as a student in Aix-en-Provence.

"I work in the café to earn money for school," she concluded, "and to visit my grandmother. She still lives on her own, but a nurse comes in mornings and evenings. Are you American?"

Chloe shook her head. "Canadian," she said emphatically.

"Really? My grandfather always used to say a Canadian saved his life during the war."

"I didn't know Canadian soldiers fought this far south in France."

"Oh, it wasn't a soldier," Rosa grinned. "It was a woman. Sylvie something."

"Sylvie Brionne?" Chloe whispered, taut with excitement.

She felt as if lightning had struck their table, as if she were lit up, sending off electric sparks.

Rosa felt it too. "I can't believe it. You know this Sylvie?"

"She's my grandmother," Chloe fumbled in her bag, handed Rosa the copy of the marriage register.

"But this is *my* grandmother!" Rosa exclaimed. "Lucie Laurion."

"Would it be possible, Rosa, for me to meet your grandmother?"

Chloe tried for a moment to identify the sensation she felt—this breathless, unreal feeling inside—and eventually decided that all the words she knew were too cold and too pale.

Lucie Laurion Clairmont was a quiet, calm woman, eighty-five years old, with the kind of dark beauty that age could soften but never destroy. Her kitchen was bright and tidy, with a shelf of stone jugs above the sink and a long wooden table running down the centre of the room, like the one that Chloe had shared with Adam and Alain in the farmhouse near Aix. A giant black stove stood in one corner, and bunches of herbs hung from low beams above the chimney: rosemary, lavender, pennyroyal.

Rosa went to the pantry and fetched a bottle of fruit wine, pouring out glasses and watching Chloe and her grandmother with curious eyes.

Chloe took the glass that was handed to her. The pale yellow liquid had a pungent aroma of freshly cut grass and apples. She took a sip, happy to let it loosen her tongue. "Sylvie died when I was two, but she had a happy life with André. Their daughter, Louise, is my mother. I know they met here, in France, and that they both worked at one time with the painter, Matisse. I'd be grateful for anything you could tell me about them."

They spoke in French, but whenever Chloe found herself at a loss for vocabulary, Rosa jumped in.

Lucie looked at her closely for a few minutes, wrapped herself in a shawl despite the warmth of the day, and smiled. Her voice, when she finally spoke, carried the Provencal accent. "You look a little like Sylvie, her dark eyes. But not her hair."

"No," Chloe laughed, twisting the dark red strands. "This comes from my father."

"I knew Sylvie a little, but we knew André better. He and my brother grew up in the port. Little boat rats, we called them. But André loved cars, learned all about them. Matteo said he could take one apart and put it all back together again. We teased him mercilessly when he became a chauffeur, but André didn't care. He liked the old man Matisse. Sylvie, he liked even better."

"Tell Chloe about grand-père," Rosa urged.

"Michel Clairmont, my husband, was a doctor," Lucie stated proudly. "During the war, terrible things happened. So terrible Rosa should not hear of them."

"Grand-maman, don't be silly. I'm nineteen," Rosa protested. "I know all about the war."

"I hope not, *ma petite*." Lucie's face changed in an instant, suddenly looking old and ruined and forbidding.

But she rallied. She leaned towards Rosa, put her hands on either side of her face. "As old as nineteen?" She laughed silently. Then she folded her hands in her lap. Her eyes drifted to a space just above Chloe's head, as if she were looking into a mirror, or some gateway into the past.

"Michel Clairmont helped people in trouble all his life. The war was no exception. He couldn't turn his back just because the Milice or the Italians or Germans said so. He had a room in a building off Place Masséna where people who needed medical treatment could go, people who couldn't go to hospitals or risk being reported to the authorities. One day, Sylvie was keeping watch for him in the square and she saw Milice approaching. She ran up the stairs to warn Clairmont. The girl he was helping slipped away with her friends, but there was no hope for Michel."

Lucie's voice had dropped almost to a whisper. She paused in her story, took a sip of her wine, and squeezed Rosa's hand.

"Sylvie figured out a way to trick the Milice," she revealed, her voice stronger now. "She and Clairmont dropped their clothes where they stood and jumped into bed."

Like an experienced raconteur, Lucie waited for Chloe's startled reaction before continuing. "It's a good story, *non*? Michel loved it. He said the Milice looked like buffoons, bursting through the door, bumping into one another, not knowing where to look, but taking a good peek at Sylvie nonetheless. A funny story, but not so funny at the time. The Milice would've arrested them both, maybe shot them."

"You see?" Rosa beamed. "Your grandmother was very brave."

Chloe nodded and took another sip of the fruit wine. It tasted syrupy and tannic at the same time, smoothing away all her tensions. She felt she could stay here and listen to stories of Sylvie for the rest of the afternoon and long into the evening. "Your husband worked in the Resistance?"

"Yes and no. At first he only helped people who were hurt or injured. He didn't report everything he should to the authorities. But then, after the raid on the port, he became more active. He took me away from Nice to hide. Saint-Jeannet was perfect. Among the country folk, the village has a reputation for witchcraft." Lucie pointed to the bunches of herbs drying near the chimney.

"Turns out the witches just make fruit wine like the one you're drinking, and potions to keep out germs. But the villagers made up some stories to scare the Germans—a potion to turn a man impotent, another to make him blind. The villagers were able to keep their stores of wine because the Germans were too spooked to steal from them. Of course the true motive behind the witch tales was to distract the soldiers from the real reason the Resistance came here—caves hidden in the rock face."

"I'm sorry to ask," Chloe began, "but did you leave Nice because of what happened to Matteo?"

The question hung in the air between them like smoke. Rosa's eyes were like saucers moving silently from Chloe's face to Lucie's and back again.

"Yes." Lucie's voice cracked on the single word, whether with rage or grief, Chloe could not tell.

Rosa stood up, slid her arms around her grandmother protectively.

"She doesn't like to talk about Matteo. It upsets her."

"Of course. Madame Clairmont, do you recognize this?" Chloe took the amethyst ring off her finger and dropped it into the old woman's extended palm.

"Oh, yes," she crooned, holding it up to the light. "Lydia's wedding present to Sylvie. I never thought I'd see this again."

"You knew Lydia?"

Lucie kept her head down, eyes fastened on the ring. "She was very kind, very strong. My brother loved her. But she was devoted to Matisse." She handed back the ring, eyes still downcast.

"Yes," Chloe replied softly, "I know."

"Matisse couldn't come to Sylvie's wedding, but he painted a picture of her."

Chloe kept very still. She felt she was in a dream, the kind of dream in which everything was on the brink of being explained, but could just as easily fall away into fragments.

"I saw it once, so beautiful. Matteo showed it to me."

"Matteo had the painting?" Chloe whispered.

Lucie nodded. "Lydia asked him to hide it. He covered it up with a different picture. Matteo was very clever. He just covered up the Matisse and hung it right there on the wall in his bedroom right under the Germans' noses."

Chloe gathered up all her courage, breathed deeply, closed her eyes. "Was the painting destroyed in the raid on the Nice port?" she asked, her voice trembling.

"Oh, no."

Chloe's eyes flew open. She stared at Lucie, afraid to believe what she'd just heard.

Lucie shook her head vigorously. "It's true. My aunt saved it. She didn't know what was hidden there, but she knew that Matteo was keeping it for Lydia. We owed Lydia, my aunt and me. She'd helped us once when no one else could…"

Lucie's voice faltered. Chloe looked up at Rosa, who was still standing behind her grandmother. She shook her head, a warning not to press the old woman any further.

"That's wonderful news. Thank you Madame Clairmont. I'm so glad my grandmother knew you."

Chloe pressed her hands briefly over Lucie's and stood up to leave.

"Auntie gave it to the nun."

"What?" Chloe strained to hear the faint words.

"When the war was over, Auntie tried to find Lydia but she and Matisse had gone to Paris. So my aunt gave the painting to the little nun across the road from the villa. I explained all this to the young man."

"What young man?" Rosa demanded, more surprised than Chloe.

"That lovely man, Jamie, with the big smile."

Rosa shrugged her shoulders and walked Chloe to the doorway. When Chloe looked back to wave goodbye, Lucie Clairmont looked far away, wrapped up in memories.

Chloe knew who the little nun was. Sister Jacques-Marie was one of Matisse's favourites towards the end of his life. Their friendship had been the impetus for the Matisse chapel in Vence, built for the sisters of a Dominican convent located almost across the road from Le Rêve. Chloe also remembered reading somewhere that Sister Jacques-Marie had died in a convent in a village on the Basque coast of France in 2005.

As the Peugeot twisted back down the narrow road to Vence, Chloe was tormented by questions. Why hadn't the nun given the painting to Lydia? For surely, if Lydia had had it, she would have sent it on to Sylvie. At the very least, it would never have been hidden from the world. If Lydia had known that the painting came from Matteo's aunt, she would not have been fooled by a different picture. She would easily have guessed that the Matisse lay hidden beneath.

Had the nun decided to keep the picture, thinking it was just some amateur drawing? Worse, had she decided to keep it, knowing it was a Matisse? Her head buzzed, but in the end, she thought a crooked nun, especially a famous crooked nun, was as unlikely as a Russian butler.

The search had come to another dead end, and Chloe's disappointment flattened her. She'd conjured up so many possible paintings of Sylvie in her imagination—different colours, different poses, different perspectives. All of them seemed so fragile, so doomed. How likely was it that one small painting had survived in the midst of the savagery that had swallowed up Matteo and millions of others?

The road from Saint-Jeannet to Vence passed directly in front of the Matisse chapel and the old convent, now called Maison Lacordaire. Chloe slammed on her brakes and parked the car. She had one half-hour before the Rosary Chapel closed.

Here, at least, was a part of the past, still living, still vibrant. The building was small, two long sides, and a tall stained glass window at one end. At the opposite end, the fourteen Stations of the Cross were drawn in black paint, stark against white ceramic tile. Yet despite its dimensions, the space seemed to soar. Light spilled through the windows on the left side, softening the large, powerful drawings of Saint Dominic and the Virgin on the right side. Chloe walked through pools of colour—bottle-green, mauvy-blue, lemony-yellow. Matisse had designed everything—the crucifix, the altar cloth, the candlesticks, even the confessional door, eight panels of exquisitely carved wood that looked like eight panels of white lace.

She couldn't begin to imagine the effort the Chapel must have demanded of Matisse. Four years of painstaking work, a thousand details to consider, when all the while his body must have been aching, crying out for rest. She took one long, last look at the serene, even joyful space, a triumphant negation of old age and pain, and turned to leave.

None of it would have been possible without Lydia. In place of the miracle of the Chapel, there would likely have been a leaky garage falling to ruin.

Chloe had been the last visitor of the day. A nun followed her up the steps to street level, locking the gate behind her.

"Excuse me," Chloe said. "Can you point me in the direction of Le Rêve?"

The nun sighed, "It's just a house you know. It's not open to visitors. People rent it for weddings and conventions. Sometimes there are painting classes."

"Please," Chloe persisted.

The nun read Chloe's pleading expression and smiled. "Most people think the house is east of the Chapel and walk halfway to Saint-Jeannet trying to find it," she laughed. "It's actually just to the west. There's a tiny road, just behind the main one. It slants up sharply, dwindles into a country lane. You'll find the house there."

Chloe set off immediately on foot. The road could only be seen from one direction, and even walking she almost missed it. It took her uphill. She turned again onto a dirt road, and suddenly there was Le Rêve, screened by yuccas and cypresses, olive trees and overgrown pines, palm trees and pink laurels. Its huge front garden was enclosed by a wrought iron fence.

The villa looked a bit like an aging movie star, repainted and remodeled over the years. Even now the paint was peeling on the pale green shutters, the pink stucco looked patchy. Though the garden was groomed, the countryside around it was wild.

Chloe put her hand on the gate, but as the nun had warned her, it was firmly locked. She remembered seeing a photograph of Matisse walking through this very gate. He was wearing a fedora, a cape around his shoulders. He was leaning on a cane. His beard shone white in the sun.

She walked around the perimeter a bit, found a place to sit on the ground in the long, uncut grass. How many times had Lydia and Sylvie crossed that garden, opened that gate, perhaps sat dreaming where she sat now? Time may have weathered the villa, but the olive trees were still rooted there, the palm fronds still pressed against the windows. She felt close to Lydia and Sylvie, as if she were glimpsing moments of their lives, like scenes in a darkly-lit play.

By the time Chloe roused herself and wandered back to the car, it was almost dark. The sky was that luminous shade of deep blue that precedes full night, the horizon striated with a deep orange. She leaned against the tall iron fence that surrounded the connecting garden between the Chapel and Maison Lacordaire. It was a formal garden, with a beautiful view across the valley of the walls surrounding the old village of Vence. She looked up at the ornate, black spire of the Chapel, towering over the blue and white tiled roof. The blue tiles traced a zigzag pattern like the edges of stars. She heard the lilting sound of soft laughter coming from the open windows of the Maison, the nuns perhaps sharing an evening meal.

A jolt of recognition, a leap of intuition, galvanized Chloe.

Almost afraid to believe what she was seeing, she counted off the signs on her fingertips: the walls of Vence in the distance, the blue stars of the Chapel roof, the nuns inside, the brides of Christ, virgin brides.

Beyond the walls, beneath blue stars,

A tree blossoms and roses veil a virgin bride.

There was a pruned tree in the garden, a trellis of roses climbing up the white walls of the Maison.

Her hands gripped the black iron rails. She slowed her breathing, tried to settle down enough to think clearly. What would Alain and Adam do? What would be the next logical step? Drive calmly back to Cap Ferrat and form a reasonable plan?

None of that appealed to Chloe. She walked determinedly to the front gate of Maison Lacordaire and rang the old fashioned bell.

Nothing happened.

She rang again and again.

Finally, a round-faced woman, dressed in a dark blue habit and head scarf, peered through the double glass doors of the Maison. She pointed to her watch and made a shooing motion at Chloe.

Chloe shook her head and rang again.

Finally, the nun relented. She opened the doors and descended the short set of stairs that led to the gate. In the fading light, Chloe could see her skin was the colour of pale coffee, and her expression was stern.

Before the nun could speak, Chloe launched into an invented crisis involving a broken-down car, and a cell-phone without reception. "I'm all alone and saw your lights. I know it's terribly rude, but I was schooled by nuns. I was sure you'd help me, perhaps guide me in the direction of a hotel?"

Chloe finished her explanation, trying to look worried and needy, but not so desperate as to seem frightening. The last thing she wanted was a hotel. The Maison Lacordaire rented out rooms.

The nun smiled, dimples that transformed her grave manner, and opened the gate, gesturing to Chloe to follow her. Beyond the tall glass doors, ornately decorated with swirls of the same wrought iron that fashioned the gate and the garden fence, the Maison was plain, even a bit shabby, but very clean.

The worn wood floor of a narrow hallway was highly polished, smelling faintly of lavender. Chloe passed a small table draped with a crocheted cotton tablecloth, on top of which were deposited slowly yellowing religious pamphlets. She saw a small sitting room to her right with comfortable-looking chairs and an old television set. The hallway ended at a makeshift office with a counter and a glass window that slid open.

The nun rattled a set of keys, lifted up a jointed part of the counter, and stepped into the cubbyhole office. She handed Chloe a reservation book of the sort she had only ever seen in 1940s movies.

"You're welcome to stay here for the night, if you don't mind leaving very early in the morning. The room is reserved for guests for tomorrow, you see, and we'll need to change the linens. Normally, there'd be no rush, but Sunday is a busy day for us."

"Of course," Chloe answered. "I'm very grateful."

"That's all right. Just sign here."

Chloe paid in cash and signed the register *Sylvie Brionne*. It was the first name that popped into her head. She felt her cheeks flush. It was different, somehow, lying to a nun.

The nun, however, seemed not to notice. She nodded and opened a door leading to a passageway and a staircase. She led Chloe up the stairs, down another hallway, past a faded watercolour of an orchard in springtime—*a tree blossoms*—and finally opened the door to a neat, cheerful bedroom.

"I hope you rest well," the nun said.

Chloe, wide-eyed, her forehead damp, nodded and said nothing.

She lay on the bed in her black jeans and white T-shirt for a long time, then stood up. First, she listened at the door of her room. Very gently she turned the doorknob. Silence. The old house seemed to exhale, settling into the profound quiet of night.

She tipped her head forward, looked up and down the hallway. One shutter had been left slightly open. The moonlight shining through the window made everything look milky, her skin paler.

She pushed the door. A board beneath her bare foot cracked. She stopped mid-gesture, listened, heard only her own erratic breathing.

Slowly she eased down the hall, hugging the wall. She stopped at the painting and worked her fingers behind it, groping for the picture hook. She coaxed the painting away from the wall, taking the weight of the heavy frame into her arms.

She retraced her steps, locked her bedroom door, laid the painting on the bed, and studied it carefully.

Matteo's hiding place was really very clever. Chloe knew that when an oil canvas is framed, there is usually a tiny gap between the edge of the frame and the surface of paint. A watercolour, on paper cut to the exact measurements, could slide into that gap quite snugly. Over time, a wood frame and an oil canvas would dry out and shrink a bit, widening the gap slightly.

She placed a thumb over the bottom left corner of the watercolour and pressed down, pushing up at the same time. The heavy paper moved. High quality Watercolour Block, cold-pressed, one hundred percent cotton. She'd used it herself dozens of times.

Inch by inch, her fingers worked around the edges until the watercolour was fully free of the frame. Then, hands trembling, she lifted up the watercolour and laid it on the floor.

Scarcely breathing, Chloe raised her eyes to the Matisse.

It was glorious, more than she'd hoped for, better than she'd dreamed. It was exactly as Alain had described it, and nothing like it at the same time. The spirit of her grandmother shone out at her through a delicate balance of line and luminous colour—iridescent oranges, a dozen shades of red and pink blended into a spray of rosebuds, the blush of a cheek, the curve of a chin, an ebony spiral of hair.

Chloe thought of her own copy—the demure bride with her doll-face, wearing the kind of meringue wedding dress that is carefully boxed and stored in an attic, clutching a stiff bouquet. She laughed out loud. Matisse had taken risks that were far beyond her. This was a portrait of a vibrant woman who would kick off her shoes and hoist the skirt of her frothy dress and dance across wet green grass at her wedding, her black hair tangled down her back. She was wild and sensual, a hundred inflections of light and shadow.

Chloe felt suspended in time, looking into the face of the long-ago girl who'd become her grandmother. The painting seemed to breathe, to pulse with yellow heat and drenching blues, capturing a moment in time like a bright scene glimpsed through a window at dusk. If she'd had one hundred years to look at it, she thought, that still wouldn't have been enough.

Reluctantly, she turned the Matisse face-down on the bed, and studied the backing. First, she would have to trim away a covering of stiff paper to expose the frame. She scrambled in her purse for a nail file and unscrewed the hooks that held the thick, twisted picture wire. A razor would cut the paper cleanly, but she didn't have one. She used the nail file again, painstakingly puncturing the paper where it met the edge of the wood frame. It was a maddeningly slow process. Her hands itched to rip the paper away, but she forced herself to be patient.

Finally, she lifted the backing away from the frame. There were smudges of paint on the back of the canvas, something that looked like a fingerprint. She smiled to herself. How many people in the world had touched this canvas? Matisse and Lydia certainly, maybe Sylvie, maybe some anonymous framer, and Matteo. And now her.

As she had hoped, the joints where the horizontal top of the frame met its two vertical sides were visible. She tapped and wiggled until the wood top came away in her hands.

The Matisse was released from its frame easily, miraculously, like a passionate letter sliding from a perfumed envelope.

Chloe set about reassembling the framed watercolour as best she could. The wood would need to be glued to hold properly. In the meantime, she used clear nail polish and band-aids and prayed that they might hold for a few days. She replaced the hooks and the picture wire. Without its sturdy backing of canvas, the image of the spring orchard wobbled a little, but it was the best she could do. She hoped it was true that a painting that had hung in the same place for a very long time became invisible to its owners.

She crept into the hallway and re-hung the watercolour, her hands slippery with sweat.

Back in her room, she rumpled the bed sheets, dumped all her makeshift tools and her sandals into her purse, and picked up the Matisse. It was slightly larger than her copy, but should fit easily into the Peugeot.

Her heart began to pound wildly.

Her footsteps on the stairs sounded unnaturally loud.

Finally she was standing in the entry hall of Maison Lacordaire.

She slid back the bolts and pushed through the heavy front doors, padded down the stairs to the front gate as softly as a cat.

Outside, the world seemed still and empty, save for the breeze whispering through pines and palm trees. Chloe glanced in the direction of Le Rêve. *It was so close, Lydia. All that time, Sylvie's painting was so close.*

She stowed the painting in the back seat and started the car.

The stars edged the tops of trees with a thin, silver light, but the road ahead seemed a tunnel through darkness. As she began her twisting descent through the hills towards Nice, she remembered that Jamie had died on this very road. He'd been murdered. She could smell the danger.

Almost unconsciously, her foot pressed more heavily on the gas pedal and the little Peugeot picked up speed.

XI

When Chloe arrived at the Countess's villa, it was almost five in the morning and even the sea was asleep. She carried the painting inside and propped it up on the kitchen counter. She looked at it lovingly, the colours glowing in the watery light of dawn. She smiled to herself, anticipating Alain and Adam's reactions as the reality of the Matisse registered on their faces.

"Bravo," a voice said from across the room.

Her heart skipped a beat and she whirled around. "Alain, you scared me to death. Don't you ever sleep? Look. Isn't it marvelous? Is Adam still asleep? What's—"

Her eyes fell to the gun in his hand and her words turned to dust in her throat.

Alain slipped the gun into the pocket of a voluminous pair of trousers. "Adam's not here. When I went to the hospital to pick you both up, a nurse told me he'd left with a young woman."

"But I didn't—"

"A young woman with black hair. Once I knew the woman wasn't you, I assumed both of you had been kidnapped."

Chloe stared at him open-mouthed. She felt the ripple of shock in her body, the instinct to deny what was happening. She groped for a chair and sank into it.

"I'll get you some coffee," Alain offered. "Drink it black. I'll put some brandy in it."

Chloe felt her life had slipped into some other dimension. Her arms clutched her middle as she tried to comprehend Alain's news. When she'd last seen Adam, when she'd kissed him, his skin had seemed feverish. He was still weak from his injuries.

Alain put a cup in her hands.

She could feel the steam of the coffee on her skin.

"Tell me everything," she said. Her voice echoed as though she'd fallen down a hole.

"A beautiful woman with dark hair, someone who didn't alarm Adam," Alain shrugged. "Who do you think it was?"

Jesus, Liliane.

"I really liked her," Chloe admitted. "Adam thought she'd followed him once to a bar in Paris, but I assured him he was wrong. I don't even know her last name."

She set down her cup, miraculously empty.

"Liliane Dupré. Sometimes Liliane Armande, or even Liliane Descambrais in a pinch. I think that last name might be her real one."

Alain's right eye was fixed on Chloe, on the pulse he could see beating in her temples. He watched her expression of shock shift to hostility.

"Who the hell are you?" she asked.

"First, I'm on your side, always have been. Just a cautionary word so you don't go up in flames."

"I'm serious, Alain," Chloe said gravely. "You have fifteen minutes before I call Julien Lejeune."

"Not a good idea."

"Why not? In fact, if Adam's missing, you should have called him already. Why haven't you?"

Alain's face was completely placid, his left eye swiveling across to the Matisse. Chloe read his meaning as if he had spoken it aloud.

"My god. The ransom. They want the Matisse. Liliane has been after the Matisse all this time? Even while she was with Jamie?"

"I think so."

"But she cared for him. She wouldn't have killed him."

"No. Kirov or Kirov's thugs, they killed my friend. Maybe Ashkar knew that, maybe not. But Liliane had no connections to Kirov and Ashkar. She didn't want Jamie dead. She was waiting patiently for him to find the Matisse and hand it to her. She knew all about it, the photograph that Jamie had, everything. When Jamie was killed, it seemed the dream was over. And then you and Adam came along. I think she might have planned to seduce him, but you were much easier—swept away by Paris, yes? She even tried to help you, told you every place Jamie had been, at least those places she knew about."

"But why didn't she just go after the painting herself?"

"I think she tried, but she couldn't understand Jamie's clue on the back of the sketch. I'm not sure I do. What does it mean?"

"If you stand in a certain place, it's all there in front of you—the walls of Vence, the Chapel roof, the convent. Matteo hid the painting behind another painting. Eventually it ended up in the hands of Sister Jacques-Marie. I'm sure she didn't know it was anything other than a mediocre watercolour. I'm guessing she showed it to Matisse and he waved it away. Lydia never saw it. It's probably been hanging in an upstairs hallway of the convent ever since."

"And the nuns just let you take it?"

Chloe looked down at her lap, twisted her fingers. Alain started to laugh.

"Not funny, Alain. Really it isn't."

"You'd have been a fine thief, had you taken it up professionally."

"And is that what you are? How did you know about Liliane?"

Alain sighed and shifted his considerable weight. One hand disappeared into his pocket again.

"I've a note here. It was left in the villa, waiting for me when I got back from the hospital. We're to wrap up the Matisse and check into the Négresco. Further instructions will be sent to us. And there's the usual threat about no police."

Chloe's eyes widened. She felt she was falling down a stairwell. "We've got to tell Julien," she insisted. "We can't do this by ourselves. The last time, Adam was almost…"

"Quite. Might have been different had Lejeune *not* been there."

Chloe glared at him and jumped to her feet. "That's it. I'm phoning Julien. I'm not risking Adam's life for the sake of your ego."

"Please sit down, Chloe." Alain's voice had shifted an octave lower. Had she imagined it, or was there an undercurrent of menace in his words?

She sat down and listened.

"I got to the hospital at about three. Raced about like an idiot for an hour or so, then came back here. The note was *already* here. Think about that, Chloe."

She stayed very still, but her mind was racing. "Adam was kidnapped before I found the real Matisse. Is that what you mean?"

Alain nodded.

"So Liliane thinks the fake I painted is the real thing?" Chloe continued.

"I'd say so. The fact that Kirov went after it probably made it seem even more legitimate. Did anyone follow you yesterday? Anyone see you leave the convent with the painting?"

"How can I know? I've never known. But I don't think so."

She paused for an instant, studying Alain's face. Then she shook her head slowly.

"I can't believe what you're thinking. And the answer is no, absolutely not. Now that I've seen the original painting of Sylvie, I know it's ludicrous to think anyone could be fooled by my fake. It was only the setting, this villa, all the rumours. People saw what they wanted to see. No, the only way to save Adam is to give up the real Matisse. Poor old George Daniels was killed because of the sketch I copied. I won't let that happen again."

"You're sure?" Alain stood up, began to walk across the kitchen. "Remember, Chloe, no more than a dozen people in the whole world have *ever* seen this painting. Liliane might easily be fooled by greed. It's worth a fortune. Its history is worth almost as much as the image itself—snatched from the Nazis, hidden unknowingly by nuns, stolen from them by the grand-daughter of the bride herself."

Chloe's face had turned to stone. She struggled to understand properly what she was hearing. With every word, every step closer to the Matisse, Alain became more of a stranger to her. Her body rocked with a desperate fear that she would never see Adam again.

She stood up, gripping the chair, her legs trembling. "Take it then, you bastard. It's what you wanted all along. Just take it, but help me get Adam back first."

In an instant, everything changed, Alain changed.

"Forgive me, Chloe. I had to be certain. Of course I'll help you save Adam."

He opened his arms to her and she stumbled into them. He blew a
strand of her hair out of his mouth and spoke into her ear. "You feel as
if you're about to collapse. Come and sit down and I'll tell you the real
reason why we can't call Commissaire Lejeune."

It was to be our last summer together. I knew Matisse was dying.

*We rented a villa far away from judging eyes. We took gentle walks together,
an elegant old gentleman leaning on a woman drenched in a black shawl.
I dragged two overstuffed, faded armchairs out onto a tiny patio so I could
read to him while he pretended to listen and instead napped in the sun like
one of his cats. Sometimes we'd listen to jazz, and hear Sylvie humming in
our ears. We held hands and laughed at how scandalous people imagined
our lives to be.*

*He spoke to me tenderly. He brushed his fingers against my cheek. The
gesture was so unexpected, the gentleness of it so long forgotten, that tears
sprung to my eyes.*

*"Lydia," he said, "I've pulled your strength around me like a borrowed
blanket. It's time to give it back. Tell me, what will you do?"*

*For a brief second, his face looked rosy in the last flare of the sunset, rosy
and young in spite of the lines and the hollowed eyes.*

*I had no answer for him. For almost twenty years, I'd stayed as close to
Matisse as his shadow, learning bit by bit what came to him by instinct.
I could have had an unremarkable life, but instead, because of his genius,
I had another. I was taught to love beautiful things and I had learned a
language in which to express beauty. It seemed inevitable that I should love
him, even though loving Matisse took practice.*

*I wrapped him in my arms, feeling the fierce engine of his heart beating
against my skin. "I'll remember," was the answer I finally gave him to the
question he'd already forgotten.*

*The summer spun itself out slowly, like childhood summers that seem to
last forever. The light danced in the green leaves, the scent of lavender hung
in the air. But gradually, inevitably, the light changed. Trees grew heavy
with fruit. Farmers sheaved their wheat and harvested their grapes. We grew
adept at the balancing of each day's small, luminous joys against Matisse's
physical pain. We knew that whatever goodbyes we might bring ourselves*

to say would be spoken here. I would not be welcome at Matisse's funeral. People would cross the street rather than speak to me. Poor Berthe, Madame's sister who'd once tried to defend me, had been ostracized, left to scratch for a living under a leaky roof in Beauzelle while Madame lived in style in a grand house in the same village.

By mid-October, there was a dark edge to the sky, an unidentifiable taste. The air was hard to breathe and smelled of wine and smoke. Matisse's jaunty smiles disappeared. His joints turned to glass. He could barely hold a pair of scissors in his hand, or maneuver his wrist around the curves of his cutouts, but he tried. Morphine rocked him to sleep, gathered him into its dark arms, softened his nightmares.

I bent over him, whispered in his ear. "It's time, my Patron."

He nodded, not a flicker of fear in his eyes.

While we waited for the ambulance that would take him back to Nice, back to the Regina, I laid my head on his chest and he stroked my hair.

It was the last time we were alone.

Marguerite was waiting for us and I became invisible.

Matisse was put in bed and propped up by cushions. The great sculptor, Giacometti, came to sketch him, his drawing pencils mercilessly seeking out the skull beneath the skin, every curve and pucker of cheek and neck.

I wandered the studio. I stood at the window where I'd once signaled to Matteo and looked out over the gardens where we'd met, still the sweetest, greenest piece of Cimiez.

At night I locked my bedroom door and smoked cigarettes. I put on the blue travelling cloak that Matisse had given me on our journey to Bordeaux. When I narrowed my eyes and looked in the mirror, I was just a blur of blue and blonde and smoke. I was disappearing and no one even noticed. Everyday I was slipping further away.

The sour smell of death hung in the air. I remembered it from my childhood. I took long baths and tried to wash the smell from my skin, but it lingered.

Matisse had a stroke. Marguerite never left his side, never said a word unless she had to, never smiled.

I entered the bedroom with my wet hair wrapped up in a towel. His glassy eyes were sunken in their sockets, his cheeks so papery I could see his bones *through the skin. The sight of him, suddenly diminished, raked my heart.*

As I stood over him, he tried to smile. His hand began to move, his fingers groped across the bed clothes seeking a stub of pencil, a pad for drawing.

He couldn't speak, but his lips moved. I knew what he was trying to say. When the sketch was done, he pressed it into my hand, and closed his eyes.

He lay on his back, still as marble, unnaturally quiet. Late the next afternoon, his worn-out heart ceased to beat.

I went to my bedroom and dressed slowly and finally picked up the suitcase I'd kept packed for fifteen years. There was no one left who needed me. I was free.

Released from Alain's bear hug, Chloe slumped in her chair. She felt like she had when she was a child, pulled this way and that by bickering parents with no control over her own life or wishes.

"Alright, I'm listening. Why haven't you called Julien?"

"First I need to give you a little history."

"Your history?"

"Art history. Two recent thefts of Matisse paintings from South America. The first occurred in Caracas, Venezuela from the Sofia Imber Museum. *Odalisque in Red Pants*, 1925. The museum didn't even know it was stolen. A Miami art collector sent an e-mail to the museum's director expressing dismay that the piece was up for sale on the Internet. The museum had had a forgery on display for more than two years.

"The next robbery was in 2006, from Museu Chacara do Céu in Rio de Janeiro. Four paintings stolen by four armed men at four in the afternoon. They grabbed paintings by Dali, Monet, Picasso and Matisse. *Luxembourg Gardens*, 1905. It was the first day of Carnival—the robbers waited until the procession reached the museum, then snatched the paintings and disappeared into the crowds. Brilliant strategy, really. Simple and clean. Stylish. Reminds me of the Norwegian thieves who stole a version of Munch's *Scream* at the Oslo Olympics. They left a note thanking authorities for the poor security."

"And your point is…?" Chloe's tone was scathing.

"The paintings were never found. There were rumours that a handsome Frenchman who used to live in an upmarket beachside apartment in Ipanema may have been the brains of the operation. I think that man is Julien Lejeune."

"You're crazy. The Commissaire is an art thief?"

"How do you know he's a Commissaire?"

"Alain, you're way off here. Adam called the police the night we found Fyodorov's body. He was put through to the Commissaire. Julien knew all about Daniels' murder. He even knew Adam had been a suspect. He'd talked to Inspector Bradley. No, this time you're wrong."

"Really? A simple device on Adam's phone could have re-routed the call. Did Lejeune ever show you a badge? Ever meet you in a police station?"

"N-no. But how could he have known what had happened in Toronto?"

"Just a wild guess—you told Liliane?"

"But the attempted burglary here—all the gendarmes?"

Alain waved his hand contemptuously. "Hired stooges."

Chloe put her head down to hide her face. She felt embarrassed and bewildered. She remembered how dizzy she felt when she'd looked into Julien's green eyes, how she'd lingered over his words as if they were poetry. She felt a fool.

"My god, they *both* tried to seduce me. How did you know about them? And I want an answer this time. I'm fed up."

Alain ducked his head obligingly. "I've been suspicious of Liliane for quite some time. I saw her in a bar once with another man when she was supposed to be with Jamie. Didn't know then that he was this fellow calling himself Lejeune."

He saw Chloe's look of growing disbelief and held up his hands. "I've got a bit of a past, *ma petite*. To make up for it, I help out now and again. Interpol. Art theft division."

Her mouth gaped open, but Alain just kept on talking. "So when you invited Lejeune down here—no doubt he'd given you his personal number—I was very curious to see what would happen. He did what I thought he might do, take out his competitors for the painting. I don't think the real police would've killed Kirov. They would've wanted him to lead them to Ashkar. But Lejeune just wanted to clear the path to the Matisse."

"But you went to the police yourself with Ju—Lejeune. You told me you had a date with him."

"I went to the police all right, but not *with* Lejeune. I went to give them a description of the pretty boy."

Chloe smiled, an ironic twist of the mouth. "And then you tested me. You seriously thought I'd try to keep the real Matisse even with Adam's life at stake?"

Alain had the good grace to look sheepish. "We'll talk later. I'll make some breakfast while you shower. We need to check into the Négresco by five o'clock."

The wretchedly long afternoon seemed surreal. Chloe's nerves were frayed, ready to snap. She swung from moments of disbelief and eerie calm to moments of sheer panic. The day had been almost garishly sunny.

Alain tapped a large watch on his heavy left wrist. "Won't be long now."

"You said that twenty minutes ago," Chloe snapped. She had to still the impulse to stand and move about the room. "Look, you don't have a paramilitary team up on the roof or anything, do you? We're playing this absolutely straight, right?"

"My days of playing the hero are long gone, Chloe. There's just us and my bottle of nitroglycerin spray. Why don't you unwrap the Matisse and take your last look at it?"

"No," Chloe could barely reply. "I think that would break my heart. I want to remember it as I first saw it, when it was being 'rediscovered'. The thought that it's about to disappear into the shadows again is almost too much, even for Adam's sake."

Chloe's phone rang, an insistent, jarring sound. She stared at it with distaste, as if it had turned into a small venomous animal.

"Easy, now. You can do this," Alain urged. "Pick up."

Her hands trembled, but she answered the third ring in a voice that was controlled, if not completely calm. "Yes?"

"Hello, Chloe."

"Liliane."

"Listen carefully. The fat man goes down to the lobby in two minutes and takes a seat on one of the red velvet benches. Once he's in place, I'll be in touch. Two minutes, starting now."

Chloe hit disconnect and turned to Alain. "She's separating us. You have to leave immediately."

Alain jumped to his feet, nimbly for his size, and shook his head. "Standard procedure. I wouldn't have expected anything less. Don't let it rattle you."

They started together for the elevators. Even in the luxurious Négresco, the elevators were of that peculiar Gallic design that encouraged closeness among the two or three people who could squeeze into the restricted space. Chloe stabbed the button several times impatiently.

"Where's the part where we demand some proof that Adam is okay?" she asked.

"I don't think they'll hurt him as long as the exchange goes smoothly."

"Why don't I just tell them that I'll walk to the balcony and pitch the Matisse into the sea, unless they give Adam back?"

"Because they know you would never harm the painting. Here's the elevator."

Alain wriggled inside and gave her a mournful smile. "I'm sorry, Chloe. I'd have liked you to keep your miracle."

She grabbed for his hand and held it briefly. Then she stepped back and let the door close.

She walked back to the room, pressed her forehead against the glass of the window. She felt suddenly exhausted. Her skin was clammy with sweat, her hair limp. She could feel the urge to cry gathering at the back of her throat.

Chloe knew exactly what Lydia must have felt when she lost the painting. Alain said it had haunted her all her life, and now it would haunt hers too.

She was expecting the ring this time. It didn't startle her. But she felt something tear apart inside her. She didn't feel rage or even fear. Just a terrible sadness for human greed, for the obsession to take, to possess, to control.

She picked up the phone. "Hello Liliane."

"Put the painting on the elevator, push every floor from six to two. Then take the stairs down to the lobby. You have two minutes."

"Wait—" But the line was already dead.

Chloe was almost glad. The horrible waiting was over. There was something for her to *do*, even if doing it meant losing Sylvie's painting forever. She picked up the Matisse, carefully wrapped in brown paper, and allowed herself one moment to say goodbye.

She heard a faint sound, felt a shift in the room's air current.

Whirling around, she saw a silhouette, as black and sinuous as a viper, standing in the doorway. Liliane, dressed in black leathers with her dark hair and almost black eyes, though now her beautiful eyes were blank as ice.

She took several steps forward into the room and smiled, a dangerous, dazzling smile. "Give me the painting."

"Give me Adam."

Liliane laughed, though it was a strangely mirthless sound. She held out a piece of plastic the size of a credit card. "Take it. When I have the painting, I'll tell you the room number. You have," she paused, pulling down the hem of a glove and glancing at her watch, "exactly one and a half minutes before Julien kills him."

Chloe felt the blood draining from her face. "It's yours," she said, stepping away from the Matisse.

"Not mine. But I'll be paid handsomely." She ripped away the brown paper, catching her breath at the image underneath.

"You'll never be able to sell it," Chloe said.

"Our client wouldn't dream of selling it. He's rich as God, and as mad as Midas."

"That's it then. Betrayal is still for sale." Chloe's voice was flat and hard.

"Don't judge. You don't know anything about me. Tell me you don't want more."

"I don't want more."

Chloe thought she saw a flicker of surprise in Liliane's dark eyes, but she sounded unperturbed when she spoke. "Bye Chloe. I liked you, you know."

Liliane moved so quickly there was no time to react. She kicked Chloe hard just below her knees, sending her crashing to the floor. She felt a sharp jab in her shoulder, the prick of a needle.

Then Liliane's hair was in her face, a black smothering curtain. She whispered into Chloe's ear, "Room two-three-nine. Say it back to me, while you still can."

Chloe's mind, scrambled by pain and panic, refused to concentrate.

"Two-three-nine." Liliane repeated.

Chloe recited the numbers, surprised at how distant the sound of her voice was. She tried to lift her head and the room in front of her swam. Her skin felt hot. She had a vague sense of motion around her, but her vision was blurred.

She managed to roll onto her side, to push herself up on one elbow, to extend a shaking hand over the floor but her crazed fingers could make no sense of what she was touching.

Black leather. As if the woman who had been wearing the clothes had disappeared like a coil of rising smoke.

Chloe crawled two meters and clutched the edge of a chair. She tried to stand. Colours swam together as if she were swept up into a Fauvist canvas, a tiny dot in an eddy of angry blues and acid greens.

Then her world went white.

Three nights later, Chloe was sitting on the strip of private beach in the cove behind the villa on Cap Ferrat, her head leaning on Adam's shoulder. They'd both been released from hospital, having slowly recovered from nasty doses of narcotics. Alain had fed them well, then ordered them out to look at the stars.

They let the conversation between them meander and stall, but finally compared what they knew about the lost Matisse.

"I knew from the first that the Négresco would be unlucky," Chloe sighed. Her thumb strayed for the hundredth time to her ring finger, but the amethyst was gone. Liliane had taken it.

Adam noticed the small, searching motion, but pretended he hadn't. "Lejeune needed a little luck, but his plan was simple, really. He knew that Interpol had been listening in on Liliane's calls for some time, and he wanted the agents to hear her instructions to you. The classic false trail. So while the agents were banging down the door of room 239 looking for me, and chasing after an elevator stopping at every floor looking for the Matisse, Julien and Liliane slipped away. Disguised, of course."

"The room number was very clever. I remember Liliane telling me to repeat it, but I was so confused I didn't know why. I didn't know I was speaking into my own phone. Liliane called Alain while he was waiting in the lobby. It was my voice telling him where to find you.

"But the painting wasn't that small," Chloe continued. "It's not like it could fit into a pocket. How did they get it out with so many agents around?"

"Ah, I see Alain hasn't told you yet."

"Alain, as it turns out, tells me very little."

"I'm sure he was waiting, hoping it would turn out differently."

Chloe rolled her eyes. "Just tell me."

"They used Matteo's trick."

"What?"

"They hid the Matisse behind another painting, hung it on a wall and waited for all the excitement to die down. The owner of the Négresco phoned the gendarmes earlier today to report a painting stolen from the lounge area of one of the public washrooms. An empty frame was found in the laundry room. Apparently, the painting was of little value."

A longing flooded out of Chloe until it seemed to fill the night. "I wish you'd seen the Matisse, Adam. It was so pure."

"Alain took dozens of pictures before he wrapped it up."

"It won't be the same. A lens could never capture the shadings, the vibrancy of the colours, the sense of life."

"But still, it exists. It isn't just conjecture or a trick of the imagination. It hasn't been destroyed."

"Oh, yes. It exists. I can close my eyes and see it, just as Sylvie and Lydia did. I suppose it cost Jamie his life, but it saved yours. We're all interconnected now, all touched by this fragment of the past captured on canvas. Did they know I'd found the real thing, or were they just lucky again?"

"They knew. Commissaire Lejeune showed up at the convent on

Sunday morning. The nuns said he was quite shocked to find you gone. You didn't know he was following you?"

"No. Nothing I ever guessed about him was right."

She let her voice trail off, her words drift over the murmuring of the sea. She shifted her position and hugged her knees.

"Go ahead, Chloe. What is it you don't want to tell me?"

Chloe turned her face towards him. She hoped her words would be heard as gently as she spoke them.

"I'm not going home. I'd like to stay awhile. I told Sammy I'd get a job, so I've offered to help Alain set up his shop again. Maybe I'll take a few art classes."

Adam leaned back, laid on the grass, his face turned up to the stars. After a long while, she felt his hand in her hair, touching the back of her neck. "Did you ever find out what that old reprobate did in the past?" he asked.

"Not yet," Chloe laughed. "I guess that's another reason why I'm staying. That, and how much I need to learn…"

"About trust, about taking risks?"

"Yes."

"I'm worth the risk, Chloe. And I'm a patient man."

"I was hoping to hear you say that. You know we've been here, on the edge of the Mediterranean, for almost ten days, and we've never even waded into the sea."

Adam stood up and held out his hand. "What are we waiting for? Time to jump in."

The room was dark, except for the moonlight that spilled across one side of the bed, illuminating Adam's shoulder and the long sweep of his back. Chloe admired him for a moment and then reached for her pillow. As her hand slid underneath it, her fingers grazed something solid and round. She gasped, heard Adam turn towards her.

"Chloe?" he whispered.

She leaned into the moonlight, holding up the ring, the purple of its stone deep and rich.

"But how—" Adam began.

Softly, she placed a finger against his lips and smiled.

"Alain, of course. The artful dodger."

The sharp edges of my memories have worn down, washed smooth as pebbles. Treachery does not cut so deeply as before. Disappointment is a soft thudding against my ribs. Lost love is a small bird dropping suddenly from the sky. Wings are a kind of miracle, after all.

It was several months before I understood the gift Matisse had given me by clinging so tenaciously to life. He gave me time. Time before our world fell apart to enjoy the feel of sun against my skin and the aftertaste of good wine in my mouth. Time to forgive a little. Time to understand my loss so that the great, empty ache I felt upon his death was one I had already learned how to carry.

As I walk now along the water's edge, the waves a lullaby, I see differently. I see colour differently, as if it were a touch, a taste, and a smell as much as a sight. Rose tastes like cherries. Green smells like lemons. I open my arms and am drenched in Matisse blue.

I believe that my Patron was not the only one on a quest: I was searching too. For a shape to my life, for a place or a name or a face that would never fade. In the end, Matisse became my muse.

Memory is a beautiful thing. It has angel wings.

Acknowledgements

This novel would not be possible without Hilary Spurling's superb two-volume biography of Matisse: *The Unknown Matisse: Man of the North 1869-1908* (1998), and *Matisse the Master: The Conquest of Colour 1909-1954* (2005). Factual information about Lydia Delectorskaya is taken from this source. Lydia's voice and inner life come from my imagination, and my story is my homage to her.

I am grateful to Inanna Publications, to Vicky Drummond, and especially to Luciana Ricciutelli for her perceptive editing and her enthusiasm. Thanks also to Fran Cohen and Alan Davies, honest in their critiques and unwavering in their support; to Merlin Homer who inspires my love of painting; and, as ever, to Arthur Haberman for sharing the journey to Nice, to Vence, and to the heart of what matters most.

Jan Rehner studied English and Canadian literature at Trent University and York University. She is now a Senior Lecturer in the Writing Department at York and has won both provincial and national awards for excellence in teaching. Her publications include poetry, a critical study of the work of Gwendolyn MacEwen, a feminist analysis of infertility, and a text on critical thinking. Her novel, *Just Murder,* won the 2004 Arthur Ellis Award for Best First Crime Novel. Her second novel, *On Pain of Death* won a bronze medallion from the IPPY group of independent publishers (2008). Jan lives in Toronto and enjoys traveling and amateur photography. She especially enjoys taking pictures of her grandsons, Jake and Kyle.